Meg Howrey

THE CRANES DANCE

Meg Howrey was a professional dancer and actress.
She lives in Los Angeles.

ALSO BY MEG HOWREY

Blind Sight

THE CRANES DANCE

THE CRANES DANCE

Meg Howrey

WITHDRAWN

VINTAGE CONTEMPORARIES
Vintage Books
A Division of Random House, Inc.
New York

A VINTAGE CONTEMPORARIES ORIGINAL, JUNE 2012

Library of Congress Cataloging-in-Publication Data

Howrey, Meg.
The cranes dance : a novel / by Meg Howrey. —1st ed.
p. cm.
"A Vintage Original."
ISBN 978-0-307-94982-0
1. Ballet companies—Fiction. 2. Ballet dancers—Fiction. 3. Sisters—
Fiction.
PS3608.O9573 C73 2012
813'.6—dc22
2012001331

Book design by Claudia Martinez
Cover photograph © Hannes Caspar
Cover design by John Gall
Author photograph © Travis Tanner

www.vintagebooks.com

Printed in the United States of America
10 9 8 7 6 5 4 3 2 1

"I AM real!" said Alice and began to cry.

"You won't make yourself a bit realler by crying," Tweedledee remarked. "There's nothing to cry about."

"If I wasn't real," Alice said—half-laughing through her tears, it all seemed so ridiculous—"I shouldn't be able to cry."

"I hope you don't suppose those are real tears?" Tweedledum interrupted in a tone of great contempt.

—LEWIS CARROLL, *Through the Looking-Glass*

THE CRANES DANCE

1.

I threw my neck out in the middle of *Swan Lake* tonight. Act III, to be precise. Everything up to that point had been going pretty well.

I've danced *Swan Lake* a lot. Actually, it was the first ballet I ever did with the company. My parents and my sister Gwen flew in from Michigan for my debut. I remember trying to describe my stage position so they would know where I was in the flock.

"I'll know which one you are," Mom said. "I'll be holding my breath the whole time. And probably squeezing your father's hand off!"

"Actually, the collective noun for swans is a *wedge* of swans," Dad said. "Although that's used when they are flying in a V formation. Otherwise it might be a bevy of swans. Or a herd."

"*Merde*," said Gwen, because that is what dancers say to each other instead of "break a leg." Some dancers say "*toi toi toi*," which is kind of an opera thing. I've always thought that was a little pretentious, but whatever works for you. The girl who had my dressing room before me was Jewish and she put up one of those mezuzah thingies on the doorway. She took it with her when she retired, but I still touch the strip of sticky tape that remains before going onstage. That isn't about superstition, or religion. It's about *ritual*. Well, maybe it's about superstition because I did it the first time as a joke and that night I had a spectacular performance and so now I always do it.

I wasn't having a *spectacular* night tonight, but it was *clean*. No real mistakes, everything neat and tidy. The first role of my evening—one of the four Big Swans in Act II—had gone well, despite Fumio dragging the tempi. That's fine for Anne-Marie, who was dancing Odette and likes things slow, but tough on the rest of us, who had to stand still and cramp through solos that felt like the length of the Old Testament. For Act III I was dancing the Polish Princess. That's a solo, and it's fairly action-packed with pirouettes, but for some reason I find it less daunting than Big Swans. Maybe it's the costume. For Big Swans I'm all in white: crisp feathered tutu, white tights, white pointe shoes, feathered headpiece. The whole thing just screams, "And now . . . SERIOUS BALLET: please be perfect." Polish Princess gear has a knee-length skirt that hides a multitude of sins, and it's all flounces and furbelows. Jaunty little headgear. I feel like as long as I keep up a general air of "I am so HUGELY PSYCHED to be POLISH!" and avoid actually falling on my ass, I'm in the clear.

It occurs to me that maybe you don't know what *Swan Lake* is all about. I haven't assigned you a face or body, invisible audience member, let alone a background in the arts. Maybe you've never seen *Swan Lake*. Maybe you've seen it and you still don't really know what happened because you dropped your program under the seat in front of you and didn't want to scramble around for it in an ungainly fashion. *Swan Lake*, like all the major classical ballets, really needs program notes because otherwise you have to follow the plot points in ballet mime, and god knows those are truly undecipherable.

You're familiar with the music though, right? At the very least you've heard it in a TV commercial for like, Mop & Glo or something, and seen that line of linked dancers in white feathered tutus clip-clopping in pointe shoes across a sparkling floor? Dun-dun-dun-DUN-duddle dundundun, Dun-dun-dun-DUN—duddle dundundun. Tchaikovsky. I'm not being condescending. I try not to think about the fact that most people don't ever go to the ballet, but I get that they don't. I do get that.

So yes a synopsis might be in order, and if you know it already you can just nap for a bit. Most productions of *Swan Lake* don't vary all that much from one another. There are one or two really funky versions out there, but those aren't done by classical ballet companies. You can't deviate too far in classical ballet or you're no longer, well . . . classical. And it's not like Shakespeare, where you can reset the whole thing in World War II, or a Mexican brothel, or something. Well you *could*, but the plotline won't stand up under a whole lot of tinkering and we've got a subscription audience to satisfy. They want the *Swan Lake* they know and love, which by and large is the one that was done for the 1895 revival of the ballet by the choreographer Petipa and his ballet master, Ivanov. Sometimes an artistic director might change a few things or restage certain sections.

Like Marius—our current artistic director—added a Prelude to our version.

The curtain rises on a nearly empty stage, with a backdrop of a lake and some boulders Stage Left leading up to a cave. Enter a young girl. She is wearing white and her hair is mostly down, so we know right away she is Young and Innocent. The girl dances dreamily by herself and all seems peaceful enough until suddenly a shadowy sort of caped figure emerges from the cave. It is the evil magician Von Rothbart. We know he's a magician because he's got the cape, and that he's evil because underneath the cape his costume is this demonic rubbery sort of thing that Roger refers to as "Mein Von Goblin Wear." Von Rothbart makes some gestures and a fog starts rolling in and darkness descends. The girl appears to lose her way in the mist. She does the big "I'm lost!" gesture: one hand in front of the face, taking tentative steps forward, peering around, etc. Von Rothbart slithers down from his boulders and makes more magic gestures, luring the girl into his arms. He swirls his cape around her, turns, and walks upstage, the cape billowing out in such a way that the girl is able to slip into the hydraulic trap and be replaced with another girl, this one in full Swan regalia: the stiff white tutu with the feathered bodice and headpiece. This is Odette, the ballerina we'll watch for the rest of the evening. The other one was a girl in the corps with a wig on to match the hair color of whoever is dancing Odette that night. It's the old switcheroo. (Be amazed by this bit of stage magic, okay? It's not like we can pull anything off with CGI.)

So Von Rothbart reveals this magically changed creature

and she beats her arms and tries to run away, but Von Rothbart is able to control her, and using more of his dastardly powers he summons onto stage two rows of women in white swan tutus who form a V and beat their arms in unison as the evil magician stands triumphant with the stricken Odette pressed against his Von Goblin Wear. Lights fall, curtain, end of Prelude.

The program notes will tell you that the evil magician has placed all these poor women under a curse and that they are condemned to be swans by day and women by night. Von Rothbart's personal motivations for such malevolent behavior are not explained. You're at the ballet. Deal with it.

Act I opens in the village green of an unspecified, vaguely German realm. We're a little hazy on the time period too. It's Days of Yore, I guess, in the yore when everyone in pseudo Germany wandered around their village green in nearly identical outfits. Ours have a slightly Renaissance Fair vibe to them, which I think is a mistake. The sleeves are too puffy and give all the girls man shoulders. Anyway, A Village Green Scene is standard issue for classical ballet, and if you've seen one circlet of peasant-dancing hoo-ha, you've seen them all. There's a garland dance and a Maypole and a lot of people standing around fake clapping or pointing out to each other that other people are dancing in the middle of the stage. This kind of random milling about drives me NUTS, but honestly there just aren't a lot of options. We can't pretend like we're talking to each other, because that would be weird and anti-ballet. We don't have props or activities like you see in plays or the opera—that would take up stage space. So everyone just wanders around greeting each other with head nods if you're a girl and shoulder thumping if you're a guy, and then one person will indicate Center

Stage like "Hey, did you see? There are people dancing! Isn't that neat!" And the other person will make a gesture like "Yes! Dancing. It is happening there!"

So here we are in the Village Green of Wherever filled with people who like to greet each other maniacally every ten seconds and then in walks Prince Siegfried, Prince of the realm of Wherever. Siegfried is greeted by his best buddy, "Ivor" (sometimes he has a different name and sometimes he's like a court jester, but in our version he's Ivor, Friend to the Prince). Ivor gets the Prince interested in some of these wonderful Maypole high jinks, the crowning moment of which is a big pas de trois Ivor dances with two local girls. The Act I pas de trois is a nice featured part, and getting to dance one of the two girls in it is a sign that things are going well for you in the company and you might not have to spend your whole career as third bird from the left.

Swan Lake floats in and out of our repertoire, so it was two years after my debut before we did it again, this time on tour, and I was cast as one of the pas de trois girls. And even though Gwen had only been in the company for about five seconds at that point, she was cast as the other girl. Our parents came to Chicago to see us, along with our brother, Keith.

"So, are you sisters in the ballet?" he asked. "Is that like part of it?"

"We're maidens," I said. "Nameless maidens."

"Everybody says we look like twins!" Gwen said. "But you'll be able to tell us apart. The one dancing better will be Kate."

Okay, so after the pas de trois between Ivor and the nameless maidens, Prince Siegfried dances a solo where he expresses (much jumping) his desire to find True Love. Then we have the appearance of the Prince's mother, the Queen. Lots of fan-

fare and aggressive pointing by all the villagers: "Look, it's the
Queen! Hey, did you see? The Queen!" She's usually played
by some old-timer—a ballet mistress or a teacher. Galina Suko-
nova is our Queen, and possesses a whole repertoire of anima-
tronic facial expressions. It's a frightening thing up close, but
good for those who can only afford seats in the top tiers. The
Queen reminds Siegfried with some incomprehensible ballet
mime that tomorrow is his twenty-first birthday and he's got
obligations, like choosing a bride and getting married. The
Prince sulks a bit at this, and makes the gesture for True Love:
one hand to the breast, the other held aloft with the first two
fingers extended. (You're gonna want to scootch down and get
that program for the explanatory notes on this action, because
otherwise you might think that the Queen is telling her son
that he needs to get a manicure and that Siegfried is respond-
ing by trying to hail a cab, or test current wind conditions.)

Siegfried cheers up when the Queen presents him with a
nifty-looking crossbow as a birthday present. Siegfried really
loves his crossbow. He runs around stage with it, showing it to
everybody Stage Left, and Stage Right, and then Stage Left
again, just in case anybody Stage Left had their eyes closed.
Basically eating up some music. Siegfried indicates to Ivor that
he wants to go hunting RIGHT NOW, and Ivor indicates that
night is falling and now's not a great time for him. Siegfried
impulsively decides to go anyway, and Ivor reluctantly follows
him. End of Act I.

Act II finds the Prince by the same mysterious lake we saw
in the Prelude. He sends Ivor off and dances around in a mel-
ancholy sort of way with his crossbow. That's another thing I'd
change if I were Marius. The Prince needs a really serious-

looking crossbow, and I'd get some kind of arms expert to come in and demonstrate how to actually hold the thing. Our current crossbow looks like a toy, and Siegfried might as well be onstage playing with a Tonka truck. Anyway, the Prince suddenly sees something offstage that at first confuses and then terrifies him. After peering around his hand and then holding it up like, "Oh. God. No!" Siegfried hightails it off Stage Right. Enter the swan corps.

This moment is actually very beautiful. One girl after another snakes onto the stage doing the same pattern of steps until all twenty-four girls are on, and then they form rows and there is something powerful and strange and, well, wonderful about it. The symmetry, the music, everyone alike and in unison, and it's serious, private in a way, because the dancers are not smiling at the audience, or acknowledging them or even each other at all. It does feel like a spell, a little. It's hammered into you from the first rehearsal: dance every step at your highest individual level while still maintaining integrity with the Group. And this works. You dance your fool head off, no matter what you feel like, no matter if you're in the back row. You can't help it. And when everyone lands from a jump you can hear it because it's twenty-four pairs of feet in pointe shoes, and when you're onstage you feel connected by that sound, by your position in line.

Maybe this is how people feel when they are in the military and performing drills. Or what it's like to be a nun, walking and chanting in Vespers.

There must have been a girl on tonight wearing my old corps tutu. Perhaps the indelible ink printing of "K. Crane" is still there inside the bodice, or half there. Like those messages on the signs outside of motels where crucial letters have fallen off and travelers are invited to sample the "HEAT D SWIMM NG POO ."

Where are we? Oh yes, well, after the swan corps dances, Siegfried gets his balls back and comes running onstage to take a closer look at these creatures, and that's when Odette—now Queen of the Swans—appears and Siegfried is all, "Who's that?" but Odette is elusive and runs offstage. More swans run in—four Big Swans and four Little Swans—and they form a kind of defensive cluster, and Siegfried is standing there with his crossbow looking like, "Um, seriously?" when Odette runs in again and stands bravely in front of all the swans like, "Don't you dare point that ridiculous toy at my girls."

So Siegfried puts down his bow and tries to get Odette to dance with him. She is shy, and otherworldly, and beautiful, and of course he falls in love with her. They dance, and the corps dances, and the Big Swans dance and the Little Swans do the linked-arm thing you are familiar with, and Odette dances and Siegfried dances and they dance together again, and Odette explains the whole curse thing in ballet mime obfuscated even more than usual by the fact that whoever is dancing Odette is totally exhausted by that point.

The deal with the curse is that it *can* be broken, by True Love, but if True Love is promised and then betrayed, the swans will lose their human souls forever and only be birds. You might think this would be a relief, that there would be at least one member of the flock who was sick of being divided in two like that and willing to forgo humanity for the quiet life, but I guess we all cling to sanity no matter how painful it is.

We cling to humanity, I mean. Not sanity. Although you can

cling to sanity. It's a matter of willpower. This is an argument I've been waging with Gwen for a long time. It's not that I think she fakes her losses of reason, but I do think she indulges them. My position on this matter might be one of the reasons she is refusing to speak to me.

Back to the *Lake*. Smitten Prince Siegfried has almost managed to overcome Odette's objections (it was a man who got her into this mess, so she's understandably a little suspicious) and the Prince is about to promise True Love when evil Von Rothbart appears! Boo! Siegfried grabs his crossbow and aims for Von Rothbart, but dawn is breaking and Odette is back under the magician's power so she stands in front of him. The Prince, unable to get a clear shot, vows to return the next night and free Odette. End of Act II. Intermission. The mezzanine bathroom is going to be pretty full so I'd try the second balcony one if I were you. Step outside, have a cigarette on me, then come on back.

Act III is the Prince's Birthday Ball, so we're at his castle. The guests of the ball behave in pretty much the same fashion as the peasants from Act I (they're the same dancers, after all), and so there's more milling about and greeting each other and gesturing to Center Stage and admiring each other's nearly identical outfits. Four Princesses are brought in to meet Siegfried, who's totally not into them although he condescends to dance a little with each one. Then the Princesses all dance a solo from their native land: a Hungarian dance, a Spanish dance, a Neapolitan dance, and—you guessed it!—a Polish dance. The Queen takes Siegfried aside to ask who he's going to choose to propose to, and Siegfried looks bummed about the selection when suddenly a New Guest arrives—a mysterious stranger wearing a mask and a cape (Von Rothbart, in disguise)—and with him he has a beautiful woman who looks EXACTLY like Odette, only instead of wearing all white she is wearing all black. This is Odile, the Black Swan. (The program notes will tell you she is Von Rothbart's daughter, magicked up to look like Odette.)

Odette and Odile are always danced by the same ballerina. It's why the role is so difficult. Not because you have to be lyrical and romantic and vulnerable as the White Swan and fiery and über-strong and confident as the Black one. That's not a huge problem, you get a different costume and different choreography and tempi and these are really all you need to change your personality when you're a dancer. We do it several times a day. The hard part in dancing Odette/Odile is the stamina and concentration involved.

Anyway, it's no surprise to anyone that the Prince is immediately taken with this fabulous Odile, and since she looks exactly like Odette he convinces himself that she *is* Odette even though she's got a totally different personality. There is a lot of bravura dancing—including the famous thirty-two fouetté turns Odile rips off—and dazzled by the pyrotechnics, Siegfried pledges True Love to the Black Swan. Just for a moment, before this happens, we catch a glimpse of Odette far upstage on a platform thing (it's not actually Odette, of course, since she's onstage as Odile at that point, but the stand-in Odette is far enough away that the audience can't see her face and she's got the Odette costume on). This is meant to show us that off at the lake, Odette has a sense that she is being betrayed and is trying to warn the Prince, but of course this doesn't work. We are in Days of Yore, and it's not like she can text him or anything: *Odile not 4 real. C U at Lake 2nite. xoxo :) Odette.*

Once Siegfried has pledged True Love to Odile, Von Rothbart throws off his cape, reveals Mein Von Goblin Wear, and claims paternity of the Black Swan. Siegfried realizes with horror what he has done. He runs offstage to go find Odette. End of Act III.

We've got another intermission here. Maybe for this one you just want to stand up in the aisle rather than trying to jimmy your way up to the bar. Or you could amuse yourself by strolling past the standing-room banister aisle at the back of the orchestra section where the super-fans and students have lolled through three acts. Walk slowly, and you'll catch them showing off their insider knowledge by using the abbreviated versions of our first names, or debating the merits of various casts. "Is it just me or is 'Sandro looking a little tired tonight? Of course, it's been a very heavy season for him." "Emmy last Saturday? She freaking *nailed* it. I was like, You better work, girl. Work it OUT."

Now settle in because Act IV is very tragic and moving. A distraught Siegfried returns to the lake to explain the whole clusterfuck to a brokenhearted Odette. The swan corps weaves in and out. Von Rothbart shows up to polish off the curse and condemn Odette and all the rest of the girls to lives as waterfowl.

Odette decides to kill herself. Siegfried, who refuses to be separated from his True Love, swears he will join her. The two of them die together, the lights indicating that they drown themselves in the lake, clasping each other. This act of love is so powerful that it kills Von Rothbart and frees all the swans. We end on a final image of Siegfried and Odette locked together, their souls entwined for all eternity against the backdrop of a rising sun.

And that's *Swan Lake*.

I didn't mean to tell it in such a smartass way. It's an incredible ballet, even if it is a dusty old warhorse in many ways. People cry at the end, I'm told.

But I didn't throw my neck out in the middle of *Swan Lake* tonight because I got all emotional. There we were in Act III and just as I was doing my first promenade around the stage with my little retinue of Polish minions it occurred to me, sort of in a flash, that the Polish Princess was actually a person. That yes, she was a character, a role, whatever, but she could also be said to be a human being.

It's funny because I'm known for being this skilled "actress," but I just think of things in, you know, general terms. Joy. Sorrow. Desire. Jealousy. So I got all tripped out thinking about the Polish Princess as an actual separate and complete human being. Because, if that were true, then she would have an opinion about things and even about being at this ball. And maybe she doesn't really want to be at the ball. Maybe she doesn't want to marry this Prince Siegfried person either. Maybe the whole time she is being promenaded around and smiling and looking so bright and charming she's just wondering where the hell the bar is and wanting to take off her stupid headpiece. All during the bits with the Prince I kept adding things to her character. Like maybe she has a slight astigmatism, and this makes her prone to migraines. She had an affair with one of her minions during a particularly bleak winter back in Warsaw. She suffers from social anxiety. She plays the tambourine.

Unfortunately, none of these attributes was at all useful for what I actually had to *dance*. But I became . . . attached to these ideas, and they sort of felt more real than everything else.

I could have passed a lie detector test about who I was, that's how real it all felt. And it occurred to me that this is the kind of thing that happens in Gwen's head all the time. And yes, it did feel a little out of my control. And I wasn't sure what to cling to.

That's what I was thinking about when I started the turns on the diagonal, and right at the first one, just as I turned my head, I felt something in my neck implode and pain shot down my right arm all the way to my hand. It felt like someone had hit me with a wrench and then set my arm on fire. For a second, I actually thought I might have . . . you know . . . died.

I finished the turns. I did the traveling mazurkas, the sauts de basque, everything. I simplified the last few bars of pirouettes and—somehow—was able to hold a long balance, which got some applause from the audience. Then I was done and my retinue came and got me, and as soon as Odile made her appearance and I wasn't necessary to any of the action, I told Julius I felt sick and had to bail and slipped into the wings. I think it's safe to say that nobody noticed the departure of the Polish Princess. Then I went to my dressing room and almost threw up from the pain. I usually share a dressing room with Tamara, but she's out this season. Hip injury.

I redid my lips and got back into my Big Swan tutu. I danced—in some fashion—Act IV. Curtain call. I stopped by Roger's dressing room and he gave me two Vicodin from his emergency stash. I came home, or rather, here. Gwen's apartment.

The official word on Gwen's absence is that she is recovering from knee surgery back home in Michigan. The real story is that three weeks ago I called Dad and said he had to come and get her, that things were bad and Gwen was out of control and that I didn't fucking care anymore. So Dad came and got her and took her home, and three days later she attempted to smash her (perfectly fine) knee through the screen door of their patio. So there's an element of truth to the official story because she tore the crap out of her knee. I'm not sure about the recovering part. I take it as a good sign that she didn't try to put her knee through the *glass* door of the patio. Nothing crucial got torn, but she did require stitches.

I don't know exactly what Gwen is recovering from, right now, or if the word "recovering" is appropriate. It makes it sound like she is getting new upholstery. From what I gather, they are trying "different things," which I assume means different drugs. This tone I am taking about the condition of my poor anguished shredded sister is sort of sick, and might possibly mean that I should be on the same regimen of pharmaceuticals as she is.

Was she out of control? Did I really not fucking care anymore? These are difficult questions to answer.

You know, there is one thing that is never quite explained in any synopsis of *Swan Lake*. That is: what's the real deal with Odile, the Black Swan? I mean, what is her MO? We're meant to believe she is Von Rothbart's daughter whom he has transformed to look exactly like Odette, but does she retain any of her own personality? Is she just a pawn? Is she evil? Misguided? Jealous? A victim? Certainly she never displays any remorse over her part in the tragedy that follows, but we leave her as soon as the big denouement. So we don't really know what she feels.

Who will weep for the Black Swan when the spell is lifted

and all the white swans are set free? All our tears are for Odette, noble, self-sacrificing, fatally tricked, and now dead in the arms of her lover.

But the Black Swan is still alive. Fluttering her midnight wings without conviction on the edges of the lake. Having to live with the knowledge of what she has done, what she allowed to happen. All alone.

Oh my god my neck is killing me.

2.

The day that Gwen put her knee through the patio door was also the day that my boyfriend broke up with me. In a surprise reversal of the usual cliché, Andrew told me that he was "in love" with me but he didn't "love" me. It may have been the most original thing he ever said to me, and for a moment I was almost proud of him. Then came the rest: how he just wanted to "be there" for me but I shut myself off from him, never let him in, didn't communicate, didn't seem really interested in building a life together. He followed this up with a catalog of all the things he had done for me that I hadn't appreciated.

I should have known better. When Andrew and I got together he kept telling me how incredible it was to be with someone who wasn't all needy, didn't have a ton of issues, was really independent. So unlike all his other girlfriends, especially Anna, his tragically doomed first love who overdosed when they were sophomores at Columbia. I should have known there was trouble the minute I heard about Anna. Never date a guy with a dead girlfriend. Because she will get to be peacefully (or however it happens) deceased, but the guy will be left alive to romanticize her out of all proportion and forever seek another flawed heroine to save.

But I shouldn't blame Anna. Probably the reason Andrew was with her in the first place is that Andrew is a giver. Givers are sneaky. If you don't present them with gaping holes, they will create them just to have something to do. Here's the twist: although the givers get quite a bit of cred for how caring and generous they are, their motives are far from altruistic. The whole time they are giving and giving, you can be sure that they're secretly keeping an account book of services rendered and waiting for just the right moment to hand you the bill.

During the breakup talk Andrew said he thought it best if we separated before anger and resentment set in, although from the length and fluid hostility of his monologue it was clearly too late for that. He said I could take my time moving out, but maybe I could stay at Gwen's since she was currently in Michigan recovering from knee/psyche implosion. And oh, yes, since I asked, there *was* someone else, but that had nothing to do with his decision, which wasn't really his decision, but rather something that was forced upon him by *my* behavior.

"I just want to be honest with you," he said.

"That does not impress me," I replied.

Our apartment was Andrew's apartment, so it made sense that I would be the one to move out. This didn't take long. I came to him with very little, like a mail-order bride from the Ukraine. Well, I was living with Gwen before I moved in with Andrew and it would have felt wrong to take any of our joint furniture or things. I already felt guilty enough for leaving her alone.

There were things I bought for Andrew and me as a couple, but I left those for him and the mysterious "someone else" to enjoy. I hope her no doubt fascinatingly vulnerable self will be very comfortable on those Egyptian cotton sheets. Yes, before decamping I really did spray my perfume on the pillowcases. Also, all over his suits. He might not even notice. He was never good at reading my signals. He always wanted me to tell him everything.

I packed up my books and clothes and a few pathetic boxes and I hired one of those "man with a van" guys to move it all for me, and now here I am. When Dad came he must have thrown some of Gwen's clothes in a suitcase, and her toothbrush and contact lens case aren't in the bathroom, but everything else is just where she left it, including the masking-tape Xs on some of the walls. (Don't ask me to explain, it's a Gwen thing, I don't know what it means.) Also Clive isn't here. Gwen's neighbor is taking care of him. That she didn't ask me to look after her cat is another sign of how furious she is with me.

My boxes are lined up against the bedroom wall. "Sweaters," "Kitchen," "Reviews/Programs/Photos," "Fiction A–F." It doesn't make sense to unpack and I don't want to disturb anything. It's a bit like living in a crime scene, actually, with the Xs and all.

I need to take those down.

I don't want to touch them.

My neck still hurt like a bitch today, and since I wasn't supposed to be performing tonight, I decided to skip morning class and do therapy.

First I went to see Dr. Ken to get an adjustment. Dr. Ken makes house calls to the theater three times a week when we are in season, but today wasn't one of those days. He'll always squeeze us in at the office, though.

Dr. Ken's waiting room is covered with pictures of the well-known individuals he has cracked to health: opera singers, boxers, dancers, musicians, and hockey players. Dr. Ken once said to me that ballet dancers are his favorite patients to treat, because we always do what we are told, and are very open to criticism. At the time Dr. Ken said this, I was facedown on the table and attached to an electric stimulation machine, so I just grunted affably, but I must say that upon reflection, being able to tell us that we aren't great seems kind of a fucked-up reason for liking us.

Dr. Ken wears polo shirts and pants with pleats in them. He has that smooth hair that doesn't look like hair, but rather a sort of fibrous cap. I'm not at all attracted to Dr. Ken, what with the pleats and all, but he's a man, and I did my girl thing anyway, as if him finding me charming or attractive would help. Help what? I don't know. You do these things.

He probed my neck for a few minutes and then said he wanted to do X-rays and that I have "a lot going on in there." But today we just had time for an adjustment. It's tricky having your neck adjusted. For it to work you have to totally relax, but it's hard to relax when the movements of the chiropractor are remarkably similar to those of the Boston Strangler.

I asked Dr. Ken if having a pinched nerve in your neck will affect your peripheral vision, and he asked me why, was I experiencing that? The thing is, I keep anticipating that something is going to come around a corner and stab me in the eye. Seriously, for the past few weeks, every time I go around a corner, on the street, or in the hallways at work, I want to jerk my head back and cover my eyes. I don't though. In fact, I have been forcing myself to take corners quickly and sharply to sort of punish myself for getting neurotic. This started before the neck injury, so I told Dr. Ken no, that I had read something online, and he told me that I shouldn't do that.

I'm sure there is some deep dark secret reason behind the stabbed-in-the-eye scenario, but really, I don't see how knowing *why* I have this fear will help stop it. That's why I don't see any point in going to a shrink. Knowing *why* you broke the glass—because you weren't paying attention to where the edge of the table was, dummy—doesn't make you less sorry, doesn't mend the glass, doesn't ensure it won't happen again, that you won't break something more precious next time. The shrink might say that actually you knew perfectly well where the edge of the table was, but you chose to miss and break the glass because you wanted to sabotage yourself or something, but please. That's like saying drug addicts are sabotaging themselves. Hello! Drugs are fantastic and you get addicted because they are fantastic and it's just bad luck that they can destroy you too.

I've read how there were so many women in Vienna talking about how they were sexually abused as children that Sigmund Freud wondered if there were some kind of child molestation epidemic going on. But no. The trouble was that even though these women hadn't been abused, they so thoroughly believed that it had happened that they exhibited all the symptoms of legitimate victims. So for all intents and purposes, they *had* been abused. Which would piss me off if I were a legitimate victim, and makes you wonder what exactly the point is of having any actual experiences if you can be just as affected by imaginary ones.

Nobody hit Gwen, or molested her, or anything like that, nor does she claim they did. Even when she's acting delusional and paranoid she doesn't say that. She knows her limits. She usually knows mine. Now I'm worried that she's deliberately acting crazy just to prove something to me. But that she smashed her own knee is . . . well. I called Dad because I was worried that she was going to harm herself, and that ended up happening anyway.

After Dr. Ken, I took the subway downtown to Dr. Wang for acupuncture.

Dr. Wang doesn't have any pictures of us on his walls, and as far as I know has never even been to the ballet. I explained about my neck and he took my pulse in about ten different places. His hands are hard but so incredibly smooth that I imagine his fingerprints to be without lines or ridges, just perfectly uniform ovals like the backs of small spoons. Sometimes Dr. Wang will ask questions or dispense wisdom, but today he just took my pulse and then did his tapping thing. He taps your whole body with his spoon fingers and when he finds a spot that interests him, he sticks a needle in. The first one went into my left hand, which made my right leg jump.

"Yes," said Dr. Wang, inscrutably.

After about ten minutes of this, I wound up with about four needles in each hand, and none in my neck or shoulder where the actual pain is. But you can't question Dr. Wang about these things. You can't flirt with him either so I tried a knowing nod, as if I realized the significance of all this.

"You are a bad breather," he said.

"Well," I said, "I'm not dead yet so I must have the basics down."

Dr. Wang looked skeptical.

I breathed deeply through my nose. Dancers are good patients. We always do what we are told and we are very open to criticism.

He shut the door softly behind him and I listened to him pad around in his outer office and, judging from the rustling, read the newspaper. Dr. Wang doesn't play gong music or burn incense or give you a pillow or anything lame like that. I rotated my ankles until they both popped, and closed my eyes. I false meditated—pretending I was clearing my mind while really planning what I was going to eat today and conducting an imaginary conversation between me and Andrew's someone else, who for the purposes of my invention, I named Janice. I waited for Dr. Wang to come back in and unpin me, which after an eternity, he did.

As I was leaving his office, Marissa called me because Mia called out sick and they had to reshuffle casts and they needed me on tonight for Big Swan/Polish Princess. Since I thought I'd have the evening off I hadn't told anyone about my neck, and you're supposed to do that, so I just said yes and went back to the crime scene and took a really long hot shower. Luckily, I found that Gwen's Advil bottle was filled with Vicodin, so I took two with me to the theater just in case.

About halfway through the very gentle warm-up I was giv-

ing myself, I could no longer turn my head to the left without
a new shooting pain running down my scapula. I broke a Vicodin into two pieces and swallowed one of them.

Roger stopped by my dressing room to check on me. "How's
the neck?"

"It feels like a yam stuck in a crimping iron."

"You see Dr. Ken?"

"And Dr. Wang," I said. "He put the needles in my hands,
though."

"Dr. Wang told me that pain has two arrows," said Roger.
"The first arrow is like, the bad thing that happens. And the
second arrow is the pain we give ourselves about the bad thing
that happened."

"How do you avoid the second arrow?" I asked.

Roger leaned against my chair.

"I forget. I think it has something to do with self-awareness?
There might be a third arrow too." Roger laughed and started
to massage my neck.

"Jesus." He prodded my yam.

"I can't turn my head," I said. "I'm stuck."

"Sweetie," said Roger, "maybe you should call out for a few
days. You're just going to keep reinjuring it if you keep dancing."

"I'm kind of hoping I'll throw it out in the other direction
and achieve some sort of equilibrium," I said.

"I don't think that happens," Roger said, gently, for him. "I
think you need to rest."

"I can't rest." I waved a hand. "I'm not in a resting place."

"You have to induce that," Roger instructed. "Smoke some
pot. Watch *Oprah*. Eat Chinese. Rent porn."

"Roger," I said. "This is a very interesting formula you have created here. *Oprah*, Pot, and Porn."

"And chicken with peanut sauce," Roger said, dreamily. "That's like, the best day off ever."

I managed to get through Big Swans relatively unscathed, although I didn't time the other half of the Vicodin perfectly and had to breathe in little puffs through my nose to keep going. Ella's got that thing with her knee again and there was a moment when we turned together upstage and I caught her eye and all pretense of stage face dropped and we were just two injured worried people dressed up in feathers with white makeup sliding down in ravines of sweat from our foreheads and I almost panicked at the sheer heartbreak of it all. But then we turned downstage and got through it, so that was fine.

Recklessly, I swallowed the second Vicodin during intermission, and was consequently a little blitzed out for Polish Princess. Got very giggly in the wings with Roger. Last year during *Nutcracker* we started making up haiku backstage. Well, very loosely haiku. We're not picky about the syllable count because 5-7-5 is too much math to do in the middle of a performance, and we're not committed to the traditional nature reference. Roger had a good one tonight:

Siegfried loves Odile
But wishes she would stop
Crapping on his tunic

And I came up with:

On my partner's shoulder
Brocade up my ass again
Smile, dummy

I'm not totally clear on what happened during my solo. I may have gone a little overboard. It's not *Swan Lake*, *The Polish Princess Story*. Did I discern a slightly more enthusiastic rumble of applause from the audience, or was that the vertebrae in my neck splintering?

What I had totally forgotten was that Gwen's boyfriend Neil called me last week and said his sister was in town and that he had gotten them tickets to *Swan Lake*. This was all planned before Gwen had her "thing," his sister loves dance, and it would be great to see me anyway, etc. We didn't discuss the thinginess of Gwen's thing. I have no idea what he knows.

Gwen met Neil on one of those trips to the Hamptons we would do with Andrew and his friends. This was after I had moved in with Andrew, and supposedly felt comfortable with his circle, and could just be myself. In truth, I had trouble being anything like myself when I was so thoroughly out of context, and usually ended up shrinking to an unimpressive version of a cliché I would make fun of in different circumstances: Andrew's ballerina girlfriend, intimidating and remote beneath a thick layer of SPF 5,000, unable to get down with the Stacis and Rebeccas who would dance on the back of someone's boat, lip-synching to rap. Having Gwen around was like seeing yourself in one of those multi-view dressing-room mirrors and finding better new angles, flattering postures, a way to cheat the overhead lighting. Gwen, reclining in a giant hat on the back of the same boat, holding a bottle of Corona like a wand, never looked dour or arrogant. She looked sinewy and self-contained and yet fragile in a way none of the Stacis and Rebeccas could hope for. Neil, who is the kind of guy who would normally have a mid-level model or actress on his arm, scented out her status as a star dancer, a rarer and thus more valuable commodity, and was titillated by her indifference. Watching him go after her was like watching an episode of *Nature*.

I hadn't thought that Gwen would go for Neil, though. The fact that Andrew had not only been to college but also to grad school, that he knew things about international politics and football stats and how to drive a stick shift, those were all weird aphrodisiacs to me. But Gwen had only ever dated dancers. I assumed Neil's cred was off her radar, because what is membership at the Soho Club, a bespoke fedora, the usage of St. Barts as verb 'cause you've been there so often . . . what's all that to being a Lord of the Dance? But they've been together, in a fashion, for almost two years now. From the outside it seems almost like they're playing a game of Who Cares Less, with Gwen always winning because she really doesn't care. My guess is that Gwen is just indifferent enough to Neil to keep him around, even though models make much better arm candy than dancers and our schedule only allows for a minimal of scene making. I've never been clear on what she gets from him. I don't ask, because it makes me feel better to pretend that Gwen has a healthy relationship.

Neil was waiting at the stage door with the dressed-up-for-the-big-city sister hovering behind his shoulder, clutching her program and goggling at the exiting dancers. He gave me a quick kiss on the cheek before hugging me, which I don't remember him ever doing before. I didn't know if this was an acknowledgment of Andrew and me breaking up, or of Gwen losing her marbles.

I took Neil and his sister to the place we take all people who come to a performance. Neil said to the waiter, "My beautiful sister would like a Cosmopolitan and the star will have . . ."

"A glass of Cabernet," I said, impressed by Neil's ability to sound both condescending and charming. He flipped open the wine list and ordered a bottle.

"Hardly a star," I said, and then to the sister, "My sister Gwen is a star. I'm sorry you didn't get a chance to see her dance."

"I know!" the sister gushed. "None of us have ever met her, even. We think Neil's ashamed of us."

"I told you she couldn't come home with me for Christmas because of her performances," Neil said easily.

"It's true," I told the sister. "We have an annual hell we like to call *The Nutcracker*. We haven't spent Christmas with our own parents since we were teenagers."

"Oh, but I love *The Nutcracker*," began the sister, and then launched into the familiar non-dancer girl talking to dancer girl conversation. "Do your toes bleed?" "I had a friend/cousin/ neighbor who danced who was really serious about her dancing until she got too tall/hurt her knee/went to college." "You must not be able to eat *anything*." "It must take a lot of discipline, I can't even imagine doing what you do." "All the men are gay, right?"

To his credit, Neil didn't try to reroute any of this, or display insider knowledge, or make excuses for his sister's gushings. He seemed a little remote, in that slightly showy way men do like they just read an article about how women find this attractive. I remembered that Gwen told me that Neil has a big dick. Eventually the sister got up to totter to the bathroom. Neil picked up his wineglass.

"So you called the cops on Gwen?"

I rearranged objects on the table. Pushed the saltshaker away. Fiddled with the cutlery. Crossed my legs. Gingerly rotated my neck.

"If you mean I called our parents when I thought Gwen was . . . was really . . . had actually sort of . . . lost it," I said. "Then, yes. I did."

Neil made a little gesture of annoyance.

"Oh come on," he said. "I admit our Gwen is a little unstable, but seriously? That's like most of the women in this city. I've dated a lot crazier in my time."

"Your time? How old are you? Like, thirty?"

"I'm just saying," Neil said, twirling his glass like he was patronizing his wine just by sipping it. "You might have overreacted a bit."

"Right, because you know my sister so well," I said, gritting my gums. "From a couple of hours at a restaurant every other week? From a trip to Cabo? This makes you an expert on her."

"I think I know her pretty well," he said. "And I know that you do consider yourself to be like, Gwen's watchdog or whatever."

"Is that what Gwen told you?"

"That's between me and Gwen."

The idea that Gwen had characterized me as a "watchdog" to Neil was not unthinkable. She often slotted me into this kind of role, for getting out of things she didn't want to do. "Kate would be mad." "Kate wouldn't approve." "Don't tell Kate." The idea that I could stop Gwen from doing anything was pretty ludicrous. The idea that I should now be in the position of defending my actions to Neil made my neck hurt.

"Everybody is a little bipolar in this town," Neil continued. "It's called being alive in the twenty-first century. Fine. She needs to take some drugs to level it all out. No big deal. You didn't have to call Mommy and Daddy. You should have called me. I know a ton of people."

I watched him take another sip of wine. I pressed the table down with the palms of my hands, but I couldn't quite finish the gesture and stand up, walk out. I couldn't believe he could sit there calmly drinking fucking Cabernet and accuse me of gaslighting my own sister. Especially since the fear that this is exactly how Gwen sees the whole thing is keeping me up at night.

I never wanted the job of watchdog.

"Look," Neil said, leaning forward and, incredibly, putting a hand over mine. "I didn't mean to upset you. Maybe she really did freak out. When I talked to her yesterday she seemed totally fine, though. She even said she wasn't that mad at you. Just frustrated. I didn't tell her I was going to see you, though. So we should probably keep that between us."

Between us? As if there could be a separate space with no Gwen. Even if she's absent, her negative space takes up so much room. It has weight, texture, scent. I nearly ordered her a vodka tonic.

"I'll be honest," Neil said. "Things between Gwen and me haven't been that great. But I care about her. I care about both of you."

That's a pretty ambiguous phrase, when you think about it. "I care about you." What does that mean? I didn't know what

to say or what to do. I was numb. I was exhausted. I was still
wearing false eyelashes. Neil leaned forward.

"Kate?"

"Yes?"

"Are you wearing Gwen's perfume?"

"No."

I looked away and saw Neil's sister weaving her way back to
us. Neil let go of my hand. When I said I was a little tired they
were both very solicitous. "Of course. You must be exhausted!"
Outside the restaurant, the sister gave me a shy hug, "You're so
tiny!" and Neil gave me a kiss on the cheek without the hug. I
got into a cab and thought about crying and calling Gwen and
demanding that she speak to me. I thought about fucking Neil
and seeing if that's what he meant about caring. I thought about
showing up at Andrew's doorstep and making a big scene. But
I would have had to change my entire personality to do any of
these things and it wasn't that long a cab ride.

When I got home I was ready for sleep, but the thought of
all the pre-bed things—face washing, teeth brushing, flossing,
getting undressed—was just too much. And my neck was throbbing. A bit of eyelash glue had made its way into the corner of
my eye. I poured myself a glass of water. I knew if I went to
bed I would just lie there, thinking, and I couldn't stand the
thought of thinking. I took another half of Vicodin, which hit
my body almost at the point of ingestion. My mood improved.
I remembered something Gwen once said about Neil. It was
after I had suggested that Neil was a bit of a player.

"He can't play me, though," she said. In another person this
might have sounded worldly, or sophisticated. But Gwen isn't
like that, exactly. What she is, is extremely honest and sort

of philosophically consistent. Once she thinks of something, that's it. That's her opinion. Faced with that, I often have to consider that what I think of as my own carefully reasoned philosophy is in fact just bricolage. A bird's nest of things I've read, things I've heard, feathers and leaves and takeout containers, single socks and song lyrics. And that I never really understand anything at all.

"He can't play you?" I prompted.

"The person he would play isn't really me," Gwen said simply. "It has nothing to do with me. So it doesn't really matter. You know?"

I did know. I actually admired her point of view, although I felt some compunction about condoning it.

"So what's the point of going out with someone if you're not really yourself around them?" I asked, trying to make the question sound rhetorical even though I was genuinely interested in her answer. "Why date someone who you know won't ever get the real you?"

"Oooh," Gwen mocked, rolling her eyes. "Oooh, the *real* me! That's so deep, Kate. Oooh!"

We laughed. Of course she was right. The real you doesn't have a fixed location. And how could one possibly find the real among all the decoys? Actually, Gwen in her madness is way more consistent than most people, in terms of fundamentals.

"Besides," said Gwen, with her heartbreaker smile. "I have you for the real me."

It's not easy to drink water, smoke, keep your neck perfectly mobilized in an ice pack, and peel off fake eyelashes. What other professions engage in this difficult form of multitasking? Glamorous but aging discus throwers? Transvestite violinists?

Okay, I was wearing her perfume.

But it's just that I used up all my perfume when I was hosing down Andrew's linens. And I hate not having perfume on. It feels like going into battle without armor. Hers was there. I'm surprised that Neil could smell it. You would think after sweating though a four-act ballet I'd be back to smelling like me again. I shouldn't have been surprised though. Everything about Gwen is so distinctive.

3.

Mara asked me today if it was strange not having Gwen around and I said, "Yes, a little bit." In truth, I feel very close to her right now. Possibly because I'm using all her products in the shower and wearing a lot of her clothes. So she's on me. Well, when hasn't that been the case?

Today in class I bit the inside of my cheek during adagio because my neck hurt so badly.

Today in class I bit the inside of my cheek during adagio because I inhaled and felt a vertiginous exaltation at all the space around me that isn't Gwen and I needed to ground myself. Grind myself.

After class I had an unexpectedly rehearsal-free day, so I came back to the apartment with the intention of maybe unpacking a few things, or at least organizing my boxes. Instead I crawled under the covers of Gwen's bed with an ice pack.

There has only been one year when Gwen and I were separated. My first year in New York. Up until that point, we had

done all our training together. It was during a summer inten-
sive in Boston that a guest artist teacher approached me and
said I should absolutely think about auditioning for the company school in New York. *We* should think, of course. The
teacher spoke to Gwen and me as a unit. He offered to talk to
our parents for us. Do they understand about these things? he
asked. That the company school was the most prestigious in
the country? That studying there significantly enhanced your
chances of getting hired by a good company, maybe even *the*
company? That it was absolutely the most elite training?

Our parents did understand about these things, but the
thought of us trooping off to New York City was pushing it a
little. All alone: two teenagers? There was no academic program affiliated with dance training, how would we finish high
school? And where would we live? Other kids do it, we explained
to them on the phone from Boston. Well, *I* explained. Gwen
and I had a system for getting what we wanted, playing to our
strengths. I would lay the groundwork with diplomacy, reason,
and conviction. Gwen was the closer. At the critical moment
she would step forward with something about "achieving our
dream."

"They may not want us, but if they do then we can't pass up
the opportunity," I explained. "This is about our whole careers."

"It's just like tennis," I said, firmly. "This is like . . . junior
Wimbledon."

At that time our parents were largely occupied with our
younger brother Keith, at twelve a bona fide tennis prodigy.
("Such gifted children!" people would say to my parents, who
would respond with "We're just happy they are finding things
that interest them," in this mildly corrective way.) Keith's tal-

ents took more parenting than ours. Not only did Mom and Dad have to constantly shuttle him around to tournaments and clinics, but every two months or so Keith would decide that he hated tennis and would quit in some very theatrical way (like, on court during the middle of a match). Gwen and I, of course, were paradigms of dedication and self-discipline. Neither of our parents could understand disinclination to perfectionism. They were truly baffled by Keith. They never told him he had to stick with tennis, but I think Keith was mostly upset by the clear inference that tennis would have to be replaced by something else, and whatever that was would demand dedication and focus too. Otherwise, what was the point of doing anything?

"It's different for you," Keith once huffed at me, as I tried to explain to him that a life spent reading X-Men comic books and riding his dirt bike into ditches would not be very fulfilling. "You and Gwen," Keith rolled his eyes, "actually like, *love* ballet."

Was there a magical love-of-the-dance moment, when the muse Terpsichore called to us and we lifted our arms and spun, at one with the divine music of the Universe? I think not. Although pride and obsession can feel like love, I guess.

We started ballet when we were little. I was five and Gwen not quite four. If left to her own devices Mom might have chosen karate or soccer, but we were girly girls, and although it probably pained her she took our demands for all things pink and beribboned and princessy in stride. Plus the local ballet school was next to the local tennis club, which meant Mom could drop us off on her way to ladies' doubles. Right away we were very good at it, and you like what you are good at, and being better than other people at something is fun. Is *that* love?

By the time we had grown out of the pink princess stage we were too good at ballet to think about whether or not we loved it. That Keith should bring "love" into the equation seemed extremely petulant, not to mention ridiculous. Why would he just want to be a "regular" kid? Where was the power in that? It was like when people talked to us about how disciplined we were to "give up" things, as if giving things up was really a sacrifice. Abstention, self-control, self-inflicted pain: these are forms of power—about the only kind you can have when you're a fourteen-year-old girl, by the way.

But Keith was more like us than he let on. He complained and threw tantrums and racquets but he kept going back to tennis anyway. And now when he gives interviews he talks about how he's always had a great love for the game and that it's this love that has always pushed him through the pain and frustration and gotten him where he is. (Number 12 in the world, according to current ATP rankings.) I don't give him a hard time about making these sorts of statements. I say the same kind of fatuous crap whenever I give interviews too.

Anyway, eventually a compromise was reached about going to New York. I was sixteen and entering my senior year of high school. If I got accepted into the company school (and received a scholarship) I could go. Gwen, still a junior and a young one at that, would have to wait a year.

Strangely, Gwen took this very calmly.

"I'm not sure I want to leave home yet anyway," she said.

"What do you mean? Why not? Why would you want to stay at home?" I was incredulous. Not that we didn't have a nice family, but we were talking the difference between New York City and suburban Michigan! And who wouldn't want to go to the most elite school for ballet in the country, practically the world? It's not like we had some intriguing social life going at high school. We each had about three non-dancing friends, people we sat with at lunch who knew better than to ask us to anything after school or offer baked goods. Mostly we took class, so why not do it at the best place possible? And we could get out of regular school, which for me was intensely boring, and for Gwen a little difficult.

"It's just one year," Gwen said. "I can wait a year."

"I probably won't get in," I said, although I fully expected to. I (we) had always gotten in. I (we) had always gotten full scholarships.

I auditioned. Got in, full scholarship. The company school gave my name to a member of their board who had offered to house a promising out-of-town student in her apartment. This woman—Wendy Griston Hedges—called our house and (thankfully) spoke to my father, who did not ask (as Mom would have) if I should bring my own sheets and was meal service included.

"Interesting woman," my dad reported. "A Schubert enthusiast."

My English teacher found a correspondence course that I could finish my last few school credits with. Someone from the local newspaper came and "interviewed" me. My picture ran next to the header: "Local Girl Dances Her Way to the Big Apple." I was described: *self-possessed and graceful* (well, obviously) *with a steely-eyed determination and discipline* (are you saying I seem bitchy?). Keith was mentioned: *a very gifted young tennis player* ("That's weird that they didn't put my ranking"—Keith). My younger sibling was duly noted: *Gwen*

Crane has been with her older sister through every step, leap, and twirl and hopes to also study at the prestigious New York school (Oh my god, seriously, *twirl*? We're not *retarded*), which led to a ridiculous concluding sentence: *But for now, Kate Crane is taking on the big city for a solo number* (suddenly we're in a 1940s musical). I found this well-intentioned but ludicrous article intensely embarrassing.

I was on a plane to New York City before I even had time to get nervous. And then the plane landed. And it was just me and eight million strangers. Disoriented, I immediately shifted into the technique I had developed ever since Miss Pat had instructed us to "always imagine an audience is watching you, even when it's just class." At that time (eight years old? nine?) I hadn't been before a lot of audiences, but I had seen a movie where people were watched with a surveillance camera, so that's what I thought of. It's a good trick. And you can vary who the audience is, whether it's behavioral scientist types who are studying you, or maybe like, a general TV viewership. Or your ex-boyfriend who needs to see how ridiculously awesome and sexy you are. Or the kids who were mean to you in grade school who are now fat and married and bored and need to see how ridiculously awesome and sexy you are. The point is, there are a lot of options. At that time I liked to imagine I was being judged by a movie audience that was comparing me to other sixteen-year-olds. (Other sixteen-year-olds: lame, bored, and boring. Me: sophisticated, exceptional, and intriguingly thoughtful.)

With this in mind, I managed to make it with relative sangfroid to the taxi stand and give the driver Wendy Griston Hedges's address—typewritten, laminated, and all but stapled to my chest by Mom.

This was 1995 and the dormitory for the school had not been built yet. The student body, mostly from somewhere outside of New York City, had to scramble for accommodations as best they could. Many came with a mother who had left husband, job, even other children in order to squeeze self and dancing son or daughter into a furnished studio sublet, five locks on the door, furniture that needed to be moved before you could pull the futon out. More enterprising moms rented slightly larger apartments, advertising bedroom-to-share or pullout couch in living room on the school's call-board. Dancers were packed into these one- or two-bedrooms, names written into the waistbands of tights to prevent confusion on the shower rod, where at least six pairs hung at any given time. Additionally there were New Yorkers connected to the school or the company in some way—donors, board members, the philanthropic elite—who took in a student or two, offering the Laura Ashley–sheeted bed of a daughter recently departed to Vassar, an unoccupied maid's room, a never-used guest room because the rich rarely have a guest importunate enough to demand lodging. But these were not numerous and so I was more lucky than I knew to have landed Wendy Griston Hedges and her Upper East Side apartment.

I tried to make a good impression on my movie audience judges as the taxi jolted through the decidedly unglamorous approach to New York City. It was difficult because I was carsick. Was this Harlem? What if this wasn't Harlem but where I was going to be living? This wasn't much better than Detroit! Where were all the fancy places? Finally, I noticed a sign: 110th Street. Okay, well that gave it thirty-six blocks to improve, which thankfully, it soon did. And then it became wonderful. It was love at first brownstone and I immediately turned traitor. I would no longer be from Michigan. I was from New York. Kate Crane: New Yorker.

The taxi stopped in front of an old-fashioned Park Avenue building with a doorman. The doorman took me up in the elevator and tried to talk to me, but Kate Crane New Yorker was filled with crippling anxiety about whether or not she should tip him, and if so, how much. Mindful of my invisible audience I pulled my wallet out of my purse and held it stagily, but then pretended to forget about it and get caught up in my bags. Wendy Griston Hedges was waiting for me at the apartment door.

Shit, I can't remember what Wendy looked like to me then. Probably because I was involved in the whole doorman thing and wanting to be perfect for my judges and hoping, as I always do, that people will not talk to me until I make up my mind about them. But Wendy hasn't changed much in the past eleven years, so I'll just go ahead and describe her: five feet ten inches bowed slightly forward, the posture of a woman who has been loved, but maybe not very well, by people much smaller than herself. Hair colored cranberry by a criminally negligent stylist on the Upper East Side, who, after achieving a juice-like maroon glaze, lightly mows the thing into an irregular orb. Bright blue eyes, very white skin, impressionistic maquillage. Back then I probably would have said that she was dressed "normally," without any idea that the blouse, the cardigan, the slacks were Mainbocher, and collectively more expensive than my dad's car.

That day, Wendy Griston Hedges let me into her apartment but neglected to give me a tour of it and for several months I

had absolutely no idea of its actual size. She led me through the
foyer directly into a dining room that I would only once eat in,
and through that into a narrow kitchen. "Here is the kitchen,"
Wendy said. I nodded. "Can you cook for yourself?" she asked
anxiously. "Oh yes," I said. I never had, all on my own, but I
didn't want my movie audience to know that, or worry Wendy,
who seemed just as nervous and uncertain as I was. From the
kitchen we progressed into a hallway lined with doors. Wendy
eyed the doors as if she weren't totally confident of their contents. "Here is your bathroom," Wendy said, opening one cau-
tiously. There was no shower, and I would have to attach a spray
hose to the tub three days later, which was a great nuisance and
always fell off. "Here is your bedroom," Wendy said, gaining
courage and leading me to the end of the hall. The room had
a full-size bed in it with about ten upholstered pillows banking
the headboard. The curtains were held back with gold tassels.
I remember those details because they were the kind of "deco-
rator" touches that I associated with rich people. On our beds
back home we just had the pillows you used for sleeping, and
our curtains were just the regular drapes that you pulled apart
with cords.

"Do you know how to get to the school?" Wendy asked. "Yes,"
I said, although I did not. "Let's see . . . what else?" Wendy
sidled back into the hallway and waved a hand at the Oriental
runner. We looked at each other helplessly. Basic social skills
were beyond me. I had never spent much time with an adult
who was not a teacher or a friend's mom. "I'm fine," I assured
her. I probably did not say "Thank you." Wendy told me she'd
let me settle in the way people on the phone say "I'll let you
go." As soon as she left, for the benefit of my movie audience I

pretended to discover my wallet in my hand and pantomimed distress at not tipping the doorman. Later I tiptoed down the hallway into the kitchen, found a phone book with maps, and spent two hours figuring out where in New York I actually was.

I *was* fine, mostly. I located the Gristedes the next day and purchased cereal, carrot sticks, boxes of raisins, yogurt, Melba toast, and all manner of Lean Cuisines. For the entire year, I did not so much as scramble an egg in the kitchen. Sometimes, as a treat, I got an Entenmann's Low-Fat Raspberry Strudel and ate most of the entire thing in one sitting, carrying the remains in my dance bag to dispose of in an anonymous trash receptacle on the way to class.

To get to the school I had to either walk across Central Park or take a bus that cut through it. Nervous of both, the first time I decided to walk, giving myself two hours to make it across. I could see the buildings of where I needed to go above the tree-tops, but the paths were curved, and I didn't want to venture into any of the low tunnels, most of which contained huddled forms of homeless people and reeked of urine, even from a safe distance. I all but ran across the park and made it to the school in thirty minutes, drenched in sweat and thoroughly freaked out. I was eager to get into something safe and familiar, like ballet class.

I wasn't afraid of stepping into a class of strangers. I wasn't afraid of competition. I had always been the best in the room, or if not the best, then so much younger than everybody else that it was remarkable I was even there. It had always been like that although my confidence had been a little bit shaken over the summer at Boston Ballet because I was now sixteen. To be amazing at sixteen is not as amazing as being amazing at fourteen. This was very clear to me because I had spent eight weeks listening to people tell me how *uh-mazing* Gwen was and overhearing things like *Can you believe that girl Gwen, she's only fourteen! She's a diva. And only fourteen! Fourteen years old, doesn't that make you sick?* But I still got a lot of attention. I still was envied and hated and courted. And Gwen was back home (turning fifteen, by the way) and I was *here*. This was *my* moment.

By the end of the first class my confidence had taken a second and larger hit. For the first time in my life I was surrounded by versions of myself. They were *all* the best girls in the room. They were all the girls that always got in, always got the full scholarship, the good part. They were all my age and they were all amazing. I was in a class of me, times fourteen. It was profoundly unsettling.

Our main teacher was Madame Dombrovski, who appeared to date from early-nineteenth-century Russia and after thirty years in America could still only speak about a dozen words or phrases in English. Oddly, one of them was "ice cream" which she used to describe things both bad and good. "Guhls (shudder, pained expression), your feet like . . . ice cream. Make better." Or "Guhls (puckering of her tiny rosebud lips), make arms nice like ice cream." She called me Katya. She was always dressed in black with thick, soft snow boots on her feet. There was a rumor (unverified) that her ankles had been broken by the KGB when she tried to defect. She didn't demonstrate combinations but muttered in French what she wanted us to do, or used her forearms and hands, standard practice in ballet class, but sometimes it was hard to believe that she was seriously asking us to do those impossible things. Her class was devastatingly hard. During grande allegro she scurried behind and shoved if we were not moving big enough. She also slapped, swatted, and pinched. Sometimes she would watch and then roll her eyes and walk away, muttering ominous Russian things that sounded like *"Plutzchushni donya snyat."* This always sounded far more horrible than the standard horrible things other teachers said in English.

Our other main teacher was Dana Gopnick—a too recently retired soloist from the company who barely noticed us at all, so intent was she on following her own still capable image in the mirror. Everyone professed to "love" her, but nobody really did. Her one main insult: "Well, you can always quit and go have babies" did not resonate particularly. None of us was going to quit, and there was already a woman in the company who had a baby and continued dancing. Dana wore full ballet attire for class: leotard, tights, flowered skirt, a shellacked French twist to her hair, painted-in eyebrows, and liquid eyeliner. She wanted all of us to look up to and emulate her, but I considered her to be a cautionary tale. For excessive eyebrow tweezing, if nothing else.

Of the fourteen other girls in my class, five had been at the school for their entire training, and the rest had been there for at least two years. I was the only new girl. This was the top level of the school and conditions were tense. After this year, selections would be made about who would get into the company and who would not. My late wild-card entry into the game was not welcomed.

By the end of my first week at the school I was deeply embroiled in class competition and speculation, which intensified as the year continued. Gradually, the fourteen versions of me began to separate into distinct entities and I was able to spot weaknesses. Suzanne was prone to injury. Laurel had great feet and legs, but her technique was weak, Paula's eating disorder was a little out of control. Shin-Li might not have enough "presence," none of the teachers seemed to really like Jenny for some reason, and Noelle was just a little too tall. Mara, Tarine, and Rachel were maybe the best of the best. Rachel was maybe the best of those three, but four months into the year she dislocated her hip in a truly god-awful way—in class—much screaming—and went home to Santa Fe. She returned near the end of the year, and struggled tearfully for a month before leaving again. We all said we felt so bad for her.

Where was I in the mix? I couldn't tell, which was also new to me. I seemed to be getting a lot of attention, but nearly every day there was a moment where I felt like I was a horrible hideous lump. I was also occasionally told, more or less, that I was a horrible hideous lump. I was also told, much more often, that I was "very good" and "excellent" and "beautiful." But the criticism, aligning as it did with my most secret fears, seemed much more valid than the praise. This was as disorienting as anything else. I had felt bad about myself before, but not with this level of sincerity. To combat my insecurity I developed a sturdier veneer: lipstick, nail polish, perfume, with an all-weather topcoat of superciliousness. I stared and stared and stared at myself in the mirror, and my imagined movie audience stared too, except for the times when I said something stupid or gauche, danced badly, used the bathroom, masturbated, or ate baked goods. During those times I pretended that some sort of electrical interference blocked their reception. This happened a lot.

That year I made friends with Mara. She was a City girl,

grew up twelve blocks from the school, had been training there since she was seven. Both her parents were lawyers. Mara knew everything about the company, all the dancers, the gossip. She had been to Paris and London and the Bahamas on vacation. She had a favorite room at the Met. She had read Camus. She could play the piano. I could not believe she was shy, because in her place I would have felt so confident, having and knowing all those things. We both made fun of ourselves and other people but never of each other. We said that the best thing that could happen was if we *both* got into the company. Once I said to her, "I won't be happy if I get in and you don't," and Mara gave me a look and said, "Yes you will." I realized that she was right and that needing people and caring about them were two very different things. I tucked this thought inside me like a fortune into a cookie. It was a secret and it made me feel powerful, even though I didn't understand why.

I mailed my weekly assignments to my correspondence course, which I considered to be a vast improvement over traditional schooling. I could hardly believe I had suffered through the tedium of sitting in chairs and listening to other people yap when I could simply read, answer, and write while stretching, listening to music, or eating Melba toast. David, one of the boys at the school who was doing the same correspondence course as I was, asked if he could pay me to do our English requirement. I was desperately short of cash because my parents had no understanding of the different world I was living in and I had no intention of enlightening them. (Mom told me to write down all my expenses and send them a monthly report, but how could I have explained Chanel lipstick, a pack of ciga-

rettes, a pashmina like everyone else had, cab fare from downtown after Mara and I got drunk with Christophe and Jenny?)
I agreed to do the Novel in the Twentieth Century class for
David. Another boy, Seth, who was sending stuff to his high
school back in Arizona, paid me even more to do his Modern
American Drama. I didn't bother creating a distinctive writ-
ing style for David. "His" papers—on Virginia Woolf's *To the
Lighthouse* or whatever—were usually just the first drafts of my
papers on the same subject. I gave him a better command of
punctuation to make up the difference, and we received the
same grades from our unknown and unimagined teachers. I
loved Seth's Modern American Drama assignments and was
sad that I couldn't write really great papers for him, lest his
teachers get suspicious.

Sex was in the air but not on the ground. Baryshnikov made
it okay for boys of my generation to take ballet, and there are
more heterosexuals around than you might think. They wear
tights and leg warmers but they're essentially jocks, and at that
age they spent more time trying to impress each other than
us. The erotic charge of half-naked sweating teenagers sliding
their hands all over each other is also not quite what you would
think. You need to imagine those teenagers under fluorescent
lighting, with a giant mirror in front of them, timing their
actions to musical cues, while being scrutinized by a portly
Ukrainian who shouts things like "Put her down, but not like
sack of potatoes, you *id-i-ot.*" The girls were more enthusiastic
about partnering class than the boys, except for David, who
was the tallest and strongest and was thankful to have one class
where he wasn't being yelled at about his feet. Everyone wanted
to dance with him. Talent equaled desirability. Talent trumped

good looks or a halfway decent personality. Talent *was* a personality.

Occasionally I ran into Wendy Griston Hedges in her apartment. This embarrassed us less over time. Discovering me once with a book in my hand, she told me that she too was a reader and I was welcome to use the library.

"Oh, great," I said. "I need to get a card, I guess."

"Oh, you don't need a card. You can just take things and bring them back."

"Really? You don't need a card here?"

"Oh, heavens, no."

I paid a visit to a branch of the NYC Public Library under the firm impression that I did not need a card and suffered quite an embarrassment at the front desk. About a week later I discovered that Wendy was referring to her own personal library, a very comfortable room on the other side of the unlived-in living room. I would often find intriguing signs of life in the library before the maid service came in on Mondays: a dry-cleaning bill on the desk that had been doodled over with really good renderings of miniature horses, the marshmallow moons and stars of Lucky Charms cereal between the crevice of a corduroy seat cushion and armrest, a fencing foil left on the window ledge. These breadcrumby clues to the inner life of Wendy Griston Hedges all seemed to lead in different directions. They made me feel fond, almost protective of my patron, who was definitely eccentric, but discreetly so. This gave her dignity.

I went home for two weeks during Christmas break. I hadn't missed my family at all until I saw them again and I became instantly homesick even though I was now at home. I felt like I had been gone a thousand years and walked around touching Christmas ornaments and holiday hand towels with a combination of condescension and nostalgia. I expected my visit to be equally meaningful for my family, but my parents seemed oddly concerned with their own lives and content to just know I was somewhere in the house. "Here we all are! All together!" Mom chirped from time to time, while she launched Christmas lights at the tree and muscled cookies out of the oven. It was as if I hadn't been gone at all. Keith was in a snit because Mom and Dad had told him he couldn't go skiing in Idaho with his friend Wes because "your sister will be home" and he either ignored me totally or stared at me with goggle-eyed fake rapture at meals.

I would have been really pissed if it hadn't been for Gwen, who couldn't get enough details. She made me describe every girl in my class as if she were memorizing them. She wanted to know how everything worked: what did we do for lunch, did we pick partners for adagio class or did the teacher match girls to boys, when would the casting for the school's top-level spring gala go up, what did I think my chances were, were there any cute boys, did everyone wear makeup for class? It seemed natural that I would be the one doing all the talking. What, after all, could have happened to Gwen in Michigan?

On my third night home I went to see Gwen perform in the same Grand Rapids Ballet *Nutcracker* we had both danced in for the past six years. My parents and Keith had already been to two of the five performances by the time I got home. (Uncharacteristically, Keith never complained about going to see us dance. Possibly there was some sort of bribe involved.) Dad elected to drive me there as the night was icy and I hadn't been behind a wheel since passing my driver's test in May.

The company had only recently become professional, with salaried dancers, so *The Nutcracker* was still mainly a chance for the schoolchildren's parents to earn back their tuition fees with a chance at seeing little Jenny and little Darla cutely out-fitted as mice or toy soldiers. Oh, those Jennys and Darlas . . . thrilled to have Mommy apply splatches of blush on their cheeks, self-importantly managing a ponytail full of rollers for the evening's required First Act Party Child ringlets. You can measure out the progress of time by your personal relationship to *The Nutcracker.*

Gwen was dancing the Dew Drop Fairy, sort of a runner-up to the Miss America role of Sugarplum Fairy. I was a little sur-prised that they had given Dew Drop to her, since now that Grand Rapids could actually hire dancers the leading roles went to them. *I* hadn't ever danced it. Last year Gwen and I had been matching Mirliton soloists, the best a student could get. Of course she was the star of the school (now that I was gone, the only star), but she was still a student.

"They say that they want to turn this into a world-class com-pany," my dad said, as we took our seats. "There's a lot of local support. Maybe you'll want to come dance here when you're done with school."

"In New York there's a live orchestra," I said, as the taped music began.

Dew Drop Fairy isn't until nearly the end, during the Waltz of the Flowers. I had applauded patronizingly through the familiar ballet, noting the lack of progress of my former class-mates and wincing at the technical mistakes and lack of polish. There was one new guy who was very good, some Polish kid who had inexplicably wound up in Michigan. The super-skinny woman dancing Arabian had great extensions, but her arms were sort of a mess. I saw nothing to threaten my com-placency. If I were still here, I thought, I would be the best. Or destined to become the best, which was really the same thing. Then Gwen came on.

I didn't so much hold my breath as my breath was somehow taken from me, like there existed some sort of high-powered vacuum from my lungs directly to Gwen's body, and she drew whatever oxygen I was capable of employing for my own puny needs in a giant powerful *whoosh*. It was over quickly, too quickly, and as Tchaikovsky fuzzed on through the auditori-um's speaker system and Sugarplum and her Cavalier gamely tipped their way through the ballet's concluding pas de deux, I tried to compose myself. My hands hurt from applauding. My feet were cold. I had a headache in my neck.

Somehow, some way, while I had gossiped and scarfed Entenmann's and flirted with my invisible movie audience and practiced hairstyles and pretended to Mara that I too was famil-iar with Kandinsky, Gwen had gotten incredibly good. Impos-sibly good. She was better than Mara, and Tarine, and Rachel even before she blew her hip. She was better than me. She was the best. I didn't understand this. Had she always been better? Maybe her performance was a fluke. One of those wacky eclipse timing things that sometimes happen where you nail every bal-ance, land like a feather from every jump, where all your single pirouettes become doubles, all your doubles become triples, everything comes easy, easy.

"I was a little better last week," was what Gwen said to me, later that night. "I felt a little rickety tonight 'cause I knew you were out there and I was nervous."

Makeup removed, the hair down her back still a little clumpy from hairspray and pins, pink-and-white poodle flannel pajamas swamping her skinny frame, Gwen sat on the end of my bed and chattered on. What did I think about so and so, and can you believe such and such and really did I mean it? She was okay?

"You were amazing," I kept saying, hating myself and her. She had tricked me. She had pretended to be so fawning and interested and admiring of my New York City life and all the while she was keeping the enormous secret of her coruscating, effortless, obnoxious talent hidden away like a bomb. *Tick, tick . . . boom.*

Under the Christmas tree were my presents for her: a Chanel lipstick, the Capezio sweater everyone in my class had, dangly earrings like I had started wearing. I had bought them in good faith, wishing to bestow a little glamour on my kid sister, be encouraging: *this is what you can have too.* Now I wanted to sneak out to the family room and take them all back. If Gwen had stuff that was as good as my stuff, then what did I have? I had nothing.

"You were amazing," I said, and Gwen curled around my knees and said that her one dream was of us both getting into the company and sharing an apartment in New York City. "I know you'll get in," she said.

I said I wasn't so sure but that I wouldn't be happy unless we *both* got in.

"I know," she said. "I feel exactly the same way."

Gwen's Christmas present to me was a huge box of stationery she had made herself, cutting things from magazines and gluing them on the paper. "She's been working on that since the time you left," Mom said. All the envelopes and postcards were pre-addressed to Gwen, and stamped too. "You can just throw them in the mailbox," Gwen explained. "I made enough so that you can write me every week." I cried a little bit and everybody said, "Awwww," even though my getting all misty was mostly guilt and shame.

And love. I can hardly bear now to remember her face, watching eagerly for my reaction as I opened the gift. Of her little shoulders under my hands as I hugged her. We always say it's the other one's shoulders that seem tiny. We always press our cheeks hard against each other before we let go.

Oh Gwen.

I couldn't believe that for three months I had basically forgotten about my sister. It was not a mistake I would ever repeat.

I went back to New York and took everything up a notch.

The newly appointed artistic director of the company, Marius Lytton, made occasional godlike descents to the school, sometimes accompanied by his balefully countenanced English Bull-dog, Ludmilla. It was the wrong dog for him. With his shaggy black hair and neatly trimmed reddish beard, his height, his giant gold watch and ability to wear a neck scarf without looking ridiculous, he should have had a Wolfhound or a Saluki. Marius lounged in the doorway of our class and watched us for a few minutes at a time. We watched him out of the corners of our eyes. Ludmilla investigated her own lady parts.

We knew Marius's history: he was a principal dancer with the company in the early '80s, left to choreograph in Europe, became the artistic director of a company in the Netherlands.

Returned to become associate artistic director here and had recently assumed the helm of one of the world's most significant ballet companies. In those early days his position was precarious, his board was watchful and begrudging of monies, his dancers insecure and therefore vaguely mutinous, but we knew nothing of this. To us he was Christ and we prayed that he would ask us to leave our father's fishing nets and follow him unto the desert.

Word circulated that Marius was looking to hire four dancers, two girls and two boys, from our class. Further word was that it might not be from our class, Marius was holding open auditions for the company. Our audition would be the final end-of-year performance, which Marius and a good many other artistic directors from around the country would attend. The open audition came and went. Justin knew a girl who had been there and told him that after twenty minutes Marius had cut everybody except for eight dancers. Eight dancers! He kept that many? Were they good? How many were girls? Did anybody get offers? Justin's friend didn't know, she wasn't one of the final eight but she knew a girl who was. That girl was *old*—twenty-five!—and already a soloist with the Pennsylvania Ballet. There was widespread panic as everyone recalculated the odds. I dug in and dug in deeper. Whenever I felt tired or listless, I thought of Gwen and pushed through. Mara and I both got cast in lead roles for the year-end performance. We knew that we had separated ourselves from the pack a little, but we didn't know if there was room for both of us to succeed. All during rehearsals we said nothing to each other that wasn't sarcastic or funny or self-deprecating. It wasn't really Mara I was judging myself against, though.

Gwenny! They brought me a practice tutu for
rehearsal today so Milos could get used to it—totally
makes a difference for partnered pirouettes, and the
lifts, etc. This week has been hard. Rain, rain, rain.
My skin is horrible and I cut bangs. Whatever you do,
don't cut bangs! (Probably be cute on you, though.
Cut bangs!) I'm doing this word-a-day thing now to
improve my vocabulary. Today's word is: noxious.
This rain is noxious and so are my attitude turns.
But I'll keep trying! Miss you! Love, K

At the end of the year it was Mara, David, and I who were
asked to join the company, along with some guy Marius found
in Brazil whom none of us had ever seen. When I was brought
into Marius's office and he offered me a contract he told me
that he was excited about working with me, that he saw real
potential, that I needed to get more confident, work hard, but
that he knew that would happen. He told me that at the end-of-
year performance he saw something "deep" in me, and I made
a "deep" face for him, for my applauding invisible movie audience, for the me I wished I was. The me who was confident and
had already fulfilled her potential.

I had dreamed that if this moment happened I would be elated
and triumphant and flooded with relief, but when you have been
keeping company with anxiety and fear for a long time it's hard
to shake them off immediately. Also I hadn't really thought about
anything beyond the immediate goal: getting in. Now I was in
and now I was going to have to *do* this thing, ballet, and not
just think about the day I would do it. I realized I still wanted to

dream about the person I would become, not actually *be* her. I was worried that I would work hard and nothing would happen, that I was as good as I would ever be. I wasn't sure I wanted to work hard anymore. I already felt kind of exhausted.

I blurted out to Marius that my sister would be auditioning the school and that he would want her too, she was amazing, she was *better*. I was then immediately embarrassed at my effusiveness and made a misguided attempt to pet Ludmilla, who nearly took my hand off.

"It's my wife's dog, actually," Marius said. "She hates everybody."

"Your wife hates everybody?" I said.

"No," Marius started to explain, and then realized I was making a deliberate joke.

"Oh," he said, surprised, and then he sealed what would become our eventual relationship. "That's very funny. You're a sharp girl."

I walked out of Marius's office and I didn't cry or jump up and down or scream or anything. I walked across the park to Wendy Griston Hedges's apartment and said to myself, "This is really happening," and "This is the happiest moment of my life." My movie audience applauded, but I didn't curtsy. I was terrified. I wanted to run away, disappear, evaporate.

I called home and Gwen picked up.

"I got in," I said. "I got a contract."

And Gwen screamed and I could hear her jumping up and down.

"You're the luckiest person alive," she said.

"I know," I said. "Totally lucky. I don't actually deserve it."

"No, you do!" Gwen squealed. "You totally do! I meant you're lucky to be *you*! I want to be you!"

"Well, you're going to come here, right," I said. "So you will be me. You'll be better than me."

"Not better. Oh my god. It's really happening. Okay, so, what do we do if I get in? Do you think your woman will let me stay at that place too? Or what? How do we do it?"

I thought of Gwen rambling around Wendy's apartment, not interested in the books, thinking Wendy was "weird." Grappling with the shower hose in the bathroom, skittering across Central Park by herself. All these things would be harder for her. She wouldn't like it. Mara and I had talked about getting a place together. That would probably happen now that we both had gotten in. We were in. It was real.

"Do you think Mom and Dad would let you move in with Mara and me?" I asked. "We could get something for all three of us if you don't mind not having your own bedroom."

"Oh my god, Kate, that would be awesome. But anyway I want to hear everything Marius said. Start from the beginning. So you like, walked into the office . . ."

And she soaked up every word and told me how I was her hero and the most amazing dancer in the world and that she knew I was scared but I shouldn't be because I had nothing to be scared of, I could do it. "Don't be scared," she said. And that she knew this about me—knew that I was scared even though I had never told her anything like that—made me genuinely want her with me in New York. Made me stop wanting to disappear. Made me see my own place more clearly, defined in relation to her place. Made me coach her like a nervous stage mother when she came that summer to audition for the company school. Made me lie to Mara and tell her that my parents insisted on my living with my sister so that Mara would agree to all three of us getting a place. Made me make a highly articulate and sensible case for this to our parents.

I remember watching her audition through the mirrors of the studio and feeling incredibly proud. She was still sweating when they pulled her into the office and offered her a full scholarship. When she came out we hugged each other's thin shoulders hard, and pressed our cheeks together before letting go.

Things have been the way they are for so long that I've forgotten about a lot of this. I've forgotten that Gwen was ever different from how she is now. I've forgotten that I got here first. I've forgotten that there was a time, if only for a little bit, when I carried a secret around. I understand that secret now. I break the cookie open and read my fortune. *Just me*, it says. Could I ever really have wished for that?

I wanted her to become a star. It was easier to want Gwen's stardom than my own. Did I push her? Did she push me back?

You can't answer these questions, of course, invisible audience member. You don't know a goddamn thing, you're just following the story like anyone else, right?

A star is mostly hydrogen, collapsing in a luminous cloud. There is something, some kind of internal pressure within the star that keeps it from collapsing totally into its own gravitational pull. Maybe Gwen and I have always stayed together by some force of gravity. Only now she's drifted away. Leaving me with all this internal pressure, lost in space, pulsing senselessly in the dark. Punishing me for the selfishness of once wanting to be without her. And then the selfishness of not letting her go.

And now it's time for me to go to work. There is a Polish Princess costume with my name on it, waiting limply on a hanger, needing to be filled. Because I am not sure that I am enough to animate it, I take another Vicodin, which seems to help.

4.

I haven't talked much to my parents since Gwen has been with them. I actually don't talk to them all that often anyway. It's not like we have a bad relationship. I love them. They're very supportive, but not overbearing, unique among both ballet and tennis parents.

Really, you can almost feel bad for them. I mean they should have had much more normal children. They should have had kids who studied hard and got good grades and maybe did one or two extracurricular activities well and then went to college and grad school and then became . . . whatever it is people become. They were prepared to be parents of such children. Maybe some parents think they want (or imagine they have) exceptionally gifted children, but I don't think that's what either of my parents wanted.

Mom was a great tennis player herself. She went to the University of Michigan on a tennis scholarship, and was an All-Star. But she never turned pro. She's always said that she knew it wasn't the life she wanted, but I've also heard her say that she knew she didn't have what it took to be the best. I can never tell from the way she says "the best" whether she's embarrassed at her failure to be it, or to aspire to it.

And Dad played the violin. He was almost like a child prodigy. But his family was sort of poor, and he went to medical school and became an oral surgeon, which he insists he finds very satisfying. He says he likes the concentration.

Dad still practices the violin, almost every day. Real practices, scales and repeating passages over and over. He says he never liked performing, he just liked practicing.

My parents believe in working hard and being disciplined, but in an effort-for-its-own-reward kind of way. Seeing any of us perform makes them very nervous. Whenever they visit New York, they never want to come backstage and are shy about meeting our friends. Which is funny, because they are really very presentable parents. (God, Roger's mom!) But it's worse for them with Keith, because with us they can sit in the dark, and with my brother, now that he's becoming such a big deal, they have to sit in the player's box, and you never know when the cameras might swing over to get their reactions. It's agony for my mom especially. Despite her background in the sport, she still worries that not applauding Keith's opponents when they play well looks "surly."

I've never been in the habit of telling my parents much about my life. Maybe because so much of it concerned Gwen, and how could I say how "things were going" without saying how things were going with her?

I know I can count on them, though. Like when I asked Dad to come get Gwen he didn't hesitate. He's very mild and gentle, my dad, but he's good in a crisis. I think this is because all day long he deals with people who are completely freaked out about whatever is happening in their mouths.

I asked Dad to get Gwen rather than Mom because Mom's way of dealing with crises is to organize irrelevant details. She wouldn't have taken Gwen away. She would have bought Gwen a houseplant (I think she needs more oxygen!) and re-caulked the bathtub (Let's get everything spic-and-span!).

I thought about calling my parents this morning, but instead I called my brother Keith.

I remember the day Mom and Dad brought Keith home from the hospital. I was six, and very excited. Gwen was less so. Keith was thoroughly boy, from the very beginning, and never picked up anything he didn't want to throw, ram, or pretend to shoot.

But I have a very sweet memory of Keith from childhood. Every summer (before summer dance programs and tennis clinics took over) we went on a camping trip to the dune beaches at Lake Michigan. It was understood that this was so our parents could "relax," although Mom treated "rough" living the same way she treated living at home. Much vigorous sweeping out of the tents every morning and a tarp over everything. Gwen didn't like the water much, so she and Dad would always make a giant sand castle together, very elaborate and, knowing Dad, architecturally accurate. Keith and I loved the water. He would hold on to a boogie board and I would push him out in front of me. Mom would stand at the shore in one of the increasingly conservative series of yellow bikinis she purchased every year, a kerchief around her hair to keep it from frizzing in the July humidity, and shout, "Kay-ay-ate! Look out for your broth-errr." Sometimes he let me carry him out pig-gyback style and we would stand there, bobbing in the waves, Keith's strong little legs in a hammerlock around my waist, his shrill piccolo scream provoking another automatic "Kay-ay-ate! Care-ful!" from Mom onshore, sitting up on the blanket, shading her eyes with a Danielle Steel romance to make sure we were still alive. Keith was three years old when he first let go of me and swam about ten feet, kicking and splashing like a madman but in a recognizable crawl. He popped his head up with a huge grin, dog-paddling furiously. "Mo-om! Da-ad! Keith can SWIM."

Two years later Mom put a racquet in Keith's hand. We all questioned the wisdom of giving Keith something that could be used as a weapon, but it worked out well in the end.

"I was just thinking about you!" Keith said when he picked up the phone.

"Where are you?" I asked. "Are you still here?" Here means Florida, where Keith touches down periodically and where he just bought a house. My little brother has a house. He has a lot of things. Between prize money and endorsements I think he's making a couple million dollars a year. A ballet dancer at his equivalent level of success might eke out a hundred grand a year, a bit more if they do a lot of guest performances with different companies. In New York City that means you might be able to rent a small one-bedroom and still be able to buy Bumble and Bumble shampoo.

"Here for another week, then I'm off to Morocco," said Keith.

"Oh yeah, clay courts, right?" Keith is awesome on clay. Last year he made it to the semis of the French.

"Yup."

"Is Famke with you?"

"Francesca, asshole."

"I know. I love Francesca!"

"You loved Famke. You hate Francesca."

"Do I? No. Wait. I loved Heidi. Famke had those pipe-cleaner legs. They made me nervous. It looked like you could bend them in any direction."

"Yeah, but she had an awesome rack."

Keith and I can go on like this for hours.

"Hey, let's Skype," Keith said.

"Can't. I'm at Gwen's. I just have my old laptop."

There was a brief pause then and a lessening of background noise. I imagined my brother muting whatever sports channel was on. Maybe stretching out on the couch.

I've seen Keith more on television and Skype in the past couple of years than in person. Last year our parents came for the U.S. Open and Gwen, Neil, Andrew, and I all went too. Keith lost in the quarters but Mom particularly was pleased with how he played and, more importantly, how he behaved. Keith's on-court behavior has been a bit of an issue in the past. When he was in juniors it was less noticeable because most of those kids are super emotional and there's a fair amount of racquet throwing and crying and so forth. But once you get to the senior level—and high up in it, like Keith—you need to pull your shit together. You're on television, for one thing, and if you spaz out then it's all over YouTube. There's a fine line to walk, though. If you're too contained and unemotional then it looks like you don't care. But if you call the linesperson a blind cunt-face, then you'll get fined and look like an asshole. Also, as I have explained to Keith, "cunt-face" is just confusing imagery. Nobody actually has that face.

"Yeah," Keith said, after a pause. "So Mom said you and Andrew were like, working through some stuff or something?"

"I think that was her way of saying we broke up."

"Yeah, I figured. I've been meaning to call you. And now. You know. Gwen."

"Yeah."

"I thought you and Andrew were going to get married."

"Really?" I felt sort of pleased that Keith had had thoughts, or speculations, about me.

"He wasn't who I pictured you'd end up with."

"Huh. Who did you picture?"

I was having this conversation with Keith while still in bed. I've been making efforts to keep Gwen's place spotless, so pretty much all my basic life things have ended up in the bed with me in order not to mess up other surfaces. I'm sleeping in between piles of books and notebooks and my computer and phone and various bags of stuff. If I had known Keith was going to answer his phone and we'd be having this interesting conversation I would have gotten some ice for my neck. As it was I rooted around under the covers until I found a bottle of water. Vicodin is very dehydrating.

"Oh, I don't know," Keith said, disappointingly. "So you're staying at Gwen's?"

"For now."

"What's the deal with her?"

I drank some water. When we were all little kids, I felt like I had kind of a special bond with my brother. That he looked up to me particularly. But maybe he identifies more with Gwen now.

"What did Mom tell you?" I hedged.

"Gwen's been having some bads and she's resting up at home right now and taking it easy," Keith said in a singsong voice. He does a very good Mom imitation, who tends to use second-grade words, or pluralize things oddly, when she wants to mitigate their possible dramatic effect. "Keith had some sads at Wimbledon." "Gramma Crane is having issues with her intestinals." "Your dad had a mole removed from his shoulder and they are testing it for ickies."

"What's really been going down?" Keith asked.

"It looked to me like a nervous breakdown," I said. My stomach had that tense crumpled-paper feeling and even though I was lying down I saw something sharp coming around the corner to stab me in the eye.

"It's, um. It's been building up for a while now," I said.

"That's what Mom said."

"She did?"

"She said, 'Apparently it's been building up for a while now but we didn't know anything about it.'"

"I knew."

"She said that too."

"Well, it wasn't my place to go around, you know, informing the family about Gwen." I put my phone on speaker and placed it on my chest so I could work on my neck a little.

"You finally did though, right?" Keith's voice bounced up from my rib cage. "You told Dad to come get her and take her back to Michigan?"

"I didn't know what else to do."

"Yeah."

I watched the phone rise and fall. See, Dr. Wang? See what a good breather I am?

"You think she's better off in Michigan?" Keith's voice was fading. Maybe he had me on speaker now too, in order to ice or heat or massage. He's always got something slightly injured.

"I didn't think she should be alone," I said.

"Well, she wasn't alone though, right? She was with you. Just saying. If I were depressed I don't think going to vay-cay with Judy and William in Michigan would be my first choice."

"So why don't you take her with you to Morocco?" I half shouted toward my ribs. "If I did such a horrible job at taking care of her maybe you'd like to try."

"Jesus, freak out much? I didn't say you, okay, never mind." Keith sighed.

I swung myself out of bed, dislodging a pile of crap, and stumped to the kitchen. Pulled a plastic bag of ice out of the freezer and retreated back to bed. Throughout this I heard the TV come back on at the other end of the line.

"Any-hoo," I sang, using the Mom voice.

"What's that sound?" He laughed.

"Ice bag. Neck."

"Oh, good. I thought it was the sound of your brains cracking up."

"How are you, by the way? How's the knee?"

And for the next ten minutes it was great, it was normal, with us giving each other shit in all the familiar ways that we haven't figured out how to replace yet. We said good-bye and I called Gwen's cell. My mom picked up.

"Hi, sweetie."

"Oh hey. Hey! I thought I'd try Gwen before I tried you. Hi! How . . . how are you?"

Mom, it seemed, was fine. Dad was fine. Gwen was fine, her knee was healing. Everything was fine. Fine and dandy. Well, Gwen had a little bit of a setback. She had had some delusionals. Some paranoias. We were just going to have to wait and see and take deep breaths and visualize Tibetan skies of blue. I didn't need to worry. Gwen wasn't really talking to anyone right now. She needed a break. Just some time to regroup. More references to Tibetan skies.

"It's actually not that peaceful an image," I pointed out. "Since Tibet is currently occupied by China. Monks have been setting themselves on fire under Tibetan skies."

"I guess that's true. Ha-ha!" Rustle, rustle, thump. Sounds of cabinets banging. Mom putting away groceries. She has this very aerobic approach to household chores.

"What kind of delusionals?" I asked. "Delusional like she's really emotional or like she thinks she's Queen of the Fairy Kingdom?

"Kate."

"Seriously, Mom."

"Well, her knee was bothering her."

"Uh-huh."

"She was concerned about the stitches."

"Right."

"And there had been some nightmares."

After some persistent questioning I got at least a partial version of the story. It seemed that Gwen's sessions with her psychiatrist had become increasingly upsetting for Gwen, and a week ago she had gotten my parents up at two in the morning telling them that the shadows in her room were smothering her, and Gwen's arms were covered with her own nail marks. She had raked them down her forearms deep enough to draw blood. Also, she thought the stitches in her knee were poisoning her and she had sort of tried to . . . undo them, I guess. They had gone to the Emergency Room, and Gwen had calmed down but not before she was dosed with lithium, which was a horrible drug and had done horrible things to Gwen but it was going to be *fine*, they just needed to reevaluate the situation.

"This is it!" I wanted to shout. "This is what I've been dealing with for almost ten years! Now you see it! This is what it's like!"

I realized how eagerly, ghoulishly, I had been waiting for this hand-off. For someone else to see what happens with Gwen, for someone else to deal with it. But I had that crumpled-paper feeling inside my stomach again.

"Why did you tell me she was fine?" I demanded, covering the side of my face with my free hand, a buffer against flying knives. "Why am I just hearing about this now?"

Mom is no dummy. She let enough silence in so I could hear what I just said.

"You haven't been telling us everything either, have you?" she asked, very calmly.

"What do you mean?"

"What do I mean about what?"

"It sounded like you were accusing me of something."

"Oh Kate, don't be so sensitive," Mom said, chirping. "I know you've always been very protective of your sister. That's all I was saying. You always think I'm implying these . . . I don't know whats."

"I just want you to keep me in the loop, okay. I don't know why you can't call me."

"I was waiting until we knew a little more. We don't really know anything about this kind of thing. We have to let Gwen do this herself is what they keep saying. I know you want to help."

"Is her knee okay, at least?"

"Yes. That they seem able to handle. These doctors, Kate. You should see some of the literature they hand you. They'll *make* you crazy! Now how's my Katie-bird? Let's talk about you for a little bit."

I told her about my neck.

"It's not serious, though," said my mom.

"I don't know," I said. "It may be. It's hard. I'm in a lot of pain, actually."

Jesus, my voice even wobbled when I said that. Luckily that jerked me back to my senses.

"But I'm taking care of it. No bigs."

"You'll be all right! Drink lots of water and wrap it up in one of your scarves."

"I will."

Conversation stalled. We talked a little more, in a desultory fashion. Like two people playing tennis, but on separate courts, so nobody could return a shot.

"How are you holding up?" I asked her, at the end of the conversation. "Is there anything I can do?" These are the things one says. Especially when there's a high-percentage chance that the response will be "I'm fine" and "No, thank you."

"You just take care of yourself," Mom said. "You just be my rock."

"I guess Gwen won't be coming back anytime soon, huh?"

"Apparently the first thing is to get the right medication," Mom said doubtfully. "But I don't really know too much about all that."

I wasn't being insensitive, by the way, suggesting that Gwen might believe she was Queen of the Fairies. If Gwen were here she'd be rehearsing Titania, Queen of the Fairies, for A *Midsummer Night's Dream*.

After we hung up I decided to stay in bed for a little while. That turned into skipping company class and staying in bed until ten. Just resting, you know. Like a rock. Obviously it was a very upsetting conversation. Actually I was pretty freaked out.

It's not a big deal—skipping company class. It's not officially mandatory for soloists and principals, although you don't want to go too long without putting in an appearance. And of course you do have to take class somewhere. It's part of our creed, daily class. And one still says "class" even when one is a professional and has ceased to actually be learning anything other than the precise amount of erosion occurring in one's cartilage. Not that one is perfect and there is nothing more to learn. But class at this point is really more about maintenance and self-evaluation. It's easy to get out of shape if you aren't always pushing yourself. It's easy to lose your edge if you don't constantly hold yourself to the highest standards. Unrecoverable torpor might not be a matter of a few missed classes, but it feels like it.

Andrew came once to watch me take class. "It wasn't like what I thought," he said, and then: "It looks weird to see people dancing up close like that." Later when we were having sex he told me that it really turned him on to watch me sweat. This is the kind of thing that happens when you date civilians. You tell your average non-dancing dude that you are a dancer and they all think the same thing, which is some version of "Wow, so I can fuck her while she's in the splits." Perhaps all these guys should be issued a dancer at some point in their sexual development so they can get over this debilitating notion and learn the truth: the splits are a terrible position to have sex in. Nobody gets any traction at all and it's just goofy. You're better off with the basics and someone who isn't either hungry or exhausted.

This morning would have been a good moment for Andrew because I was very upset, somewhat theatrically so really, but I didn't long for his comforting arms to be around me. Andrew was security, maybe, but not solace. Then he turned out to be neither, right, so the joke is on me. And I'm in the splits, getting no traction.

I took class with Gareth before going to rehearsal. Gareth teaches at a big studio on the Upper West Side.

So here's the thing with ballet studios around town. For the most part, all the classes are technically "open." Which means if you have a pair of ballet slippers, you could go take Gareth's class too. Most classes are rated: Beginning, Intermediate, or Advanced, but teachers rarely throw anyone out. They need the money. So at a class like Gareth's you might get major company members, some unemployed dancers, Broadway kids, serious students, and then a handful of freaks. The freaks never miss a class. Proof that one can maintain a residence in New York City, have enough surplus cash to pay for dance class, feed and clothe oneself, learn choreography, wear pointe shoes, and still be an absolute stranger to Reason. There's one regular at Gareth's who spends the entire class standing in the corner and arranging himself in elaborate Diaghilev-era postures while talking to his reflection in the mirror. It should be noted that these whackjobs are probably the happiest people in the room.

Gareth is always pleased to see me or any professional, really. Since he only teaches at noon he doesn't get a lot of us. Wendell, who teaches at ten at the same studio, is the popular choice for most company dancers, since his class is by invitation only. It's always packed. He's quite the little guru. People get very nervous when they know Wendell is in the audience. His "Not bad at all, sweetie, there were some very nice moments here and there" means more to some dancers than an "Absolutely radiant and virtuosic" from the *New York Times*. I don't like him, or his class, or the atmosphere in the room. He's a big fan of Gwen, though.

Gareth is English and I find his accent and irony soothing. I'm happy when he comes to a performance, because I know he'll have something funny to say to me when I see him next. Sure enough, he gave me a wink before class began and during pliés he sauntered over to my spot. (I like to be at the barre near the window. For the fresh air and in case I need something to throw myself out of.) "Darling," he said. "I was there last night. I saw what you did."

"What did I do?" I laughed. "I can't remember a thing."

"You made me want to be a Polish Princess," Gareth drawled, doing a sketch of a mazurka with his hands. "You made me forget that I've seen the ruddy ballet five thousand times. Where did *that* come from?"

"Powerful analgesics," I said.

"Oh?" Gareth raised an eyebrow. "Well, keep it up."

Class.

First thirty to forty-five minutes are at the barre. There's an order and a logic to it, but it's not always the same exercises. Some teachers might start class with a little guided stretching: rolling the head, the shoulders, swinging out the hips, the lower back. Some teachers may have a set sequence for the first couple of combinations, and if you're new to the class and don't know it, you just follow the person standing at the barre in front of you. Always the left hand on the barre first, then turn around and repeat with the right hand on the barre. Hand on the barre lightly, please. It's not a crutch. Along with basic warm-up of the muscles it's also about finding your center, your balance. You'll need that later on.

That's the other thing Andrew said. "How do you guys know what to do? The teacher was like, just mumbling stuff and not even dancing and then you'd all spring into action and it looked nothing like what he was doing."

Pliés, tendus, dégagés, fondus, rondes de jambe, rondes de jambe en l'air, frappés, développés, grande battements. You do all this from your first ballet class and it's part of you. Gareth might say, "Okay, tendus." And we'll watch him for a moment as he half demonstrates in his big white sneakers. "IN, IN, IN, and IN, IN, IN, and IN, IN, IN, and OUT PLIÉ. Front, side,

back. Yes? And then port de bras. SIDE, to the front. SIDE, to
the back. Plié, sous-sous, soutenu, OTHER SIDE." This makes
sense to us. We know what to do.

And IN, IN, IN.

When you are a student, class is as serious as everything
else, which is to say that it is very, very serious. Even the most
basic, most beginner-level thing, first position, is loaded with
rules. Heels OUT. Legs STRAIGHT. Knees pulled UP. Stomach IN and FLAT. Rib cage IN and UP. Shoulders DOWN.
Arms OUT. Elbows LEVEL. Thumb curved slightly IN, first
finger slightly EXTENDED, the next two following in a gentle
descent, the pinkie finger RELAXED and slightly RAISED.
Neck LONG. Chin LEVEL. The teacher circles the room,
watching, correcting. Technique. There's one right way to do
everything. Every other way is wrong. But it can never be stiff,
or robotic. The amount of technique you need to master before
you can be decently said to be dancing classical ballet is enormous. But there does come a time when a great deal of this is
automatic.

For most of us professionals, class is self-assessment, like I
said. Namely, what hurts? And, how do I feel? Do I feel okay?
Do I need to worry about that twinge or will it go away once
I'm warmed up? There's also a kind of zone. Some days you
feel great right away. From the first couple of pliés you feel centered, you feel in control. It's going to be a good class, a good
day. All is right in the world. And IN, IN, IN.

Other days the zone eludes you. Nothing feels good. You
look in the mirror and it does its funhouse thing and you feel
sour and heavy. And there are days when it is possible to be
fully engaged in what you are doing and be completely, mind-

numbingly, tooth-achingly *bored*. But you still have to do it. And IN, IN, IN.

As a professional, class is a safe place presumably. No audience. If you look like hell, it's okay because who cares, it's just class. Theoretically. In practice, a terrible class can have you feeling almost as wretched as a terrible performance. If a ballerina falls in a forest and there's no one around to see her, does she make a noise? Yes, she does. It is the sound of the ballerina saying, "Oh fuck me."

After barre comes center. Depending on the number of students, groups are formed, usually two, so everyone has room. Maybe if you pick up combinations quickly (a mini-art in itself) you'll step up for group one. Maybe if it looks like there is an abundance of eager beavers going in group one you'll hang back for more floor space in group two.

In the center, we arrange ourselves in slightly staggered lines, facing the mirrors. There is etiquette for a mixed class like this one. A student should never stand in front of a professional. A man should never stand in front of a woman. If you sense that you're crowding someone in the middle of a combination, you should gracefully step back or forward. Failure to do this will result in hostile stares or a drubbing from the teacher. Occasionally an etiquette-oblivious freak or whackjob will get tossed out of class. Gareth did it once to some poor dear who didn't have her hair tied back properly.

"Either you leave or I will cut that goddamn mop off your head," he said. She hesitated, and he pointed to the door.

Center is maybe forty-five minutes. Again, individual teachers and classes differ, but order and logic are maintained. There is an adagio combination—slow lifting of the legs in different positions, balance, control, extension. Some bright tendus, shifting the weight quickly and moving in different directions to get the blood moving. Maybe a little traveling step, a waltz. Pirouettes. More pirouettes. Small jumps, traveling jumps.

The teacher issues corrections, shouting above the music, or maybe seizing a moment in between groups to elaborate on some point, issue a general admonishment, or work with an individual. A correction given to one person is usually taken up by others. No one ever refutes or argues a correction, because it's not a subjective thing. If someone tells you that you are doing something—raising a shoulder too high, cheating a preparation for a turn, rushing the music—then that means you are absolutely doing that. And you correct it. Sometimes a teacher might ask someone to demonstrate: "Julie, do it. Everyone, watch Julie. This is how it should be done." And everyone will watch Julie and when she's finished, we will applaud, and Julie will make the gesture for modesty.

Class always ends with big jumps on the diagonal. First from left to right, then right to left. Groups are smaller: three or four dancers at a time, the rest forming a snaky line at the back of the studio, men waiting at the end so they can go together. (The pianist will slow her tempo for the men, who jump higher. Intrepid women will sometimes tag on to a men's group to push their elevation.) Many professionals opt out at this point, saving their knees, their ankles, their backs, for the day's rehearsal or evening performance. To this too there is an etiquette. You don't just walk out of someone's class. You catch their eye, mime a thank you, blow a kiss, pantomime a bow.

If class is running late (over ninety minutes), a teacher might just clap or wave their hands after everyone has gone across the floor a couple of times, and say "Thank you!" or whatever. Or they might bring the entire class back to center for a formal révérence. (That's curtsy and bowing to you civvies.) Conscientious teachers will instruct the students to include the pianist in the révérence. At the end of all this, you applaud. The teacher and the pianist, I mean. Not yourself. Then everyone heads for whatever corner they stashed their dance bag/discarded sweater/water/towel and shuffles out, chatting, sweating, checking cell phone, trying to catch the teacher's eye for last-minute approval or correction, dodging the freak who after class likes to practice some macabre version of fouetté turns in the middle of the room, lost in some *Swan Lake* of her own invention, oblivious that the audience has left.

Today in class my neck was still in a pretty shitty state, but I pushed myself anyway, mostly because I knew I had Gareth's attention, and also to punish myself for skipping class yesterday. Gareth asked me to demonstrate the adagio—"Everyone, watch Kate. Ideally, this is what it should look like"—and everyone watched me and I watched myself dance beautifully, acknowledge the applause, wave it off with the gesture for modesty. "You see?" Gareth addressed the class. "You *see*?" And various people nodded or murmured or looked at me admiringly.

I was fairly tanked out by the end of class and my neck was really throbbing, so after one pass at the big jump combination, I dropped Gareth a curtsy from the doorway and made the gesture of time on an invisible wristwatch. Gareth nodded, but then waved at the class to keep going and ran over.

"Great class, as always," I said. "Sorry to bail. Rehearsal."

"Seriously, Katie dear," Gareth said, grabbing my hands. "Last night? Brilliant. Marius needs to promote you. It's time."

"Oh, I don't think that's going to happen," I half laughed, shouldering my bag and trying not to wince. "There always seems to be some Russian or Argentinian diva to hire next."

"You have to fight," Gareth said, very intently. "Fight now while you still have something left to fight with."

And then he turned back to the earnest students, the talented jobless, the ones who plow through eight shows a week on Broadway, and the ones who just don't, and never will, have it. The freak with the enormous bun and rainbow-striped leg warmers on her arms launched herself from the diagonal into the grande allegro, scattering enraged dancers in her wake. Having the time of her life in a way that I don't think I ever have.

Something to fight *with*? How about something to fight *for*? IN, IN, IN, and OUT.

5.

I really wanted to get through today without drugs so I booked a half-hour session with Irina before rehearsal.

Irina, our massage therapist, is worth her weight in gold. More, since she can't weigh more than a hundred pounds. We have physical therapists on staff as well, who patch and tape and ice and invariably give you some sort of gentle exercise to do that doesn't feel effective. Iri pummels the shit out of you. She doesn't bother with scented candles or CDs of falling-rain music or what have you. Nor do you slip discreetly under a sheet on the massage table. You go in, strip off whatever clothes are near the affected area, and get to it. Roger tells a great story of his first visit to Iri, where she shoved his cock and balls to one side in order to get to his psoas muscle.

"Just full-on moved my junk," he said, "with her forearm."

Iri has a tiny cubicle at our studios. She greeted me with a kiss and asked, "What did Gwen do to knee?".

Iri manages to roll her rs even in words with no rs. Although she must be at least fifty, she shops at those stores for trendy teens and is always in some complicated getup: painted jeans that lace up the back and shirts with plunging sequined neck-lines. Her skin is alabaster white and clear, which she will tell you can only happen if you rub real butter on your face every day. I love Russians.

"Tore her ACL but she's okay," I said. "She wants to be care-ful and not rush things."

"What is it with this ACL?" Irina demanded. "We never have ACL before. Now it's oh, my ACL, my ACL. I think this made-up thing by doctors. Like ADD. We don't have anybody in Russia with ADD. Nobody have ACL. Don't tell me you have ACL because this is not real thing."

"I rotate vertebrae," I say, because after two seconds in her presence, I too start dropping my pronouns and articles.

"Of course, shit, no," she says. "Lie down."

I'm not entirely certain Iri is really a licensed massage thera-pist. Her cousin Dmitri is one of our rehearsal pianists, and he got her the job. Over the past six years I've heard most of her life history and she's never mentioned any kind of mas-sage school. Iri was a gymnast in Russia back when it was the Soviet Union and had one of those incredible childhoods like you hear about when they profile Eastern European athletes during the Olympics: the two-room apartment shared with par-ents and grandparents; the mother mopping floors; the hours spent searching for a store that carried milk. Iri tore her Achil-les tendon and missed the Olympics, but she ended up mar-rying her coach and "everybody life get better." Her husband, Yuri, managed to get visas to come to the U.S. and now he runs a fancy gymnastic training facility in New Jersey. Iri helps out at the gym, but Yuri "makes me so crazy, I don't even know," so she prefers to work at the ballet. I assume the kind of massage technique she uses on us is what was used on her in 1980s Moscow: a mixture of extreme stretching and what can only be described as thumping. It's terrifically painful and fabulous. Like most Russian women she is full of practical relationship advice that only works if you are dealing with another Russian: "Of course, when I want something, like new refrigerator, I tell my husband, 'I think your idea is good and we should get new refrigerator,' and he say, 'Eh?' and I say, 'Yes, yes, at first I think you were wrong and we not need this thing, but now I see you were right and so maybe yes,' and even though he never say these things about refrigerator now he say, 'I told you this was right thing,' and 'You should listen to me, Iri,' and I say, 'Yes, yes, you were right,' and he go to store and bring me refrigerator next day."

I'm not sure "passive aggressive" translates into Russian. They are too credulous and too crafty for such noodling about. A direct appeal to the ego is totally fair play. Masking your strength is just good politics. If you get what you want in the end, who cares who was right?

"So," said Irina, pressing a thumb forged with Soviet steel into my neck, "how is Mr. Boyfriend?"

"Oh, I didn't tell you?" I mumbled, wondering if it's possible for cervical vertebrae to be ejected out of your eyeball. "We broke up."

"Whaaaaat?" Irina moved her thumb slightly and I visualized the yam in my neck breaking in two. "How this happen?"

I was emotionally withholding. I made him insecure because I wasn't needy. I rewarded his efforts to "be there" for

me with sullen hauteur. I reacted to intimations of marriage/
children with disdain. I didn't try to kill myself. I demystified
sex in the splits.

"He cheated on me," I said to Irina.

Her hands paused.

"He tell you, or you find out?"

"He tell me."

"And you do what? Leave?"

"Um . . . yeah."

Iri sighed and resumed her Vulcan death grip on my neck.

"He wants to be with her," I explained, through my teeth.

"He don't know what he want," Iri snorted. "But you don't
know what you want either, so it's better little time away. Just
remember. Nobody dance forever."

Irina has an eleven-year-old daughter, Alisa, who is, of
course, a gymnast, and on track to get on the U.S. Olympic
team. Iri has a corkboard nailed up in her cubicle covered with
pictures of her daughter coiled around a variety of apparatuses,
each rib sharply etched through her Lycra leotard as she arches
toward . . . what? A gold medal? Her father's approval? Her
mother's love?

A gymnast's career is even shorter than ours. You can have
the whole business wrapped up and done with by the time you
are twenty and ready to go to college and deal with the fact that
your body now resembles that of a very muscular gnome. I think
athletes operate under the same basic motivating principles as
us. You may start off dashing toward the vault and wanting to
stick that triple twist double flip so Daddy will say "Good job"
or so you will win or so your double flip will be better than little
Susie's, your rival with the swinging blond ponytail and a better

leotard than yours, but at some point, maybe even mid-twist, as it were, none of that matters. At some point you did something perfectly and now your whole life is a search to re-create that. This is your doom, your bloody pact with the devil. Because while all other motivating factors are either attainable or surmountable, BEING PERFECT will never—not ever—happen for any length of time that will prove satisfying.

My brother is lucky. He at least gets moments where he knows he won. Also, he's a freaking millionaire.

After leaving Iri and her magic rs, I had to go down to the third floor to pick up my shoe order, and I passed the studio where the school kids were rehearsing *Dream*.

Marius's *A Midsummer Night's Dream* will close the season for us, and it's a world premiere, so there will be much fanfare, for the handful of people still interested in these things. I think he's done a fantastic job with it, but there are a host of problems with turning complicated stories into ballets. (*Romeo and Juliet* would be an exception. I would argue that the ballet is better than the play. If you disagree, it's only because you've never seen the balcony scene pas de deux or you are made of igneous rock.)

There are some obvious things that shouldn't be made into ballets, like the life of Louis B. Pasteur or shark attacks. But a tale of warring fairies and love potions gone awry seems like it would be an easy match. Unfortunately, any story ballet is going to need pantomime and require acting, and here's where we run into trouble. You try coming up with a very clear and specific gesture that indicates "Hey, why don't you sprinkle the juice of that flower into the eyeballs of these characters" or "I'm really attached to this changeling child and you can't have him" and you will see what I mean.

Also there is the problem of Mendelssohn's score. For Felix, fairies translated musically into extremely fast twittering tempi, and it's hard to dance to without looking as if you're on crack. Like Balanchine, Marius has incorporated some other Mendelssohn works to flesh out a full-length ballet, but I find most of his music sort of academic and perfunctory.

Marius was smart, though, because he also borrowed Balanchine's idea of using young students to fill out the ranks of the fairies, and they are very touching to watch. The school rehearses the crap out of them and they are totally psyched to be onstage with us.

The girls are ten and eleven years old, so for many of them *Dream* is the last time dancing onstage will be so pure— dancing at all, really. Round about next year the competition will start getting fiercer, their bodies will start changing, and the simple delight in just whipping around as fast as you can and wearing your hair in a pretty way will be over. Little girls are romantic. We learn quickly though, how to suffer, how to endure suffering. By the time a little girl has become a young woman she has learned how dangerous a thing it is to Dream.

I watched them through the studio window for a little bit. There is a girl in this class, Bryce, who during *Nutcracker* last season shyly waited outside my dressing room and asked me to sign a pair of pointe shoes for her. Lots of girls do this, but Bryce told me I was her favorite dancer in the company. Mostly the kids only look up to the big stars around here, so I was inordinately pleased by this.

Bryce's face lit up when she saw me and I waved at her and she looked proudly at her friends to make sure they saw her being singled out by a company member. I don't know whether to hope she is incredibly talented or not.

In the rehearsal studio, Bryce ran to her spot. She raised up her arms and fluttered her fingers as she has been taught to do. She turned in place as fast as she could, as fast as any little girl can turn. You could see her counting the beats in the music under her breath. Her hair came loose from a pin and whipped up into the air, but she kept her balance. She already knows how to turn. You must pick one spot to focus on and look at it while your body is turning until the last possible second, and then whip your head around to find the spot again.

Bryce has never had a neck injury, or an injury of any kind. If she has been in love already it will be remembered fondly, if at all, when other greater loves have come and gone. She has not thought about the middle or the end of her life. She is not as tall now as she will be, nor as beautiful. She has not thought her first cynical thought. She does not appear to have a sister.

I grabbed my shoe order and hustled myself to *Dream* rehearsal, only to find out that Justin, who is my Demetrius, was at the doctor's having his knee looked at. Partnerless, I sat in the front of the studio and watched Nina, one of our ballet mistresses, rehearse Lawrence and Yumi, who are Cast B for Helena/Demetrius. Behind them, moving less fully so as not to take up studio space, were two new kids in the company, Klaus and Maya, who are learning the roles in case everybody else is struck down. Unofficially, we call this the "Plague Cast." Nina was counting the music aloud using her preferred form of musical interpretation: the deedle. "And a-deedle-deedle

FOUR and a-deedle-deedle SIX." It's enough to make one insane. I'm no fan of Mendelssohn's score, but Nina and her deedles are even worse.

Nina stopped the rehearsal to harp on Yumi's turn-out. "Yes, but it's not modern, dear. We still have to turn out. The supporting leg too. It's not just about being cute. We still have to dance with at least a little technique."

Yumi has been told she needs to work on her turn-out her whole life. I'm sure she did all kinds of torturous things to herself in school to try to improve it. She is a gorgeous dancer; she has great feet and legs. They just don't turn out naturally, and Nina being so condescending about it completely shut down anything free or spontaneous in Yumi's dancing and she got all strained and stiff looking. You can see these things really clearly from the front of the room. While this was going on, I sewed ribbons on my shoes. When someone is getting berated in rehearsal, the polite thing to do is to look like you aren't seeing or hearing it. What I wanted to do was take over the rehearsal. Nina has that old-school break-you-down approach, and that doesn't work with everyone. I could get Yumi to turn out without making her feel like crap.

I coached Gwen a lot. Right from the beginning, even when she was in the school. I've coached Gwen all through her career. Not on her technique, necessarily. Gwen is a phenom. It's not really possible to dance as well as she dances. On my best day ever I am really, really good, but I'm _never_ that good.

But I could be helpful to Gwen in some ways. I could say, "Let your head fall back there," or "Stay looking at him for two more steps back and then turn away, but let your left hand trail behind you, no, break the wrist, that's it, more, better, good."

And I could talk and talk and talk to her about Giselle, and Juliet, and Sleeping Beauty, and while I was talking I could tell I had her, you know, I was filling her up, making it real. Because even if I couldn't do it myself, I knew how it could be done. I could see it so clearly in my mind. And then I could see it right in front of me, because there would always be a moment when Gwen would see what I was seeing and she could make it happen.

It's not something I can do for myself, though. I sometimes wish I had a me for me, if you know what I mean. Maybe then . . . well.

You know, if I danced almost anywhere else but here I might be a principal dancer. If I went to Philly, or Cleveland, or Boston? I might dance Odette/Odile, and Juliet, and Giselle. Might. Maybe. It's hard to say just now because I've kind of lost track of where I am, but definitely this used to be the case.

But it's too late now. I'd always know the truth. My stardom would be conditional. How could I have the balls to step forward and accept roses and ovations at the end of *Swan Lake* when I know that I am only wearing the crown because I have shrunk my *Lake* down to a manageable size? Odette, Queen of the Puddle.

I'm not really clear on what it is I am supposed to do now.

Oh yeah, what I should do is focus on myself now, right? Get out from under my sister's shadow? Spread my wings and learn to fly? Fuck you.

Now don't get excited. I'm not crazy. I know this because although I keep talking and talking to you, I don't really imagine that you are saying anything back. I like how quiet you are, which allows me to go on performing.

.   .   .

After rehearsal I met Mara for a chat and a bite to eat. Another ritual. You can trace the trajectories of our lives through the progression of our "bites." First they were blueberry muffins toasted with butter, or chocolate croissants. A once-a-week treat. Then it was whole-wheat toast. Then fruit salad. Now it's usually just tea lattes. Green tea for the antioxidants. Soy milk. So it's really more of a deterioration than a progression.

But I'm grateful that Mara and I have more or less kept our friendship intact. It hasn't always been easy. I know she thinks that Gwen and I have a fucked-up relationship. I know she would take my side if I ever complained about Gwen, which is one of the reasons I never do. There's also the difference in our careers.

Something happened to us both in our first year in the company. What happened with Mara was that she went on for an injured girl in *Giselle* with only five minutes' notice. The girl's position downstage left meant that Mara had to reverse every step from her own position upstage right, and reverse every swirly corps traffic pattern, and in some cases move eight counts earlier in the music than she was used to, or four counts later. She didn't make a single mistake. This sealed her fate. Mara became "dependable" and "useful." The girl you could go to in any jam, the girl who could teach incoming corps girls the choreography. It changed her. I mean physically changed her. She has become more square, more solid looking. Inasmuch as an underweight ballerina can look substantial, she looks substantial. She no longer makes fun of herself, and is only occasionally sarcastic. It's not good when you feel you can no longer afford to be self-deprecating.

What happened to me in our first year was that I was given the second cast lead in a new ballet, a world premiere, by an important German choreographer. Being second cast meant that I would get to dance all the matinees and the Wednesday nights. A huge honor for a new girl.

The ballet was called *Those Who Are Left Behind*. Very modern, which in dance tends to mean no pointe shoes and everyone wearing drab costumes in colors like mustard and olive, and lifts where you're held by something odd, like your knee. I played the role of a young girl whose fiancé must go off and join the military (green tunics with black sashes) because there is War. The village of the girl is then destroyed by the attacking army (all in puce with beige sashes), after which she is forced into prostitution (red sash) to save her family. At the end, the soldier returns, but the girl is too ashamed and broken to face him. War has killed their love (and, apparently, wiped out the supply of sashes). In the last moment of the ballet, I had a little limping step that carried me downstage away from my soldier love. Then I had to pause, begin to turn around, decide not to, then limp slowly offstage. A moment that the *New York Times* would say "contained all the pathos, the loss, the brutality of war itself. This is the new dancer to watch."

It wasn't a great ballet—the little meaningful gestures were not terribly original, the music was on the wrong side of atonal, and the sashes were a bloody nuisance—but I loved it anyway. I had hung on every word the choreographer said during rehearsals and read books set during World War II to try to get myself "into" the role. I thought about it all the time, although

I suspect that the little limping movement at the end of the ballet had more to do with the pathos of my own ambition than the pathos of war. But I had that moment onstage, that moment when you're not thinking about steps, and you're not counting music, and dance—real dance—comes out of your body and you are extraordinary and it is beyond any small, dull word like "happiness" or "satisfaction." You make the gods jealous in such a moment, I suppose.

To keep the gods from destroying me, I've held on to my sarcasm and my self-deprecation. And they've become my alibi for whenever it occurs to me that I have not quite become the person I wanted to be. I suppose I do have rivals in the company, but none of them is as challenging as the ever-present, alternate version of me: always one giant unreachable step ahead. And then there's Gwen. Even with a splintered knee and god knows what swirling around in her head, she will be forever better than messy, middling me, and we both know it.

When I got to Café Margot later this afternoon, Mara had a table and was flipping through a brochure.

"Columbia," she said, turning it over so I could see the cover. "They have that program for performing artists? I'm thinking of taking some classes."

"Really?" I dumped my bag in the extra chair, on top of Mara's bag. "Like what?"

"I don't know. Mike and I have been talking about it. I've also been thinking about . . . . you know . . . . maybe. Having a kid."

I raised my eyebrows.

"I know, I know," Mara said. "But I feel something changing in me. It's weird."

"Actually, it's natural, right? It's a normal thing for a woman? To want to have a baby? I feel like I read that somewhere."

Mara laughed and put her elbows on the table, cupping her chin with one hand. She's got the mother of all diamond rings. Her husband, Mike, is a hedge fund dude. He and Andrew really bonded over the whole "being an outsider in the ballet world" thing. At gala events they would beeline for each other. I think Mike was more upset than I was that Andrew and I broke up. And that's another thing that keeps things cool with Mara and me, I guess. I may be a soloist, and she's still corps and unlikely to ever be promoted, but she's got a loft in Soho. And someone who loves her. And maybe a shot at being happy with a normal life.

"So what's going on?" Mara asked.

I've been sort of waiting for Mara to instigate a big "talk" about Gwen. She should think about taking some psychology classes at Columbia, she's really good with all that shit. And she's pretty much the only one who has a clue about how things really are with my sister and me. I appreciate her perspective, but Gwen isn't her sister. She can't understand.

"Gwen's doing really well, actually. But the doctors want her to take her time rehabbing."

"I meant with you," Mara said.

"A pinched nerve, I think," I said. "Iri worked on me for a bit. It's not great but I think I can muscle through it."

"You don't want to talk about it, do you?"

I didn't, and so I shrugged and changed the subject and

Mara let it pass. But, for a second it was like a little window opened up between us. And I could see through it to Mara and a place where we could be truly good friends, truly important to each other and intimate and trusting. Almost like a time portal, back to the days when it was just me and her and there were no husbands or sisters or ballets I got and she didn't, or visions in mirrors we couldn't escape or smash.

6.

There is always a beginning to everything. The house lights go down and the audience settles into their seats. The conductor comes out in a spotlight. The people in the first few rows applaud the conductor and the rest of the audience starts clapping too, even though they don't see him yet. The conductor bows, turns to the orchestra. There's usually a nice moment where he seems to be taking them in, focusing their attention. Then he raises his arms, inhales, and the overture begins.

In life though, most beginnings are so quiet you don't even know that they are happening. Suddenly you're in the middle of things as if there were no beginning at all. Maybe you'll try to retrace your steps, but it's a useless endeavor because you're always going to miss the essential, initial clue. You might say, "Oh, here is where it all began," but you're always going to be too late.

My second year in New York. Gwen was at the school and Mara and I were in the company and the three of us shared this apart-

ment. Mara and I took the bedroom and Gwen slept on a futon in
the living room because she was the neatest and if it had been me,
certainly, the thing would never have gotten folded up or the bed-
ding put away in the closet. Mara's parents cosigned the lease for
us, and gave us some old furniture, even though they were upset
that their daughter felt the need to move out. City parents are very
protective, maybe because they know more about what can happen. Our parents were still operating under the impression that
my life in New York—and now Gwen's—consisted of one Teflon-
coated bubble of ballet. This was largely true, but there were all
kinds of things inside that bubble with us. Just because you are in
a nunnery doesn't mean you won't get fucked.

It started with small things. I wonder how many of them I
missed before I noticed the "first" one?

Mara and I had come home early from rehearsal. Gwen was
still at the school. We were doing Pilates in the living room and
needed an extra pillow. Get Gwen's, I told Mara. She went to
the closet.

"Kate, come here."

Mara was holding Gwen's pillowcase. Only there wasn't
any pillow in it. It was stuffed with paper. Paper dolls, that
is. The kind you cut out from books like *First Ladies of the
United States* or *Film Stars of the Golden Age*. Mara handed
me one—a Josephine Baker costume, maybe. Meticulously
cut along every thin line and around every octagonal bead and
with every feather expertly delineated.

"Your sister plays with dolls?" Mara whispered, laughing.
She wasn't being mean. She liked Gwen. But it was so odd.

"Oh god, no," I said. I was mortified for Gwen. "That's her
old collection from home."

"There's like, a thousand of them in here," Mara said.

I had never seen Gwen cut out a paper doll in my life and I knew that she hadn't moved in with these things because I had helped her unpack. I was surprised, though my concern was not so much for my sister but for how she might be perceived by others.

"Yeah, it took her years," I said.

"And now she sleeps on them?"

"She must have just put them in there. Look, here's her pillow."

Later I asked Gwen about it and she told me that she couldn't sleep at night and it was just something to do with her hands. She assured me that she didn't *play* with the dolls. She couldn't turn on the TV because it might wake us up, and she needed to do something. She would knit, she said, if she knew how.

"You could do your homework," I suggested. Gwen was taking the same correspondence course that I had done.

"That takes me like, five minutes," she said.

I didn't really buy this because Gwen had never been that great at school, but I let it go. I told her that if Mara asked, it was an old collection that she hung on to for sentimental reasons. Gwen asked if there was something wrong with cutting out paper dolls and I asked why she hid them if she didn't think it was weird. Gwen did not reply to this, and, impressed with my sophistry, I forgot to ask her why she couldn't sleep, or if she was in fact sleeping on Eleanor Roosevelt and her collection of hats.

Maybe the second thing was the baths. There is only one bathroom, and since we all needed to soak our muscles there were rules. Twenty-five minutes, tops. Long enough for the

Epsom salts to dissolve. No adding more hot water once you were in and depriving the next person of a necessary scald. Still, by the third fill the water was noticeably less hot, so legal-minded Mara suggested we rotate bath order. But Gwen said she liked going last, she didn't mind.

Gwen started staying in there for a really long time. She took a little portable boom box and played music. At first I assumed she was masturbating, frankly. Since I shared a bed with Mara I had to take care of my own business on the bathroom rug, lying on a towel in the fetal position that I still use today for such purposes. Anyway, halfway through the year Mara started dating this boy in the company, Fabrice, and on the nights she spent with him I would hear Gwen in the bathroom talking to herself, a steady monotone under the music. If I knocked on the door or called out, "Gwen, what are you doing?" she would say, "Nothing," and then after a moment start mumbling again. After I complained about needing to pee and brush my teeth, she started waiting until I had gone to bed. Sometimes she didn't even turn the water on, she'd just go in, shut the door, and monologue, or whatever. For hours.

I didn't tell Mara about it, but eventually Gwen started doing it when she was there, so I invented a story about Gwen reading aloud to herself because it helped her dyslexia. I thought this was such a good idea that I convinced myself it was true. And I started reading out loud to myself when I was in the tub. I liked the way my voice sounded with the acoustics.

But the big thing turned out to be the mouse. We all saw it one night, in the kitchen, and we all screamed and jumped on chairs, like cartoon housewives. Then there was a big debate over what to do, and we ended up getting one of those humane traps because none of us was prepared to deal with some sort of mouse carcass or chewed-off leg or something. The guy at the hardware store gave us a rough time about the stupidity of releasing a mouse into our rodent-choked city, but we held firm. The trap was a simple little boxcar-like thing, weighted so that the door would shut on our unsuspecting guest once he had wandered in to grab his cheese. We had to upgrade the bait twice. In New York City, even vermin have aspirations. The little bastard ended up with Roquefort.

But lo and behold, one day we all trouped in from doing laundry and the trapdoor was down on the cage and the thing was rattling, sliding a bit over the floor. Again with the screaming and the leaping onto chairs.

Mara and I just started laughing hysterically, arguing over who was going to take it downstairs: "Pick it up!" "No, you pick it up!" "I don't want to touch it!" "Well, I'm not touching it!" I started to pick it up, but my hands were shaking and I dropped it. Mara screamed. I screamed. The mouse screamed.

And that's when Mara and I noticed Gwen. She was cowering in the corner of our apartment and like, clawing the wall. Literally standing with her face to the wall and . . . scraping it, and sort of squealing. Like she was the one in the trap.

"Oh my god, stop!" Mara said. "Gwen! Stop! That's so creepy!" Mara was still sort of laughing. She thought Gwen was being funny.

I knew that it wasn't Gwen's sense of humor, to do something like that. But it was so outlandish and over the top that I was laughing too.

"Oh my god, she's freaking out!" I shouted to Mara. "Quick, help me pick this up."

But we were both sort of . . . transfixed by Gwen. It almost seemed as if she was pretending, but she didn't stop. You know how in sci-fi movies a robot might malfunction and start sparking off electricity or repeating "System failure, repeat, system failure" while it runs itself into a wall? That's what it looked like. Like a gizmo inside Gwen had busted.

"Wait, is she for real?" Mara asked me. "Gwen? Gwen, calm down. It's just a mouse."

"Gwen, stop it," I said.

But she didn't.

"Kate?" Mara looked at me.

"Let's take the mouse down," I said. "Gwen, we are taking the mouse away, okay? We'll be right back. It's *fine*." I found the dustpan and slid it under the trap and turned with it to the door. Mara was trying to put her hand on Gwen's back, but Gwen crouched down and covered her head with her hands. She wasn't screaming exactly, because her mouth was closed, and the sound was coming out of her nose.

"GWEN, STOP IT," I shouted.

"DON'T YELL AT HER," Mara shouted.

Gwen started beating her head against the wall.

"Oh my god," said Mara. "Oh my god, Kate, you have to stop her."

"FUCK," I yelled. "OPEN UP THE FUCKING WINDOW."

The window of the living room opens onto a fire escape, so you have to unlatch the door with bars first, and swing that open. Mara did this and I crawled out the window, holding the dustpan in front of me. This apartment is on the fourth floor, the back of the building. Below us are the trash cans and a locked storage unit that belong to the building's superinten-

dent. I threw the trap with the panicked mouse still freaking out inside it into the alleyway as hard as I could. Actually, I served it, overhand, like a tennis ball. It smacked against the storage unit and broke apart. I was already crawling back inside.

Mara was standing in the living room with the phone in her hands. Gwen was still mewling in the corner and bumping her head against the wall.

"I think we should call someone," Mara whispered.

I went over to the corner and crouched down next to Gwen.

"You want me to call Mom and Dad?" I asked her. I put my hand between the wall and her head. "Is that what you want? Because if you don't stop right now then I'm calling them."

Well, she heard that all right. She quieted down instantly.

"Kate, seriously," Mara said.

"No, it's okay," I said. "She's fine."

I patted her back for a while and Mara came over and sat with us and we both said things like "Talk to us" and "The mouse is gone" and "We were scared too." Eventually Gwen unfurled herself and went into the bathroom and shut the door and we heard the water turning on.

"Should we let her do that?" Mara whispered.

"I'm just going to take a bath," Gwen called through the door. And then, after a moment, "Sorry."

Mara and I had both started smoking that year although w hid it from Gwen. We stared at the bathroom door for a mome and then at each other. Mara mimed taking a drag. I nodded.

We crawled out onto the fire escape and mostly shut the w dow, something we had done before. We lit cigarettes and pe down into the alley, but it was getting dark and we couldn' anything.

"We should get a cat," I said.

And we just smoked and then went back in and sprayed bo\
mist around the living room, and eventually Gwen came out o\
the bathroom and Mara asked her if she was feeling better and
Gwen said yes and that she didn't really know what happened
and I think we all played cards or something like that. By the
time we went to bed it was more or less okay.

But the next day, Mara told me that she thought Gwen
should go to therapy. Mara's mom went to therapy every week,
and she had sent Mara to a psychiatrist when Mara was twelve
and her mom thought she was crying too much. We spoke very
seriously about it, in the kinds of voices that women use when
they are talking to other women about issues. This was new
to me. Mostly I made jokes or complained or imitated other
people or was sarcastic. So I really enjoyed listening to myself
be so thoughtful and adult.

Later, I tried out the voice on Gwen. It seemed to work pretty
well, and she agreed to go to therapy if I promised not to tell
Mom and Dad.

"They'll just want me to come home," she said, which was
true enough.

Mara got the name of a doctor, and I made the appointment.
I went with Gwen to make sure she actually did it, and because
I was paying for it. The psychiatrist's office was on the East
Side. Sure enough, Gwen balked outside the building.

"You're going to have to do it," she said.

"Gwen, come on," I said.

"No, you have to be me," she explained. "You have to go.
You're eighteen. I'm a minor. They'll need parental consent or
something."

"No, they won't," I said. "You don't even need that for an abortion, I think. It's like, confidential."

"They won't give medication to a minor," she said.

"It's talking," I said to her. "You just talk to them about what you're feeling."

"Not if you need medicine," she said. "Then they have to tell the parents."

"You don't need medicine."

"I do. I know I do."

So we had this whole long ridiculous argument on the street and I said that if Gwen didn't go then I would call Mom and Dad, and she said if I called Mom and Dad then that meant I wanted to ruin her life, and we went back and forth and I said, "Well, let's just forget the whole thing," and then she started crying.

"Please help me," she said. "Please just this one time. I would do it for you. You're the only one I trust."

It's a heady thing, to be handed a role like that. Or maybe I thought I really was helping her. It all seems kind of insane, now, in a way it didn't then. Then it seemed like an extension of every other thing that was more or less pretend, which was pretty much my life. My name was on the call-boards for rehearsals, in the programs, on the list for dressing room C, but it never really felt like me.

Also, I didn't want Gwen to go home.

"My name is Kate Crane," I told the receptionist. "I have an appointment with Dr. Freiburg?"

And all the girl did was cross out the name Gwen and write Kate. While my sister and I waited in the chairs, we wrote notes to each other.

What do you want me to say?

Say that you can't sleep and that you get really nervous and have a hard time calming down.

What if she asks why?

You don't know why—that's why you're here

That's why you're here

Whatever. Don't overdo it but be really upset

This is so stupid

It's just one time

But of course it wasn't.

My first session with Dr. Freiburg went well. I was nervous, so it was a pretty realistic performance. She had to keep telling me to breathe and I actually cried a little at one point. We talked about my history and being in a ballet company, and the stress and how I felt about it. She asked me to describe my panic attacks and what techniques I used to calm myself down. I did a lot of shrugging and gripping the arms of the chair. At the end of it all she told me that she wanted to see me once a week and that I should practice the breathing/counting thing she had demonstrated and we'd see "where we were" in a couple of sessions. There were "things" she could give me, she explained, to help, but there were side effects with these and it was always best to try other methods first.

"You'll have to go back," Gwen said, when I told her about the counting method. When we got home, Mara asked how it went and Gwen gave her a big hug and said that she was really

grateful that Mara had suggested it. Mara said she was very proud of her. And that night Gwen didn't take a freakishly long bath. The three of us played cards and watched television, and Gwen seemed relaxed and happy.

"I feel better, don't you?" Mara said, as we went to bed. "I think she'll be okay."

I didn't sleep much that night. Or the next. But I won't lie. Eventually I started sleeping just fine.

It took two more sessions before Dr. Freiburg prescribed benzodiazepines for me/Gwen. By that time I had opened up a little in our sessions. By this I mean that I had started inventing things. Conversations, situations, dreams. I was very careful not to tell Dr. Freiburg anything that I actually felt, because then it would be like I really *was* in therapy, which I obviously didn't need. And I couldn't tell the doctor what *Gwen* was feeling, because when I asked Gwen, she wouldn't ever describe it beyond saying that she just got stuck in her head sometimes, and it wasn't a big deal but she needed something to help with the feeling so she could sleep. Dr. Freiburg told me that the drug enhanced a natural chemical in the body that would help calm me down.

Dr. Freiburg wasn't all that sharp. She never smelled a rat (or a smashed mouse). Not even when my fount of invention ran dry and I started describing feelings cribbed from Ibsen or Chekhov. "Sometimes I feel like I am a seagull," I told her. "Oh, that's interesting," she said.

Every six weeks I got my/Gwen's prescription filled. At first I doled out the pill to her every morning, but eventually I just handed her the bottle. If you do something like take a whole bunch and overdose, I told her, I will absolutely never forgive

you. She said she would never betray my trust like that. She said it in the adult woman discussing serious issues voice, which I guess she learned from me.

There are things you do when you are a teenager, or a dancer, or just a girl, I guess. You cut your food up in special ways, or you cut yourself, or paper dolls. You pretend that there is an invisible audience watching you all the time, and you do things to impress them or pretend that they didn't see what you just did because their live video feed was interrupted somehow. You steal things or tell lies or speak to strangers in a Russian accent. You have sex with someone you love, or with someone who gets you really drunk. You lie to your parents, your boyfriend, yourself, your therapist. You cheat on your homework or do other people's homework for money. You get up, you take class, you rehearse, you perform, you go to bed. How do you decide which of these things are truly crazy and which are just being alive?

You realize, too late, that you are that sneakiest of all beings. You are a giver. You gave your sister drugs. You started her on a path from which there is possibly no return. You should have said no. You should have ruined her life then, instead of letting her ruin it in much worse ways later on.

But Gwen got better that year. She seemed fine. She seemed happy, or at least not unhappier than anybody else. Who's happy? Gwen didn't make a ton of friends in her class, but she was so clearly a star in the making that it would have been impossible anyway. There were no more hysterical scenes. For Gwen's birthday, Mara and I got her a cat, and she named it Clive. She even made jokes about it catching mice, although we never saw one again. At the end-of-the-year performance,

Gwen made my heart stop, she was so beautiful, so serene, so absolutely perfect. When Marius gave her a contract I was waiting outside in the hallway and she flew into my arms and we jumped up and down, hugging each other. She told me that I didn't have to go to therapy anymore.

And she became a star for real.

You buy a humane trap and you end up killing the thing anyway.

I've been ignoring the pain in my neck, which I can't do anymore. I need to get out of here. But to get up and leave would be to pass the corner where Gwen crouched and banged her head against the wall. I shouldn't have left her here when I moved in with Andrew. I should have forced her to move someplace else. Oh, the things I should have done.

If you were recording my story, this tape would be Exhibit A. Oh Gwen.

7.

Okay so when you're trying to sort out what's crazy and what's not and where you might lie on the spectrum and how much guilt you can absorb, it is possible that ballet is not the most useful arena in which to position yourself for perspective.

You have to keep your head in the game. Keith, who is unabashed about his clichés, always says that. When you're in the middle of a match, you can't start doubting yourself or your ability, or imagining how the commentators are ripping you a new one on ESPN, or getting upset over how the trash talk that went down in the locker room is going to make you look like an ineffectual ass when you blow the match, or how when this whole bloody mess is over you're going to relive every single point while you lie next to your palely disappointed Icelandic girlfriend, and you're still going to have to get up the next day and hit balls, and it just never really ends or gets any easier.

My nerves felt flayed today. Everybody bothered me. Company class. Joan with her pile of pointe shoes and therapy tools,

rolling and stretching away and sewing ribbons with that goddamn earnest conscientious look on her face. Yuri and his ridiculous warm-up pants in DayGlo colors. Simone with her sexy
leotard and her perfect glossy bob and her air of living a considerably better life than everyone else because she's married
to a gazillionaire and does live a considerably better life than
everyone else. All the gay guys being so gay. All the straight
guys being so straight. All the South Americans being so South
American. Everybody who seemed perfectly fine about taking class and not at all tortured. Like Andrea, who never just
throws her hair up in a clip, but always has this perfect cinna-
mon roll of a bun. The upside-down Us of each and every one
of her symmetrically rayed hairpins oppressed me all through
barre. And Nicole was teaching because she's rehearsing this
Balanchine ballet we'll be doing in rep in a few weeks and so
we all have to suffer through her ridiculous class, even those of
us who aren't cast in that ballet. Former Balanchine ballerinas
make me crazy. None of them have ever recovered from being
in the presence of the Master, and they have this weird mystical
sexual love of dance that utterly confounds me. I would envy it
if it looked less fucked up . . . like they weren't all still hoping
Mr. B will stop by and pat them on the head, that their entire
lives weren't an offering to a dead man, that they all didn't
still get up every morning, draw on black liquid eyeliner, brush
out the dry ends of their waist-length hair like it was 1969 and
they're still wondering why you can't get Tab anymore.

While we're on the subject of unrequited whatever, why do
I still want Charles to make a move even though the two times
I've had sex with him were vaguely disappointing and he went
into these elaborate mini-dramas afterward of avoiding me and

flirting with other girls just in case I thought for two seconds that he actually liked me. Which was painful every time even though I don't like him. (Hello, Charles, I still don't want to be your girlfriend, so fucking relax!) Why does the sight of Hilel make me say to myself, "My mouth is filled with ashes." I'm over that whole situation. I just read that somewhere, "mouth full of ashes," and the phrase stuck and now I think of it every time I see him and since I have the thought, I kind of get the feeling as well. My mouth gets dry.

Why why why. Why must Emma and Tyler act like they have some secret inside information about what Marius thinks of all of us and who's going to do what next season, and why do I spend whole mornings thinking of situations where I triumph over them in some very witty and cutting way? Why do I spend other mornings imagining being treated horribly by various people just for the pleasure of having a legitimate complaint against them?

Why am I acting like I'm stuck on the island of *Lost*? It is possible to quit dancing. I don't have to be here.

But aside from having nowhere else to go, I guess I still, on some level, care.

At one point when Nicole was rhapsodizing about the HEEL, the HEEL, I caught Mara's eye and she made this funny mad-scientist face, and I thought, Well, okay we accept that we are all a little crazy. It's an act of defiance in today's world, to care about ballet. To care about the HEEL, the HEEL.

And for a moment I saw the room and everyone in it a different way. Gods and goddesses, rebel angels, gorgeous, impossible, improbable us, refusing everything that is ordinary and sane and reasonable. Champions of the extraordinary.

I watched Yuri in his ridiculous pants execute a breathtakingly beautiful adagio. And I was overwhelmed with pride and humility that I was in the same room with him. That this is the company I keep. That this is what I do. Such moments are fragile, too fragile to cling to. I tried to hold the feeling lightly, with the tips of my fingers.

After class I had rehearsal for this ballet *Look At Me*. It's another one we'll be doing in our mixed repertoire, for the evening that's been labeled "New Directions." Three ballets by contemporary choreographers. When I got to Studio B there was a small camera crew and a reporter setting up in a corner.

"What the hell?" I said to Simone, who was stretching at the barre.

"*New York Times*." She shrugged. "They're doing a piece on James." James King is the choreographer for *Look At Me*. He's a big Broadway guy—won a bunch of Tony awards. Done a couple of movies.

"Okay, but why are they filming?"

"For the *Times*," Simone repeated.

"Um, the *Times* is a newspaper." What was I, speaking Greek?

"Video blog," Simone explained patiently. Right. I *was* speaking an ancient language. Everything now has to be YouTube-able.

"Were we told about this?" I asked, kind of frantic.

"Of course not." Simone rolled her eyes. "Abby is running around somewhere. She said they might want to interview some of us."

"Shit, shit." Not enough time to dash over to my dressing room at the theater and get some makeup on my face. I ducked across the hall into the ladies' locker room, scrabbling in my bag hopefully.

"Does anybody . . . ?" I dumped my bag in front of the sink. One of the new corps girls, Holly, offered me the candy-pink lip gloss she was applying to her cherub mouth. Luckily, Mara joined me at the mirror and handed me an eyeliner, wordlessly. I commenced smudging.

"Thanks. God, Nicole today," I grumbled. "Her class just kills me. And I'm not even warm. How do you get through rehearsals with her?"

"She's pretty intense," Mara said, leaning against the sink. "But I mean, we never do Balanchine here, and it feels amazing. You can see why his dancers were obsessed with him. For giving them steps like that. You feel beautiful. Powerful. I know you think Nicole is ridiculous, but she has a lot of important things to say. You know, the whole passing on the tradition of it."

"It's like the Holocaust," chirped up Holly, blotting her fructose lips.

"It's like the *what*?" I paused in my smudging.

"You know . . ." She faltered. "Like, there aren't many people left that survived the Holocaust, so, like, it's really important to get their stories. Before they get lost."

"Oh yeah," I said. "Yeah. It's like the Holocaust. That's a really good analogy, Holly."

Holly blushed. Mara followed me out of the locker room.

"You're so mean," she said, taking back her eyeliner and poking me in the ribs with it. "She was just trying to sound smart in front of you."

"I know. I'm very mean." I sighed. "And I've got to get to

rehearsal now. You know, rehearsal?" I added, in Holly's voice, "It's like the Siberian labor camps?"

Mara rolled her eyes. I surreptitiously fished a Vicodin out of my bag and swallowed it. It was easier to swallow than my jealousy. Jealousy of Mara, for feeling beautiful and powerful while dancing and for being in general a much kinder and more receptive person than I am. Of Nicole, for having interesting things to say about dance. Of Balanchine, for being a genius. Of Holly, even, for being twenty and adorable and sort of stupid.

Back in Studio B, James was talking to the reporter, a guy with a huge handheld camera was filming them, and Abby— our PR woman—was hovering nearby, anxiously smiling.

"Getting to work with this company is a dream come true," James was saying. "But I knew I would be asking many of them to step outside their comfort zone. On every level they have surpassed my expectations. They're just brilliant."

This was kind of him. There was a bit of skepticism about his ballet in early rehearsals. A little undercurrent of snobbery. We'll do anything we're asked—but please don't ask us to do dazzle hands.

Actually, I've liked working with James. He's funny and respectful and appreciative, which is a nice change. And he gave me a great solo. My character, who is called "The Celebrity," has this moment alone onstage where I am supposed to be performing for myself in front of a mirror. Preening, adjusting my postures, checking in with the mirror to see what sort of effect I'm making. Posing. It's funny, and then, at the very end, sort of sad, because I end up dropping all pretense and walking toward the mirror all doubtful and vulnerable and so forth.

Also, I get to wear heels instead of pointe shoes for *Look At Me*, and so my feet get a break for a few hours a day. Dancing this ballet isn't some sort of transcendent the-magic-of-Balanchine-is-entering-my-body experience, but in my current state of mind I'm not sure I'm capable of getting that anyway. And it's a special thing, having something created for you, even if the something is a ballet that will probably disappear forever after we do it twice. Things like *Look At Me* are really more attempts to attract a wider audience, give people something fun and "accessible."

I wasn't mentally prepared to be filmed today, though. Not that I'll watch whatever they shoot. It only takes a few times of watching films of yourself dance before you learn: *never* watch yourself on video. There's a reason why we are a performance art. Photographs are fine, if it's a photographer who knows what they're doing and which image to select. Then you get a picture of yourself looking perfect. But film is totally deflating. If it's rehearsal footage it looks flat and uninteresting and the mistakes are glaring. If it's performance footage, you think, Really? That's what my face looks like? And the mistakes are humiliatingly permanent.

Ballet and film have an uneasy relationship in general. And god—while I'm on the subject—can we please stop making movies about ballet? Enough already! Okay, so *The Red Shoes*: campy greatness. *Turning Point*: yes, because it's real dancers dancing and anyway it's worth it just for the scene where Shirley MacLaine and Anne Bancroft spank each other in evening gowns. *White Nights*: Baryshnikov in full force, and we should all be grateful that one of the greatest dancers the world has ever seen is also a smokin'-hot Russian with a genius for communicating passion. So okay, those three are great, but now: everybody stop. It's just embarrassing. And haven't we all gotten our fill of the clichés? Does the world need another close-up of bleeding toes? Do we really believe that a stuck-up ballerina can learn to love and be free with just the liberating influence of hip-hop?

Full disclosure: I have participated in this mockery and am actually in one of the recent dance movies. Not as an actress, of course, but they shot some footage of the company performing, and class stuff. We're not in it a whole lot, because the movie centers around the supposed prima ballerina of this fictional ballet company, and she was played by a movie star. They got some girl from National Ballet of Canada to be the dance double, and hired five million coaches to get the actress into some semblance of basic ballet for the close-ups. For everything else, it was necessary to move the real dancers several leagues away from the actress so the illusion wouldn't be shattered. Not that there was much illusion, per se. Between the actress's lobster-claw hands and biscuit-shaped feet, no one could mistake her for the real thing. Except for the millions of people who completely loved the movie, of course.

I'm in a hallway scene of that film too, just hanging out and chatting with a group of people. It's so funny, to see the situation reversed. The actress looks all stiff and graceless when she is dancing, and all of us look totally weird and stilted when we're supposed to be talking. Even the pretty girls don't look pretty. We look like Edward Gorey drawings. The actress looks insanely gorgeous.

But whatever. We got paid nicely. And as Marius kept saying, "If it gets even one person interested in coming to see what we really do . . ." I don't know. I should think people would be disappointed if they watched that kind of movie and then came to see us dance and none of us slit our wrists onstage or made ourselves vomit or got on the backs of motorcycles while wearing tutus and started fucking each other.

The camera guy swooped down on me as I was putting on my heels for rehearsal. I hope I had the sense to suck in my stomach while that was going on. And that my dance bag was out of frame and the bottle of Vicodin wasn't peeking out from under a leg warmer.

Sometimes when you are a miserable complaining bitch you find yourself unexpectedly having a really good time doing the things that are making you crazy. There was a good vibe in the studio, even with the camera there, or maybe because of it. Or maybe because I was sort of high. Abby grabbed me after rehearsal and asked if I would do a brief interview. Possibly because I was the highest-ranking dancer in the room right then, and because Abby knows that under normal conditions I can speak in coherent sentences. I tried to pull myself together.

"How has it been?" the reporter asked me. "Working with a Broadway choreographer? Has the different style been challenging?"

It's "challenging" for me to find reasons to get out of bed. Which right now is the bed of my sister, who has lost her reason to have reason.

"It's been great for us," I said. "We have a very diverse season this year. Full-length classical ballets like *Coppélia* and *Swan Lake* and the *Midsummer Night's Dream* we'll be premiering in a few weeks. Important repertoire from the twentieth century. And then some very contemporary works. I think *Look At Me* is something our audiences are really going to enjoy."

Abby, who was stationed just beyond the reporter, shook her head at me and made a "Kill it" motion across her throat, like I said something wrong. Which made me afraid that the Vicodin had given me crazy eye. But the reporter was still looking expectantly at me, so I kept going, switching tracks.

"One of my favorite dancers of all time is Cyd Charisse," I said. "So I feel like I'm getting to live out my Cyd Charisse fantasy! I love it."

I gave a quick glance over at Abby, who was nodding and grinning approvingly. This was quick and random recollection on my part. I'm not much of an old dance musical buff. But James had brought in a Richard Avedon book of photographs for me to look at—celebrities posing, I guess, was the idea—and there had been a gorgeous shot of Cyd Charisse. My favorite was the one of Marilyn Monroe. In a beaded halter dress, looking like she's retreated inside her own image, and so her beauty is like clothes she took off and threw on a chair. I'm trying to get the expression on her face down for the closing moment of my solo.

The reporter finished with me and I grabbed my bag. On the way out, Abby hustled over.

"Thank you, Kate. That was perfect."

"Yeah, sure. What was wrong with the first thing, though?"

"Nothing!" She waved her hands. "It's just exactly what Marius said. Like, almost word for word."

"Ha! Well, you know I'm going to be artistic director of this company someday, so I guess that's only fitting."

"Right on!" said Abby, moving to give me a hug before realizing how sweaty I was. "You've got my vote."

For a second I had that feeling back again. That breakable love in the palm of my hand feeling. I wanted to go sit quietly with it for a moment, but I had *Leaves Are Fading* rehearsal. Turns out there was one section that everyone was counting slightly differently, and so it was this long technical rehearsal over about twenty seconds of dancing. These are the most tiring rehearsals, where you start to feel every little pain, and even though it's necessary to break everything down, you lose the ballet a little and all you hear inside your head are notes and corrections. Christine was on a trip about how none of us were pointing our feet when we were running, so we had to keep doing that over and over. I think at one point, a few months ago, I was looking forward to dancing this ballet more than anything this season, and now it's gotten so submerged in everything else that it takes all I have to kick and kick and kick up for air. There was a moment in our first rehearsal when I thought I made a connection between the way Tudor choreographed the arms in this ballet and the way time and memory are bent. I almost had it again today, for a moment. But then rehearsal was over and I was angry at the return of my waves of anxiety and my bad breathing and my pain and I wanted to be luxuriating in this not being a performance night and I needed to *rest* and where, oh where, could I lay my weary head without drowning?

"What are you doing tonight?" Roger asked me.

"Oh, the usual," I said airily. "Sewing pointe shoe ribbons and living a life of quiet desperation. Maybe having some soup."

"That dance show I'm obsessed with is on," Roger said. "Let's get high and order Thai food."

"No," I said. "I don't know. I feel a bit . . . right now, nothing feels real."

"Because you're stoned."

"No, I mean in general nothing feels real. Look at what we do. It's completely unreal."

"What's real?" Roger asked, reasonably. "And who the hell cares?" He switched back to the dance show, where another couple was rehearsing a "contemporary routine." The camera showed a close-up of the choreographer, who explained that the piece was about a man and a woman who were at the end of their relationship. "It's about how we don't want to let go," she said. "It's about how we hurt the ones we love."

"Ugh," I said.

"Yeah, but this girl is fierce. She has feet like you."

"I guess it's not supposed to be real." I sighed. "I mean, you're not going to see the Swan Queen flossing her teeth. The Nutcracker Prince doesn't scratch his balls."

"Honey, trust me," said Roger. "You can't even get to your balls with that headpiece on. Can we talk about how everything I'm dancing this season comes with some sort of giant headpiece? Hello? Have you seen what they've got me in for Bottom in *Dream*?"

"You're never going to see Romeo get annoyed by Juliet," ambled on. "It'll never look like a real relationship. Like, meo loves Juliet madly and all, but sometimes she gets on nerves. No one makes a ballet or a symphony or a painting expresses dating or looking for an apartment or switching af. You're not going to make a sculpture that represents I kinda like him, but I'm not going to call him, because ks desperate.' It's all on this elevated and unrealis-

"I shouldn't," I said. "I'm on tomorrow."

"So am I. Come on. I'm not saying let's get trashed. I'm saying let's relax. You look totally fried."

One hot shower, half a Vicodin, half a plate of chicken curry, and two hits off Roger's pipe later, I was feeling better. I *was* able to relax more at Roger's place. It's very comfortable, untidy in a healthy way. To live among Gwen's things is to live among her rules. Roger's stack of empty CD cases strewn about the desk, the tangle of cords visible behind the computer, this morning's half-drunk cup of coffee on the window ledge, these things were very reassuring. At Roger's there is actual stuff on the coffee table, not just Thai food detritus but magazines and candles and a stack of marble coasters and a small iron Statue of Liberty that, when you pull back the head, reveals itself to be a lighter. The kind of silly object a person might have when a thing is just a thing and doesn't hold mysterious esoteric threats. Roger's refrigerator was covered with photos of his two nieces, postcards, a letter from the older niece: *Dear Uncle Roger, Thank you for my birthday presents I love them so much and I love YOU! xxxOxxx Natty*

It was the O in the middle of those Xs that got to me: kiss, kiss, kiss, HUG, kiss, kiss, kiss. A perfect musical phrase.

Roger's not close to any of his family except the nieces, and so he's sort of invested in the idea that Gwen and I are best friends. I've never told him about any of the bad shit that's gone down, and I don't think Mara has either. I told myself to take a vacation from thinking about Gwen and just enjoy the safety of Roger's apartment, and the comfort of Roger himself.

Beautiful gay men are God's gift to women. They're like a consolation prize for . . . well, for everything else about being a woman. It's nice to take aesthetic pleasure in a man and feel neither insecure nor acquisitive. Intimacy without desire. Roger is a satyr. Elfin curls, sculpted shoulders, slim hips, muscular thighs, hairy toes. He's also an excellent cuddler.

Roger hooked me up with an ice pack for my neck and we lay on the couch, occasionally extending our legs toward the other for foot rubbing or just general limb holding. We'd both had full afternoons of rehearsal, and let the not-unpleasant torpor settle in, along with the weed.

I haven't been paying too much attention to these dance competition shows. Roger loves awful TV, not with irony but with genuine pleasure, like a Roman citizen at the Coliseum cheerfully eating a lamb sausage while a Thracian guts a Gaul. He flipped the channels back and forth among the dance show, *South Park*, and *Rebecca*.

"Do you miss Andrew?" Roger asked me, as we watched two teenagers thrash through some kind of disco on the dance show. Every second of the routine was choked with flips, spins, splits, and even backflips, which the teenagers performed as if their lives depended on it. The crowd screamed appreciatively.

"This morning," I said, "I woke up and realized I hadn't taken my socks off last night. I had on these knee-high socks, right, because I was wearing boots yesterday? So my feet were hot and a little bit uncomfortable. The elastic around the knee had dug in. And so I took my socks off and it was this fantastic release. The feel of the cool sheets on my legs, and the freedom, and I just rubbed one foot up a leg and then the other and my legs felt *soooo* good."

"Your legs do feel good," said Roger, bringing one of my legs

up against his cheek and rubbing it. "So, wait. Was that you feeling free from being in a relationship?"

"No, I'm just telling you that's what happened this morning," I said, and we laughed the laugh of the stoned. The dancers finished their routine and a beautiful blonde in six-inch stilettos strode over and embraced them. "My goodness," she giggled warmly. "Disco FEVER! Fantastic stuff! Well, we know the crowd loved it, but let's hear what the judges think! Judges?"

"Whenever I get sad about sleeping alone," Roger said, "I make snow angels in the bed. Because you can't make snow angels if someone else is there." He flipped the channel over to *Rebecca*. A drab and nervous Joan Fontaine was wandering forlornly around Manderley, and was startled by the appearance of dead Rebecca's cocker spaniel.

"I don't really feel sad," I said to Roger. "I feel . . . I don't know. Like I don't know what happens next, I guess."

"You're making it happen, though," Roger said thoughtfully, stretching his arms above his head and cracking about four different things.

"What do you mean?" Joan Fontaine had knocked a china figurine on Rebecca's desk and was hiding the pieces in a drawer.

Roger squinted at me. I put a pillow over my face. He knocked it away with his foot.

"You've never danced better," Roger said. "For rehearsal. Otherwise, I have to say you're dancing like someone just shot your dog. No dog. Is it Andrew?"

tic level. But we have to do it. And we're real people. There's this . . . gap."

"Not really," Roger said. "Unless you think that what we're doing right now is more real than what we'll do onstage tomorrow. Shit, look at what you can do, Kate. That's you. That's *you*."

"Okay, turn up the volume. I want to watch this," I said, because I was starting to feel like I might cry.

The dancers started performing the piece about the end of love, which, surprisingly, involved just as many backflips and splits and crazy lifts as the disco routine, only occasionally the dancers crumpled, or stared longingly at their own hands, or messed up their hair and stalked away from each other. The music was some sort of arty chick rock. The guy flailed like he was being attacked by wasps, glared at the girl, then vaulted across the stage with some really excellent barrel turns. The fierce girl clutched at her skirt, shook like an epileptic, tossed off four perfect pirouettes, then jumped up and landed in the splits. The audience screamed their heads off.

"Isn't this piece supposed to be about the end of love?" I asked. "It looks more like the end of that girl's hips."

"Seriously."

The piece ended with the dancers shadowboxing on their knees. The guy caught the girl's fist and then beat it against his chest as her face crumpled in agony. The lights dimmed, then brightened, and the two struggled to their feet as the show's thumping theme song kicked in and the cameras panned to the ecstatic crowd, some of whom were holding up signs. "WE LUV BECCA!" "AMERICA WANTS MORE JOSH!" The blond hostess embraced the dancers, who were struggling to catch their breath and waving at the crowd. "Oh *wow*," said the blonde. "*Powerful* stuff. *Wow.* Okay, breathe, babies! And now let's hear what the judges think. Judges?"

Roger hit the mute button.

"That is the sound of us officially becoming irrelevant," I said. Roger reached for his beer.

"Or old," he said, taking a swig.

"If this is what the next generation thinks of as dance," I asked, "then who the hell is going to come watch *Sleeping Beauty*? There are like, no backflips in *Sleeping Beauty*!"

"America wants more Josh," Roger agreed.

On the screen, one judge had finished his critique and the next one was speaking.

"Look at that little faggot cry," Roger said, hitting the volume.

The judge was, in fact, weeping copiously.

"You ARE what dance IS," the judge sobbed. "And dance IS what you ARE."

Roger and I looked at each other and burst out laughing. We laughed for about an hour. By the time we thought to check in with *Rebecca*, the creepy lesbian housekeeper had set Manderley on fire and Joan Fontaine, still drab but now liberated from the ghost of the terrible Rebecca, was tending to a slightly crispy Laurence Olivier.

"You want to stay over?" Roger asked. "It's late."

I did want to stay over. I wanted to curl up next to Roger, beautiful talented Roger who will never ask America to vote for him and who doesn't bother about what's real or not and who says that the person who is dancing is me. I wanted to wrap myself up in our little bubble of untelevised revolution and wear it with pride.

But then Roger's phone beeped and he looked at it and chuckled. He started texting something back.

"I'm telling Gwen you're here," he said.

"That was Gwen? Gwen texted you?"

Roger nodded.

"Yeah, we talked yesterday for like, an hour."

I picked up the dripping remnants of my ice pack and walked into the kitchen. Roger followed me.

"So you guys talked?"

Roger yawned and nodded.

"How did she sound to you?" I asked, tentatively.

"Bored. But I guess her knee is healing good, right? She said she might be back in a week or two and rehab here, since you'll be around to help her. It'll be like the old days, with you guys living together again."

I kept Roger chatting for twenty more minutes, but his phone never beeped again. So I just came back here and got into bed with my piles of stuff and put on my socks. And then I did a few snow angels and sent everything flying. Something broke, I think, but I didn't really want to look.

8.

Shortly after Gwen got into the company, Mara decided to get a place of her own. Well it *was* sort of crowded in the one-bedroom. I felt torn, because I think Mara really wanted us to still be roommates, but it wasn't like I could just abandon my sister.

The *New York Times* ran a little article on Gwen and me, that first year. "Dancing for Themselves, but Together" was the header. The journalist was from the Arts section, but not a dance critic. Therefore, most of the article was devoted to an examination of our daily life, with all the attendant adjectives: grueling, Spartan, demanding. Our quotes were a purpler-prose version of an athlete's "I love this game/I'm here to support my team/I just want to give it one hundred percent."

> "All the hard work is worth it when you step onstage," says
> Kate, her eyes lighting up. "That's the ultimate reward."

"Onstage is where I feel most me," admits Gwen, shyly. "That's where I'm free to really express myself."

"I'm thrilled," Kate says, regarding her sister's acceptance into the company. "I'm really proud of her. She's worked really hard and she really deserves it. She's going to do great here."

(My first lesson in how fucking stupid you sound when someone accurately reproduces your colloquial English.)

The reporter got Marius to weigh in on us.

Marius on me:

"Kate is a very musical dancer. And she connects with her characters in a very spontaneous way. A natural actress."

Marius on Gwen:

"When Gwen came to the school we were all impressed with her technical facility. That drive for perfection is one of the things you look for in a dancer. It can't be taught."

Probably the interviewer thought that this was an even assessment of our skills. Fair. Each of us getting praise. But for me it might as well have been written in capital letters and stamped on our foreheads: Kate is funny and dramatic, but it's Gwen who can really dance.

The reporter confined her own comparisons of us to a quick paragraph at the end:

As befitting their different dance styles, the sisters display quite individual personalities. Older sister Kate is more outgoing, quicker to laugh and joke. Gwen is more reserved, and her smile, though just as endearing, is slower to come. On one subject, however, Gwen is all enthusiasm: "I'm her biggest fan!" she says, hugging her sister. "She's my inspiration!"

The article, when it appeared, embarrassed us both. Me, because I thought I sounded like an idiot and was worried that Marius was implying that I lacked technical ability and was just a funny drama queen. Gwen because she thought the accompanying photograph made her look fat. (We were pictured in a silly pose by the fountain at Lincoln Center, in our street clothes, and the wind caught Gwen's dress, billowing it out around the midsection.) I crept around shamefaced for about a week before I realized that mostly people just ignore this kind of thing. I once did an editorial spread in *Vogue* with some other dancers and a few people said, "Nice pictures," or whatever, but nobody made a fuss. It's not jealousy. It's more that it's hard to shift one's monumental ego over to acknowledge other people. And looking pretty in a magazine, or doing an interview? They don't really count. What counts is what happens in class, in rehearsal, onstage. That's the only measure.

"I'm her biggest fan!" she says, hugging her sister.

And she was. She seemed to take it for granted that I was wonderful, that I did well, that life in the company was easy for me and that I was happy.

What needed work, what needed discussion and prevention and codes and rules and effort, was securing Gwen's happiness. That Gwen needed to be made happy seemed obvious. Her talent was too extraordinary. And I, the stronger one, the outgoing one, the one quicker to laugh, had been given this task. What was I going to do, let her fall apart? The only reason not to help Gwen would have been that I was jealous of her and wanted her to fail.

I couldn't see the future. I didn't know that little waves might become a tsunami. How could I have possibly known that my puny canoe wouldn't be enough for Gwen? That I would have to lash myself to a lamppost in order to survive the storms to come?

Being in this apartment again has brought back all those early-years feelings. But I see them differently now. If this place is a crime scene, then everything in it is a clue. No wonder I have trouble falling asleep.

I can't sleep, and I can't sleep in. I wake up exactly three minutes before the alarm, and the anxiety of the sound the alarm is going to make propels me out of bed and across the room to the dresser.

A hot shower, normally one of my favorite places to be, seems to have become yet another thing to endure. There's just so much . . . work to be done in there. Because of all the crap I have to put in my hair to get it up in performance-worthy smoothness, I have to shampoo every day. And then condition. And then there's facial cleanser. And then scrubbing of various body parts with exfoliant. And then shaving, because I'm not a fan of waxing. Actually, the shaving is the best part, because in order to shave my nether regions properly I must hike one leg up high on the shower wall and it's kind of a nice hip opener. After I've finished with one side I rotate on the ball of my foot and bend forward slightly and get the first deep, satisfying crack of the day, right where the femur attaches to the pelvis. *THWONK*. So funny: when I did that in front of Andrew he would wince; if I do it at work, people say, "Oh, good one."

And then more work. Toweling. Combing. Scooping up hair that comes out when I comb. Deodorant. Moisturizer for body. Moisturizer for face. Ear cleaning. Skin examining. Eyebrow tweezing. Nail trimming. Tooth cleaning. It's just fucking exhausting and then there's doing my hair and attempting some sort of makeup and then clothes. If I hadn't reinstituted my invisible audience/judges for this whole segment of the day I just wouldn't be able to get through it. Gwen's wardrobe helps too. It's very well organized, by color and within color, by season. She doesn't have a ton of random things that she never wears, like I do.

All of Gwen's apartment is very well edited. Which is not to say that it's barren or cold. She has very good taste.

It was a thing we enjoyed, those first years of living together. Shopping, choosing, fixing up our apartment just so. Even something like getting a corkscrew was special, because we would hunt around until we felt like we had found the absolute *best* corkscrew. And we were just making corps salary, which doesn't go very far in New York City, so everything had to be very carefully thought out. Lots of things we did without until we could afford exactly what we wanted.

It was like a game. I thought it was all about the aesthetics of our life. Were we not artists, after all, tuned in to the finer details and existing on a somewhat more elevated plane than the common folk?

But Gwen has a way of multiplying the rules of any game. And things snuck up on me. I would lose focus, get involved in some drama of my own, and not pay attention to what Gwen was doing until it was already there, a fact of our life together, something I had been colluding with for months without really being aware of it.

Like the switch from extremely neat to obsessively neat. Emptying the wastepaper basket every time I left anything in it, like a lipstick-imprinted tissue or a hank of floss. Washing the dishes and then drying them and putting them away and then washing and drying the sink and then the kitchen floor and then taking pots and pans that we hadn't even used out of the cupboards and washing them too. Vacuuming. Oh god, the vacuuming. She'd vacuum and then empty the bag out onto newspaper and comb through all the detritus. And then do it again and again. Examining. Like an archaeologist with short-term memory loss. There's always something, she'd say. Until there wasn't, but that didn't always bring the relief she needed.

Sometimes she would refer to objects like floss or bobby pins sucked up from the rug, with gender pronouns.

"Look at her," Gwen might say, holding up a miniature bird's nest of hair plucked from the bathroom wastepaper bucket. At first I thought she was being whimsical.

"Here he is," she said, seizing upon two or three crescent slivers of toenails.

"Um, that was probably me," I would say. "Sorry."

She would smile her sibylline smile.

No. I knew it wasn't right. That it wasn't just eccentricity. Her face, as she organized, scrubbed, aligned objects at right angles, hung and re-hung and re-hung towels, was eerily blank of expression. She was there and she wasn't there. If I interrupted her, she might cower, or yell, or even cry. If I left her alone she would eventually either exhaust or satisfy herself and things would continue on. It was all very private. And at work she began to blossom. Her dancing got more confident. She worked hard. I know this because these were the very things I was supposed to be doing, but my results didn't look like Gwen's.

If I joined in the cleaning, and did it with her, it would often wear itself out and abate more quickly. Sometimes not. Sometimes it would lead to her doing other, stranger things. I guess the paper dolls were an early typical example. Things would start . . . appearing. Like, keys were a big thing for a year or two. Not her own apartment keys, but ones she had picked up from god knows where. Keys to nothing. She collected dozens of them and hid them all over the place. They would be sewn inside curtains, placed in a Chinese takeout box, and stored in the freezer. I'd find keys in Clive's cat litter.

"Hey, Gwen," I would say, going for casual and curious instead of slightly freaked out. "What's with all the keys?"

"Oh, I just like them."

"Okay, why are they taped to the side of the oven?"

"Why is anything anyplace?" she might ask. And since this was both funny and true, I usually let it go at that point. I started removing the keys from wherever strange place I found them and dumping them in an unused glass flower vase. Gwen didn't mind. She put the vase on the kitchen table like a centerpiece and it was almost like an Easter egg hunt for me. When the vase got full, it would disappear.

Well, look, it's not like Gwen staggered around in a constant state of looniness, thinking she was the ghost of Napoleon or doing big Jekyll-and-Hyde mood shifts. I probably did some weird stuff too.

This morning, after the interminable five-act opera that is basic hygiene, I dismissed my viewing audience so I could smoke a cigarette with my morning coffee. This is terribly sloppy of me—I've trained myself to only have one or two cigarettes a week and then only after a performance—but I've slipped into this new habit and now it's hard to break.

In all other ways though, I'm basically living by Gwen's house rules. The only thing I haven't been able to avoid is collecting a pile of mail on her desk. Gwen hates piles like that. She keeps a paper shredder on her desk so that after she opens and deals with everything, she can utterly destroy it. (For someone with such a shaky sense of her own identity, she's really paranoid about identity theft.) I've been paying her Con Ed bills, etc., but I don't know what to do with the catalogs and various other things. Gwen has a very particular system for everything.

The New York City postal service has been forwarding my own mail in little rubber-banded caches. This morning, after the cigarette, I finally sat down to go through a few. It was still early, too early. Hours before morning class and I couldn't think of anything else to do. Amid all the junk—the usual stalking from Bed Bath & Beyond—I found the familiar envelope from Wendy Griston Hedges.

I didn't need to open this to know what it contains.

During my first years in the company, I would see Wendy at all the donor events, and we would talk, but she never initiated anything more, and it did not occur to me to suggest it. I was always happy to see her. She felt mine, in a particular way. My own private thing. She didn't seem especially interested in Gwen. It was always about what *I* was dancing, *my* performance, how *I* was feeling about things.

When did she invite me to tea, that first time?

Oh, of course I remember. Gwen had just been made soloist. Ahead of me. And the whole thing with Hilel had just gone down. I guess I was feeling kind of low. Anyway, there was something—an invited dress rehearsal, I think—and a few days later I got a formal invitation in the mail from Wendy to have tea at her house. A little bemused, I responded in kind, by mail.

My arrival at her apartment coincided with the hanging in her foyer of an enormous glass chandelier, recently purchased in Venice, comprised of enormous glass fruits and vegetables. Pink grapefruits. Red pomegranates. Green peppers. Purple eggplants. Something that might have been butternut squash. Wendy ushered me in and we stood watching together as this monstrosity was hoisted overhead by an electrician.

"That is really something," I said.

"I think it should be lower," Wendy said, fretfully, to me.

"Um . . . Mrs. Hedges would like you to lower it," I addressed the electrician.

The giant thing sank a few inches.

"Too low, and it'll bang on someone's head," the electrician counseled.

"I want to see it, though," Wendy said to me. "So I can enjoy it."

"A bit lower," I instructed.

He lowered it another few inches.

Wendy stepped directly under the chandelier. The electrician, freaked out, grabbed the chain with both hands and nearly fell off his ladder.

"Lady," he squeaked.

"There," said Wendy, smiling. The fruits and vegetables sparkled a foot above her head, like a celestial produce tiara.

"Okay, good!" I shouted, hauling her out of the way. "Lock it down there, please."

"I'll get the tea," said Wendy, happily.

And so it went on. The first Monday of every month, Wendy and I would have tea. A week or two before the Monday a formal invitation would appear, and I would send a reply. Of course there were gaps. Tour. Vacation. Wendy occasionally took a cruise, or spent a month or two in Greece. But it's been a kind of staple in my life. I've pieced together bits of her history over the years, although she's not one for talking about herself. I've gotten used to her shyness, which hasn't really abated with time. It's not a lonely shyness, though. As happy as she is to see me, I think she's equally happy when I go and leave her to her books and her occupations. Considering the shyness and her extreme privacy, I wondered what made her take in a student ballerina. When I got up the nerve to ask, she took a moment to reply and then said, "Henry couldn't have children. He told me that when he asked me to marry him. I think it's why he asked me, actually. He thought I wouldn't mind. Oh, and I didn't. I didn't want children. But I did wonder from time to time. How do you know you won't like something if you've never tried it? So when the company asked if I would consider hosting a student I thought, Well, here is my chance to experiment. And Henry was already dead, you see, so it couldn't hurt his feelings."

"I guess you realized you really didn't like it!" I laughed. "Since I was the only one you let stay here."

"That wasn't you." She patted my knee. "I liked you very much. Very much. But oh, my dear, it made me so nervous and uncomfortable." She shuddered. "They say it's different if it's your own child, but what a risk! What if it's not different? No, I satisfied my curiosity."

Our teas have been mostly instructional. Wendy usually has some book ready for me. She reads Latin and Greek. She knows a lot about ancient civilizations, mythology, classical drama, and poetry.

"The life of the mind," she told me once. "That's what I really wanted. My fairy tales were filled with ivory towers. And then I met Henry. So that was a different life."

"Well, it's sort of an ivory tower," I said, gesturing around the Park Avenue living room. "Ivory-colored upholstery, anyway."

"Yes. That's why I never sit in here unless you come. I'm afraid of spilling things."

"We can sit somewhere else."

"Do you think?"

After that, we always had tea in her library, which had moss-green corduroy armchairs.

Occasionally, I went with Wendy to "pay calls" on some of her favorite art around the city. She didn't believe in prolonged museum visits; she preferred to visit one or two favorite pieces and leave it at that. Since her apartment wasn't far from the

Metropolitan Museum of Art, she liked to check in fairly regularly with Jean-Baptiste Carpeaux's *Ugolino and His Sons* in the sculpture garden.

Ugolino, a Pisan traitor, was imprisoned with his sons in a tower and condemned to starvation. The sculpture is sensuous and grisly and disturbing all at once. Ugolino is depicted gnawing at his own fingers. One child is perhaps already dead, collapsed against Ugolino's left leg. Two other sons are coiled around him, the eldest digging his fingers into his father's calf in a way that makes your teeth hurt. Wendy explained to me the history of Ugolino, which led to a mini lecture on thirteenth-century Italian politics, the differences between Guelphs and Ghibellines.

"According to Dante," Wendy told me, "the sons pleaded with their father to satisfy his hunger by eating them."

"Father, our pain," they said,
"Will lessen if you eat us—you are the one
Who clothed us with this wretched flesh: we plead
For you to be the one who strips it away."

"It would be really horrible to look at," I said, "if it were in color. But it's so . . . white. And their bodies are so beautiful."

Wendy nodded and we walked slowly around the sculpture, examining it from every angle. Her face, so quick to paper-crease itself with mild anxiety, was utterly serene, and her manner oddly confident.

"You would have made a great teacher," I said, as we left the museum.

"A good researcher," she corrected. And then added, with

one of her oddly girlish giggles, "I'm very selfish. I never wanted
to teach. I just liked knowing things. You would be a good
teacher, Kate."

"Only I don't actually know anything," I said, which made
her giggle again.

I was selfish too. I never brought Gwen to Wendy's. Nor,
when Gwen questioned me about her, did I reveal how much
I enjoyed going there. Disloyally, I made it sound like a drag,
something I felt obligated to do. Gwen, sympathetic, would
sometimes try to talk me out of going.

"I mean, she volunteered to have you in her house. It was
only a year. You don't have to keep thanking her!"

"She donates to the company," I would say. "It's polite."

"Yeah, I guess. Well, it's really nice of you."

This morning I pulled the envelope from Wendy out of the
packet and walked to the fridge so I could post it up and remind
myself to send a reply. But of course Gwen doesn't have refrigerator magnets.

I went back in the bedroom to make the bed—tricky, since
I've stashed so much crap in there with me. And yes, I did break
something last night when I was doing Roger's angel wings. A
glass.

Sweeping up the remnants of this, I found a piece of paper
under the bed. It was taped to the floor. I pried it up.

3333333333.

My neck hurt. I sat down on the floor, in between the dust-
bin of glass and the bed.

Gwen and her numbers.

And this one she told me about, didn't she? I can say, "Oh, it
crept up on me," and "She wasn't stark *raving* mad," and "I was

focused on my career too," but Gwen actually told me about the numbers. So I have no excuse.

We were doing laundry and I was going through her jeans pockets before I threw them in the wash. I thought they were my jeans and I had a bad habit of leaving books of matches in my jeans and then washing them. I pulled out a piece of paper with "55533555" written on it.

"Do you need this?" I asked, holding it out to Gwen. She paused, her arms full of sheets, and leaned over.

"No, that's old," she said. "You can throw it away." Which I did without comment because it wasn't particularly interesting or striking. Maybe my disinterest irked her, or maybe she genuinely wanted to share something with me, but after a moment she said, "Fives and threes are my favorite numbers. They're like, similar but they do different things in different ways."

"Huh?"

"Well, they're both really comforting, right?"

"What do you mean? You mean like, the numbers themselves are comforting?"

"Yeah. Threes are like anchors. Fives are like rocking chairs."

"What they look like, you mean? The shape?" I drew a 3 in the air between us.

"Not really that. Threes are more protective, and fives are more soothing."

"Okay, so in what way is the number five soothing?"

"I can't explain it."

"Is this a numerology thing?"

Those were the only kinds of books Gwen would read. Crystals and tarot cards and astrology stuff.

"It's my own thing. If I feel anxious I might just repeat the number five to myself, or count to five for a while. Or if I feel scared I might say '33333.' It makes me feel better."

"Huh."

And that's all I ever said about it.

And even now I'm tempted to just stick the piece of paper back where I found it. Except that I'd have to sleep over it knowing it's there, and I'm already not sleeping.

Maybe it's not really that bad.

How different is this from touching a strip of tape on your dressing-room door? Or believing that you have a better class when your nails are done? Or maintaining an invisible audience in order to inspire more perfect behavior?

Who is to say that these things aren't the mark of the extraordinary? Nobody says about a genius, "Well, they were really boring and normal."

3333333333.

I threw the number in the trash, along with the glass.

Sometimes, when the cleaning and the numbers failed to do their job, Gwen would take pieces of masking tape and make Xs on the wall. This wasn't something I could reasonably ignore. It was too strange. It was frightening.

"Talk to me," I would plead. "If you talk to me, I might be able to help you."

"You wouldn't understand. You don't believe."

"What? What don't I believe?" I would try to stay calm. I would make the gestures for sympathy, for calm, for understanding. But the body doesn't lie. Gwen knew I was just pretending to be patient and kind. I didn't feel those things. I wanted to run. I wanted to run away from her.

"Just leave me alone," she would say. "Just pretend you don't see. It's worse if I feel like you're watching."

And so that's what I did. I pretended I didn't see.

I was never there when the tape came off the walls. But by their absence I knew that things were okay again. I could unclench my jaw, sleep through the night, stop trying to act like I wasn't watching her, stop waiting for the thing to come around the corner and stab me in the eye.

When Gwen comes back, things will be different. I won't let it all happen again. I will take better care of her.

I'm not ready for her to come back.

I don't want her to come back.

3333333333.

It's not a code. It's an accusation.

9.

I dragged myself through company class. I dragged myself through *Look At Me* rehearsal. I dragged myself through the rain across the street to get some sushi before dragging myself back to the theater for another round of *Swan Lake*.

At the theater: high drama. Marianna, who was supposed to be dancing Odette/Odile tonight, canceled. Her ankle. Gia, who was supposed to make her debut as Odette/Odile on Sunday, now had to go on. Four other people had called out in addition to people who were already on the injured list. The call-board was full of cross-outs and big red arrows and circled names. I read that Mara was going on for Big Swan/Hungarian Princess. She's third cast for that and hasn't performed it this season.

I ran into Yumi in the hallway.

"I just ate huge dinner," she said. "And then they call me. Tell me Kim is out and I need to come. I tell them, Okay I come, but I puke up onstage."

I found Mara in the dressing room I usually share with Tamara, slicking her hair back into a bun.

"Is it okay if I dress in here with you?" she asked. "My dressing room feels like a high school locker room. Everyone is screeching."

"Is Mike coming?"

"I just left him like, five messages," said Mara, jabbing pins into her hair. "I think he's still at work. He works late when he knows I won't be home."

"Don't worry about making the front perfect," I said, taking the pins out of her hand. "Both headpieces will cover it."

"Oh, right, right. God, what is this?" Mara asked, picking up an orange stuffed animal from the dressing table.

"It's Tamara's lucky bunny."

"Jesus Christ. We're in a company of children."

"I would like to remind you," I said, "of a certain teddy bear that gets taken on tour with a certain dancer. A certain dancer who, I might add, takes care to pack this said teddy bear in such a way that he has 'room to breathe' in her suitcase."

"I'm nervous," said Mara.

"Really?" I asked, surprised. "You've done it before. Didn't you do it last time?"

"Once," Mara said. "Big Swans only once. And I did Neapolitan Princess. Not Hungarian."

"You'll be fine. You'll sail right through it."

Mara gave me a level look through the dressing-table mirror.

"I don't get all that many chances, you know. I'm not ever going to get promoted. I know that. I don't even care anymore. I just want to have a few things to look back on where I knew I was really good. I don't want to sail through it. I want . . . I want to own it. You don't know what it's like."

"Okay," I said.

"I feel old," said Mara.

"We're not old," I told her. "We're in our prime."

"Yeah?" Mara asked, twisting around in her chair to face me. "How good do *you* feel?"

I would have looked away, but that would have meant turning my neck. Mara and I confronted each other for a moment. There have been a lot of things that have come between us in the past ten years, but we are both, after all, women.

"Well, if that's the way you feel," I said, "don't get nervous. Get even."

"Okay," said Mara. "Get even."

"Get even," I repeated.

"With who, exactly? You?"

"Why would you need to get even with me?"

Mara laughed.

"No, seriously," I said.

"I don't want to get into this now," Mara said.

"Okay. Just get even with fucking ballet, then."

"You're the one with the problem with ballet."

"Fine." I pointed at Mara's reflection in the mirror. "Get even with her."

Mara squinted her eyes at herself.

"Oh, you," she said.

When you put on stage makeup you are basically painting on a face that will transmit up to the second balcony. It's great. You can white everything out and then draw whatever you want on top of it. I quickly assembled Beauty, stepped into my Big Swan tutu, layered every available knit over it, and popped a pair of puffy down slippers over my pointe shoes. Mara went down to the warm-up room, and I stopped by Gia's dressing room to wish her *merde*. She was in that excited state of nervousness where you can't get your eyebrows to match. I told her that she would be magnificent and I would send Andrea in to do her eyebrows.

"Will you watch?" Gia asked. "In the wings? Take notes for me? I was thinking to ask you before but I was . . . I was shy."

Why do people pick me? I'm the last person someone who needs someone should pick.

"Of course," I said.

In the hallway, I passed Roger.

"I'm on for Von Goblin," he said.

"Oh, goodie," I said. "I love your Goblin. Wait. Who's doing Ivor?"

"Alberto."

"Really? He knows it?"

"He knows the pas de trois," said Roger. "He's a little sketchy on everything else. I told him that when in doubt, just point at something, smile, and slap Siegfried's ass."

"Oh dear god."

"Should be quite a show," said Roger, who disappeared down the hallway shouting, "You ARE what dance IS! And dance IS what you ARE!"

Normally cast changes are typed onto slips of paper and stuffed into the programs, but there wasn't time for that tonight. Theo, our production stage manager, had to make an announcement on the mike. The changes were so extensive and the list so long that the audience actually started to laugh a little. You could hear them through the curtain. I was in the wings, watching Hilel and Gia run through a few last things together. It's a little ballet in itself: dancers before a performance. Hilel would sketch a lift with his hands. Gia would nod. They would do it. Then stand apart, nodding. Gia would walk in circles, hands on her tutu. Stop. Look at Hilel. Mime a pirouette. Hilel would nod. They would do it. Then stand apart, nodding.

I decided to stay in the wings and watch the Prelude. When Gia made her first brief appearance there was tremendous applause from the audience. I could see her shaking in Roger's arms. It was so beautiful, how vulnerable she was. It was real fear though, so I don't think she'll be able to re-create it with the same simplicity. Once you start practicing emotions they look less cool.

Act I. Hilel as Siegfried got a nice entrance ovation. I watched Alberto scamper up to him and gesture either "Hello! Welcome! We are all having a good time and dancing! Please join us!" or "Thank god you are here, as I have been milling and mugging for what seems like an eternity! Do I slap your ass now?"

Things seemed to be going moderately well, so I retreated deeper into the wings to warm up until the music for the pas de trois began. Alberto, clearly grateful to have actual steps to dance, looked great. Galina came onstage as the Queen. It's like she's able to unhinge part of her jaw or something. No wonder Alberto got a little spooked. He nearly clipped Hilel with the crossbow.

The lake sets dropped in and the stage was bathed in blue. Hilel entered, woefully. Alberto entered, a full thirty-two counts early, and all but shoved the crossbow in Hilel's arms, before fleeing, *fleeing*, the stage. He ran right by me in the wings, crying, "Shit, shit, shit," then doubled back and we watched Hilel improvise.

"It's okay." I patted Alberto.

"I fuck up," he moaned. "Did you see me fuck up?"

"It just looked like Ivor was really scared of the forest," I assured him. "Hilel is fine."

But then it was time for the swans to make our entrance, so I ditched the knits and slippers and had a dresser hook up my bodice. Mara was right behind me. On and on we came, one after another, like heartbeats, like thoughts, like memory, like grief.

It's not really the audience that one is frightened of, onstage. One is chasing ghosts, shadows, time. One is using the word "one" because to say "I" is to acknowledge that I might feel differently about dance than other people. As Mara pointed out, I'm the one with the problem.

Worth it? How do you measure that, please?

How does Gwen measure that?

Gia almost fell. There must have been a slippery spot just at the edge of the wings, and she stepped on it and skidded. I don't think she was far enough onstage that the audience saw it, but the six or seven of us who did see it all sucked in our breaths simultaneously. Gia's face went whiter than her makeup, but she composed herself quickly into the stricken ethereal femininity of all the White Swans who have come before her. I watched her out of the corner of my eye. We were all watching, holding our breaths for her inside our narrow bodices. In moments like these, the family closes ranks. We want her to do well. We know how much it means to her, we know exactly how she feels. The empathy onstage was almost palpable. We danced our best, wanting to help.

She's not there yet, Gia. She's fabulously gifted, of course, but all the talent is still inside her body. She hasn't yet learned how to think about this role in her own way. Phrases floated inside my head, things I could say to her. The kinds of things I said to Gwen.

Big Swans. Mara wasn't my direct opposite, so I couldn't really see her, but I could feel that we were in unison, and her spacing was perfection. At one point, when we were in a diamond formation, I saw her shoulder blades ahead of me, glistening sweat, every little tendon visible. She'll never know how extraordinary she looked. How fragile. How noble. How perfect.

Intermission.

Mara was giddy with relief in the dressing room. Everything had gone well, very well, felt good. I hooked her into her Hungarian Princess tutu, fluffed out her skirts like a bridesmaid, took pictures of her with her iPhone. She rubbed Tamara's lucky bunny and I touched the tape where the mezuzah used to be.

Act III, the birthday ball. Each Princess has a little retinue. I came on last and let myself be led to make my curtsy to Hilel. He took my hand and bowed over it politely, but without interest.

After our "Hey, we're the Princesses! Check our shit out!" group dance, we all trouped off Stage Left, except for Mara, because her solo was first. I stood as far into the first wing as I could to get the best view.

The Hungarian Princess solo has a folk dancing flavor to it, and a lot of little hops on pointe. It's also very fast. Mara was dancing like she got shot out of a cannon, just ripping through things, huge smile. I guess I can see why she's never been promoted. There's something withheld, an academic quality to her dancing that's wonderful for corps work but not necessarily inspiring. Still, she is super strong. And very musical. Maybe if someone had just taken more of an interest? If she had been less willing to be useful? More demanding? There are roles that she'd be right for if she had just been given the opportunity and the right coaching. Phrases began forming in my head, things I could have said to her, long ago, that might have helped.

I was thinking about that when all of a sudden—in preparation for an easy jump—Mara's supporting leg went out from under her, and she landed flat on her ass, hard. Even from the wings, I could hear the audience gasp. Mara scrambled up so quickly it was almost as if she bounced, and she launched herself right back in.

From the dancer's point of view, falling isn't the worst thing that can happen onstage. Falling is either a fluke or the result of going for too much, and as long as there's no injury involved it's embarrassing and a little shocking but it's possible to laugh about it or shrug off later. A splashy fall isn't as bad as knowing you gave a mediocre performance—that's really the worst thing.

Except if you don't get many chances to dance by yourself. Except if you're just wanting one moment where you know yourself to be really, really good. I could tell from the way Mara was moving that she hadn't hurt herself and after a moment she resumed smiling, but her eyes were dead.

Of course she fell. She fell because there was maybe a jewel from a costume that came off, or a stray hairpin, or something, and she stepped right on it and slipped. And because a million, a hundred thousand million pliés and tendus and a life spent sweating and aching and wanting and wanting and wanting could not stop her from falling. She fell because earlier in the evening Gia didn't, and the stage demanded a blood tribute. She fell because life isn't fair.

The audience started applauding her before her solo was over, and there were some cheers when she finished. I heard that, the cheer, and I sobbed out loud, a horrible sort of choked honk that scared me a little. I covered my mouth with my hand and watched Mara take her place upstage as the Spanish Princess came on. Mara was still smiling her leaden-eyed smile and breathing through her nose, the tight bodice of her dress holding in her heart so it wouldn't fall too. And after Spanish Princess, and Neapolitan Princess, I came on and I danced . . . wonderfully.

I mean, absolutely flawlessly. My neck felt like it was jammed up into my right ear and I hadn't stayed warm properly and I wasn't paying any attention to what I was doing, and I have never danced that stupid thing better. I held every balance, and floated every jump. I could see the conductor leaning in to tell the strings to pause for me, but I wasn't really listening to the music. The solo ends with a series of three slow turns in a diagonal coming downstage. As I prepared for the first one, I thought, "Fall," because if I fell too, it would be the performance that Mara and I both wiped out in, and we would be even. But I didn't fall, I just did an extra pirouette, and for the next one I thought "Fall" again, and I didn't, and then "Fall" once more, and I whipped through four pirouettes, balanced like I was made of stone, and finished. I made my révérence to the Prince, who will never be mine, and stepped sedately back to the upstage corner. I passed Mara on the way and we looked at each other and I thought, You don't know what it's like either.

After the solos we all briefly danced with the Prince. I was lifted and promenaded and returned to my place. The Queen demanded that Siegfried make a choice. Hilel took his customary regretful bow over my hand. It's not that I am not beautiful and worthy. I'm simply not special. I'm not the One.

Then Roger as Von Rothbart entered with Gia as Odile, the Black Swan. I was supposed to join everyone else with some "Who is she? Who is she?" gestures and then move to the far side of the stage, but I just watched everyone else do it. I knew who she was. I let myself be led by my escort to Stage Right, and I watched the betrayal unfold. It looked, as it sometimes can, better than the thing it betrayed.

Second intermission. We end at the lake, of course. Whenever I wasn't onstage I wedged myself into the wings. I promised Gia I'd watch, and it's important to see these things through to the bloody end.

You could tell she was almost cashed out, dancing on adrenaline. She looked almost enthusiastic about killing herself, eager to end the ballet and sit down. That might be the right way to do it, actually. Not mournful, or resigned, or pathetic. Excited.

Is that what you would feel?

I was in the wings the first time Gwen danced Odette/Odile. Of course I was. Where else would I be?

Forgiveness. That's what the last act is about.

What is forgiveness all about?

You shouldn't ask for forgiveness.

Because if you ask someone to forgive you, and they do, then that's twice that you've taken something from them. First the betrayal, and then the absolution.

God, Odette can't even die by herself. Siegfried jumps in after her.

Better to be dead than live with forgiveness, maybe.

Curtain call took forever tonight. The audience was kind.

In the dressing room, Mara did not allow me to say anything about her falling. When I asked her if she was okay, she said, "Fine!" as if nothing had happened. Then we talked about Gia and, for some reason, about some new wine store on Twelfth Street. Mara was furiously rubbing off makeup and tearing down her hair like she wanted to get out of the room and away from me fast. Perversely, I kept pace with her. I didn't want to be in the room by myself. The intercom buzzed to let Mara know that she had a guest waiting for her by the sign-in board.

"Good night!" Mara said, still unpinning her bun. "Thanks for your help tonight!"

"Oh, I'll go down with you!" I said, shoving my sweater on inside out and grabbing Kleenex.

Mike was waiting with a bunch of roses in his hand. He was wearing his suit, from the office, I guess. He looked like something from another planet, amid all the dancers—half-dressed visitors from yet another planet.

"You were awesome!" he shouted, hugging her. He actually jumped up and down.

"I fell," she said softly. "Mike, I fell."

"Wait, what?" he cried. "You did? When?"

"Oh, honey!" Mara gasped, and started to cry.

"Wait, that thing where you sat down on the stage?" Mike pulled her to him and started rubbing her back. "It happened so fast I was sure that it was supposed to be there. It looked like you were doing a fancy trick."

Mara started laughing and buried her head in Mike's chest.

"I know you get mad that I think everything you do is incredible," he said. "But I do. I really do."

"Tonight I don't mind," I heard Mara say.

I left the theater and walked to the subway. There were people on the platform with *Swan Lake* programs in their hands. I moved to the far end, set my bag down on a bench, and my arm suddenly went numb. I remembered that I have an injury. I stood there for a moment, gently rotating my head to assess the damage. I would've liked the platform to open up and slowly lower me into another realm, but of course there were no violins and no painted moon and no one to go with me.

It's been a lot of years now of worshipping in a church where the gods have left, and my neck is broken from praying and my knees are tired. I could have changed my life years ago. I could have been another person and I could have done other things. I did not. I was talented and I didn't want to give that up. It wasn't that I always loved dancing so much. But what I always liked, what my poor crooked soul still likes, is being a person who is talented. Talented at one of the most difficult and rare things to be talented in. Almost nobody gets to be a professional ballet dancer. Those of us who have made it here have watched nearly everyone we knew who was also trying to get here have to drop off at some point. We are the elite, and we have paid for the right to be. How could we possibly walk away from it when it is offered to us? I couldn't then, and I still can't now.

Forgiveness.

No, I don't think so.

10.

Sort of an odd day. I got myself out of bed and to ten a.m. company class and it turned out to be one of those days when Marius was teaching. He doesn't usually anymore. The temperature in the room goes up about 20 degrees when he does, and everybody turns it on. And there I was looking like total hell again. Like I just shot my dog, as Roger put it. I used to take so much care with how I looked.

"You need a signature thing," I told Gwen when she joined the company. Mine was dark red lipstick, inspired by that photograph of Marguerite Duras on the cover of *The Lover*. She looks deep, there, and also alluring, which is how I wanted to be seen. I parted my hair in the middle and wore it in two braids a lot, and always had a little skirt on for class and rehearsal.

I broke a Vicodin in half and swallowed it with my takeout coffee. Sometimes caffeine will accelerate the effects. I was hoping to stay more or less invisible, but Marius came up to me before barre and squatted down beside me.

"Come see me after class," he said, patting me on the foot.

I just nodded because I didn't want to breathe Starbucks on him. Absolutely everyone in the room saw this little exchange. Marius walked away and I stood up and turned to the wall and pretended to stretch. Then I fished out the other half of the Vicodin. I actually felt like I was having a panic attack, because all of a sudden the only reason I could think of as to why Marius wanted to see me was that I was going to be fired. Well, that's it, I told myself. You're done. It's over.

Class started. Marius gives very difficult combinations of steps. Very complicated musically. You have to really pay attention. He always confers with the pianist on what she is going to play. "Let's have . . . dum-de-dumdum-dummm-de-dah," he says to her, humming some piece, and then he claps softly along with the rhythm. Marius counts out the phrases for us, but he never uses any number but one. "And a ONE and a ONE and ONE," he chants. He says things like "Try to look like you are happy when you do this" and "Don't be stingy" and "Why is everyone sweating? Ballet is so easy." Marius himself always looks perfectly composed.

The first part of class passed not so much in a blur as in a glaze. Like there was a shiny hard coating over everything. A stone kept dropping and plunking into my stomach.

Things got worse after barre, because then we move into the center of the room, and I could no longer avoid my reflection in the mirror. I was so distracted that I had trouble following Marius's adagio combination and had to fake my way through it, a few counts behind.

I looked around the room, but I couldn't connect myself to the people in it. I felt like I had slipped into some sort of bubble inside my head, where it was impossible to reach the rest of my body. *Soutenu, soutenu, step, step, arabesque. None of this makes any sense. I'm like fucking Helen Keller in here. I can't do this. There, it's done, but who did it? Because it's not me. This isn't me.*

I thought I would be okay, kind of hiding in the back of the room, but when it came time to repeat the adagio to the left, Marius stopped class and said, "Kate, come demonstrate."

"Oh shit," I said. People laughed and moved off to the sides.

Marius took me by the left wrist and said, "Arabesque," and I snapped into one like a trained pet. Left leg supporting my weight, toes, knees, and hip all rotated 90 degrees, right leg held up behind me, a good two inches higher than I would go if no one were watching. Still holding on to my wrist, Marius took a step back. "Resist me," he said, as my torso leaned toward his in order to keep my balance. I did, tightening the muscles in my back. "More," said Marius, taking another step back. He slid his hand from my wrist and gripped my fingers, pulling me. I pulled back as hard as I could. "Look at me," said Marius. I looked at him, at his eyes, which are a dark brown. Tiny crow's-feet surround them now and his hair is turning gray. We are both getting older. I took a breath that was filled with the scent of Marius's cologne: lemons and something secret and sweat. "There," said Marius. "There." He released my fingers and I remained positioned, stretched, flattened, wired, strung. "Rest," said Marius, and I brought my right leg down, relaxed my arms.

Marius walked away from me, addressing the class.

"There must be tension always, before the release. Otherwise there is no dynamic, everything just bleeds, yah, yah, yah, no up, no down. And so it's boring. Your audience sits back in their seats and wonders what the babysitter is doing. Always tension, then release. I say tension, but I do not mean this"—Marius screwed himself up like a scalded cat—"I mean like the bow of an arrow." Marius turned back to me and held me in front of him, encircling me with his arms. He moved me into an archer's stance, pulling back an imaginary string. The knuckles of his left hand pressed against my heart. My right shoulder blade slotted into the ridge of his sternum. "Aim," said Marius. I pressed back into him and swiveled us a half turn to face the mirrors. I closed one eye and found my reflection's heart in the mirror, lowered the imaginary arrow, and pointed it directly at myself. There was some chuckling and applause from the class. Marius let go of me and stood back. "All right, then," he said. "Fire when ready."

When class was over, I grabbed my bag and caught up with Marius in the hallway. I was still playing through the YOU ARE FIRED narrative in my head. I imagined taking everything out of my locker and going to someplace horrible like McDonald's and getting french fries and a milkshake and then going to a deli and getting those Zingers cakes that are filled with fake frosting and lard and then purchasing a bottle of wine and a pack of cigarettes and then staying in bed for a week. And then. And then. And . . .

My plans for a life after ballet didn't seem to go much further than immediate consumption of disgusting food and sleep.

In the hallway everyone was milling around, talking, heading to rehearsal or to the lounge or down to the alley for a smoke. Marius was standing by the call-board, speaking in French with Claudette, our ballet mistress. I rocked back and forth in my pointe shoes a few feet away. Claudette saw me waiting and every few seconds her eyes flicked over to me, but she kept chatting away. They spoke too fast for me to understand more than the beginnings of sentences. I heard:

"Next week I want to—"

And:

"Yes, it's always good to—"

And something that sounded like:

"Your eyes are like cake."

I edged forward and touched Marius on his wrist, to get his attention. He grabbed my hand, but continued talking to Claudette. I felt like a little girl waiting for Daddy to finish speaking with another grown-up. Marius was saying something about shoes, about how the girls' shoes are so loud and we sound like horses running around in class. We must break our shoes in more thoroughly before we perform. Claudette shrugged her shoulders in sympathy. Yes, yes, it is terrible. The noise. The clip-clop. The new shoes these days. So loud. She will speak to the girls. So true. Like horses.

Finally they reached the *"D'accord, très bien"* stage and Claudette moved off to wage war with the clip-clop. Marius turned to me.

"Let's go up to my office."

Ludmilla the Bulldog is no longer with us. I miss her. She became very mellow in her old age, and I kind of bonded with her. Marius's wife is gone too. Not dead, but they divorced. Not amicably, people say. He's got a little son, Oliver. There's a picture of him on Marius's desk, holding a tiny football. The kid has giant feet and they are flexed in demi-pointe.

"Oliver has good feet," I said, pointing, hoping to delay the inevitable.

"Every time I play music in the apartment he dances around." Marius sighed. "And every time he dances I give him the football and try to convince him to throw it at something. Or bang on the piano. Or play with his toy stethoscope. Possibly I'm inflicting psychological damage."

"You'll know in about twenty years, I guess."

"Right. Listen, I spoke to Gwen this morning."

This was the last thing I expected. I had no clue as to what face or gesture would be appropriate. My first thought was that I wished I were wearing clothes, which was odd, because I'm fairly naked for most of my working day and you would think that would insulate me better from the metaphorical nakedness.

"She says she'll need six months off," Marius said. "Well, I'm sure you know all this. Her spirits sound good though, don't you think? I thought she should come back here and let Dr. Yates handle her rehab, but she said your dad has hooked her up with some top guy at his hospital and she wants to stick with him."

I nodded.

"Listen, I need you to help me out," Marius continued. "God knows, in this climate, I'm grateful that we had the tours, but Japan was cutting it close, and everybody is getting injured. Every day I come to work and Carlotta hands me a list. And we already had gaps. Tamara, Natalia, Gwen. Now Marianna.

Five years ago I had too many women and not enough men to partner them. Now I have too many men, and all my women are injured."

This didn't seem like a prelude to being fired. Marius seemed to have completely accepted the torn ACL story. Six months? Gwen would be gone for six months. Why was she apparently carrying on these elaborate conversations with everyone but me? What part of this latest story was true? I tried focusing on the matter at hand to calm my nerves.

"Justin is out," Marius said heavily. "For at least three weeks, and I don't want to risk putting him back on too soon, so that leaves you without a Demetrius for *Dream*."

I nodded. If Justin was out, then Marius was probably going to bump me from *Dream*. Well, considering my neck, this was probably good news. My season was already packed, Helena spends a lot of time frantically throwing herself at Demetrius, and I was having problems looking both ways before crossing the street. Still, the immediate relief at not being fired was replaced with disappointment at losing out on *Dream*. And what would I do with the extra time on my hands?

"I'm replacing Justin with Klaus," Marius said. "He knows it, and I think it's going to be a good match. The kid is on fire, and frankly, Lawrence needs a little competition in the room. You'll have to coach Klaus a little, but I trust you. He's very macho, but a little stiff. Shake him up for me?"

"Okay," I said, heart sinking. Extra rehearsal. Macho ego to overcome. Shaking up, yet. What the hell was going on with Gwen?

"Oh, and I want you to do Titania," he said, almost casually. "David has two performances of Oberon in his contract, and now Marianna has this issue with her ankle. She says maybe, maybe not, but I don't have time to deal with any drama. So. I'm splitting the performances between Anne-Marie and Hilel and you and David. You'll start rehearsing on Wednesday. It's not a lot of time, but you're quick. I'm not worried. David isn't worried."

Marius pushed a calendar in front of me. One Thursday and one Saturday at the end of the month were circled.

Marius's phone buzzed and Carlotta's voice announced, "Marius, I've got George Roffola from Chase Manhattan on line one."

"Potential new sponsor," Marius said, crisply. "So get out of my office. I don't like anyone to hear me beg."

I stood up. Sort of. It was more of a lurch. I made it a few steps to the door and then turned back. Marius was already reaching for the phone.

"Did you tell Gwen about this?" I asked.

Marius's hand hovered over the phone.

"No," he said. "Because this isn't about her."

I nodded and shut the door quietly behind me.

Was it really five years ago that Marius came up to me before class in just the same way and asked me to come to his office? I wasn't nervous then. It had been an incredible season. Kylián's *Black and White Ballets*. Manon in *Lady of the Camellias*. The lead in a new ballet, *Illuminata*. I had moved in with Andrew and suddenly I was in love with dancing again and there were pet names and late-night sex and a feeling that I was no longer a house divided. Even when I felt like shit—and *Illuminata* rehearsals were exacting and sort of nerve-racking because the choreographer was Czech and only spoke through an interpreter (although I soon learned Czech for "bad," "wrong," and "not enough")—still, even in those moments when I felt like dance was being cut out of me with a knife, I at least felt some relationship to the knife. I knew why it was necessary, I braced myself, even leaned in to it.

Five years ago Marius called me into his office to tell me that he was promoting me to soloist. He offered it to me like an opening-night gift. I didn't tell anyone right away. I didn't tell Gwen. Or Mara, or Roger, or Andrew. I didn't call my parents. I kept it all to myself and danced Manon that night with a kind of fearless abandonment. After the performance I went home. Andrew carried my roses. For some reason the hot water in our building had been shut off, and Andrew heated up pots of water on the kitchen stove and carried them into the bathroom to make me a bath. Me protesting that it was too much, he didn't have to, and him saying that nothing was too good for me. We had just gotten to sleep—around two in the morning—when Gwen called.

"Something's wrong," she said, sobbing. "I can't walk. Kate, I can't walk."

I couldn't get her to calm down. I couldn't get her to explain. I pulled on sweatpants and Andrew's camel-hair coat. Andrew said, "I'll go with you," and I said, "No, no. It's okay."

There wasn't anything wrong with Gwen's legs. She could walk perfectly fine. The problem was with her floor, which she said was so dirty that she was afraid to step on it. She was sitting outside her apartment in the hallway when I arrived. I didn't know what to expect when we opened the door, but everything was perfectly spotless. I knew better than to explain that to Gwen, though. I gave her Andrew's coat to hold so it wouldn't get dirty. She waited outside while I vacuumed and mopped. When I was done I stepped out in the hallway and Gwen thanked me.

"Marius promoted me to soloist," I said.

"He just made me a principal," she said, handing me the coat and shutting the door.

I was still holding the Swiffer mop.

11.

So I guess it's time, once again, to take it up a notch.

Look, I'm not kidding myself. This isn't some big *Star Is Born* moment. Maybe if it had happened a few years ago, and I had the sense that Marius was grooming me, and I had been cast originally for it, then yes. But it's really just a case of all these people being injured, and Marius thinking that if he puts me on there won't be a lot of fuss. And Titania, while definitely a principal role, isn't Juliet, or Sleeping Beauty, or Odette/Odile.

It's not a huge deal.

Except maybe.

Well.

Anyway, after my little convo with Marius, I had trouble sleeping last night, so I decided to open up my boxes labeled "Dance Clothes." Costuming makes the character and I can't go around looking like crap anymore. My sister is irreplaceable, but I am, in fact, going to have to replace her. Or save her a seat on the bus until she's ready to get back on board. I thought it was appropriate, considering how close we are, that she make a contribution to New Me, so in addition to the pile of my own dance clothes on the living-room floor, I added all of her dance stuff as well.

As I shifted through the collection I started thinking how cool it would be to do an installation art piece thing with them. Each piece could be hung up on its own hanger and be accompanied by a piece of prose on its own historical significance or place in my personal mythology. This is the leotard I bought when I went on the pill and my breasts got a little bigger and I was so excited about how I looked in it that I spent the entire first class I wore it looking down at my own cleavage. This pink skirt was from Gwen's ultra-feminine phase and I told her she looked like Ballerina Barbie in it, and we got into a fight that was less about the insult and more about the fact that she had finally seen another doctor and started taking antianxiety medication but the drugs made her feel "wonky" so she was also doing a little coke. This unitard always shows the patch of sweat in between the breasts and, more unfortunately, the patch of sweat at the crotch and, moreover, retains a musty smell from being stuffed in a corner of the dressing room for most of a season, but I can't throw it out because Charles told me how a bunch of the guys in the company once had a whole long conversation about how good my ass looks in it. (Hello, Charles, I still don't want to be your girlfriend! We were on tour! It was Cleveland! Get over yourself!) These cut-off sweatpants are divine and blessed and I would as soon part with them as I would my soul.

I think such an exhibition would be very interesting. I could throw in some real-people clothing too. This is the sweater that was Andrew's and now it is no longer the Boyfriend Sweater but the Ex-boyfriend Sweater, and soon I will pull it on and take it off without thinking of him because love can die. This is the Givenchy dress Gwen wore to the opening-night gala last year, the night she told me that she was sorry for how she had been acting and that she was going to make it up to me and I told her that she had nothing to apologize for and she said, "Oh, well, then maybe you should apologize to me," and we both had a good laugh, although . . . in retrospect . . . not so funny.

I made a giant bag of discards but didn't throw it away. Which is silly. It's not like I can donate this stuff. What isn't nasty is full of holes, and what needy person wants a leotard? But you never know. There might be a starving one-legged blind peasant child in China who needs some leg warmers. Or one leg warmer, I guess.

I'm working on a blend of Gwen's stuff and mine. Nothing too obvious.

After clothes sorting, I painted my toenails red. My pinkie toes don't actually have nails, just disk-like calluses where the nail would be if I had a different job, but I paint the calluses red so you can't really tell. Then I took a long bath and iced my neck and made a list of ways I am going to be this week. One is grateful, because even without Titania, this is a very good season for me, with lovely roles in good ballets. I need to cultivate more perspective. I should spend some enervating moments meditating on the crushing misery of the greater world in general, although perhaps the irrelevance of my sadness is just as sad as anything else.

I had my first rehearsal with Klaus for *Dream* today, so I decided to take company class and get a proper look at my new partner. He is ridiculously good-looking, but a bit short. I am going to end up towering over him when I'm on pointe. I suppose Marius thought of this, no doubt with hilarious intent. Klaus is almost barrel-chested, which is unusual in a ballet guy. Klaus and I are going to look like Popeye and Olive Oyl.

Yumi came up to me during class.

"Rawlence is so mad," she said. "He say it bullshit Klaus be your partner now. Rawlence is more senior dancer than Klaus."

"Oh, well, Marius probably just wants to keep you and Lawrence together as a couple," I said, because one of the ways I decided to be this week was diplomatic. "You guys work well together, right?" I asked.

Yumi nodded vigorously, but what she said was, "Oh no, he is crazy maybe."

Roger told me after class that Marianne told Hilel that she didn't consider Titania important enough to risk hurting her ankle on, and that's why she pulled out. Mara told me that Maya, who was Klaus's Plague Cast partner, was crying in the dressing room. She and Klaus are dating, or fucking, or are Facebook friends with benefits, or something. Seems Maya saw me talking to Marius in the hallway, and thinks that I asked for Klaus to be my partner because I want him for myself.

"It's just drama," said Mara. "Don't worry."

Little flares like this happen, from time to time. We're not a bunch of cutthroats (who has the energy?), but it's understandable that bad feelings—resentment, jealousy, frustration—occasionally arise. There are only a certain amount of performances, and our days are numbered.

I did notice some tension, to say the least, in the studio for rehearsal today. I was feeling a little cautious because of my neck, and suggested that we start with working out the more straightforward Act II pas de deux. The Act I sections, where Demetrius first spurns Helena and then, under the influence of fairy juice, falls grotesquely in love with her, seemed a little complicated for a first date.

"Yeah, cool, whatever you need," said Klaus.

Klaus's solution to our height difference involved muscling me around. I wouldn't have minded that but he kept rushing ahead of the music, so it was all very fumbly. Yumi and Lawrence took to repeating perfectly whatever thing Klaus and I were bumbling through. At first they did this right behind us. Then they moved up next to us, forcing Klaus and me to move over. When a lift went poorly, Klaus summoned Maya, forlornly stretching in the back corner, to demonstrate how *they* do it.

"See?" said Klaus, looking at me while he flipped all forty pounds of Maya over his head. Maya simpered at me from atop Klaus's shoulder.

"Yes, I see," I replied. "That's very nice."

Lawrence bounded forward and started telling Klaus how to change his grip.

"Do," said Lawrence to me, yanking me up on his shoulder.

"See?" he said to Klaus, plopping me down flat-footed.

I looked over at Yumi, who looked at Lawrence's back and rolled her eyes. Lawrence patted me on the shoulder and looked at Klaus's back and rolled his eyes. I looked around for someone to roll my eyes at, and found no one but a harassed version of myself, red-faced and sweaty in the mirror, in Gwen's green leotard. It didn't seem worth it to roll my eyes at myself.

All of this could have been defused, or controlled, anyway, if Nina had run the rehearsal properly. But she was saying very little. Nina has never liked me, possibly because I've never bothered much to conceal my loathing for her. She piped up eventually in classic form.

"You'll have to make adjustments, Klaus," she trilled, "when working with a taller girl. You won't always have a little wisp like Maya." Nina turned to me. "And you'll have to adjust too. I know you're used to Justin doing everything. You're going to have to pull your weight a little more."

And with that masterstroke Klaus was no longer the lucky kid from the corps who gets to dance with the first cast soloist. He became the poor wunderkind who has to haul the spoiled fatty around. Klaus looked at me from under a blond wing of his hair.

So I spent the rest of the rehearsal partnering my own resentment, barely opening my mouth to say yes or no. Klaus became overly deferential, treating me as if I were some sort of dowager royalty. Lawrence and Yumi moved from working beside us to working slightly in front of us. Nina turned her attention to them, which made Klaus summon little Maya again, in order to show Nina how good he could be. Maya started giving Klaus these very sympathetic looks.

I was working up the nerve to storm out of the rehearsal studio when Nina said, "We'll pick up here on Thursday," and Klaus dropped my hand without a word and went over to his bag. I watched him throw a towel over his head and slump against the mirror, pull a tennis ball out of his bag and lie down on top of it, rolling it under his shoulder blade.

Of course, I would never have stormed out of the rehearsal room. Other people do that kind of thing and get away with it.

Gwen actually threw a chair at the mirror once.

After rehearsal, Nina called me over to the piano.

"So Marius told me that we're going to start rehearsing you

for Titania," she said. "And I'm a little concerned that it's going to be too much for you."

You can always tell when people don't like you because their voices will sound like they're acting when they talk to you. That's how you know that they spend a certain amount of time rehearsing in private the biting and cutting things they wish they could say to you in person.

"I'm not worried," I said to her. "But I think Klaus and I should work on our own for a few days. Just the two of us. It's hard when the room is like . . . crowded."

"Well, you can sort that out yourself," said Nina, walking away before I had a chance to say, "Great," or "I'll do that," or "Eat me."

I spent the dinner break with Mara, and she was congratulating me about Titania and I felt weird about that and I still don't actually believe it's going to happen, so I told her about rehearsal and how stressed out I am, even though one of the ways I was going to be this week was completely cool and positive and calm. Mara was very sympathetic and it was only when we were paying the bill did I realize that, of course, Mara would love a chance to do Helena with *anybody*, instead of dancing one of Titania's attendant fairies—one of my attendant fairies, actually. There was no way to rectify my tactlessness without making it worse, so I had to just leave it alone.

Back at the theater, the next day's rehearsal schedule was posted, and there my name was with David's for Titania/Oberon rehearsal. Roger was waiting in my dressing room.

"DIVA!" he said. "Do you know what this means? It means I'm going to be your Bottom. We are going to tear it up."

"What's the word on the street?" I asked, indicating the hallway outside. "Are people like, 'Has Marius lost his mind?'"

"Since when do you care what other people think?" he sniffed. "People are like, 'That's so great.' What are they going to say? You scare the shit out of everybody."

"I do? What? No, I don't."

"Whatever." Roger kissed me on the cheek. "Just try not to fuck it up. See you later."

I stopped by Mara's dressing room before the performance. She shares it with five other girls, so I pulled her into the hallway.

"Hey," I said. "I'm sorry I went off about Klaus and *Dream* and all that stuff earlier. I don't know why I was complaining. You should just smack me when I start talking like that."

"What are you talking about?" Mara asked.

I was apologizing for apologizing when the half-hour call was announced. Sometimes it's just better to suck up the fact that you are an asshole and decide that tomorrow is the day you will start being the person you intend to be.

I was dancing the pas de trois tonight with Roger and Yumi. Roger was waiting for me in the wings with a leg warmer stuffed in his dance belt.

"Hey, if that's what you're packing," I said, "I'll be *your* Bottom."

Roger pulled the leg warmer out and Yumi joined us. She gave me a sweet little hug.

"Conglaturations," she said. "You be awesome Titania. This good time for you."

"Ask my dance belt
What it understands
About time"

Roger said as the Prelude finished and we got ready for our entrance.

"You haiku suck," said Yumi, plastering a bright smile on her face.

My neck is still bad. I felt very restless onstage, although I was glad that ballet is a silent art and I was temporarily safe from yet another unsatisfying conversation. I danced okay, but I had that nervous energy that comes over you when you are in a small shop filled with breakable objects and it's too quiet and some little chime is tinkling and you think you might suddenly go "*Yaaaargggh!*" and smash things.

As I was leaving the theater, I saw Klaus having a smoke outside.

"In the name of all that is holy," I said, "give me a cigarette."

He laughed and gave me the cigarette he was smoking. Lit a new one for himself.

"Listen," I said. "I don't think we got off to the right start today."

"What do you mean?" He leaned against the wall, all black leather jacket and cowboy boots, holding his cigarette with his thumb and first finger like he's in a gangster movie.

"You seemed a little pissed off at the end there."

"Nah, it's cool," he said. "You shouldn't take things so personally."

The only thing worse than taking things personally is being told you take things personally. And how am I supposed to take things, if you please? Why bother talking to anyone at all if you are not supposed to consider anything that is said to be at all personal? What would Gwen do in this

situation? She might cry. She's sort of a crier. It's very effective. If people think you are sensitive, they are very careful. If
you scare the shit out of people, then they are automatically
defensive.

"I'm sorry," I said. "I am just going through . . . kind of a
tough time right now. It's not you. It's me." I took a feminine
puff and waited.

"Hey," Klaus said, reaching out and rubbing my shoulder.
"I'm sorry. I'm here for you, you know? Whatever you need."

Jesus god, is it really that easy?

I gave Klaus one of Gwen's fragile smiles, and by gum he
actually hugged me and said that he was glad we were going to
get some separate rehearsal time and he was really psyched to
dance with me, I was so fantastic, blah, blah, blah.

I decided to walk the twenty blocks home instead of taking
the subway. It's a nice walk, especially if I detour a bit and take
Central Park West, and I had my iPod for company. In truth, I
was not quite ready to be home, to be alone. I wish it were safe
to go in the park at night. When you go through it in a cab the
trees look so secretive and sexy.

As I pulled my iPod out of my bag, the earphones got caught
around a tangle of warm-up clothes, and in the struggle to get
them free everything went flying out to the concrete. Lurching
after stuff, my neck sent an atrocious dart of pain down my
shoulder. I stood absolutely still and realized how little I can
afford to cry. I still had to come here and be alone. I must not
take things too personally.

I wasn't in the room when Gwen threw the chair, but of course I heard about it instantly. People were laughing about it. Gwen was laughing about it.

She said it wasn't like she had actually lifted a chair over her head and hurled it. And she hadn't hit anyone, or broken anything.

"Yeah, but Gwenny, honey," I said. "You can't do stuff like that."

But she told me that was where I was wrong. She could do stuff like that.

I saw that she had gone to the place inside her head where the rules were entirely her own. The place that separates people like Gwen from people like the rest of us. Furniture might get broken in these places, but who cares about that?

I will never be so talented that I have the right to break more than a toothpick. I'm not allowed to throw a chair, or a fit, or even the towel in.

"You can't do stuff like that," I said again, miserably, failing her.

She stood there slowly beating her thigh with her fist and glittering her eyes at me. Glitter, glitter, thump. Glitter, glitter, thump. Harder and harder. A diamond-encrusted wrecking crane. It wasn't the first time I had seen her hit herself. I watched her fist descend over and over again, smacking against the side of her leg, sending the muscles rippling across her thigh. There would be a bruise later. There would be more to come.

"Please stop doing that," I said.

Make me, her eyes glittered. In defiance? In appeal?

Make me.

Make me.

make.

me.

12.

Big relief that Claudette was running rehearsal today, and not Nina and her deedles. Claudette, like many French dancers I have known, has a deeply philosophical approach to ballet. To her there is no greater art, and no greater artists. It's an approach born in a country where ballet companies are subsidized by the government, where the performing arts are considered important, and where the public is educated about them. France does not want more Josh, *merci beaucoup*. It's a thing to envy.

Today, as always, Claudette was neat as a pin in her trim little blouse and kitten heels.

David is the David that I once did homework for when we were at the school. He's now the only American male principal dancer in the company. All the others are these wunderkinds from South America or Russia. What David lacks in virtuosity, he makes up for in elegance, height, and perfect partnering. He's still the guy all the girls want to dance with. He married a girl in the corps, Catherine, about five years ago, and she immediately quit and got pregnant. They just had their second kid. David is the guy who hangs out with the stagehands and talks about playing *Halo*. He and Catherine have a house in New Jersey. I think he might even know how to use a grill.

I gave extra thought to costuming today and arrived in pink and black, less severe than my usual gear, and with my hair piled up in twists. Perfume, of course, and earrings. Rings on four of my fingers. A perfectly timed Vicodin flowing through my bloodstream.

David was on the floor, stretching out his Achilles with a towel. I went and sat down next to him, looped my arm through his.

"David," I said.

"Kate," he said.

"We are going to dance together."

"Yes, we are."

"Tell me how you feel about this," I asked. "Honestly. And when I say honestly, I mean let's get our cards on the table right now and work from there."

"Honestly," David said, after a moment, "I haven't really thought about it. I think it will be good. I'm more worried about how I'm going to look next to Manny."

Manuel Ortega is dancing Puck. He trained as a gymnast in Cuba, but then the Commies shifted him over to ballet. I've seen him do fourteen pirouettes. On a bad day. As Puck he will be wearing pretty much nothing but a dance belt and his skin is a shade of copper that only exists in $800 cookware. You could probably sauté something on him. Still, I was surprised that David admitted to feeling insecure about him, because at a certain point nobody does that. It's too risky.

"Yeah, but he's *Puck*," I said. "He's your henchman. You're King of the Fairies, big guy."

"Exactly," David said. "I'll be standing there in green eye shadow with my dick in my hands while the audience goes ape shit every time Manny's onstage."

"If we could get back to the subject of *me* for a moment . . ."

"Sorry, hon." David laughed. "I haven't slept more than a few hours in six weeks. I'm not even sure I'm a man anymore. I'm just a large person that moves toys and tries to prevent infant death and wipes up spit and poop and sticky things. And even though that's all I do, Cathy is still doing more, so I can't complain. Everything in my house is sticky. If you don't throw up on me or cry or run face first into a wall, we're basically cool."

"I can wipe my own ass," I said.

David kissed me on the cheek.

"Also, I'm horny as hell," he said. "If I get wood, don't take it personally."

"Okay, *mes enfants*," Claudette said, placing a binder on the piano and flipping it open. "Let's begin. Kate, we'll teach you the Act II pas de deux and then if we have time, I'll go over the beginning with you."

Marius choreographed *Dream* months ago, so I saw Gwen dance it with David in rehearsal a couple of times. Things were very tense between us then, and it was difficult to watch her. I was so anxious about her state of mind that I didn't watch her dancing the way I usually do. Anne-Marie is dancing Titania too, but I can already visualize her performance because she does everything the same way. She will be lyrical, she will be pretty, she will make the face she makes when she's not making that other face. Butter will do as it has always done with Anne-Marie, and refuse to melt in her mouth. Or a soy-based butter-like substitute, anyway. I've always thought she was dull to watch, but she has a big following.

Gwen's in a class by herself, so I can't make direct comparisons between us as dancers. It's not . . . unreasonable that we are sisters, to look at us. I'm a little taller. Less than an inch, but it seems like more, probably because my shoulders are wider. From the waist down we are nearly identical, although we've different scars now.

Nothing is ever too hard for Gwen, too fast, too slow, or too tiring. Her technique is complete, like a mathematical theory for everything. When Gwen makes mistakes, they seem to come from some external source: seismic tremors, cosmic vibrations, the wobble in the axis of the earth. Her worst day is nearly as good as her best.

If ballet didn't exist, they would have to invent it just to give a name to what Gwen can do. So yes, there's something a little frightening about that. Ballet is such an unnatural act, so a body that looks made to do it must therefore be an unnatural body. Not really . . . *human*. Which again is perfect for ballet, because it's not like there are ballets about Sheila, a registered nurse from Hoboken, or Janet, realtor and mother of two. No, it's all somnambulistic princesses and tortured birds and dead virgins who have been Betrayed. Even in ballets without plots, you're embodying music or an ideal or some notion like Regret or Hope.

Take a thing like the second act pas de deux for Titania and Oberon. After all their jealous feuding in Act I they are reconciled, and they demonstrate this by dancing perfectly with each other. So, Harmony. That's basically it. Be beautiful together.

When you represent Man and Woman Together, as opposed to actually being them, you can approach the sublime. The classical pas de deux is a nice example of this.

In classical pas de deux, the man controls everything. He picks up the girl. He puts her down. He turns her, takes her weight, stops her, and she must always go where he leads. The woman submits to all of this completely. But her submission is not feeble. In fact, the only reason she can submit so utterly is because she is very strong in herself. In her center. She does not collapse, or cave, or stutter-step, or flop. No, she holds herself very consciously, very confidently. She is centered within her own weight. So the man always knows where she is. He can feel her. He can absorb her strength.

This is good partnering. It's really the only way partnering can work.

Of course it doesn't always happen.

Sometimes the man isn't strong, or he doesn't care about partnering, he just wants to solo. Then the girl collects bruises and jammed ankles and feels abandoned. The woman goes back to the dressing room and says to the other women, "I have to do everything!" and "I can't trust him!"

Sometimes the girl tries to control everything herself. Or doesn't hold her own weight. The man tires because he's having to fight with her on every step. Or muscle the girl around because he can't get a good grip. The man goes back to the dressing room and says to the other men, "I don't know what she wants from me!" or "Fuck, it's like hauling bricks!"

But in the ideal situation it's perfectly balanced. The woman is strong enough to give everything; the man is sensitive enough to take it all. And because they are listening to the same music, they are always in rhythm. Not just on the same page, but the same note. There is no past to regret or future to fear, everything is present tense. There is no talking, no "What did you mean by that?" Nothing mundane or trivial. What everybody needs is absolutely clear.

There is no actual sex, only the infinite promise of it.

You think actual sex achieves this sort of sublimity? Do you really? And have you ever had that sex? With another person, I mean. Because I've had perfect sex in my head, but with another person it's only ever been great.

We worked for two hours today. Marius's choreography is good. It's more than good. And from the first touch, David and I danced well together. Our musicality is the same. I felt something stir in me. That feeling dancing well can give you. I was almost scared to take in that drug. It's so easy to get hooked.

"*Très bien*," Claudette said at the end of rehearsal. "*Très, très bien.* But, yes. Lovely."

"I like the way you look at me," David said. "You really *look* at me."

After rehearsal, I didn't know what to do with myself. I didn't want to go home. I didn't want to go to the movies, or do laundry, or steam vegetables. I didn't want anything to intrude upon this clear space where I felt sort of safe from myself.

Cast B was on tonight, so I decided to do a thing that I rarely do anymore. I decided to go to the ballet.

Carlotta got me a seat in the first balcony, toward the back. Luckily I sort of dressed up today. People still dress up for the ballet, and this is kind of them. A party of four took their seats in front of me. Two older couples. The women's figures were pear shaped past the point where evening dresses look elegant, and they were sensibly clad in tunic-style silk blouses and pants. Their hands and wrists were laden with enormous chunky jewelry, which rattled against the gold chains on their handbags. Their men, one with hair, one without, wore identical sports coats.

"Howard, you go in first. I know Heime will want the aisle."

"Alice, are you sure you don't want to check your jacket? You won't be warm?"

"Loretta, I have your program here."

"Alice, where are my glasses?"

Alice had an Aladdin's cave of a handbag and handed out mints and tissues and Howard's glasses. I was filled with tremendous love for all four of them, for their willingness to come and watch. The number of people who will accept being an audience to anything is getting smaller and smaller. Mostly people seem to want to be the person looked at, even if they don't know what they are doing, even if what they are doing is horribly embarrassing.

Is there a better sound than when the house lights are brought down and a lowering murmur takes hold of the audience? Alice, wedged in by her coat and handbag, wiggled forward when the overture began. God! Strings! Oboes! Timpani! Are you fucking kidding me? Why, when we know what human beings are capable of doing, do we not turn our collective heads in shame at the sight of rich housewives screaming at each other on television?

The curtain rose, but I was still looking at the orchestra, swaying gently over their instruments. From them I moved to the first rows of the audience, row after row of dark heads. I could see people in my section pretty distinctly, so I watched them watch us. People's faces become so smooth in the dark, so innocent. So trusting. They know what they are seeing but they must know a little too of what they are not seeing. They know the jewels are fakes. They know the moon is painted. They know it is not easy to turn and jump and they know that a great deal of effort and perhaps pain is being hidden. They do not linger on this. They let themselves be told, be led. They are grateful for being told, being led, being tricked. Our tricks will never hurt them. We will never say the wrong thing, because we never speak. They are never as happy as when we make them cry.

They got babysitters and picked out shoes and turned off cell phones. The woman sitting next to me pressed a hand to her rib cage when the rows of the corps de ballet began their hops in arabesque. A man two rows in front of me craned his head around the man in front of him: not wanting to miss a step.

I was so absorbed that when the first intermission came I hadn't given more than a cursory glance at the stage. Alice turned to Loretta and patted her hand.

"Glorious," said Loretta.

"Happy birthday," said Alice.

"Wonderful," said Heime, thumping his program against his knee. "Just marvelous."

I decided that I didn't want to hear anybody say anything more than that. I wondered if it was possible to get home, brush my teeth, ice my neck, and fall asleep without anything else entering my head. Threading my way through the lobby, I ran into Marius. We stood for a moment together by the bar, and I felt my euphoria cocoon splinter as people passed us, talking about ordinary things, checking their phones.

"What do you think?" Marius asked.

"It's scary to see them all like this," I said to Marius. "In the light, I mean. They look more interesting in the dark."

Marius smiled his inscrutable smile.

"I meant about the ballet you're watching."

"Oh that," I said. My second Vicodin was wearing off and I was beginning to crash. "I've been thinking that you should restage the whole thing actually. Less artifice, more humanity. But maybe I'm wrong. Maybe it's better this way. Maybe it's better to be remote."

"Remote?"

"Well, we're nothing if we're not inaccessible," I said. "People can't judge us when they barely understand what they're seeing. I was just sitting behind people . . . they aren't here because they want to relate to us, to what we're doing, what we're telling. They're here because they want to be awed."

"I was thinking," Marius said, "the opposite. That it's wrong for us to be so inaccessible. What does this story have to do with anything anyone has experienced? There's something . . . something at the heart of it . . ."

"Yes," I said. "But everything is up for interpretation. David said he felt like I was really *seeing* him when I looked at him in rehearsal. But I think what he meant was that the way I was looking at him was the way he wanted to be seen. Is that him? I don't know. What does he see when he looks at me?"

"No one will ever judge you the way you do yourself," said Marius. "Nor will they love you properly either."

"Are you talking about an audience or a lover?" I asked. Marius is the sort of man you can say the word "lover" to without sounding pretentious. But he gave me this very penetrating look and "lover" seemed to hang awkwardly in the air, inflating, like a vulgarly shaped balloon.

"I'm sorry," I said. "I know we're talking about different things, but I *am* hearing what you're saying. If you followed the trajectory of what I'm talking about it would eventually get to what you're talking about."

"Sometimes I think you are the only person in the room who understands what I'm saying," Marius said. "It's why I keep you around, you know. As hard as it's been to watch you diminish yourself."

He put a little space before the word "diminish," and then served it. An unreturnable shot, directly into the body.

A couple of our donors approached, claiming his attention. I watched Marius smile and shake hands, kiss cheeks: so smooth and confident, knowing just what to say, and how to say it. I said a few words to the donors too, because I'm not bad at these things. I can make the gestures for charming and gracious. I can walk away from Marius and what he said to me and I can come here to the crime scene and take off Gwen's makeup and Gwen's scarf and crawl into Gwen's bed while back at the *Lake* another swan kills herself and the audience rises to their feet, applauding.

When you are asleep you can't tell whether or not you are alone, or diminished, or whatever. *I have nothing,* I thought. But that's not true. I have her absence. You can see it clearly. Look for the edges of my existence that surround it.

13.

I read on the schedule this morning that Klaus and I had a two-hour private rehearsal today to work on Helena/Demetrius for *Dream*. I was a little indignant until I realized that this was something I had requested. I meditated on the problem of what to do with Klaus all through class. I was tired, my neck was hurting, I was feeling cruel and angry. I was in a dangerous mood, and I was wearing a lot of lipstick just in case I needed to leave an imprint on anything. Try diminishing Chanel Shanghai Red, motherfuckers!

In the end, I decided to take Klaus through some of the "acting" bits. Nothing shakes up a dancer more than having to emote.

The lovers in *Dream* have a rough time. Hermia and Lysander are in love, but Hermia's father wants her to marry Demetrius. Helena is in love with Demetrius, but he utterly rejects her and wants to be with Hermia. All four go tearing into the forest, Hermia and Lysander to elope, Demetrius to follow Hermia, Helena to follow Demetrius. Oberon takes pity on poor Helena, and arranges with Puck to pour a little love juice in Demetrius's eyes when he is asleep. This will cause him to fall in love with the first person he sees when he awakes, which Puck will arrange to be Helena. Of course Puck gets confused, puts the love juice in Lysander's eyes, and leads Helena to him. So then Lysander falls in love with Helena and Hermia is distraught, and more than a little pissed off at Helena. Puck tries to fix things by squeezing love juice into Demetrius's eyes, and getting Helena over to him, but then both guys are in love with her and want to kill each other. And Helena is dismayed because she thinks they are just punking her. And Hermia is very much WTF. Oh, it all gets sorted out, with Puck removing Lysander's spell, and it ends with everyone getting married, which is how you know it's a comedy. The tragedies are what happen *after* everybody gets married.

Klaus was waiting for me in the studio, doing push-ups.

"Hey," he said.

"Hey." I put my bag down and considered Klaus's arms, which are, frankly, very appealing.

"Klaus, I'm thinking we should play around with the first sections," I said.

"Okay," he said, popping up. "You're the boss."

So we started working. He's a strong little critter, this Klaus, and he's got the technique for sure. And the ambition. I see what Marius was alluding to. But Jesus, he was boring. He trotted out all the standard-issue male ballet stuff: the proud chin lift, the doleful chin lowering, the arrogant arm sweep, the dejected arm droop. It pissed me off. I'm dragging myself to rehearsal through injury, fatigue, and a mounting anxiety level that's damn near choking me, and this kid thinks he's too cool to get into character?

"I think we need to ramp up the acting," I said to Klaus. "It might work better if we start really getting into it."

"For me that always happens in performance," said Klaus.

The old "It will be there on the night" gambit. I've heard it before.

"Oh, I don't know," I said, as airily as I could manage. "That's sort of like planning out how witty and sexy you are going to be on the date while you are still in the shower. I'm fabulous in the shower, then suddenly I'm at the restaurant and all I can think of to say are things like 'Ranch dressing tastes good.'"

Klaus hesitated, clearly not sure whether I was funny or a complete dork. He probably doesn't go on dates. Most likely he just shags whatever ballerina is nearest to hand. There's probably a sign-up sheet in the corps girls' dressing room.

"I'm kidding," I said. "I'm always witty and sexy."

"Just tell me what you want," said Klaus. "I don't know what you want."

Ah, we had come to this. Since the dawn of time has man said thus to woman.

I thought of our massage therapist Irina, and her special Soviet tactics for man handling. Klaus is not Russian, but he's young and stubborn, so . . . close enough. It was worth a try, anyway.

"What I love," I said, "is what you are doing in that first moment. When I come on and throw myself at you, you're doing this thing where it's like you see how crazy I am and then you turn to the audience, like *Oh Jesus, not her again*. It's great. That's why I wanted this time to rehearse. So you could keep finding moments like that for yourself, without everybody telling you how it should be."

This was utter fabrication: Klaus was indeed turning his head to the imagined audience when I ran in, but only because he had been told that is what he does on that count.

"Cool," said Klaus.

"Let's do that again and work through the next bit," I said.

And by golly, it worked. He actually did it. I told him that it was nice to be working with someone who has such great musicality, and he stopped rushing the tempo. "I love the way you are walking like a football player," I said, and shazam, Klaus lost the tight-assed noble gait. Cunning and deft, I played both sides of the court. I hit my shot, then leapt over the net and hit Klaus's for him, then scampered back over the net to thank him for having sent me such a perfect return. Then we played the point again and, like magic, there it was, just what I wanted. How come I never thought to use this system before? I caught myself employing a slight Russian accent. We moved on to the moments when he suddenly falls in love with me.

"It's good the way we are starting to exaggerate our height difference," I said, when Klaus was still pretending to be tall. "We need some shtick." After I was done explaining to him what shtick is, I came up with a really cute thing for when he tries to embrace me. I made him bend his front leg so he was basically sticking his nose into my breasts.

"Can I change stuff like this?" Klaus asked anxiously.

"It's okay," I assured him. "Marius wasn't totally happy with what he had choreographed, I could tell. If he doesn't like it he'll change it, but he's going to like it. It works."

After two hours, Stefan and Rochelle, who are the first cast for Lysander and Hermia, joined us. Rochelle is tiny and adorable, perfect casting for Hermia, and Marius had fun with our little fight scene. We just marked through it today, on account of my neck, and then Klaus, Stefan, and I worked on the part where they both declare their love for me and end up fighting each other. Stefan is the tallest boy in our company, so their fight looked legitimately hilarious, not just ballet funny. I was exalted with my successful foray into manipulation, and kept on making suggestions in Klaus's name. At one point, instead of doing the classic male dancer fight move (an incredibly lame pushing of another guy's shoulder and then a spreading of one's arms as if to say "Do you want a piece of this tunic, my friend?"), I told Klaus to do cartoon fisticuffs while Stefan held him off with one hand on Klaus's head.

"I can't even look at you," said Stefan to Klaus. "You're going to crack me up. Great idea, man."

I had Klaus propose that he do a professional wrestling–style drop on Stefan. This seemed to me very Shakespearean.

"No way," laughed Rochelle. "Marius will never let you guys do that."

"It's too over the top," said Stefan.

"That's why it will work," I say. "They are so insane that they can no longer do ballet. They are reduced to brute animals. And the audience gets to see that you're not just ballet dancers, you're dudes. Marius will love it. He's very into accessibility these days."

"The whole ballet is about duality, anyway," said Klaus.

"He's so cute," whispered Rochelle in my ear.

After this amusing and strategically complicated rehearsal, I went to see Irina for a massage.

"Iri," I said. "You are a genius."

"Of course," she said. "Why?"

Klaus was in the elevator when I staggered out of my session a half hour later, and he suggested getting a bite to eat. He'd apparently just come from a shower. He had on the black leather jacket. He gave me a very charming smile. I said yes.

Over salad he told me all about himself. Klaus, as it turns out, is in love! The object of his affections is, of course, himself, and what a changeable and contradictory and endlessly fascinating person he has discovered himself to be!

He told me all his theories on dance and male dancing and the nature of the masculine artist. He likes to speak in what he calls "mythic terms." He elaborated on his theory of *Dream* as Shakespeare's expression of man's duality, and how matter and spirit are in conflict in the soul. He has had two quite complicated love affairs, both of which were very "intense." He writes poetry. He suggested I read *The Fountainhead.*

I made the sympathetic face, and the interested face, and even the impressed face. I did not say, "In the name of all that is holy, cease this incessant drivel, you pretentious ass." I did not say, "Ayn Rand is fascist garbage." I didn't even say, "You smell good and that's a great jacket, so please be quiet." I made faces and he kept going. It was like feeding quarters into one of those tennis ball cannons that shoot the balls at you. I let them smack me in the forehead, and said nothing.

It started to rain. We had finished eating, and neither of us was supposed to be on tonight. I could feel the notion of extending the evening hovering over our table. Klaus had talked himself into a froth of heightened awareness, and I could sense his need to watch himself making love to me in order to round off his evening. I excused myself on the pretense of needing to ice my neck, which was true enough, and came back here.

I talked briefly on the phone with Keith, who is through to the quarterfinals in Morocco. I sent e-mails to my parents.

I sent a text to Gwen.

Please talk to me.

Gwen and I used to play a game when we were little girls. Not really a game as such, it didn't have rules, no winner or loser, not even a name. It must have grown out of some other game. I don't know exactly how it started.

We'd stand on opposite sides of the bedroom we shared and press ourselves to the wall as if we were pinned there. We'd watch each other, waiting to see who would move first. And that was it. That was the game. Sort of stupid, and you can stand against a wall even in fairly baroque positions for a really, really long time, so it wouldn't have looked to anyone else like an action-packed game, but it was terrifically dynamic. At first it's easy not to move because you know the person wants you to, but then it becomes weirdly hard not to move because the other person wants you to. It's a hook and an embrace.

Move. Don't Move. Move. Don't Move.

What do you want me to do, Gwen?

14.

At work today, Nina had something up her ass and everything out of her mouth that wasn't a deedle was some sort of thinly veiled jab.

"Klaus, you take her by the *left* hand. Or is that something Kate told you to change?"

"I think this recording is slow. But Kate probably likes it that way. She hates to move fast."

"Kate, I know you'll be wearing a dress, but you still need to keep your hips square. You can't cheat *everything*."

I guess my hand was going reflexively to my neck every time we stopped working, because suddenly she was all, "What's the deal, are you injured?" She actually did an imitation of me, mock rubbing her own neck and affecting a babyish pout.

"It's a pinched nerve, but I just got an adjustment and it's a lot better," I told her, in a very measured tone.

"Look, if you are injured, you need to let us know now so we can make arrangements," she huffed.

"No, I'm good!" I chirped. "Just getting a little older, ha-ha!"
That was a tactical error.

"Oh well!" Nina trilled. "We can't do anything about that!
But if you're not one hundred percent, it's really not fair to
Klaus, or to David. He's already got a lot to deal with."

"May I speak with you privately for a minute?" I asked.

I knew she wanted to say no and was weighing the odds of
how much of a cunt she thought she could get away with being.
And how much of a cunt I might turn into. Basically, it was a
cunt-off.

Technically, all the power was in her court. The rest of the
dancers in the room were all examining their feet, or the walls,
or pretending to practice steps. I had no idea what I wanted
to say to Nina other than "Get off my back, you shrew," but I
couldn't say that. I couldn't say anything. It just doesn't work
like that. But I also couldn't let Nina continue. She was under-
mining my authority with Klaus.

"I'd prefer not to stop rehearsal," said Nina.

"Well, we *have* stopped rehearsal," I said. I put my hands on
my hips and jutted my chin. The gesture for defiance.

At this moment, the door opened and Marius strode into the
room. If he noticed the tension he did not acknowledge it.

"May I have a look?" he asked, drawing up a chair. "I want
to see what you're up to."

"We're having a little bit of trouble today," Nina said, all low-
cal-syrup regretfulness.

"Yes? What's the trouble?" Marius looked at me, standing by
myself in the center of the room, my defiance posture drooping
a little.

"Kate's having trouble with her neck."

"You're having trouble with your neck?"

"My neck is fine," I said coolly. Inspiration came. "My mood is terrible, though," I said brightly. "I was just about to throw a temper tantrum!"

"Oh, this I'd like to see," Marius said. "Don't let me interrupt you."

"I'm driving Nina crazy today." I grinned, fake ruefully. "She's at her wit's end."

Marius looked at Nina, who half laughed, uncertain. She doesn't know how to play these scenes. But I do.

"I'm sorry," I said to Marius. "Did you want to see some dancing?"

Marius folded his arms. "If it's not too much trouble."

I dropped a curtsy. Marius gave me a complicated look. I realized then that he'd read the situation perfectly. That it was something . . . some kind of test. Maybe he even told Nina to give me a hard time. The Machiavellian touch is not beyond him. Nina isn't clever enough to push my buttons toward anything but frustration and bad dancing, but Marius?

As hard as it's been to watch you diminish yourself.

"From the beginning, please," he commanded.

"Full out," I said in a low voice to Klaus. "Like it's a performance. Anything less and I'll throw you under the rails."

The adrenaline kicked in where today's Vicodin failed. I was not feeling any pain, but I danced way beyond what I should have, whipping my head around recklessly. Klaus started out a little tentatively, but soon he was mugging, he was pouting, he was storming. Stefan and Klaus did their WWF fight. Marius actually jumped up from his chair, laughing. He waved a hand at Nina.

"I don't need to see any more," he said. "This is all very good. Really, I don't think you should rehearse much more. It will ruin it. Just try not to kill each other." Marius headed to the door; turned to look back; shook his finger at Klaus. "I love it," said Marius, "when I am right." He looked at Klaus, gave another laugh, and then shot me one sliver of a glance, his face emptying of expression, before exiting.

Nina looked at the clock. "That's it for today," she said. "Thank you, everyone."

I fished a towel out of my bag. I wanted to lie down. I wanted to collapse. But I couldn't even touch my neck until Nina left the room.

"See, that was what I was trying to get out of you, Kate," Nina said, on her way out the door. "That's why I was pushing you."

I didn't trust my neck enough to nod. I blinked amiably, since you should never spoil being right with being righteous. She left. I sat down slowly, not trusting my spine, and inched into a supine position. Stefan and Klaus and Rochelle exchanged relieved chatter.

"You okay, Kate?" Rochelle called over.

"I'm good," I said. Actually, I did feel almost good. I felt sleepy.

Klaus playfully assumed the push-up position over me. I encircled his wrists with my hands. A little something passed between us.

"You're sweating on me," I said.

"At this point, what's the difference?" He looked down at his T-shirt, drenched with the both of us. I brought a knee up and knocked him gently against his ribs.

"That's my boy," I said. "Well done."

"Dude," he said. "That was pretty awesome."

"Don't call me dude."

"Yes, my lady. Hey. For a minute there I thought you were going to rip Nina a new one."

"Mhmmm. Help me up?"

Klaus pulled me up. I felt a little metallic taste in my mouth. "I think I bit my tongue," I said.

I experienced a drowsy desire to . . . have sex, bizarrely.

"Rub my neck for two seconds?"

"This isn't my fault, is it? I know I've been a bit rough." Klaus turned me around and placed one hand on my sternum so he could pull me back into the tips of the fingers of his other hand, which traveled up and down my neck.

"It wasn't me, was it?" he murmured. Actually murmured. Do they teach this sort of thing at hottie school? "I didn't hurt you, baby, did I?" he asked softly.

No, it's sexual, but also maternal, what I feel for Klaus. But no, not maternal. It's more sort of . . . fatherly. Or something. I was confused, so I turned around and gave Klaus a kiss. He still had a grip on me, so it was slightly more than a peck. I made the gesture for fondness, cupping his face with my hands.

After rehearsal I headed down to Capezio for some new dancing duds. And who should I see there but Bryce, the little girl from the school who is my fan, looking at a rack of leotards. I almost didn't recognize her in normal clothes and with all her hair down. I hid myself behind a rotisserie of leg warmers. I'm not sure why. I suppose I am a little uncomfortable with the idea of someone looking up to me. Also, she was with a woman who I assumed was her mom, and ballet moms can be a little hard to take. They gush and roll their eyes, and their own particular daughter is always very special and gifted.

I am guessing Bryce is about eleven, but I am not very good at figuring ages. At any rate she has that kind of body that happens around eleven or twelve. Just past the overgrown-puppy look that is so cute, and not quite into the awkward stage that can go on for years.

Bryce had on a blue cardigan sweater, a khaki miniskirt, and pink tennis shoes. I appreciated the outfit's lack of sexuality. It looked like something Nancy Drew might have worn. Bryce's light brown hair (a few years away from being highlighted red or blond, depending on her personality) is shoulder length and a little bit bushy. She should grow it a little longer so it won't do that awkward triangle thing. Her skin still has that creamy look of youth, but she isn't exactly beautiful. Her face is too changeable. Really pretty girls always look the same. She will be just lovely when she grows up, but these years of not being beautiful will get in the way of her recognizing it. When she is a teenager, she'll wear too much makeup. Her mom, because it was her mom who was with her, is absolutely beautiful: tall and thin and expensively dressed in cashmere. I circled around the leg warmers. Bryce disappeared into a dressing room with some leotards. Her mother hovered outside the curtain of her cubicle, peeped in, was evidently rebuffed. She turned around, and our eyes met.

"Oh, hello!" she said, advancing with a perfectly manicured hand. "I'm Jane Pritchett Ford. We met briefly last year at the Winter Gala. I'm on the board of the company. Congratulations, by the way. On Titania."

Not just a ballet mom, but a power ballet mom. I didn't, in

fact, remember meeting Jane Pritchett Ford, but I made the gesture for "Ah, yes."

"My daughter Bryce," Jane pointed at the dressing room, "has convinced me of the utmost necessity of getting a new leotard for Friday." She smiled and shrugged her shoulders. "I'm sure the fact that you will be there is a factor. She has your shoes wrapped around her bedpost."

On Friday we have a full studio run-through of *Dream*, and that means the little fairies will be rehearsing with us.

"I'll just be doing Helena for that rehearsal," I told Jane. "I'm still learning Titania."

"Ah, well, you'll make a great Helena too. But I'm really excited to see what you do with Titania. And what Marius has done with the whole ballet. It's time for something new." I liked the way she said it. I liked that she's wasn't asking me about Gwen, which was what I expected.

"I don't know what I'm doing yet," I said. "It's . . . tricky. Like, in the play, Titania is a mess in the beginning. She's just become a mother to the changeling boy. Oberon is jealous that she has shifted all her attentions away from him to the child. They're fighting and it's throwing everything in the natural world off-balance. *'The nine men's morris is filled up with mud!'* I kind of wish Titania would come on with some sort of frizzy hairdo and food on her clothes, all sweaty and irritable."

"Like a new mother," Jane said, getting it. "That's very interesting. I mean, you're very articulate about it. That's unusual, if you don't mind my saying. With dancers."

"Oh, some of us can talk," I said. "It's just easier not to."

Jane laughed.

"I should stop talking to you," she said. "Because Bryce saw you earlier and I told her she should go up and say hello, and that was apparently just too incredibly gauche and mortifying and uncool. I think she's afraid I will embarrass her. She's hiding now in the dressing room. And when she comes out, please pretend this conversation never happened."

I laughed and Jane smiled and mouthed "Thank you" at me. She went back to the curtained cubicle. I grabbed a few things off a rack and ducked into another dressing room. After a bit, I could hear Bryce and Jane leaving.

I sat down in the dressing room at Capezio, suddenly exhausted. And missing Gwen.

There must be tension before there is release. That's what Marius said. *Otherwise it is boring.*

But it's Gwen who provided the tension and the release. Without her it's just . . . silence. I don't know where I am. Before a storm, or behind it.

"It goes away," Gwen said to me once, after a crisis. We were standing in adjacent dressing rooms, at some boutique in Soho. I was struggling into a dress Gwen had insisted I try on, something I would never have pulled off the rack for myself.

"What goes away?" I asked. We had just been laughing over a dress I had picked out, which, when on, had been so spectacularly awful that we had both cracked up when I had revealed myself.

"Take it off!" Gwen had shrieked. "Oh my god! Get it off your body!"

"It goes away," she repeated, tapping on the wall that separated us. "Kate, it always goes away."

"Yeah," I said, to the wall. "Yeah, I know it does."

Five months before, we had been on tour in Spain, and Gwen had refused to unpack her suitcase, or let me unpack mine, because everything was "unsafe." A few weeks after that, we were vacationing in Ibiza and staying up all night in clubs, and Gwen, tanned, blissful, smiling, kicked off her shoes, and we danced all night. "Happiness!" she screamed, over the music. And then we were back in New York and the long baths and the talking to herself started up again, and I found myself holding my breath whenever I saw her with a pair of scissors in her hands, or a knife.

And then. And then. And then.

But that day in the dressing room, I stepped out of my cubicle in the dress Gwen had picked out for me and she held me by the shoulders and examined the length of my body, turned me around to face the mirror.

"You see?" She grinned, exultant. "I was right. It's perfect."

"You were right," I agreed.

"Who knows you better than me?"

"Nobody."

She pressed her cheek against mine hard, before letting go.

15.

I went early this morning to Dr. Ken's office to look at my X-rays. It's weird to look at your own skeleton. It's so much smaller than you think and that's sort of sad. Like a dog standing forlornly in a bathtub, dripping wet, revealed to be quite puny without all the fluff.

I didn't know what I was supposed to be looking at, but Dr. Ken put an X-ray of a "normal" person next to mine so I could see the contrast.

"So, should I have that curve?" I asked, pointing to the civilian skeleton's neck, which had an S shape. Mine was pretty straight. You would think that straight is better; it looks more stable. You can't build anything on an S.

"Your life would be considerably less painful if you did," Dr. Ken said cheerfully. "Now look at this."

He slid another X-ray next to mine, and this skeleton had the same straight line of vertebrae as mine. Dr. Ken tapped it with his finger.

"This is a person who has whiplash," he said, like he was giving me the punch line of a joke. "Fairly serious car accident."

"I have whiplash?"

"Most people who are in the amount of distress you are in are given a neck brace and kept more or less immobile. I'm not really certain how you are dealing with the pain, in fact."

I smiled modestly.

"My concern," Dr. Ken continued, "is that you will go on working in this condition, and do permanent damage to yourself." He explained how an S absorbs shock and how I have blown back my S so completely that it's now slightly bowed in the other direction. That this is the actual problem, and the pinched nerve is just a symptom.

I gazed at the bones on the screen. Is it really so bad? They all appeared to be there. Once again I was struck by how small my skull is. I can't believe you can fit a whole personality in there. How do you stuff everything you own or have ever owned and all the things you will own in the future till the end of your life into something smaller than a handbag?

"I don't want to alarm you, but we should approach this very seriously," Dr. Ken said.

"Well, we need to make a deal," I told him. "Because I need to make it to the end of the season. That's a few more weeks. After that I'll take a good rest, but not now."

Dr. Ken crossed his arms in front of him and took a wider stance, rocking back and forth, flattening out the pleats in the pants, considering.

"You know, now that I can conceptualize what the problem is," I told him, "it's great, because I can sort of see what I might be doing that's causing it. I feel like if I adjust my technique and stay really mindful and aware then I can protect myself." I brought my hands up to the occipital bones and gently bobbled my head, demonstrating how I am going to balance it out.

"If you can, stay off the rest of the week." Dr. Ken sighed. "Come see me every day and I'll keep giving you adjustments. Let's fit you with some orthopedic pads. I want you wearing these every moment you're not in toe shoes. I know you dancers think anything can be cured by icing, but it's not necessary. Stretch it gently. I'll give you some exercises. After the season is over, then we'll evaluate. There's something fundamental about the way you are working that needs to be changed."

I stood on this weird fibrous substance so Dr. Ken could get exact measurements of my feet for the orthopedic pads. He gave me a good cracking and fifteen minutes on the stim machine. I lay there, the muscles in my neck jumping slightly.

Gwen, you look too fragile, there.

We were rehearsing the ballet *Giselle*, another classic from the Douchebag Prince/Betrayed Maiden archive. Giselle is a young peasant girl with a heart condition. (Seriously, there's choreography where she has to stop dancing and sort of clutch her heart and be tremulous and fainty.) There is a sweet local boy, Hilarion (no really, that's his name), who is in love with Giselle. But Giselle has met and fallen in love with another boy, a peasant just like her but from another village. He visits her in secret, and promises to marry her, but jealous Hilarion spies on them, and he is suspicious. He follows the stranger and sees that he's not really a peasant at all. He's Prince Albrecht, wearing a disguise. It seems Albrecht is already engaged to a

noblewoman and he's just amusing himself with Giselle. Hilarion exposes Albrecht in front of the entire village and Giselle
goes mad and kills herself. With a sword. Although possibly
she had a heart attack too—preexisting medical conditions.
Anyway, that's Act I. In Act II a stricken and grieving Albrecht
visits the grave of Giselle and is attacked by the "Willies." I am
not making this up! Willies are the ghosts of women who died
before their wedding day. Gotta love a ballet that literally gives
you the willies.

Gwen was Giselle.

Gwen, you look too fragile there.

What do you mean?

You look too . . . vulnerable.

I am vulnerable, she insisted. *I've got a heart condition,
remember?*

Yeah, I said. *But you're in denial about it. And you're a peasant. A sturdy peasant girl, filled with life. When your mother tries
to stop you from dancing, you've got to really push her away.*

I pantomimed the mother's actions: grabbing Gwen's hands,
insisting. Gwen gave me a big shove and then flipped me off
with her middle finger. We both laughed.

You can really be irritated with her, though, I said. *You want
to dance. She wants you to sit still. She's being a pest. You think
you're going to live forever.*

Okay, do it again.

That's it. That's better.

I did take a Vicodin after leaving Dr. Ken's, but I had a very full day. Two hours for *Leaves*, then a little break, then two more hours with Claudette to start learning Titania's solos, and then the final performance of *Swan Lake* tonight.

Hilel came up to me in *Leaves* rehearsal and asked if I read the review.

"Where?"

"*Times.*"

"Walter or Pauline?"

"Walter."

"When was he here?"

"Plague Cast night. Me and Gia. You should read it."

"He doesn't talk about Mara falling, does he?"

"He mentioned it, but he didn't say her name. He had an interesting thing to say about you, though."

Then Anne-Marie joined us and Hilel started talking to her but he put his hand on my back in this casual, proprietary way that gave me a bit of a jolt.

I was twenty-two when I fell in love with Hilel, if that's what it was. It was during *Nutcracker*, and two or three times a week we would go out to a restaurant after a performance and then go back to his place, because Gwen and I were still sharing a bedroom. I was dazzled by him, which made me nervous, which made me act a lot tougher than I really felt. Now, everyone had told me that Hilel was a total player, and it was for that reason that I asked him if we could keep it on the down-low at work. I didn't want people thinking I was a fool and really liked him. Gwen knew I was sleeping with him, of course, and

Mara, but even with them I kept up an air of "Oh, it's all just totally casual, I don't really like him that much." But often in the elevator, or on the stairs, or in the wings, he would put his hand on the small of my back and just before he moved it away he would run it over the curve of my hip. A little promise. You would think such subtleties would be lost on people who spend all day touching each other, but it was secret, so it was special.

I began to entertain the thought of Hilel and me as an actual couple. They were fantasies, of course. A smarter and funnier Hilel and a me with smaller pores and perfect French for our romantic trips to Paris. I imagined bringing him home to Michigan and him getting along really well with my dad. I decorated the apartment we would live together in.

Then it was New Year's Eve and he said he would be at Chris's party, but he never showed up. I called three times and the third time I was drunk and I told his voicemail that I loved him. It was awful. Three days later he called me from Hawaii, where he had gone to surf. "Yeah, didn't I tell you? Yeah, it's awesome." And when the season started up again it was over. No talk or anything, just over. I would've sooner shot myself than let him or anyone else know how miserable I was.

Four months later during a rehearsal for *Sleeping Beauty* I saw him put his hand on Gwen's back in a way that seemed very familiar. I held my breath and waited and watched. And sure enough, there it was. The slow soft brush of the hand over the curve of the hip. Her hip. Gwen turned around and saw me. Her smile was as sweet and as innocent as a child's, inviting me to fall in love with her too.

·   ·   ·

So what's going on with you and Hilel?

Nothing.

I hope you're protecting yourself, Gwenny.

I got a diaphragm.

What? Since when?

Since last year. I don't know. Just before Christmas.

Okay, wait a sec. Who were you sleeping with at Christmas?

Omigod, Kate, don't freak. I wasn't sleeping with anyone.

So you just got up one day and thought you'd go get birth control.

You know. Just in case. But he uses condoms. He used them with you, right? That would be sort of funny. Because you know how they say that when you have sex with someone, you also have sex with everyone they've ever slept with. So that means I've had sex with you.

Gwen.

Marius said something to me about Giselle, next season?

Really? Oh my god, GWEN!

I know. I know. Do you think I can do it?

What are you talking about? Do I think you can do it? It's the perfect role for you. Perfect! Congratulations, Gwenny.

So you see, this whole thing with Hilel. It's like, just more so I have something to do other than think about things, you know? Otherwise I get too nervous.

What could I say? Hilel was a better option than the keys, or the cleaning, or the masking-tape Xs. I even thought that maybe all of that was sort of a weird expression of sexual frustration, or thwarted hormones, or something. I trained myself not to be jealous.

And Hilel was actually in love with her. Totally. Everybody was amazed. He was publicly devastated when Gwen broke up with him. And he never went back to his playboy ways. He's become a big star, though.

So the touching of the back thing today was interesting, and made me oddly nostalgic. Possibly it didn't mean anything at all, and never meant anything. I rooted through my bag, broke a Vicodin in half and swallowed it dry, enjoying the powdery chalk tang. I didn't feel very good. I needed to eat something.

I went across the street and picked up the *Times*, then went to the good salad place. I had an hour, and I needed to be out of the studios for a bit, so I took a table, flipped open the paper.

Walter Short and Pauline Offenfeld are the two main dance critics for the *Times*. Pauline is very sentimental and protective of Marius, and our company. She gushes, and in return she always gets invited to galas and parties and things and we are all really nice to her. Walter I've only met once. He's an odious little egg of a man, frequently more mean than critical, but he's also pretty perceptive.

This review started with a paragraph about how lengthy our injury list has been this season, and how this has led to some chaotic scrambling of casts, as in the other night when blah, blah, blah. According to Walter, there is something very dispiriting about catching us with our tights down. "In theatrical comedies blatant errors such as a mangled bit of dialogue or a fumbled prop may often be acknowledged and even elaborated upon by experienced actors, who know that the audience relishes an opportunity for inclusion, self-deprecation, complicity. The so-called fourth wall between audience and actor is a flexible affair. Frequently, this is not the case at the ballet, where a mistake is only a mistake. However, . . ." He went on to praise Hilel to the skies, but was more cautious about Gia. He's always much harder on women. He admired "Alberto Leon's deft partnering in the pas de trois," and "a heightened clarity, especially in the upper body, from the corps de ballet," one of those typical critic sentences that always read oddly. It all seemed more or less okay until toward the end, where I found this paragraph.

> Although an awkward fall marred the beginning of the Act III Princess solos, Kate Crane shone brilliantly in the final divertissement. Miss Crane's performances of late have shown an increasing level of technical proficiency and confidence to add to what has always been a sensual richness and purity of line. Earlier today it was announced on the company's website that Kate Crane will be replacing her younger sister as Titania in the upcoming premiere of *A Midsummer Night's Dream.* (Gwen Crane is yet another principal dancer absent this season due to injury.) One can only wonder if the elder Crane isn't seizing the chance to storm the castle walls. If so, more power to her.

I read this over and over, and it got worse with each reading. Did Hilel actually think this would make me happy, to read this? That I would take it as praise or something? I wanted to crawl under the table. I don't think I could have felt more exposed than if Walter Short had described my vagina in the *New York Times.*

As I was leaving the restaurant I passed Marius, who was also sitting alone. He didn't look up as I went by his table, and so I didn't stop. From where he was sitting, he must have seen me during lunch, though. Seen me reading the *Times.* And I was incredibly angry that we were sitting in the same restaurant and he didn't come up to my table. Offer to have lunch with me. Talk to me a little. I wonder what my face looked like while I was reading. Maybe he saw me and saw that I was suffering and he simply didn't care. I know what that's like. I took the other half of Vicodin.

Titania's solos are a bitch. I kept trying to picture how Gwen skates through stuff like this, but nothing felt right. It's like my body was made of tin cans, clunking around and fitting improperly. Claudette kept saying that today was just about learning the choreography and that we'll finesse everything later. I would've preferred to stop and work slowly on each little thing until it looked good, but I just couldn't see in my head what that was supposed to look like. I needed to see Gwen do it so I could try to imitate her.

At one point, Claudette had to refer to the video of rehearsal to remember a sequence and she snapped open a laptop on top of the piano.

"Come watch," she said.

And there was Gwen. Three months ago. Marius had just finished the ballet and we had a full cast studio run-through.

They often video these so future dancers can refer back to them
when they are learning the roles.

Well. Dance always looks terrible on video. Also, the lighting was bad. It was just rehearsal, anyway.

No. No, she wasn't dancing well. She looked terrible. I could
barely watch. I couldn't look away. These are the castle walls
that I am storming?

On the tape Gwen ran to the left, every cord in her neck
standing out like the tangle of wires that lead to a bomb. You
could see a few other dancers, sitting on the floor, lounging
against the barre, warming up. You could see me, although I
had my back to the camera. My back to Gwen. I remembered
this day very well. I remembered what happened two days after
this day. I won't remember it. Not now.

"It's not so good," said Claudette. "She was maybe already
injured here?"

"I think so," I said.

"Ah, see, yes, it's soutenu, soutenu, and then cross downstage, no?"

"Right, right. That makes sense."

After rehearsal I ate the rest of my salad and took a little
nap in my dressing room. By nap I mean I stared at the ceiling
and practiced swallowing without throwing up. I popped two
Vicodin and quickly ate the bag of M&M'S I keep hidden in
the bottom drawer of my dressing table. I'm not really enjoying dancing on Vicodin. I can't feel the floor properly, and it
makes the time go too fast. But it helps with every moment that
I'm not dancing. It makes my mind race ahead of the present,
which, in non-dancing moments, is moving way too slowly.

I thought about dancing the last *Swan Lake* of the season.

Possibly my last *Swan Lake* ever. I decided I should really pay attention to it. I looked at myself in the dressing-room mirror. I painted on a face.

There may indeed be something fundamentally wrong in my approach to dancing that is causing this injury. I might be able to correct it, and I might not. It might not ever get better. I might not ever get better. I could just be facing a long struggle not to get worse. The descent of the body has begun. I have passed my peak, my prime. This is the reality. This is the physical reality that conquers all others. This is my body, and there are things happening to it that cannot be imagined away.

"It's you," I said to myself in the mirror. It didn't sound as bad out loud as it did in my head. I tried it again. "Look at what you can do."

But I can't see. I can't see anything.

When you step from the wings onto the stage you go from total blackness to a blinding hot glare. After a moment you adjust, but there is that moment. Like being inside lightning.

It's terrifying.

It's wonderful.

My neck was stiff. I hadn't sewn in the tail ends of the ribbons of my left shoe smoothly, and the bump they made knuckled into my ankle in an annoying way. My stomach felt too full from the candy, and one of the pins in my hair was jabbing into my scalp. My sweat didn't feel right. I just wanted to stand in a hot shower and scrub everything off and off and off me. I had a hangnail.

And yet. And yet. I had tears in my eyes during curtain call.

I cannot bear this love. Nor the loss of it.

16.

In truth, I don't even know how painful my neck is anymore. I don't want to know. What I know is that if I drink two full glasses of water and eat a banana before my first Vicodin of the day, the stomach cramping seems less.

All week I kept thinking that when I got to this day off I was going to be able to relax and rest and maybe rent some kind of *Masterpiece Theater* something and eat a cookie. I realize, though, that there might not be enough hours in this day for me to feel better. Even if I remained more or less immobile this would be true. So I might as well carry on, in my fashion.

Laundry, sewing of pointe shoe ribbons. What else? A day off. By myself. It used to sort of exasperate me, how Andrew always wanted to run around doing all this stuff on his days off. He thought an afternoon on the couch watching movies was a waste, not really living. He was happiest with me when the company was on layoff, and except for daily class I was free to "live" with him.

I met Andrew at Tamara's birthday party. He was her next-door neighbor and she had been telling me for months about him, in installments. "Suit Guy" was what she called him, even after she learned his name. Only, just before her birthday she got together with Roberto, so she was a little embarrassed about having already invited Suit Guy to her party. I remember seeing Andrew for the first time, walking into that party. He wasn't wearing a suit, but I felt like I could almost see the ghost outline of it surrounding his T-shirt and jeans. He was tall and very self-possessed. He should have been a little uncomfortable, walking into an apartment populated by dancers and not knowing anyone but Tamara, who was already pretty drunk by the time he showed up. But he didn't look uncomfortable. He looked almost haughty. I was impressed. I was intrigued. I was also, to be perfectly honest, totally depressed. Gwen had started seeing Hilel, and where once my days had been colored by the secret thought of him, I had now the utter blackness of watching his very public devotion to my sister.

Earlier that evening, when Gwen and I had been getting ready for Tamara's party, Gwen had asked my advice about what to do with Hilel.

"He says he's in love with me." Gwen shook her head. "And I don't know whether I should say it back or not. Should I say it? I should say it, right?"

"Well, do you mean it?"

I hated talking about Hilel with Gwen. The whole thing should have been weird, right? She was sleeping with someone I had been sleeping with four months before. There should have been at least one offering of "Hey, are you okay with this?" That wouldn't be unreasonable, right? Even though I was being so perfectly poker-faced about the whole thing? But I couldn't even be justifiably resentful. I had completely concealed my real feelings for Hilel, and I couldn't expect that Gwen could magically divine them. So I had to suck up the price of being so guarded. It was all very complicated, but only inside my own head, which made Gwen's blitheness even more exasperating. What should have been the pink elephant in the room was just my own personal invisible elephant. Sitting on my chest.

"I thought I loved him the other day," Gwen had prattled on. "When I was watching him in class? He had on those black sweatpants? You know which ones?"

"Ummm . . . maybe," I lied.

"He's just got that thing. I know it's like, wrong or whatever, but I couldn't be attracted to someone who wasn't an amazing dancer. I love watching him dance. And it lasts, you know, knowing that he's so great. Because even when we're just talking or having food or hanging out, or sex or whatever, and he's not actually dancing, I still know that he's a great dancer."

I knew exactly what she meant, although I would never have admitted it. There is a particular glow to being with someone who is supremely gifted. It's not just the status it gives the person. Talent is its own kind of romance. You can make out with it all by yourself if you have to—which is frequently the case, since really talented people are often thinking about things other than yourself.

"It's not all about that though, right?" I asked, half to Gwen, half to myself.

Gwen pursed her lips, thoughtfully. We were doing our makeup together in the bathroom. The thing about Gwen is she's very honest, in her own way. Sometimes this gives her a savant-like quality, her ability to reduce complex questions to a singular basic component. It can be amusing or deflating, depending on your point of view at the time.

"Why does he think he loves *me*?" Gwen countered. "Isn't it the same thing, really? Would he love me if I were just some normal girl?"

I looked at Gwen's reflection in the mirror, and then at my own beside it. That's when it became very clear to me that as Hilel was to me, so was Gwen to Hilel. Of course he was besotted with her. He was sunning himself in her glow. He was making out with her genius. The answer to her question seemed very clear. No, he wouldn't.

"So what do you do when he says, 'I love you'?" I asked brightly, so as not to collapse in tears and whatnot.

"Eyes, napkin, corner, inhale," Gwen said calmly. "But I can't keep doing that."

"Eyes, napkin, corner . . . ?"

"Irina told me about it," Gwen explained. "I forget what it is in Russian. You look at the guy's eyes, and then you look down at your napkin—or your lap or whatever—and then you look up at the corner of the room, and then you inhale."

Gwen demonstrated, turning to look deeply into my eyes, her lips slightly parted. Then she lowered her eyes modestly at the bathroom sink as if overcome, then raised them to the corner of the ceiling as if seeking divine help for the storm inside her. Then she inhaled sharply, a little gasp.

"Jesus," I said. "Well, that should hold him for a while."

"Good, right? You're supposed to do it to get the guy to fall in love with you, but it also works if you don't know what to say." She smiled the Gwen smile I love best, the one where the corner of her mouth indents and her shoulders curve girlishly, making her delicate collarbone stand out in the prettiest way.

I let the subject drop, but I remember that I felt fairly tormented, at the party, watching Hilel watch Gwen. I imagined him telling her that he loved her, and then falling even more deeply in love whenever she did eyes, napkin, corner, inhale at him.

And then Suit Guy walked in. I noticed him right away, but I was too depressed to do anything about it. I was also pretty drunk. And even though he was standing there so confidently, who was he, anyway? Tamara had reported that he was an investment banker from Connecticut, two things that seemed to rival each other in dullness.

Knowing Andrew as I do now, it makes perfect sense that he would pick out the most miserable girl at a party. He always said he was attracted to my independence and my calm, but I think he must have some sort of internal divining rod for buried drama.

How did I let that relationship happen? As fucked up as I was at the time, I wasn't deaf, I wasn't blind. I could see that he fell hard for me, that he wanted me very much. I could even see the red flag of his great need to be needed flapping in the wind, but I ignored all these things. I moved in with him six months later.

I wanted to get away. I wanted something of my own. I wanted to be someone's star.

These are the kinds of wants you should probably ignore when it comes to relationships. In fact, you should probably ignore all wants when it comes to relationships, including "I want to fuck him." Wait until someone hits you over the head with a rock and drags you back to his cave. This is a decent, honest method, and it's the only way to circumvent how terribly shaming it is to be unsatisfied when all your wants are met.

One thing that definitely scrambled my judgment was the sex. This would be the most positive aspect of Andrew's giving nature. He had even read a book about going down on women, *What She Wants and Where She Wants It*, which in my judgment has been egregiously overlooked for the National Book Award and the Pulitzer Prize. Previously, my only sexual experience had been with male ballet dancers, who, probably due to the sultan-like nature of being a straight guy surrounded by innumerable willing girls desperate for someone to stop yelling at them and tell them they're pretty, never expended a great deal of effort in that department. There were lots of things to like about Andrew. Even the things that irritated me were the sort of great things other girls would really want. I just wasn't used to someone wanting to be "there" for me. It never occurred to me that there was a "there" there, if you know what I mean, and so I was always making sins of omission. Like not inviting him to come home with me for Grandpa Crane's funeral so he could be supportive. Not telling him about little disappointments at work, or not waking him up when I had a nosebleed.

Never really explaining about Gwen.

I didn't tell Gwen much about Andrew either. Certainly in the beginning I was cautious. Like my real affection for Wendy Griston Hedges, I kept it secret, which is the only way to maintain ownership of something. And like with Wendy, I passed it off publicly to Gwen as something of a joke.

"So how was it?" Gwen asked, after the first time I spent the night with Andrew.

"He's got a hairy chest," I said. "I was totally frightened."

"Ew. What's his furniture like?"

"That sort of dark wood/brushed steel kind of stuff."

"Weird. So, are you all in love now or something?"

I always said no. To Gwen. The first time Andrew said it to me it was just after amazing sex, so I'm not to be blamed for replying in kind. But I was surprised by how good it felt to say it. It was something I could give him, something that made him happy, something that worked.

Gwen broke it off with Hilel, saying only that she wasn't ready yet for something "more," and that Hilel made too many demands on her.

"It's hard to concentrate," she told me. "With someone around you like that all the time."

"Hmmm." I was frequently exhausted by the time I saw Andrew at the end of a day, but he worked hard too, and so we mostly had sex and then went to sleep. On Sundays, which I had off since we were in rehearsal, we added food to this routine, sometimes supplemented with an "event," since Andrew worried about our lack of dating rituals. He was surprised by how many things I hadn't done in New York. ("You've never been to Coney Island? You've never been to the Blue Note? You've never gone to a Knicks game?")

"I like my routine," Gwen said. "I like to be able to do my own thing."

This sounded ominous to me, with my knowledge of what Gwen's routines could consist of, and I wondered if we were in for another spell of obsessive cleaning and paranoia. But things seemed more or less under control. Hilel was miserable, and his misery was still painful for me to witness, even though I was officially getting what I wanted, where I wanted it.

At that time I was worrying constantly about my place in the company. I was dancing a lot of soloist roles, but Marius hadn't promoted me. And most of my good parts tended to be in the more contemporary dances of our repertoire, which signified to me that Marius didn't see me as a serious ballerina, someone worthy of the white tutu and tiara. Gwen had been made a soloist a year earlier, had danced her first Aurora in *Sleeping Beauty.*

I kept everything in boxes. A box for work, a box for Andrew, and a box for Gwen. But the lids to all the boxes wouldn't stay shut. Their contents kept spilling over, demanding more room. The company had a three-week tour in Europe, which I planned on using to recommit myself totally to dance and showing Marius what I was made of. I sprained my ankle slightly the second night on a rain-slicked raked stage in Spain, and lay on my single bed in the hotel room I shared with Gwen for four days, reading—for some reason— *Middlemarch*, watching Spanish television with the sound off, and feeling a general sense of thwarted desire. My ankle was better by Lyon, where Gwen suffered from a bout of stage fright and woke me up in the middle of every night, convinced she had "forgotten" the choreography. Andrew offered to fly to London for our final stop and was hurt when I said it wasn't a good idea, I wouldn't be able to spend time with him, I needed to focus. The company returned to New York. Andrew had cleared a drawer, a bathroom shelf, and three inches in his closet for my use. I saw the words "Move in with me" hovering in a cartoon thought bubble above his head. I sensed he was waiting, scanning the air above *my* head to see the words form in my own cartoon bubble, where the letters were still hopelessly garbled. I brought over a bag to his apartment filled with contact lens solution, underwear, sweaters I never wore, and I did eyes, napkin, corner, inhale at him, hating myself. The company went on summer break. Gwen and I flew back to Grand Rapids to dance a benefit gala for the ballet company there. I felt myself eclipsed within my own family. My younger siblings were flush with success. Two years on the pro circuit and Keith was already making a name for himself—endorsement deals, a *Sports Illustrated* article, a Scandinavian model girlfriend. Gwen had danced Giselle for the queen of England. Marius had cast her as Juliet in his new staging of *Romeo and Juliet*. When my mother turned to me at dinner and asked, "Well, and so how are things with you, Kate?" I wanted to crawl under the table.

Back in New York, we began rehearsals for *Romeo and Juliet*. I learned that Marius had given me the role of Lady Capulet, Juliet's mother.

"It's actually a very good part," I told Andrew. "There are hardly any featured roles for women in *Romeo and Juliet* other than, obviously, Juliet. Lady Capulet is a soloist role."

"You should be Juliet," said Andrew. It took years before he learned that I didn't find it helpful when he was indignant on my behalf.

"No, no. You see, we're all pretty much the same age in the company. I mean, there's not a big spread," I explained. "So someone has to dance someone's mother. It doesn't mean I'm old."

"You're twenty-three," said Andrew, who was himself thirty. "You're a baby."

"Not really. We're like dogs or something. You know how you say a four-year-old dog is like, twenty-eight or something, in human years? That's how it is for dancers. I'm only a baby to you."

"I still think you should be Juliet."

"I don't want to be Juliet. Lady Capulet gets to act up a storm. When I learn of Tybalt's death, I actually get to rend my garments."

"I'll rend your garments," said Andrew, who wasn't usually funny on his own, but could piggyback on my funny pretty well.

I told Gwen that things were becoming more "serious" with Andrew.

"I think he wants me to move in with him," I said.

"Oh no," Gwen said. "Poor you. How are you going to get out of it?"

"I don't think I want to get out of it," I said. "I think I want to get . . . into it."

"Oh."

"You could afford this apartment on your own," I said. "And it's really too small for two people. I mean, it was fine when we were all students, but . . . anyway, you'd be happy not to have to pick up after me all the time, right?"

"Huh."

"He hasn't asked me yet. I just thought I'd let you know what direction things seem to be moving in."

I said that as if I had no control over the direction things were moving in myself. In fact, I was desperate for something to control. Gwen would have understood that, I think, if I had told her. I did not. After a while she went into the bathroom and shut the door. I listened to the taps of the bath come on.

That was all for a week or so and then Gwen sat me down and gave me a long speech about how she thought it was really great that I had found somebody and that she could "see" me having this really great, happy life. "A normal life," is how she put it.

But I didn't want a normal life. I wanted an extraordinary life. I didn't know which box that life was in, although Gwen seemed to be destined for one. But that was her own box, and I couldn't fit in there.

Gwen went through another crisis of nerves, worse than the one in France, or maybe she felt more comfortable freaking out in the privacy of our own home. I went to Andrew's—"fled" is really a more accurate verb—when the masking-tape Xs started appearing again. One day I came home to find all the house-plants missing.

"Gwen, what happened to our plants?"

"Your plants? They died."

"They died?"

"Your plants died last week," she said, turning a leaden face to me. "So I threw them out. You didn't even notice."

"They were *our* plants," I said. "You could have watered them too. They were ours."

"I can't take care of everything," she said, her face crumpling. "If you don't take care of things they die. I didn't know what to do."

Frustrated, I stormed out of the apartment. Got about a block away. Then came back. Gwen was curled up on her futon bed with Clive in her arms, crying into his fur. I sat down next to her.

"I'm sorry," she whispered. "I'll get you new plants. I'm sorry I'm not being better. I promise I'll try harder."

I knew she meant it. Mostly I tried to pretend her suffering was just excess theatrics, and sometimes . . . maybe . . . it was, but when the tears weren't pretty, when her hands shook and she destroyed things I knew she cherished (she had given those plants *names*, for fuck's sake), what could I do?

I put my arms around her, she curled into them, and Clive jumped off her lap.

"See?" she sobbed. "Even Clive doesn't want to be around me anymore."

"I'll try harder too," I told her. "We'll do better together."

Later that day, I called Andrew and told him that my sister was going through a difficult time, and that I needed to spend a little more time with her.

"What's wrong?"

"She's just . . . she's feeling a little lonely, I think. She's used to me being around more."

"Is this about your sister or is this about us?" he asked.

I wasn't going to plead with Andrew. The minute he heard the coldness in my voice he switched tactics.

"Maybe we could include her more," he offered. "Saturday? I'll take you both to the Hamptons. It's the last weekend we have the house. You won't have to do anything, just lie in deck chairs and eat barbecue. Tiny amounts of barbecue. Low fat-barbecue."

"Thank you," I said into the phone. "Thank you for being such a great guy."

"Everything will be okay," Andrew promised.

Because of my whole separate-box program, Andrew and Gwen hadn't spent much time together at that point. On the car ride out to the Hamptons, I let Gwen ride in the front seat, knowing how carsick she got. I had warned Andrew that my sister was a little "depressed" and to be kind. Totally unnecessary, of course. Andrew took one look at Gwen's wan little face and switched into hero mode. By Sunday, she had worked her magic. She lay on her deck chair and accepted the things Andrew brought her: a blanket, a gin and tonic, a sun hat, the Style section of the *Times*, grilled asparagus. Gwen made fun of herself, of her incompetence, always pointing out how stable and capable and competent I was by contrast. I saw her put her hand on Andrew's forearm. Her fingers trembled. I thought I might actually throw up. That night we drove back to New York and I insisted on dropping Gwen off at our place and continuing on to Andrew's.

I knew I had to move fast. I also knew I couldn't out-Gwen Gwen. That night I climbed on top of Andrew in bed and held his wrists down with all the strength I had while we were having sex. I told him—in the most indelicate of vocabularies— how much I wanted him. Basically, if I had had access to a hot iron, I would have branded him. Afterward I coiled around him and said the three words I knew he most wanted to hear.

"I need you," I said.

By the time we fell asleep, Andrew had asked me to move in with him.

Let me just say right now that even then I had some inkling of what I was doing. And what I was doing wasn't securing my boyfriend against my sister. I was *stealing* my boyfriend from my sister. Gwen and Andrew would have made a great couple. He would have taken care of her, would have taken pride in taking care of her. She would have felt protected. She might have been saved.

I told Gwen the news the next day, right before rehearsal, like a guilty boyfriend breaking up with his girl in public so she won't cause a scene. To my surprise, Gwen threw her arms around me.

"Oh my god! I'm so excited for you!"

She was jumping around so much I had to jump too, or be knocked over.

"I can totally see it!" Gwen laughed. "You're gonna get married to him and have a million babies. I'll be crazy Aunt Gwen!"

"I'm just moving in with him," I said, alarmed.

"It's what I wanted for you," Gwen gushed. "I was hoping this would happen. I knew it would."

"You did?"

"Of course," Gwen said, smugly, as if she had arranged the whole thing. "Oh my god, I'm so excited I have to pee." She ran into the bathroom, leaving me in the hallway, slightly stunned. After a minute, I went in and found her sobbing over the sinks. There were a couple of other people in there. Someone, I forget who, was trying to pat her on the back.

"Okay," I said, waving everyone off. "Okay. She's okay."

"I'm okay!" Gwen choked out. "I'm okay!"

It's not a totally unusual thing, meltdowns in the bathroom. People carried on with their business. Gwen stopped crying. I wet a paper towel and wiped her face. I smoothed her hair.

"Oh gosh," Gwen whispered, when everyone had left the bathroom. "I don't know what happened! That was weird."

We went into rehearsal. Gwen seemed totally calm. I was a wreck.

When Marius is working on something new, he frequently sounds like he's asking for input, but he's not really. He's talking to himself. So if he stops and says something like "And now what should you do here?" the standard thing is to say nothing but just sort of hold yourself in readiness while he figures out the answer. There are only a few of us who will offer suggestions. I might be one of the very few. Maybe the only one, now. That day Marius was working out the bit where Juliet pleads with her mother not to have to marry Paris, and Lady Capulet totally gives her the cold shoulder. Marius had Gwen running at me and flinging herself into my arms, and me icily peeling her hands off my shoulders.

"And then you slide down her body," Marius instructed Gwen. "Until you are at her feet. And then Kate, that makes you . . . what?"

I looked down at Gwen, huddled pathetically at the tips of my pointe shoes, her arms around my ankles. Several options occurred to me. One was to reach down and embrace her, set her on her feet, tell her I would do whatever it took to protect her. Another option was to kick her in the face.

"Can you sort of step out of her arms?" Marius sketched a movement in front of me. I elaborated on this, letting one foot trail behind me.

"Yes!" Marius nodded. "Right. And so then Gwen, can you grab that leg? No, higher up. Yes, that's right. You're still pleading with her. And Kate, you . . ."

I looked down at Gwen's hand on my leg. Then at Gwen's face. I wondered how she could look so composed, so business-like. I myself was shaking.

"Perfect," Marius said. "That's exactly the right feeling. And so, having your mother look at you like that, Gwen, that's what makes you let go. You know she's not going to help you."

17.

Marius came today to watch David and me rehearse the Tita-nia/Oberon pas de deux. We got about thirty-two bars into it before Marius stopped us, waving a hand at Dmitri to stop play-ing and jumping up from his chair.

"This love is autumn, not spring," he said, pushing his giant gold watch up his forearm, intent, electrified. "This isn't young love. Young love is given. Mature love is earned. This is mature love."

How do you dance mature love? I wondered. What would that look like? I pictured Titania coming onstage with a hot water bottle, inquiring about Oberon's sciatica. Usually I enjoy it when Marius goes all arty and talks about abstract notions or character development, but today I just wanted to dance and get it over with.

"Young lovers grab at each other," Marius continued, look-ing at David. "You can't wait to get your hands all over her, it's greedy and loud." Marius turned to me, and for an extremely bizarre moment I thought he was actually going to demonstrate this with me. I was totally unprepared and it sent a wave of heat through my body. I haven't felt that in a while. I've been under the impression that my sexuality is in deep freeze.

"But mature love . . ." Marius took my hand, looked me in the eyes, and smiled. Brought my hand to his lips and kissed it. I wasn't sure what to do, how to respond. I couldn't think of a gesture that signified mature love as differentiated from the other kinds of love.

"So, less passionate?" David asked.

Marius started humming a phrase and marking through the choreography. I followed along. When we got to the first lift he got a good grip on my hips and said, "Do," so I pliéd and up I went. Marius was always a good partner. He wrapped an arm around my legs, securing me against his torso, and started walking backward. Some lifts you have to be supporting some of your weight with your arms, or working hard to keep your center or make a platform for the guy's hands with your back or thigh or whatever, but this one was one of those nice floaty lifts that Marius is good at choreographing and where you feel quite beautiful doing it. Does mature love include the almost childlike pleasure in being picked up and carried? Marius slid me down close against his chest. I was supposed to fall back then, and I started the movement, arching my upper body, but Marius stopped me, keeping me upright and facing him, pressed against his chest, hands flat against my scapula. I could feel his heart beating under his soft T-shirt. I felt almost sleepy. Marius softened his hands and I arched back, Marius lunged with me, then brought us both back to standing.

"See?" Marius said, over my shoulder to David. "Still passion, but passion with authority. Titania and Oberon know each other very well. They've been fighting and now they've been reconciled so there's a relief. A deeper harmony. Acceptance. Titania has given in to Oberon's demands with the full knowledge that next time it will be him giving in, but it really doesn't matter all that much. There's almost a sense of humor here—a kind of 'Yes, darling, you are a piece of work and I'm a pompous old windbag, but we're a pair, you and I, and life is better when we stick together.'"

Marius turned back to me. "I'm speaking of the characters," he said with a smile. "Of course."

Marius walked back to his chair. David and I studied each other for a moment. It's hard to translate these kinds of notes immediately into the body. Sometimes it doesn't happen at all. We are neither poetry nor prose, exactly. We have gestures for tenderness, and sincerity. Denial. Rage. Passion. A gesture for true love. A gesture for betrayal. But it's a limited emotional vocabulary. You can think of metaphors before and after you dance, but it's hard to dance a metaphor in real time. Between my neck and my fatigue and my nerves and my fear, I wasn't sure if I was even capable of an adjective.

"It's the mood," Marius said. "Just be human with each other."

We began the pas de deux again, and this time Marius didn't stop us. Something must have seeped into both of us, because it did feel quite different. David and I kept sort of smiling at each other, and everything went much more securely. It felt great, actually. So real. Like we were human beings. I wished I had danced more like this from the beginning of my career, when I wasn't so beat up. We finished and separated, catching our breath, looking up to nod at each other, then turning to Marius, who was squinting.

"It doesn't . . . quite . . . work," he said.

David snorted. I looked down at my feet. They seemed very far away. And so sad. The veins stood out in vivid blue relief to the pale skin. I shifted my weight to the backs of my heels to give my toes a little breathing room inside my pointe shoes. I wondered how much longer I could remain standing. It didn't seem like that much longer.

"It's not you," Marius said, jumping out of his chair and pacing. "That was lovely, actually. It was lovely, but it wasn't Titania and Oberon. I don't know . . . hmmmm . . ."

When Marius goes to this phase you just let him pace and talk to himself and wait it out, stay ready for instructions. David caught my eye and blew me a silent kiss, then bent over to stretch his hamstring. I calculated that I had about five more minutes of dancing left in my body before I started disintegrating. Less, if I just had to stand around.

"I think," I started, not having any real thought formed but out of desperation to keep upright, "I think that was valuable though, in terms of how we are relating to each other? It just needs to be, maybe, it just needs to be more formal."

Marius stopped pacing and considered me.

"You know how after you've had a fight," I continued babbling, "you're all polite and really respectful and considerate? Well, not me—after I fight I just get sullen and resentful until enough time has passed or I get bored with myself or whatever— but I think that's how people *should* behave. You know, in a better . . ." I waved a hand around the studio. The bare floors, the box of yellow rosin in the corner, Dmitri yawning at the piano, the grime of New York City on the windows too high to see out of, the fluorescent lights blotted with occasional shadows of dead insects, David's and my dance bags under the barre spewing towels and water bottles and sweatpants and Advil and time. And despair. And fatigue. And desire.

"In a better world," I said. "A better world than this one."

"A better world," Marius said.

"And a better me," I added. "Obviously."

Marius nodded. I looked down at my feet again. This time they appeared to be quite close, almost under my chin. *Stand up*, I told myself. *Stand up*.

"Let's try it," Marius said. "From the beginning."

18.

Dress rehearsal today for Program One of our mixed repertoire evenings. In the morning we were all called to company class onstage.

Swan Lake had disappeared, back into storage. New backdrops had been lowered in. The front of the stage was freshly taped with the markers that help us form properly spaced lines. Portable barres had been brought in, along with a rosin box in the corner. It's always a bit weird, taking class onstage since you don't have mirrors. On the other hand, it has sort of a dramatic feel to it.

A few house lights were on, and you could see the entire theater. Usually all you can see are the green EXIT signs and the shadow thumb shapes that are people's heads. The orchestra pit was empty, except for Dmitri, at the piano. It's disorienting to take class without a mirror. And to be onstage without an audience.

We had an audience today, though. An assortment of elegantly dressed people, sitting in the center orchestra block.

This was one of those days, as Marius likes to say, where we were paying some bills.

Individual sponsorship of dancers has now become a normal thing for ballet companies. You pay a set fee and your name will appear next to a dancer's name in the program. "Tina Ballerina's performances are sponsored by Bruce and Brenda Moneybags." It's been proven that people will be more generous to the needy if the needy are given an individual face, a personality, a story line they can sympathize with. And it's not like the dancers have to wear their sponsors' names on their costumes.

But Marius has resisted this trend. So our individual donors have to be content with the usual perks: a private bar at the theater, the best seats, meet-the-dancers dinners, invitations to rehearsals, etc., etc. There's a whole tiered system of Friendship with the company. As in life, some friendships are more meaningful than others.

And some of them are real friendships. I spotted Wendy Griston Hedges sitting in the third row, wearing what looked like a brown cloche hat. I waved. She waved. I hadn't seen her in a while, we'd missed a couple of our first-Monday teas. In January she was away, visiting her sister, and in February we were just getting back from tour, and this month . . .

That's when I realized that the first Monday of this month was . . . yesterday. Did she send me an invitation? Yes, she did. I remember looking at it. Did I even open it? No. No, that was the day I found the numbers under Gwen's bed. I couldn't remember what I did with Wendy's letter.

Class hadn't started yet, so I quickly ran down the steps by the side of the orchestra pit and over to Wendy, smiling and waving in a general way to other donors.

Wendy is extremely shy, and not very physically demonstrative, so we never hug or kiss cheeks or anything like that. She was sitting at the end of a row, and I sat down on my heels in the aisle, holding on to the armrest.

"Hello," Wendy said.

Once I was next to her, I saw that it wasn't a brown cloche hat.

"Wendy, your haircut is fabulous!" I told her. I'd gotten used to the cranberry frizz, and our relationship is such that I would never have suggested anything different to her, but it was an incredible improvement. Even her skin, normally quite dry and chalk-ish, was shining with a pearly glow.

Wendy patted her hair self-consciously.

"Oh," she said, with an almost girlish giggle. "Oh, well, thank you."

She turned to the woman next to her, a beautiful black woman, ageless except for the gray in her dreadlocks.

"Kate, this is my friend Karine," she said.

I reached across Wendy and shook hands with Karine. My hand disappeared into her giant one. Karine had a West Indian accent. Wendy watched us, alert, smiling nervously. The hallmarks of someone introducing a loved one.

Wendy in love? There definitely was something . . . almost bridal about her.

"Wendy, I feel terrible," I said in a rush. "Monday. It's been . . . I got injured and this season has been and I . . . I moved. My boyfriend and I—"

"You're injured?" she interrupted. "Are you okay?"

"Oh fine, yes fine. But listen, Monday. I'm so sorry. Can we do this coming Monday?" I was almost pleading, as it suddenly did seem very important that I see Wendy.

Wendy turned a questioning face to Karine.

"Monday?" Wendy asked. "Is that . . . do we . . . ?" She put her hand on top of Karine's. Despite Wendy's general glow and fetching new do, her hands looked very old and crabbed. I was glad that she was with someone who didn't mind, if that's what was going on.

"Or . . . whenever, really," I said. "I mean . . . we can pick another time or . . ."

"Monday will be just fine," Karine said to me. "Not too early though, I think."

"Oh good." Wendy beamed. "That will be lovely."

"Oh good!" I said, although I was a little concerned now about the relationship. Had Wendy fallen prey to some sort of lesbian heiress hunter? "Good!"

"We'll talk then," Wendy said.

"Yes. Okay. It's so good to see you."

"It's good to see *you*, Kate."

I vaulted back up the stairs and took my place at the barre. Marius strode onto the stage and welcomed our guests charmingly. We applauded them. Class started. My Vicodin kicked in and I gulped water in between combinations like mad, trying to get rid of the dry-gum feeling. The mood of the company was good, Marius was making his little jokes, people were smiling, showing off a bit. Everyone was doing a stage version of themselves, including me. This is the public version of our lives. Yes, it's incredibly hard, taxing, draining. Yes, we are super dedicated.

But we love what we do. We wouldn't be here otherwise. And we support one another. It's a family. And you, lovely well-dressed people in the front rows, you are our generous aunts and uncles, our doting grandparents. You love us. We love you. Especially when you watch. You are our mirrors, reflecting magnificence.

I think the Vicodin I got from Stefan yesterday is stronger than what Gwen had. I felt a little too high. It was almost fun.

"Snazzy," I said to Roger, as we waited to go across on the diagonal.

"What?"

"I feel snazzy." I snapped my fingers. "You know. My mojo. I feel it."

"Right on," said Roger. "Or whatever."

I zip-zip-zipped across the stage, confident, a little daring, sparkling like a Venetian glass vegetable. I can't believe I've been performing on this shit. It's a miracle I haven't tipped off the stage and into the woodwinds. Impaled myself on a bassoon.

After class, I went to Wardrobe, and Fiona pulled my *Leaves* costume off the rack.

"While I have you here," she said. "Let's see where we are with the *Look At Me* dress." She disappeared into the racks and I stripped off all my junk and stood in my tights and pointe shoes, trying to work a little saliva into my gums. My neck was starting to throb a little. People filtered in and out, grabbing costumes, chattering. I closed my eyes.

"Hey." It was Mara, prodding me on my shoulder.

"Oh hey. Hey!"

Mara had her *Symphony in Three Movements* costume on. Well, it's not really much of a costume, *Symphony in Three*

Movements being prototypical Balanchine modernism so the dancers just wear pale tights and leotards with a little belt around the waist. Mara's leotard is white.

"You don't have a straightening iron, do you?" Mara asked. "The one in the Hair Room is broken and we're supposed to have high ponytails. It looks like I've got a sheep on my head." She pointed to her curls.

"There was a character in one of the *Oz* books," I told her, "who was like, an evil princess. And she wore the same thing every day. But she had a whole room full of different heads. She collected them. And so when she wanted to look different, she just changed her head."

Mara stared at me. I guess I did look a little crazed, standing there naked holding on to my boobs, pouring sweat and gabbling away.

"Tamara does, I think," I said. "Have a straightening iron. Check my dressing room."

Fiona emerged with a red cocktail-style dress, glittering with beading, and shook it at me.

"It's not done," she said, grabbing pins.

I watched Mara leave. She seemed a little less friendly than normal. I've been neglecting her too. I stepped into the dress and Fiona started fussing with the fit.

"Don't you dare lose a pound between now and opening. Oh, and James said we should use these." She handed me two flesh-colored gelatinous half circles.

"What the hell are these?"

"They're called cutlets," Fiona said, raising her eyebrows.

"What do we do with them?"

"For your cleavage." Fiona pointed at my naked chest.

"Huh."

"Broadway, darling. Those girls have boobies."

Mara was waiting for me in my dressing room. Holding the bottle Stefan gave me in her hand.

"You find the iron?"

"What are these?" Mara shook the bottle.

"Vicodin," I said. "For my neck."

"How many are you taking a day?"

"Jesus, Mara." I rooted around in Tamara's stuff until I found the iron. I pretended to be a little annoyed, but really I was relieved if all Mara was mad at me for was my becoming a drug addict.

"Here." I handed her the iron and held out my hand for the bottle. After a moment, she gave it to me.

"Kate."

"Look at what I got," I said, shaking the cutlets at her. "Fake boobs."

"Kate."

"Try them on. They're fabulous."

Mara looked for a minute like she was going to throttle me, then rolled her eyes. I took the iron from her and plugged it into my outlet. She fitted the cutlets into her leotard.

"Nice, right? You look hot."

"Oh my god. Take a picture of me so I can send it to Mike?"

And we spent the next fifteen minutes posing her around my dressing room, and I gave her a smooth and swinging pony-tail, and when she wasn't looking I shut the bottle in a drawer, because what your friends can't see can't hurt them.

.   .   .

On our dinner break a couple of us went to the salad place. I asked Klaus if he wanted to join and I could tell he was a little psyched to get an invitation to the cool kids' table.

The waiter brought us huge glasses of water with straws in them and we all laughed at the fact that we were too tired to actually pick up our glasses and instead just leaned forward and sucked on our straws like little kids. Roger instigated a game of trying to look sexy while sucking on a straw. During this, my phone rang, and I saw that it was my parents' home number. I jumped up and walked outside the café onto Broadway.

"Mom!"

"Oh! Hello! I thought I was going to get your voicemail."

"No, no, I'm here. What's going on?"

"Well, I just wanted to give you the latest news."

I struggled past some skyward-gazing tourists and turned down Seventieth Street, phone jammed hard against my ear as taxis blared at each other. A ubiquitous clipboard-holding activist on the corner lurched toward me and then hastily backed away as I glared at her.

"Yes, yes. I'm here. Go ahead."

"Where are you? Should I call back when you're home?"

"It'll be late then. No. Tell me. How's . . . how's Gwen. What's happening?"

"Gwen is doing much better. She's in this . . . well, she's in a program, I guess you'd call it. She goes five times a week to a therapy situation."

"A therapy *situation*?" I stepped over some trash and plugged my free ear with my palm.

"I guess just therapy, you would call it. For the next eight weeks, and then they'll . . . I guess . . . reevaluate."

"What does her doctor say? I mean, do they have a diagnosis?"

"Your father knows more about all the medical terms and he's consulting with everyone. Hey," Mom chirped happily, "did you know that one in every four adults has a psychotic episode?"

"Um, no."

"It's not an uncommon thing, is what I've learned. It's very common. Especially for people with stressful jobs."

"So like, what." I wandered up a few steps of someone's brownstone. "We're saying that's it, it was a one-time thing, and she's actually totally normal?"

"What do you mean? She had to take a test."

"What kind of test?"

"That's one of the little evaluationals."

"Evaluationals?"

"How they evaluate. All these questions. So they could know whether they needed to admit her or she could be an outpatient."

"Okay, is this a legitimate thing? It sounds like a *Cosmo* quiz. Where is all this happening?"

"Kate." My mother's voice lost its cheerful getting-all-our-ducks-in-a-row reportage and became quite crisp and formal. "It's happening at Two Rivers Psychiatric Clinic and your father and I are making sure that she's getting the best treatment possible. I really don't appreciate . . . I'm not sure you have the right to criticize."

"What's that supposed to mean?"

She sighed heavily. "Here we go again."

"She still won't talk to me, answer my calls, texts, nothing.

And I mean . . . it's not just one flip-out, okay? What if she's really messed up? What if she's got schizophrenia? Is anybody checking that?" Someone was coming out of the brownstone, so I retreated, hunching my shoulders up to try to get some privacy.

"I don't think we should rush to put a label on it," Mom said firmly. "And I know you're upset that she hasn't talked to you, but you have to understand, sweetie, that she was angry with you for calling your father and forcing her to . . . that's part of her depression. I think there is a sense of some betrayals. Some hurts."

"JESUS FUCK," I yelled into my phone. "Can you stop talking in that fucking stupid *kiddie* voice? She didn't just all of a sudden get *sad*. And she was going to *kill* herself! I was *there*!"

The line went quiet. I had managed to get "JESUS FUCK" out about the same time that a Mommy and Me–style Mommy was passing with a stroller. The woman, now halfway down the block, was still scowling at me over her shoulder.

It's amazing how quickly all emotions just hurtle through me. I can't hold on to anything. Immediately, I felt horrendous. The conversation was ruined.

"Kate?" It was my dad's voice now. Mom had apparently abdicated.

"Hi, Dad."

"Kate, why are you yelling at your mother?" It's probably been about fifteen years since I last heard that tone from my father. Although the disappointed timbre sounded remarkably like Marius's voice when he told me how hard it was to watch me diminish myself.

"She just . . . she just . . ." God, I was sweating like a maniac inside my hoodie.

"She has been working very hard to stay positive in what has been an extremely stressful situation."

"I know . . . I'm . . . she's just . . ." I started to cry. It wasn't tears, exactly, but all the rest of the crying activity.

"Kate," my father said firmly. "Kate. I know you are upset, but this is not the way to handle it."

"She's my *sister*," I choked. A couple passed me, arm in arm. Their eyes flickered at me and then snapped back to each other. I turned my back on them, huddling next to some garbage cans.

"And she is our daughter," Dad said. "And we are making sure she is getting the best care possible. We are doing everything we can. Gwen is working very hard. And what she needs most right now is space and privacy and to not have additional emotional demands placed on her."

Gwen doesn't need emotional demands placed on her? Gwen doesn't need? I swallowed hard.

"Kate?"

"Yes. I'm here."

"Do you understand me?"

I nodded silently.

"Yes."

"I love you, Katie. I want you to be strong."

"I love you too. Okay."

"I'm going to give the phone back to your mother now. Are you able to speak calmly to her?"

"Yeah. Yes. I'm sorry."

"We'll talk to you soon."

"Okay. Bye, Daddy. I'm sorry."

"Bye, sweetheart."

The line went quiet again, and I scrubbed my cheeks with one hand and took a deep shaky breath. I'm such a bad breather.

"It's me." My mom's voice, sounding tentative. I could picture her: a canary-yellow polo shirt, maybe with a sleeveless fleece over it. She gets her hair cut at a Supercuts and colors it herself with L'Oréal. She wears a visor when she plays tennis. Gwen and I always give her a hard time about her visor. We have a jingle that we sing at odd moments—"VI-sor JU-deeee!"—meant to convey in four syllables the totality of steel-jawed perky obliviousness that is the birthright of the Midwestern Mom.

"I'm sorry, Mom," I said. "I didn't mean to shout at you."

"Oh, it's okay, honey. I know you're worried. Where are you?"

"I'm on the street. We're at dinner break."

"Are you with your friends? Is Mara there?"

"Roger. Bunch of other people. Not right now. They're in the café."

"Well, I think you better go back and get some food in you!"

"Uh-huh."

"It's going to be just fine, honey. Take deep breaths."

"I am."

"We're all just taking deep breaths. And you know your sister loves you. She just needs a little more time."

"Okay."

"Okay?"

"Okay," I repeated, trying to sound like I meant it. I made the gesture for calm, which helped slightly.

"Guess what your daddy and I did today?" she asked—or rather, begged.

"Uh-huh. What did you do?"

"We went to yoga! We got a free pass in the mail for some new place that opened and I said, 'Bill, I think we should check this out.' And your father did very well! He didn't think he would like it but he *did*."

"That's . . . that's great!" My exclamation point was faint, but I got it in there.

"Did you talk to your brother?"

We spent a few minutes regaling each other with the same information we both had about Keith, who had won the final in Morocco in straight sets and was now headed to Italy. By the time this was done, we were speaking normally to each other, and my nose was no longer running, although I could feel the cakiness under my eyes where mascara had pooled and dried. We said good-bye and I checked out my reflection in the window of a dry cleaner's, licking my fingertips and repairing the damage. My phone beeped. A text from Roger:

Food here. Where U?

When I got back to the café, I was informed that Klaus had figured out a way to suck on a straw while still looking sexy. He demonstrated this for me and I laughed along with everyone else.

"You better hit that," Roger whispered to me, nodding at Klaus.

"Ha-ha," I said. "Ha-ha."

Back at the theater, dress rehearsal dragged on. Our sponsors had departed, and free from adult supervision, Marius grabbed a microphone and commenced shouting with something less than the afternoon's geniality. My brain felt hot and uncomfortable, like the way you feel bulky and irritable inside your winter coat when you're slogging through a department store in January. I swallowed another Vicodin, more for my guilt than for my neck, and it did bring me a certain amount of mental ventilation. In the wings before my first entrance for *Leaves* I was champing at the bit, so badly did I want to get onstage and just dance. Every time Marius stopped us to correct the lighting, or confer with the orchestra director, or yell about our spacing, I wanted to scream.

Marius announced that we were running the whole ballet again from the beginning. Everyone nodded obediently and bitched in the wings. "Are we in overtime?" "He doesn't expect us to do it full out, does he?" There were many complaints about our costumes for this ballet, which is an old one from our repertoire, and it must be admitted that there is a faint reek of mildew coming off the chiffon.

"I think the last guy who wore this is dead now," Roger said to me. "I'm wearing a dead man's blouse."

"That's very poetic," I told him. He nodded.

"Sweat lingers on
In a dead man's costume
Don't order the brisket!"

Roger said.

I laughed, and it felt like the sound broke something free in my head.

It's not my problem anymore, I told myself.

It's not my problem.

It's just me now.

When you exhaust every possible emotion, you make space for the unexpected. For the rest of the hour I loved everything. I loved standing in the wings and looking upward into the fathoms of the theater: the flies, the iron catwalk, the lighting grids and scrims. I loved that the sound of Dvorak was so comprehensible to my muscles that the phrases seemed to be emitting from my own bloodstream. I loved the drama of running into the wings and dashing around the narrow crossover backstage that is set up for us with glow tape. I loved that I'm able to turn on one foot, run, run, run, glissade, and then jump into the air, half turning, so that Adam is able to lean down and catch me, one arm circling my legs, and I loved knowing in a hundred tiny indescribable ways that it was done perfectly and that Adam was glad that I have a good jump and make it easy for him. I loved the sight of my own hand in front of my face. I lifted my arms and felt the muscles undulating down my back, and this too I loved.

And then it was over and Marius said, "Better. Thank you, company. Go home. Get some sleep." And we all filed offstage and Fiona shouted out a reminder for everyone to *please* hang up their costumes in the dressing rooms, *do not* leave them on the floor, and people crowded into the elevator or pulled themselves up the stairs, and I told myself that this night would be fine.

This night I would end the evening perfectly, ride the subway home quietly, put my things away neatly when I got back to the apartment. Not smoke or watch something stupid on TV, or stare bleakly at Gwen's masking-tape Xs on the walls and construct grim fantasies in my head to work out all my resentments. I would perform nightly ablutions methodically and peacefully and perhaps spend an hour reading Peter Holland's essay on *A Midsummer Night's Dream*. I would do this all for me, and not for the benefit of an invisible audience.

But back in my dressing room I was afraid. I was afraid that with the removal of each layer I would slowly be reduced, like a series of glittering, mildewed, sweat-stained Russian nesting dolls, until there was just one tiny feeble me, so easy to knock over, so easy to lose.

19.

I told Mara I would meet her at the Russian Baths downtown this morning. Two Vicodin and my iPod meant I could get on the subway and down to lower Manhattan with artificially induced cheer. I wanted to cancel on Mara. Usually I love having a good long sweat in the steam room, but I was afraid that under intense heat the backlog of Vicodin in my pores was going to waft out in a noxious cloud, and I wanted it in me. I have this idea that my toxins are acting as a kind of force field.

The Russian Baths are coed, so you wear bathing suits. The saunas are mostly populated by extremely large Central European men who watch us impassively and speak to each other in thick wooden-block sentences. From time to time an attendant, wearing a special peaked cap that seems to serve no purpose other than the ludicrous and ceremonial, will appear and offer to whack you with special branches. There are buckets in the corners and chests with ice water. You can also step outside the sauna and stand in a shower cubicle while the peaked-cap guy throws buckets of ice water at you. I never do that though, because I hate the feeling of cold water.

Mara and I arrived at the baths at the same time, changed into suits, and took our usual benches in the sauna. It was early enough that it wasn't too crowded. Most of the dancers in town come to this place, even though there's a fancier one in the East Village where the attendants don't scowl at you. Eventually we'll all switch over to that one, I suppose. When there's a signal from the herd.

Mara and I spent a few minutes gossiping about the week. Mara seemed distracted, which suited me just fine. I wasn't up for any big talk. I asked her about Mike.

"Yes, so, actually, kind of big news," she said. "Mike surprised me last night. We've been talking about doing a little trip, after the season is over, but I was thinking maybe a long weekend at a B and B in Vermont or something. He's got all this vacation accrued. Anyway, last night I came home and the kitchen table was covered in this red-and-white-checked tablecloth and he had music playing, and a bottle of red wine, and cheese and prosciutto and this whole itinerary printed out. A week in Venice!"

"Ohhhh," I said, squeezing her sweaty knee. "Mara, that's fantastic. How sweet. He set it all up for you?"

"Can you believe it?"

"With prosciutto and everything waiting?"

"Uh-huh."

"He's the best," I said. "And you deserve the best, but I mean . . . when do we get what we deserve? So it's even more the best that he's the best."

"He is the best."

"It's just what you need," I said. "And Mike too. I love that he's so romantic."

"So I got a little carried away." Mara bent over her legs and looked up at me sheepishly. "Because later, in bed, I asked him what he thought about us trying to get pregnant."

"Wow." I laughed. "That must have been some cheese."

"Sort of starting in Venice, because it's better if you're off the pill for a cycle or two before you start trying. So I thought, well, I could go off the pill now, and then we could start when we're on vacation. To make it even more special."

"Oh my gosh. You're serious?"

"We were both sort of crying and laughing too. I mean he was laughing at me for having this whole logistical plan, but he was also really, really excited. He said that he's been thinking about having a baby a lot lately, but he didn't want to say anything and make me feel pressured, and he thought we were still a few years away from me wanting to do that."

"Right, right." I tried to breathe shallowly because the heat was hitting me faster than it usually does, and I was dehydrating rapidly. "I thought you were too. You said something about it, a few weeks ago, but also you were talking about taking some classes, so I just assumed it was all very hypothetical and—"

"And you know, after I said it," Mara continued. "To Mike? I just felt so happy and I thought, if I get pregnant in Venice then I won't come back next season. And then I thought, well, maybe I'll just retire altogether."

"Wait. What? Retire?"

"Yup." Mara extended a leg out in front of her. Three of her toes were taped up, there was a bruise on her knee, and clusters of lavender spider veins traced their way down her shin. But this is how we look. These are the signs of our commitment.

"I thought," I said. "I thought you were feeling good about things. The other day, you were talking about *Symphony* and saying how great it felt to be dancing that. And I mean, you look great, you're not injured . . ."

"In a way, that's sort of a reason to quit now," Mara said. "Finish with dance before dance finishes with me, you know?"

I breathed in nausea.

"This isn't about what happened in *Swan Lake?*" I asked. "When you fell? Because that happens to everybody, and you were dancing beautifully. It was a total freak accident."

I looked at the topography of Mara's bent-over back. Stone footpaths of vertebrae. Cresting ribs like sand dunes. Shoulder-blade cliffs. When she pulled at the tape around her big toe, the muscles of her back volcanoed new islands into the valley. It's not the terrain of a retirement village. Or a nursery.

"No," Mara said, straightening up. "Of course not. I'm not that egotistical. It's just that when I think about all the things I want now from life, they're more like, life things, you know?"

"You can have life things and still dance, though," I said, blinking sweat out of my eyes. "It's not either/or. People have babies. People take classes, get degrees. Sometimes it's better, right? You have more to give onstage when you have a full life."

"Okay, why are you being like this?" Mara asked. "Are you seriously trying to talk me into more dancing? When I'm actually feeling happy about the thought of doing something new with my life?"

"No, I know, it's just that it seems really sudden," I said. "Are you sure you didn't get carried away, like you said, in the heat of the moment? He pulls out the whole spread, he's booked this great vacation, you're feeling the postcoital glow . . . you were in a chemical rush."

"*I'm* in a chemical rush?" Mara asked pointedly.

I waved that away.

"Guess I just feel like I missed a chapter in a book," I said. "We haven't really talked about any of this."

"That's not my fault."

And just like that, we were in a fight. Neither one of us is a yeller or screamer and since we were both physically exhausted and in a public sweat lodge, there was no arm waving or extra energy being expended. We basically sat very still, perspired, and spoke sedately of betrayal.

"You know, Mara, I've had a few things of my own going on."

"And you shut me down every single time I try to talk to you about Gwen."

"Because I don't want to talk about her. Sorry. I know I should. But I don't want to right now. How hard is that to understand? I'm not like, obligated to talk about it."

"I don't think you realize how difficult it is to be friends with you."

"Because I don't dump my problems on everybody?"

"Because you're sad and you won't talk about it."

"I'm not sad all the time."

"No, lately you're high all the time."

"It's Vicodin. It's not heroin."

"It actually does affect your personality. I know you don't want to believe that, but it does."

"Well, according to you I have a bad personality anyway."

"I didn't say that."

"You know, I haven't really noticed that you've made some huge effort to reach out to me."

"That's what I'm saying. You make it impossible."

"God, that's what Andrew said."

"This isn't because I'm jealous, Kate."

"What? Who said you were jealous?"

"You think I'm being hard on you because I'm jealous."

"Can we just get past this idea that you might be jealous of me?"

"I *am* jealous of you. But that's not why you're pissing me off."

"God," I said. "Jealous of me. What a fucking joke."

Mara stood up and left the sauna.

I sat there dripping sweat for a few minutes. I had that special kind of rage that comes when you've ruined your legitimate right to be mad by being an asshole. I stood up and clambered down from the benches, cartilage in my knees creaking, dizzy and desperate for water. I pushed open the sauna door. Mara was standing right outside it. She pointed to the shower cubicle. In one hand she held a bucket.

"Stand in there."

"What? No." I tried to walk past her, but she was blocking me.

"Stand in there," she repeated.

"You're not throwing that on me." Mara knows I absolutely hate cold plunges. They make me feel like I'm having a heart attack.

"Go." Mara put a hand on my shoulder and shoved. She

shoved me into a shower like we were a couple of frat boys. She didn't look crazy, exactly, but she did seem very determined.

"Okay, seriously, stop this. I'm injured." I tried to brace myself against the wall, but my hands and feet were slippery with sweat and I couldn't get any traction on the floor.

"You can't do this," I said. "This is . . . this is stupid. What's wrong with you?"

Mara held up the bucket.

"Don't do this," I said.

She started to swing the bucket backward.

"This could actually kill me," I said. "I MEAN IT."

Mara threw the ice water straight into my face.

I took a huge shuddering inhalation and groped blindly for the sides of the shower stall. I could feel my heart jump up into my throat and it didn't stop. I could feel my heart on the back of my tongue, in my nose, my forehead. My lungs sucked in more air and my knees collapsed a little. I could sense movement in front of me and hear the slosh of water and a metallic bang.

"Oh my god," I said. "Oh my god." I was too dehydrated to cry tears, but my lungs and throat started crying.

She did it again, only I was a little bent over, so she emptied the bucket on my shoulders and the water coursed down my back. It was horrible, outrageous. Like being flayed by ice. I could hardly get enough air in my lungs to deal with the violence of it. My heart was banging against the top of my head, like a bat in a shoebox. I made a huge effort and stood a little more upright. Spit some water out of my mouth. I looked at

Mara, who was still holding the bucket. "Okay, one more," I choked out.

The third time she tipped the ice water almost tenderly over my head.

"John the Baptist," I said to Mara, fighting for breath. "Come-to-Jesus moment. Right? Where I admit. I'm a drug addict. And my sister. Has gone insane. And I knew. I knew it was happening and did nothing. To stop it."

I rubbed my eyes. Wrung out my hair. Two enormous Armenian men walked by, and their dark eyes flickered over us with instant assessments: women, too skinny, emotional, keep moving. They entered the sauna.

"Kate, I'm really sorry." Mara handed me a towel. She was crying a little bit. "This thing with Gwen . . . it's not your fault. You have to know that."

"I can't talk about it," I said.

"Okay. It's okay."

"Really, Mara. The only thing that helps right now is . . . I don't know. Please don't cry."

"I don't even know why I'm crying," Mara said.

"Can we go to the Turkish room now?"

Mara nodded.

The Turkish room is not steamy, just warm, and almost always empty, which means you can stretch on the heated benches and not worry that you're putting your foot in someone's face. Mara and I spread out towels and lay on our backs. I pulled my knees to my chest, wiggling so the knobs of my spine fit into a break in the wooden slats of the bench. I reached over and brushed Mara's arm.

"I think you should have wild unprotected sex with Mike in

Venice," I said. "But what if you don't get pregnant right away? Will you come back after the break?"

"I haven't decided. Maybe not, maybe I'll start school, see what happens. I'm going to the doctor this week, make sure everything is okay in there."

"I'm sure it is," I said. "I'm sure it's perfect."

20.

"Is better," Irina said, prodding my neck.

"Oh. Is it?" I asked, trying to concentrate.

"What? You no feel?"

"That's sort of a complicated question."

Irina sighed.

"Dr. Ken says I have what, in a normal person, is like whip-lash," I said, defensively.

"So?" Iri sniffed. "Normal person is not you. Is not impor-tant, the bones, if they are not normal. If the muscles work, then bones can be anything."

"Huh. Maybe you're right," I said, because this sounded bet-ter than "We need to treat this seriously."

"*Normal.*" Irina dismissed the word with some majestic *r* roll-ing. "Some people think I'm bad mother, for not letting Alisa have normal life. She should lie on couch at home. Watch tele-vision and eat Twinkie."

"She doesn't want to do that, does she?" I asked, gripping the sides of the massage table.

"She want to be gymnast." Irina reached under my back and moved my scapula about four feet. "She can be normal later if she want, but at least then she'll have medal."

Unless, of course, she doesn't get a medal. But it's probably too late for that. If she quits, she'll always wonder what would have happened if she hadn't. If she tries and does not succeed, she'll spend the rest of her life feeling like a failure for events that occurred while she was a teenager. The only good outcome would be getting a medal.

"You have to try to be more soft," Irina said sternly.

"More soft?"

"Yes. Make soft."

I took a shaky breath and tried to imagine the muscles of my neck melting. I thought of those cold packets of butter they give you in delis that are such a nuisance. You can't spread them. You can only roughly chop them up with your plastic knife and then you get too much butter on some things and not enough butter on others. Of course, I no longer spread butter on anything.

"Make soft!" Iri commanded.

I tried loosening my jaw, which has become increasingly hard to do because of the whole Vicodin thing.

After leaving Irina, I had about an hour to kill before *Dream* rehearsal and I was consumed with a desire for one of those giant deli muffins. Blueberry. With butter. If you ask, they will grill it for you and slather butter on, and you can avoid the butter-packet disappointment. I told myself that it was okay to go and get one of those muffins because I've been losing weight recently and Vicodin on an empty stomach is a bad idea and if anyone caught me I could claim that I was having low blood sugar.

Today was the first truly nice day of spring we've had, so every New Yorker was in a frenzy to soak up the sun. I sat in one of the iron chairs in front of the Vivian Beaumont Theater and hugged my muffin bag to my chest like a wino. I kicked off my shoes and stretched my legs out so the tips of my feet could get some sun.

I watched the tourists. I listened to chatter from a passing group of students—Juilliard actors probably, from the animated way they pronounced their vowels. I watched a young man with brown curls pushing a cello in front of him. I watched an older man go up to our box office and pull out his wallet. Was he buying seats for himself and his wife? His companion? His mother? Will he come alone to the ballet tonight, sit quietly in his seat during intermission, reading the names of all the dancers in the next piece, which is his favorite? From a chair at Lincoln Center, humanity doesn't look so bad, especially if you squint your eyes and imagine that what you are seeing is all there is, and that nobody has anything concealed.

I broke the muffin up in the bag so I could extract discreet pieces at a time, and just as I was about to take my first delicious bite (my god, my mouth was watering so much it hurt) I saw my little fan, Bryce, sitting on a chair near mine. She had a book in her lap and there was a white paper bag next to her on the table. I was annoyed, since I really wasn't in the mood to be someone's idol. I just wanted to eat my goddamn muffin.

Bryce turned a page of her book and looked up, and even

though I was glaring at my own feet in an attempt to create some sort of invisibility barrier, I could see out of the corner of my eye that she had seen me. I tensed myself, waiting.

But no. Bryce ducked her head down and twisted her shoulders away from me. She scrunched up her paper bag and crammed it into the backpack at her feet.

"Hey, Bryce?" It was out of my mouth before I could stop it.

"Oh, hi!" she said, doing a fairly credible job at surprise. Her little face turned pink.

"How . . . how are you?" I called out. There was about six feet in between our chairs.

"I'm good," she said, fiddling with her dance bag. She was trying to stuff her book inside it, but it was too full.

"We should be sitting in the sun," I said, pointing to the sun, like she might not know what I was talking about.

"I don't have any sunblock," she answered, solemnly. "And Mrs. Darya told us that if anyone got sunburn or tan lines she would take us out of *Dream*."

Mrs. Darya is the director of the company school. She was director when I was there too. She will probably be director of the company school until the apocalypse, and when there is nothing left on earth but cockroaches she will organize them into levels, assign them colored leotards, and make them feel insecure.

"Do you know what Mrs. Darya told me once?" I said, leaning forward in my chair so we were closer. Bryce scooted her chair toward mine.

"She called me into her office," I started, "and told me I needed to dress better. Not for class, mind you, but just for walking around. Just in my normal clothes."

"Why?" Bryce asked, round-eyed.

"She sat me down," I said, warming to the story. I've been telling this one for a decade. People request it at parties. "And she said, 'Kate, dear, you need to wear nicer street clothes. And more rouge. For class. Because you're plain, dear.' And then she took a moment and it was like she was actually suffering over how plain I was. Like it physically pained her. And then she shook her head and sighed and said, 'So very plain.'"

Bryce looked horrified. I realized that you kind of have to be on the safe side of adolescent agony to find this story funny. When I tell it at parties, people howl. Then they tell their own Darya or a similar ballet-school-sadist tale.

"But," Bryce said. "But you're so pretty!"

"Oh, no," I said. "I mean, that's sweet, but . . . anyway, my point is that you don't have to listen to everything Mrs. Darya says."

"So you didn't like, start wearing different clothes?" she asked.

Actually I did. I started borrowing Mara's clothes. And I wore more makeup.

"No," I told Bryce. "I was kind of a rebel. But I got into the company anyway so you see, it's more important that you be yourself."

"I hope I get in the company someday," Bryce said. "It's all I want."

She wants everything I have. I could see that. Of course she does. I want everything I have too.

"What are you reading?" I asked.

Bryce turned from pink to red.

"Oh, just . . . something. I . . ."

"What is it? I'm a reader too." I was using this silly voice like I was some sort of exceptionally kind person. Reluctantly, Bryce slid her book out of her bag so I could see the title.

Little Women.

I couldn't help smiling.

"I've read it before," Bryce defended. "When I was younger. I was just like, kind of in the mood for it today. Whatever."

Bryce looked nervously over her shoulder and I noticed a couple of company school girls clustered together a few tables away. Bryce's classmates, I figured from their ages. They were all looking at us. What is the collective noun for a group of ballet students? A pride of ballerinas? A threat of ballerinas? And here Bryce was, reading alone with very possibly a blueberry muffin stuffed in her bag. I picked up my things and sat on the other side of Bryce, shielding her from the threat of ballerinas.

"What kind of mood are you in?" I asked.

"Sometimes I wish I had sisters."

I felt a chunk of my heart break off. There must have already been a substantial tear, I think, for it to come apart so easily. Is there a single thing Bryce dreams of that would be as good in reality as it is in her dream? If only we could crawl inside our dreams and live there. Why can't I live inside my dream? Why couldn't Gwen, whose reality was even better than mine?

"It's a really good book, *Little Women,*" I said. "What part were you reading? What's happening now?"

"Um, it's the part where they go for a picnic with Laurie and the Vaughns and Mr. Brooke talks to Meg. And Jo . . ."

" . . . gets mad during the croquet game and they all play that game where they take turns telling a story," I finished.

"Yeah." Bryce nodded, all unembarrassed enthusiasm now. "And you can totally tell that Mr. Brooke is in love with Meg. I wish we all dressed like that still."

"Totally. Which girl do you like best?"

"I like Meg, but she just ends up getting married and having babies. I wish Amy became like, a really great painter. I mean, I'm happy that she ends up with Laurie but it's sad that she doesn't get to be a real artist."

It *is* sad. It's Jo who gets to have fulfillment as an artist. But only after she goes through great pain. Loneliness. Struggle. The death of her beloved sister Beth, who was just too delicate, just wasn't meant for this world.

"Is that one illustrated?" I asked, pointing to her copy.

"Yeah," said Bryce. "But they're not very good. I mean, they don't make any of the people look like how I imagine them."

"I hate that."

"Me too."

"Hey, I've got rehearsal now. I should get back."

"Me too."

Bryce and I walked together back to the studios. On the way, I tossed my uneaten muffin into the trash. Bryce pulled her paper bag out and threw it in too.

21.

Up way too early for the kind of day I have today, which won't end until about midnight and involves class, two long rehearsals, the premiere of *Look At Me,* and then a little champagne reception at which I must make some sort of cocktail-gowned appearance. I'll have to wear something of Gwen's. The five minutes of actual sleep I got last night were totally corroded by one of the two recurring dance/anxiety dreams I have. The other one is standard: I'm in my dressing room, naked, no makeup, hair not done, and I can hear the music for the ballet I'm about to dance playing. I'm late, I can't find the right pointe shoes, everything is taking forever, and I realize that I have no clue as to what the choreography is, I missed rehearsal, etc. The one I had last night is the odder but no less irritating one. I'm doing these amazing multiple pirouettes, seven, eight, nine turns, but my supporting leg is bent at the knee, so they aren't proper pirouettes. They don't count. I keep telling myself to PULL UP, PULL UP, STRAIGHTEN YOUR KNEE, but

I can't. I can't . . . quite . . . straighten it. It's a really horrible dream.

No coffee and so I threw on yesterday's sweatpants and T-shirt, Gwen's rain boots, and a bulky coat I found in her closet that probably belongs to Neil. On the way out the door I grabbed my iPod so I could block out all the shit that's in my head with really loud rock.

Outside of Zabar's I ran into Andrew.

The whole thing was terribly awkward. For one thing, I was exiting and he was coming in, and there was that homeless guy who likes to pretend that opening the door at Zabar's is his real job and who shakes his cup at you and shouts, "God bless you, ma'am, and have a beautiful day," in this highly antagonistic manner when you glare at him and insist on opening the door for yourself. So I was balancing my extra-large coffee and packets of Sweet'N Low and stuffing my wallet in my purse and lurching after the door in a fruitless attempt to preempt Homeless Guy, and Homeless Guy was mid-blessing/rebuke, and there, suddenly, was Andrew, resplendent in a business suit and looking perfectly composed.

"Oh," I said. "Oh. Wow. Huh. Hi." It just could not have been worse. I hadn't washed my face before coming out. I hadn't even brushed my teeth. Or combed my hair. Someone behind me said, "Excuse me," and I stepped back into Zabar's, knocking the Sweet'N Low off my cup and banging my elbow on the door.

"Careful," said Andrew mildly. God, I hate it when people say that after you do something clumsy. "Careful." How fucking smug is that? And what was he doing on this side of town in the morning? He must have had a sleepover with Miss New

Thing. I guess I should count myself lucky she wasn't with him, in some deluxe New York girl getup.

"So . . ." Andrew smiled. "What are you listening to?"

"What? Oh." I pulled my iPod earbuds out and looked blindly at the device. "You know. That song. By that band. You know, with the name I can never remember. It's got like, a number in it? And a verb? And something else? Four Dyspeptic Giraffes? Six Lugubrious Pencils? Ha-ha. Hahahaha."

One Garrulous Spinster.

"Ah," said Andrew.

"So what's up?" I tried to inhale while talking so my morning breath didn't waft out. "What are you doing here?"

"I thought I might get some coffee," Andrew said, in this new bland and slightly sarcastic tone. There was not a trace of feeling for me in his face. Even his sarcasm sounded indifferent. He looked incredibly handsome.

"Yeah, good." I nodded. "There's coffee to be had. Here. You've come to the correct . . ."

I seemed to have lost the ability to form nouns. I had no name for where we were. Andrew waited, raising his eyebrows slightly.

"Okay, see ya," I said, trying to move my hideous bulk around him.

"See ya," Andrew said, as if that was all the conversation he wanted to have with me. As if he had never loved me at all. Homeless Guy threw open the door for me.

"God *bless* you, ma'am, and have a joyous morning," he accused.

Back in Gwen's apartment I headed straight for the bathroom mirror. It was even worse than I had thought. Oily skin.

My hair hanging lank from a center part. Gray smudges under my eyes. Chapped lips. Plain. Very plain.

And I had forgotten to get more Sweet'N Low, so I had to drink coffee as bitter as I am.

After some ferocious cleansing, I stomped around the apartment trying to get everything I needed into a bag. I rifled through Gwen's closet, looking for something to wear tonight. This took time, as all her nicest things are covered with their own individual dress bags, so I had to unzip and peel back the second layer of dry-cleaning plastic to see what was what.

But this activity calmed me down. All of Gwen's hangers go in the same direction. All the clothes are arranged by color. Everything is hooked or buttoned or zipped and perfectly pressed. It's hypnotizing. It soothes the nerves. I get it, Gwen.

If I stayed there long enough, would I start to see the point of the masking-tape Xs too? Maybe I would make some of my own. What number did she say was like a rocking chair? Five.

5555555555555.

Rehearsal today for the Titania/Bottom sections of *Dream*. Yesterday I watched Anne-Marie and Tyler go through it, and I marked along in the back by myself because Roger had to be in another rehearsal. But it was good. It gave me an opportunity to really see what Marius was going for.

It's a moment of hilarity: Oberon and Titania have been fighting and Oberon decides to teach Titania a lesson. So he gets Puck to sprinkle love juice in her eyes and then he makes sure that the first person she sees upon waking is Bottom. Bottom is a local yokel who has wandered into the forest with his yokel posse and whom Oberon has naughtily transformed so that his head is now the head of a donkey. So, how funny.

Except when has it ever really been funny, watching a woman throw herself at an ass?

Love in ballet is as codified as everything else, so there are certain gestures, characteristic movements, that generally travel from one ballet to another. For example, a woman in love will almost always do the thing where her feelings of love overcome her and she has to run a few steps away from her partner and be in love all by herself for a few counts.

Anne-Marie, by the way, is really good at all this. She's the resident Beauty of our company. Physical beauty doesn't mean the same thing to us as it does to the rest of the world. Here, someone can have a hook nose, a sty in one eye, and half a head of hair, but if she's an incredible dancer we will all say, "Oh, she is gorgeous." But Anne-Marie is beautiful even by normal-person standards. She has a bouncy cascade of strawberry-blond hair and big brown cow eyes and adorable freckles on her chest and arms. No one can look demurely out from under false eyelashes like Anne-Marie, with the possible exception of *Sesame Street*'s Mr. Snuffleupagus. She doesn't walk around like that, though. She's a totally normal person and has kind of a crass sense of humor. She can be chatting away, chomping on some gum, "Oh my *gawd*, that's so funny I think I just *peed*!" and then—*poof!*—the music starts and she's more lyrical than lyricism, trembling with romance, goddess divine.

These two sides of Anne-Marie are perfect for Titania and I can see why Marius cast her. I would have too. And Marius made good use of all the classic ballet clichés in the Titania/Bottom pas de deux so it's almost a little satire of love.

If love weren't already a satire of itself.

"Is everyone just pretending to be in love?" I asked Roger, before we started rehearsal.

"I never pretend," he said, loftily, before donning his giant donkey head.

Claudette came in and we worked for an hour. By the end, I was enjoying myself very much, in a kind of grim, vengeful way. Claudette, who is normally all about steps, steps, steps, actually offered up some artistic advice. She told me, very gently, not to overdo it.

"I think it is more . . . it should be sincere, no? Otherwise, it might seem like Titania is being . . ."

"Sarcastic?" I offered.

"Yes," Claudette said, relieved. "Yes, it is looking, maybe, a little sarcastic."

"It's funnier if she really means it," I said.

"Yes."

"Or you could say it's more tragic if she really means it."

"Well . . ."

"I'll work on it," I assured her.

After "notes and fixes" rehearsal for *Leaves* I took a nap in my dressing room, which left me groggy and hungry, but by then it was too close to performance time to eat anything real. I went to the corps girls' dressing room and scrounged for candy. Someone offered me almonds. Someone else had dried prunes. "What's happened to all of you?" I joked. "This is pathetic. Who has M&M'S?"

I had better luck in the boys' dressing room.

I took a hot shower to warm up. I coiled my wet hair into a series of mini pancakes all over my head so it would be nice and flat for the Celebrity wig. Josie brought me the wig and skewered about four thousand pins into my scalp to make it secure. She did my makeup too, since I'm meant to look ultra glamorous and fabulous, and while she was shellacking away at my face, I thought through every step of my choreography.

It was a pleasant moment, preparing for a role I was about to dance, feeling excited and a little nervous. If only it could always be like this, I thought. And then, Wait. It *is* always like this. This is how it is.

A very nervous James stopped by to wish me *merde*. He also had a gift for me, a small and very beautiful antique silver hand mirror.

"You've been such a joy to work with," he said. "You're going to be just stunning."

We joked about the fake boobs, which got cut after yesterday's dress rehearsal. This would be a big night for him, and I realized that it was potentially a very good night for me too.

James left. I tried to imagine what the evening would be like if Gwen hadn't gone over the edge and everything got so twisted up. I tried to imagine what it would be like if none of the events of the past few months had happened and I were still living with Andrew and it was all going along like normal.

Strangely, none of these imaginings were appealing. I wished my neck didn't hurt and I wasn't a quasi drug addict, but wherever I'm going I don't really want to go back.

So where, then?

It's a funny thing, when everybody leaves the stage but you. *Look At Me*. Look at me? There's nothing else for anyone to look at.

I'm alone, but not really. There's a whole audience in front of me, witnessing my privacy, watching. It's meant to be terrifying for me—for my character, The Celebrity. Whoever she is.

Whoever she is, she is not a real woman, with a real history. She is not a replica of a real celebrity. She is not an assemblage of character traits: lost, insecure, vulnerable. She is not this red dress, these heels, this blond hair.

This is who she is. She is this movement here, these steps, this turn, this raising of this arm. It's a waste of time to think of oneself in any other terms. For what of us, what of reality, cannot implode, evaporate, contort, evade, disappear? But the body doesn't lie. At a certain point it's impossible to dance loneliness without feeling genuinely lonely.

For another minute it will all be mine. There is no other place in the world, no better way, no more powerful aphrodisiac than being gorgeously, achingly, perfectly lonely in front of two thousand people.

22.

Karine opened the door to Wendy Griston Hedges's apartment. She was wearing nurse's pants and a brightly colored blouse. I had only seen her sitting down. Standing up she was imposingly tall. She had to duck slightly to make it under the Venetian glass chandelier in the foyer.

I was expecting to go to the library, but Karine took me through the living room down the hallway to Wendy's bedroom. I snooped in there once or twice when I was her houseguest. There was a massive jewelry box filled with things I never saw her wear. I tried on a few rings before I got nervous.

Other than the library, I don't think Wendy was terribly comfortable in her own home either. Every time she turned on a lamp she would have to peer under the shade and inspect the mechanism. Her apartment is decorated with that waxy, shiny reproduction Louis XVI furniture you see in antique stores and wonder, Who buys that crap? Actually, some of it might be real Louis XVI. The only comfortable chairs are in the library, where we always had our tea on an elaborate Minton service.

Wendy's bedroom door was closed and Karine knocked softly on it. It was not until that moment—until Karine called out, "Meeses Hedges, I'm here with your friend, a' come to see you now"—that I took in the fact that something was definitely wrong, and that nurse's pants are usually worn by . . . nurses.

Wendy was propped up in bed.

When I had snuck into Wendy's bedroom years ago, it was decorated in the same marbled and filigreed style as the rest of the house. It was all still there, including a large oil painting, ornately framed, hanging across from the bed. But what was once a massive four-poster had been replaced with a single metal-railed hospital bed and there was a plastic upright tray next to it. And there was a . . . smell.

"Here you find me, lazing about in bed," said Wendy, faintly, struggling to sit up. "Karine, will you bring the porter's chair over for Kate?"

I helped Karine drag over this giant ridiculous canopied chair, upholstered in yellow silk. The seat was too low, and Wendy in her hospital bed hovered above me. Karine left to find some cushions.

"I did manage to get my wig on." Wendy patted her little brown cloche hairstyle. "Karine and I have a joke that she's going to get me some dreadlocks like she has. She's from Haiti, did she tell you? It helps me a great deal, knowing that. I complain much less. She lost her whole family."

"How are you . . . how, I mean . . . what . . ." I couldn't sit in the chair. I stood up and leaned against the metal bed rails, but Wendy shrank back a little into her pillow.

"I am not contagious," she said, as if I were the one recoiling from contact. "It's ovarian cancer. Or it began that way. It's spread, so now I suppose it is everything cancer. Like everything bagels, you know? Sesame, onion, poppy seed, cinnamon-raisin. I never liked those. Did you like them? You never ate anything when you lived here. I did notice that. You probably think I never noticed anything."

The sharp, distracted way she said this was so unlike Wendy's usual shy professorial manner of speaking that it took me a minute to understand what was going on. Wendy tapped out a staccato rhythm with her ring finger against the bed frame.

"You should sit down," she said.

Obediently, I sat on the edge of the yellow silk chair. Karine came in with an armful of sofa cushions.

"Maybe you should bring a phone book," Wendy ghost-giggled. "Poor Kate."

"I start the kettle for tea now," said Karine, peacefully. "I'll bring some nice tea for you and your friend."

"Oh, wonderful. Thank you, dear. I think when it comes we should go out on the terrace. Don't you think that would be nice?" Wendy asked me.

"Yes," I said. "Yes. Um. If you feel up to it?"

"It's actually very tiring, being in bed. It makes you feel as if you should be rested, and you're not, so that is fatiguing."

We watched Karine leave and then turned back to each other, nervously. Wendy tapped her ring against the bed again. I adjusted the slippery pillows underneath me.

"How long have you known?" I asked. This came out in the adult woman talking about issues voice, and I couldn't stand it. I couldn't stand that I too was buzzing on pharmaceuticals and couldn't focus, take in the moment properly. Time zigzagged.

"December," Wendy said. "I didn't go to my sister's in January, like I told you. I was here. Being excavated, as it were. I apologize for the subterfuge. But it was already stage four, so you see they do things, but it's only because they have to do something. It seems almost disproportionate, the things they do, but you're meant to let them do it all. And one does sort of hope. Well."

"Wendy." I tried to find my normal voice. "I am so sorry."

Wendy looked down at her lap, as if someone had just placed an amusing and slightly inappropriate gift there.

"I don't have very long," she said. "I'm sorry to say that to you. I wish there were another way of saying it, without saying it, if you know what I mean. I keep thinking of phrases. *Arma virumque cano, Troiae qui primus ab oris.* 'I sing of arms and a man, who first from the shores of Troy . . .' But of course that doesn't relate to my situation."

"Are you in pain?" I asked. "What can I do for you?"

Wendy brushed away the ribbons of the invisible gift in her lap and looked at me. Yes, I thought, recognizing it. Yes, you are in pain.

"That's a very ridiculous chair, isn't it," said Wendy. "I have to make arrangements for things, where everything should go. But they'll sell all of this together. You don't want that chair, do you?"

I looked down at the yellow silk arms of the chair which I did seem to be clutching with some force.

"We'll talk about that another time," said Wendy. "There's a little bit of time. I will see you again."

"Of course," I said. "I'll come, I'll come every day if you like."

"Oh, no, dear. Not every day. You have so much to dance. And you said you were injured too."

"It's nothing," I said quickly. The extent of its nothingness was shameful. What right had I to be doping myself to the gills? Detaching myself from what? From what?

"I don't think I'll be able to come and see you dance *Dream*." Wendy sat up a little straighter. "I wish I could. I wish I could see you dance so many things."

"It's okay." I leaned forward on my cushions, almost pulling the chair up with me. "No, no. It's okay."

"When I was a little girl," Wendy said, closing her eyes, "my father used to go into his study and listen to the baseball games on the radio. He would draw a grid on a piece of paper and he taught me how to keep score. I would mark it all down. K, for strikeout. F8 was a fly ball to center field. P6, a pop-up to the shortstop. I haven't thought of that in years. Oh, how I loved doing it."

For a second I saw in her face, which didn't look ill at all, a ghost of her childhood. Of a whole life, a whole person, about to go forever. I couldn't speak.

"I'll be thinking of you dancing," she said. "I'll be imagining how lovely you are."

She looked at me, with something like a plea on her face. I swallowed.

"It's too bad," I said, "that they don't air ballets on the radio. That way, you could follow along and keep score."

I switched into a sportscaster voice. "Titania successfully dances the first solo. A little wobbly on the pique turns, but nice tight fifth position on the bourrées. She makes it into the downstage left wing safely and now . . . it's Oberon, who's been having a rough season so far, let's see what he does tonight!"

"Yes, that's just what I mean!" Wendy said. "You understood me perfectly."

But I didn't understand. I don't understand anything.

Karine came in, not with Wendy's cumbersome silver tea service but with two mugs, tea bags hanging off the sides. I wanted to tell her that's not how we do it, Wendy hates teabags, but I was cowed by her air of competent authority. I could never do that. I could never pull back the covers and scoop a dying woman out of bed, set her gently on her feet, fold her arm under mine to help her walk.

"Oh, I've got my energy back," said Wendy, patting Karine on the arm. She walked by herself, upright and stately as she rarely was in . . . in what? In life?

Wendy made it to the terrace, stood in the sunshine. Her face, when she turned to look at me, was radiant and smooth, not the face of the woman I have known for the past ten years. It was the face of a woman I have never known.

Will never know, apparently.

When I left Wendy's I walked across the park. The path I took when I was a student, when none of what has happened had happened.

The other night I thought I wouldn't want to go back, but

now it's all I want to do. Or stay forever now, with things only as bad as they are, not worse. Not gone.

I can't imagine a Gwen returned who I could live with. And yet I also can't think of how she will ever be gone enough.

And Andrew. Of course Andrew left me for someone else. I gave him nothing. I gave him the shell. Now I can't even remember why it seemed so important to not need him.

Wendy said she is not gone yet. But she is evacuating, I could feel it. And she is afraid, I could feel that too.

I wanted to sit down on the grass. For what? To say to myself, I am sitting on the grass and grieving for my friend? I don't have the right to sit down. Not with all the time that I've wasted standing.

I went to the theater. Tonight I danced *Leaves Are Fading* for the first time. There is a synopsis of the ballet in the program, although in this case it's not necessary. It's simple. A woman walks on the stage and looks thoughtful. Men and women appear and dance, in groups, in pairs. The lights dim and the woman comes on again and walks across the stage, satisfied. The dances have been her memories, and they have been good, they have been filled with love.

In my dressing room I told myself that I would dedicate my performance to Wendy. I would offer it up to her as a gift, I would send her grace for wherever it is she is going next. Let her exit gently across the stage, satisfied.

But I couldn't hold on to that. Things kept getting in the way. I was fussing about my shoes, which felt a little too soft, so I changed them for a harder pair and those were a little too hard. I hadn't taken any Vicodin, so I was worried about seizing up with pain in the middle. I could tell in the opening that our

timing wasn't as good as it had been in dress, people were rushing, Marius would have a fit. And, at a certain point, my desire
to dance well was just simply my desire to dance well. I could
say that it was a desire to dance well for Wendy, but it wasn't
that. What I was thinking, in that strange way you can think
without words while you are dancing, think in glyphs, think
in numbers, was how stupid it is that any of us are here, living.
What an absurd game we play with ourselves, as if it mattered.
We are all mad, all insane, all deluded. It is all for nothing,
really, in the end.

The woman, at the end of *Leaves*, she shouldn't walk serenely
across the stage. That's sentimental drivel. She should run. She
should get off as quickly as she can, and not look back.

23.

I took Gareth's class today. As I was going to take Gareth's class
I said to myself, over and over, *I am going to take Gareth's class.*
Sentences are trenches you can take cover in. They are not
wildly comfortable. They are not bulletproof. But they can give
you the illusion of safety.

I am going to take Gareth's class today and here I am at the
place where Gareth's class can be taken.

There were a group of girls in the changing room. Teenagers, maybe fourteen, fifteen years old. One had her fingernails
painted yellow with blue daisies. A little Thai girl with plump
shoulders was chomping hard on a wad of strawberry gum.
The blonde had an angry dash of acne across both cheeks. A
thick-calved brunette dabbed the wrong shade of pink lipstick
on her lips.

The girls chatted, which meant I could listen to them and
stop repeating, *I am going to take Gareth's class.*

"Oh my *gah*, it took me like, forty-five minutes to get my hair up today."

"I love your hair."

"Elle's always like, I love your hair, I love your hair, and I'm like, please, it's a hot mess."

"I need Starbucks."

"I totally need Starbucks."

"I want that maple scone thing they have."

"Oh my *gah*, I was totally thinking the *same* thing. Like, *right* as you said it."

In the hallway outside of class, more students clustered in little groups on the floor or benches. I spotted two in the corner who, indignities of adolescence aside, had the imprint of serious dancers. Sleek hair, perfect bodies, the self-absorption of hungry animals. One of them pulled an elastic band out of her bag and stretched out her Achilles tendon. The other worked a pointe shoe between her hands, softening the box, flexing the sole. Achilles Tendon Girl looked up, saw me, tapped Pointe Shoe Girl with the side of her foot. They widened their eyes at each other, and one of them smiled tentatively at me.

"Hi," I said. Somewhat aggressively.

They looked a little startled.

The class before Gareth's finished and I took my spot by the window, trying not to gag on the haze of sweat. I looked out the window at Broadway. See how it all goes on, I said to myself. See how it all goes on. See how it. See how it. See how it all goes on.

Gareth tapped me on the shoulder.

"Darling," he said, giving me a kiss on the cheek.

He is a kind man. His T-shirt smelled like Tide.

"So, I've a friend in town from Stuttgart and he got tickets to opening night of *Dream*," Gareth explained. "But I want to see your Titania too. So I'll come back."

"Oh!" I said. "Oh, gosh. You don't have to. I mean, it's no big deal, really."

"This is your season," Gareth said.

"No."

"Yes."

"Well, by default, maybe."

Gareth put his hands around my throat and pantomimed strangling me.

"I got standing room for *Look At Me*. You broke my heart. And *Leaves* the other night? I've never seen you give more onstage."

Gareth looked at me expectantly. What would Kate say? Oh, yes.

"You should have been there opening night," Kate jokes to Gareth. "I think I actually gave birth."

"That's my girl." Gareth laughs. "Diffidence does not become you, darling. You're not going to turn into one of these head-case dancers, are you? That would be too tragic."

"Not me," I said, as if in horror. Tragic? I don't get to be tragic.

Gareth nodded. Over his shoulder I saw Klaus and Maya entering class, and, right behind them, David, who spotted me and pointed to the space at the barre next to mine, claiming it.

"See, we're all needing your class today," I told Gareth.

"Only by default," he mocked, over his shoulder. "People must have overslept Wendell's class."

A few more members of the company filed in. Rochelle, Gillian, Tyler. People probably had slept in.

Except for me. I just couldn't get out of bed. Mostly because I was repeating the phrase "I can't get out of bed" over and over. This is pretty much how I've been doing everything for the past week. First I say, "I can't do this class/rehearsal/performance," over and over until it's time to do it and then I somehow do it. A second performance of *Leaves*. A second performance of *Look At Me*. I didn't think I could do them until I was onstage, and then they were over too quickly.

Before I left Wendy's apartment, I gave Karine my cell phone number and asked her to call me, anytime, if there was any news. Yesterday she called to tell me that Wendy was in the hospital, but should only be there for a day or two. She suggested that I visit once Wendy is back home. There was not, she told me, so very much time.

"Is she in pain?" I asked.

"I can give her morphine for this pain," Karine said. "I tell her that she does not have to be strong, now. She must be easy."

"What about her family?" Wendy has a sister, she has nieces and nephews. She has a couple of cousins.

Karine sighed.

"They are asking her if they should come, but of course she says no. She does not want to trouble nobody. This is how it is, for some people. But her friend, from Greece, she does not ask. She just comes. She will be here tomorrow. I will call you. Maybe Friday? This is the time to just come. Not to ask."

My mother called me. Gwen is doing better. She is on a different medication. She was having trouble moving well, her joints were stiff, possibly from the previous medication, possibly from muscular atrophy from not dancing.

"Is she in pain?" I asked.

"Your father can explain it better. Something about dopamine and if you have too much, that's bad. But it also helps a person's body move fluidly. So if you take away the dopamine, it might hurt their, what do you call it?"

"I don't know. Grace?"

"Something like that. I'd like to see her get off medication entirely."

"How can that be the goal?" I asked. "You wouldn't say that to a diabetic. You wouldn't say, 'Well, the goal is to get you off insulin.'"

"The new medication is much better," Mom said. "She's taking class now, with the Grand Rapids Ballet. I think that's helping more than anything. Some normalities!"

"Well, that's good," I said. I couldn't picture any of this. I tried imaging Gwen doing better under new medication, or even a Gwen who would consent to *taking* medication. A Gwen chemically engineered to be normal. It was like having a dream where you know who someone is but they don't look at all like themselves.

"Now, let's see," Mom chirped. "You've got two more weeks left of the season?"

"About that, yeah."

"And so then you have six weeks off . . ."

"Yeah."

I've been avoiding thinking about the break. I should've tried to book myself some guest artist gigs or something. What the hell was I going to do? Gwen and I usually went home for a week when we had the long break. Andrew and I had talked about going to Paris, seeing Keith play in the French Open.

"I should probably come there, right? If Gwen is okay with that. You probably want me to come there?"

"We can talk about it when the time comes," my mom said.

"That's almost now, though," I said, feeling pinned somewhere in my rib cage.

"So, what's new in *your* life?" Mom asked.

I flailed about on my pin and I kept talking even after I knew Mom's interest was gone. I didn't say the thing she was wanting to hear. If she was wanting. If any of us knows what it is we want anymore.

Keith called me. He had to pull out of the tournament in Madrid because of a strained gastrocnemius. He wants to be ready for Rome, and then the French Open. He's frustrated. Clay is his surface, a chance to boost his ranking. He can't be injured for Roland Garros.

"Are you in pain?" I asked.

"Nah. It's more a question of like, holding up. And I don't want it on my mind, you know. I don't want to be thinking about it."

"So maybe you should totally rest before the French?"

"It's like, a mind thing. I have to stay mentally tough, you know? I think of you guys a lot."

"What guys?" I asked.

"You and Gwen. It's this thing I'm working on with Gary. We're collecting like, images of heroism. Watching all these tapes."

Gary is Keith's coach. Gary is way more intimate with my brother than I am. But then, I've always had Gwen.

"So I was telling Gary, remember when I came to New York and saw you guys in *Swan Lake* that one time?"

"Years ago, you mean?"

"Yeah. At the end of your thing, you held this pose, and Dad had given me the binoculars so I could see really close. And you were both just like, totally drenched in sweat. Standing on one toe with the other leg all up. It looked fucking hard! And then I put the binoculars down and it was like—*bam!*—it looked easy. Like, no one else watching would know that you were trying hard."

"Oh. Huh."

"I always tell people like, 'Yeah, my sisters are ballet dancers, and that's like an extreme sport, you know?'"

"I'm really proud of you, Keith," I said, trying to concentrate. "You know that, right?"

Keith laughed a little bit at this. It was Dad's laugh, the one he gives after he puts down his violin and you tell him how amazing he just played.

"I was going to ask Mom and Dad to come," he said. "You know, to Roland Garros. I know it's France and everything and Dad is working, but I kind of . . . I kind of wanted them to come."

"Did you ask them?" I always assumed that Keith was like Gwen and me in this respect, so totally into his performance in a private way that it didn't much matter who was watching.

"I feel bad, 'cause you know . . . Gwen and everything."

"Have you talked to Gwen?" I held my breath, waiting.

"Just stupid stuff. Jokes. Is she really okay?"

I shook my head, knowing he couldn't see this.

"You there?" Keith's voice sounded really far away. Probably because I had dropped the phone onto the bed and was sort of swaying over it.

"Kate?"

I knelt on the bed and curled myself around and in between everything on it.

"I'm here," I said, picking up the phone. "Listen. Keith. Don't worry about Gwen. She's going to be fine. You just concentrate on you right now. This is your time, buddy."

"Yeah. Maybe. Yeah. It's kind of weird, right, because you have to seize the moment, but you also gotta be *in* the moment."

"It's better when you're just doing it," I agreed. "The hard part is all the stuff before you're doing it, and all the stuff after you're doing it."

"Right," he says, sounding relieved. "That's what I mean."

"Life," I say, clarifying.

"Yeah," Keith agreed.

But if life is what can be called the time you spend preparing for the event, and then dealing with how the event went, then what would you call the event itself? Is that not life? Is that not the best part? Except sometimes, of course, it isn't. Sometimes it's the place where you injure yourself. Sometimes it's the horrible mirror of your inadequacy. Sometimes it's just sweating and running from one side of the stage, or the court, to the other, trying not to fall down, or start screaming.

"Life," I said again, uncertainly.

"Fucking life, man!" Keith laughed.

David dumped his bag down behind the barre and gave me a kiss. I thought, I can't possibly make small talk with David.

"Isn't today a day off for you?" I asked.

David pulled on an extra T-shirt.

"Yeah, but I had yesterday off. We went to Home Depot. And Bed Bath & Beyond. And then I played Princesses with Jayla. Which was cool because I got to lie on the couch and just wave a wand at Jayla every few minutes. Thank god she's still too young to be telling friends at school that Daddy is a Fairy King. Anyway, you're not on tonight, are you?"

I shook my head.

"What are you doing today?"

I shrugged.

"Awesome," said David.

Class began. And IN, IN, IN, and OUT. And IN, IN, IN, and OUT.

There were enough company members that Gareth had us all go as one group in the center. We were celebrities there in the dingy studio, sweat fogging the windows, the sounds of taxis and buses from two floors below punctuating the pianist's plonk-plonk-plonking of the stuff all accompanists play for class. When I wasn't working, I watched those two serious students, who were both very good. Like whippets: lean, muscled, focused. Watchful. I glanced over at the group of girls from the dressing room, who weren't bad, but who were soft and sloppy. The little Thai girl was a turner, though. Strawberry-gum girl had nice feet. Oh, what will become of us all?

David, Klaus, and Tyler showed off—for one another, for the four or five other men in class who will never jump like they do, for the girls, who all gawked. Klaus tied a bandanna around his blondness. David had his eyes half closed. Tyler removed three layers to reveal a Ramones T-shirt. Gillian touched me on the shoulder and we whispered a few exchanges, I said something funny as I always do, she laughed soundlessly. Gillian had a thin gold bracelet on her wrist. I think she always wears it. I'm not sure. I've danced with her for six years and I can't tell you. The universe is filled with things I've never noticed.

The crazy lady with the rainbow leg warmers was there today too, Kleenex poking out of the V of her leotard. I smiled at her but she did not smile back. The features of her face were drawn tightly up and out, and she jerked woodenly across the floor, a stringless marionette. She was once a little girl. We were all little girls once.

Leaving, I saw the students pulling on pairs of identical Ugg boots. They would go get Starbucks, and that scone thing they were talking about. It's totally possible to walk completely away from dance and go get Starbucks. Not everybody can, but it is possible. Preferable? I can't say. I didn't envy them their freedom, though. None of us is getting out of here alive.

I was early to meet Mara at Verdi Cafe. Actually, Mara and Roger. I asked Mara if it was okay if he joined. Partly because Mara's been looking at me in this worried way all week and also because I needed the extra voices. The more noise, the better.

On that note, I took half a Vicodin. It's not so much that I need it for performance, now. In fact, it's making me too paranoid and nervous to dance on it. I need it more to start my day, to occupy space in my brain until I can get to performance, and then to make artificial chatter with me after so I don't have to go back to Gwen's alone. I thought I wouldn't need it for meeting Mara and Roger and all, but it was raining, they were late, I didn't have my iPod, and I can't read now. Obviously everything in the newspaper is awful but even a stray sentence from a *New Yorker* left on the adjacent table—*When he came home from work, he would make himself a snack and eat it by himself in the kitchen, standing up*—I mean, what the hell? Stop right there! You have already plunged me into a fathomless gloom from whence there is no solace and no return, an endless twilight of loss and pathetic aspirations, a forever-empty kitchen where sad little snacks are patiently, lovelessly eaten.

Even imaginary nice sentences: *The sun shone. Beauty is all around. My sister is my greatest inspiration.* Isn't there something inherently heartbreaking about all of those?

"Sorry, sorry." Mara bustled in, dropping her bag on the empty seat. Her coat was wet. She folded up an umbrella.

When it rains, Mara's hair goes into these mad tendrils, all around her face. She looked like a Victorian paper doll, round faced and ringleted, pink cheeked.

"Roger's late too," I said. "What busy lives you all lead. I've been sitting here for ten minutes twiddling my thumbs. Twiddling, twiddling away. It's like tweeting, only more existential. Nothing actually gets sent."

Mara smiled indulgently, but only with her mouth. From the deliberate way she was handling her umbrella, rearranging the silverware, placing her palms against the menu, I could see we were on the verge of a talk. I thought we pretty much covered things at the Russian Baths, but apparently not.

"First off, we are ordering you some food," she said.

"I was just thinking we should eat," I said, talking fast, not really minding what I was saying. "I was thinking about salmon, you know, lox and bagels. I had never heard of lox in Michigan. It seemed so exotic when I came here. The most exotic we ever got with food was port-wine cheddar cheese at Christmas. It comes in like, a tub. It's fucking delicious. Crackers and port-wine cheddar cheese."

I moved Mara's umbrella out of range so I wouldn't have to look at the little metal rods sticking out from the fabric. Those things could just fly out and hit you in the eye at any time.

"You need to eat," Mara said. I could feel the overture to Adult Women Conversation beginning.

"*We* need to eat!" I grabbed the menu. "We're both completely gaunt. It looks better on you, though. I look like a slightly aerobicized Jane Eyre. But you need vitamins and shit for baby making! Hey, did I tell you I ran into Andrew?"

Mara shook her head. If I had managed to stop shrieking and rolling my eyes, it could almost have passed for typical gossip between girls. I needed Roger to show up though, make it a party, interrupt me, tell bigger, more embarrassing stories. My right leg thrummed up and down, under the table.

"Oh god, Mara, it was so ridiculous. It was early in the morning and I was coming out of Zabar's—the coffee shop part? And I had my iPod on and he was all, 'What are you listening to?' And I was a complete mess. No makeup. Morning breath. And I . . . I . . . well, actually I guess it doesn't really matter at all."

I grabbed a fork and tapped the table with the tines. No, none of it mattered. That was good, actually. If none of it mattered then you didn't have to feel bad about a sad man making a sad snack for himself in a sad kitchen.

"No, come on," Mara said, putting her hand over mine and the fork. "Of course it matters. You haven't seen him since the breakup. You're allowed to be upset, Kate."

"I mean it in a really positive way." I turned the fork so the tines were sticking into my palm. "It's actually really liberating. Nothing matters except what you decide to make matter and so I could just say—*poof*—I don't matter to Andrew and I don't and it's all nothing. And he doesn't matter to me. And all the little awkward clumsy little mechanical machinations? All those things we do in our minds? None of those matter either. Especially those. So it's not a sad thing like, 'Oh boo-hoo, the world has no meaning, what a drag,' but more like, 'Hey! Nothing matters! So I can just . . .'"

I used my free hand to make a gesture.

"You can just . . . what?" Mara asked.

I guess my gesture needed program notes. It could have been the gesture for the end of existence, or it could have been the gesture for carrying on. Luckily the waitress arrived.

Under Mara's stern watch, I ordered a Cobb salad. "Bacon!" I said, defensively. "Blue cheese! I'm like a wild woman here."

"Are you sleeping at all?" Mara lifted my hand off the fork, turning it over.

"Read my palm," I said, thrusting my hand up. I did it a little too fast though, and with too much strength. I almost hit her nose. I think I was almost trying to hit her. She dropped my hand.

"Sorry, too much coffee." I shoved my hand under my leg for safety.

Mara bit her lip and took a breath. She was going to be careful with me. She had probably already talked over "what she was going to say" with Mike. I could imagine them tucked up in bed, Mike with one hand on the remote, muting CNN while Mara explained how she was worried about me. A memory surfaced, Mara and I in the apartment before Gwen came, lying on our backs in the bed with our feet in the air, laughing about something. That kind of laughter where you laugh and laugh and then stop and then start laughing again and then it almost seems fake that you're laughing so hard, but then it becomes real again.

"Wendy is dying of cancer," I said.

"Oh my god." After a moment of comprehension, Mara's eyes filled with tears. I watched this jealously, greedily, guiltily.

"Oh my god, how terrible. When did you find out?"

"Last week," I said. "She's been sick for a while, but I didn't know. I mean, I haven't seen her for a little bit. She told me she was visiting her sister, but I think she just didn't want me to see her when she was going through chemo. But the chemo didn't work, I guess. So it's the end." I made the gesture again. Yes, it was definitely the gesture for dismissal, for exiting Stage Left or Stage Right, whichever wing you could throw yourself into.

"Kate, I am so, so sorry." Mara moved as if to touch me, but I was sitting on both my hands, and it was awkward. She had to half get out of her chair to hug my shoulder. Bones embraced bones. She knocked over the fork, which clattered to the tiled floor horribly, as if it were a thousand forks. Bending down to retrieve it, I considered seriously the notion of staying under the table. It took everything I had to come back up.

"Thank you," I said, as if Wendy's dying were a thing that was happening to me. "I didn't really want to bring it up because, you know . . . what do you say after that?"

Mara shook her head.

"Is she . . . ?"

"What? In pain? Is it better or worse to be in pain when you die?" I forced myself to let go of the fork. "It's like you want to say, 'Oh, she's not in pain and she had a good life,' but then isn't it better, in some way, if the person *is* in pain, and *hasn't* had a very good life, because then they get released. It might look like she's had a good life, because so many people have just horrific circumstances, you could spend your life in total squalor, running from drugged-out African warlords and starving to death, so who's going to cry over a Park Avenue heiress making herself a little snack in her kitchen, all alone?"

"You can cry about both those things," Mara said, frowning, trying to keep up with me as I crashed about the stage, groping for the wings. "One doesn't mean the other isn't . . . just as sad. In its own way."

"I know," I said, because I wasn't making much sense. "It shouldn't have this big justification, anyway. Death. You shouldn't have to make grand statements about it. We don't even know what it is, right? Except it's not this." My eyes circled the room. An old woman was vigorously shaking out an umbrella at the front of the restaurant. The cashier was shoving a receipt onto a metal spike. A waitress was taking a giant white frosted cake topped with strawberries out of the glass display case. There were playbills and magazines and newspapers in a pile on top of the piano in the corner. Two gentlemen, one bald, one not, were eating sandwiches by the window, identi-

cal Barnes & Noble plastic bags hanging off their chair posts.
People, other people. Tables. Posters on the wall. A crumpled
paper napkin on the floor. Glass containers of brown sugar,
white sugar, fake sugar. So many spoons. An EXIT sign, lit up
in green. GO.

"Kate," Mara said.

"Yeah?"

But it wasn't what I wanted. Sympathy. Understanding. Or
whatever Mara was offering. I didn't want to be scolded either.
Told I was being selfish, melodramatic, that my indiscriminate
drug use had to stop. I didn't want my perspective altered, or
my spirits lifted. I didn't want to eat Cobb salad.

Roger walked through the door, drenched and looking thoroughly irritated.

"Ugh." He tossed his bag on the floor with a wet *thwonk* and
threw himself into a seat. "I hate rain. I hate it! This place better have cheeseburgers with fries or you bitches are in trouble.
Cover me now. I am not sitting here in these wet pants." Roger
took a pair of sweatpants out of his bag and whipped them
under the table.

"Poor kitten." I reached over with my napkin and blotted his
face. "Poor soggy puppy." Keep making noise, I prayed, laughing. Bang drums. Clamor and ring bells for I cannot stand to
hear the tired beating of this almost heart. Get me to the event
that is neither before nor after. The event that isn't life.

24.

To dose, or not to dose, that is the question. That's another play, though. About a prince who goes mad. Or is pretending to be mad and then gets confused and really does go mad. You can see how that could happen quite easily.

I was standing in my dressing room in my Helena costume when my phone beeped a text message arrival. I was so convinced it was Gwen, and I felt such relief, and such anger, that I almost didn't pick up the phone. How dare she, after all this time, just fucking text me? I snatched up the phone.

SPRINT222freedownloadforyourphone!

I swallowed a Vicodin, to punish myself.

Marius called us all onstage before the performance. He said things. I wasn't worried about how I would dance. Klaus was excited. His eyebrows were dark with liner, his blondness gelled into a quiff. There were flowers from him in my dressing room. The note attached said, "To the sexy librarian, *merde* and thank you, from the captain of the football team." I was confused until I remembered describing our characters like that to him about a hundred thousand years ago. In Klaus's dressing room is a copy of Harold Bloom's *Shakespeare: The Invention of the Human* and a DVD of WrestleMania. The card attached to them says, "Dear Klaus/Demetrius: for the development of your duality with love from Kate/Helena." Just before getting to the theater tonight I remembered to pick up a little bouquet of tea roses for Bryce. Knowing that she would probably keep the card, that it would mean something to her, I threw away several attempts before settling on "Have fun tonight, Bryce. You will be a beautiful Fairy in this Dream. Kate."

After Marius finished, the stage cleared out a bit. Klaus asked me if there was anything I wanted to run. "I think we should just do it," I said. "I think we're good." Klaus nodded. He trusts me. I sipped water and swung out my hips. Klaus did push-ups in the wings. My feet were cold, too cold. I tried to warm them up, doing a quick series of relevés at the barre. I could feel the floor underneath the tips of my pointe shoes. You're supposed to feel the floor. You want to. When you're a student, feeling the floor is painful and you pack the toes of your pointe shoes with padding. In the old days they used lamb's wool. Now they have these sort of gel cushions you can put in there. I used to cut off the tips of thin socks. As you get older, you need stuff like that less. You just use tape, or maybe half a rectangle of a paper towel, folded over the toes to absorb sweat.

Of such things is my life composed. I am constrained by

layers, hooks and eyes and tights and hairpins and satin and ribbons and music that I count, under my breath.

My hands have small discs of calluses at the base of each finger, from holding on to a barre all my life. When I released the barre, my hands smelled like metal.

In the wings, the schoolchildren were lining up. You have never in your life seen such straight backs. Translucent wings, stiff with wire, jutted out behind downy shoulder blades. Someone whispered, "Hi." I looked down. Stage makeup had swallowed Bryce's heart-shaped face. "Hi," I whispered back. I took her small hand in my metal one. There was a little ripple in the line as the girls looked back at us. Over the top of Bryce's head I saw Mara, backlit from stage lights, screwing her pointe shoes into the rosin box. Mara also had wings, grown-up wings, mother wings. "*Merde*," I said to Bryce, because that is what dancers say to one another. When the fairies ran onstage I stepped into the wings to watch Bryce. I wanted very badly for her to be good. Bryce turned in place, ran, dropped to one knee. I saw her eyes quickly check her position in line, making sure she was equidistant from the fairies beside her. She straightened a leg out in front of her and bowed over her foot, toe pointing, wings straight up in the air. Her foot was a perfect arch, her thin hands graceful over it. She popped back up and then down again, over and over, right on the music. Her face was alight, alight, alight.

And then I was onstage. I threw myself at Klaus, who rejected me, so funny! I fell asleep, dejected, on a forest floor, so sad! I awoke and found two men were now in love with me, so confusing! I got in a fight with a girl, so entertaining! I got another dose of flower potion just in time, and then my love loved me back, so sweet! So satisfying! So enchanting!

Then—*pop*—it was over, and I went back to my dressing room. What now? What now? Luckily I had a drug for now.

There was a little gathering happening on the mezzanine. A champagne toast. It was packed because the student fairies and their parents were invited and of course they were all there. I grabbed a flute of champagne off a tray, looked for Marius.

Abby flagged me down and shuttled me over to three tables where posters of *Dream* were spread out. The photo shoot was done months ago. Manuel Ortega as Puck, all burnished-copper sinews, flying over the heads of Gwen as Titania, cradling Roger with Bottom's donkey head on. Next to each poster was a black Magic Marker. It's a souvenir, for the students, to get posters signed by the cast. Presumably they will take them home and hang them on their walls until such time as they have ceased to Dream of *Dream*. How long will this take?

I signed my name. A big swirly *K* and smaller, delicate *a-t-e*. Another swirly *C* and tiny *r-a-n-e*. I held myself back from forging Gwen's signature underneath her left foot.

"Kate?"

Bryce's mother, Jane.

"Congratulations," Jane said, reaching as if to touch me on the elbow and then not doing it. "You were so fabulous," she said. "I'm in awe."

I made the gesture for modesty.

"What a fantastic production," Jane enthused. "Just enchant-ing. And so funny! Especially the things for you and your part-

ner, and the Hermia and Lysander. That's a new partner for
you, isn't it?"

"Klaus," I said. "He's new to the company. I don't know that
we'll get matched up outside this, though. I'm too tall for him.
He's great though, isn't he?"

"Well, you're great together. And he's gorgeous!" Jane
winked conspiratorially.

"Did Bryce have a good time?" I asked, trying not to too
obviously look around Jane for Marius.

"Oh god." Jane fluttered her hand again. "I think so. It's
all become so . . . serious for her all of a sudden. I miss the
time when we could give her like, ballet slippers for her charm
bracelet. A ballerina music box. I mean, I'm thrilled for her
that she's having this experience, but it's also a little . . . God, I
sound like such a *mom*."

I made the gesture for empathy, although it's only Bryce's
position that I've experienced.

"You have been so great with her," Jane said. "She just
thinks you're the most incredible person on the planet. And the
flowers? She's putting them in the car, now, so they won't get
crushed. I think we might have to bronze them for her."

"We hang them upside down," I explained. "So they dry
out. That's what my sister and I always do. Even when they
are dead, they'll keep their shape. They'll be these like, perfect
little dead things."

Jane looked a little alarmed, as well she might.

"I haven't done anything special," I said, trying to lighten
the mood. "We've just chatted a few times. I like her."

"It makes a difference." Jane shook her head. "Just your
noticing her. She's had a problem lately, with self-confidence.

I guess that's why I'm a little worried. About the dancing. It's so intense. It puts such unreasonable stress on—" Jane broke off, shook her pretty head ruefully. "God! Two glasses of champagne and I'm explaining the stress of being a dancer to an actual dancer. Arrrgh!"

My mind leapt far ahead, and also off to the side, and on the diagonal.

"Well, Jane," I said. "There are girls who take ballet class and then go get the maple scone thing at Starbucks. And there are girls who don't."

"The maple scone?" Jane puzzled it out. "Oh, discipline, you mean? But that's sort of my point. There's no reason why any of these girls shouldn't eat whatever they want. It's hard enough when you're just a regular woman to feel good about your body—"

"I don't mean discipline." How does anyone ever explain anything? "I ate all kinds of shit when I was a student. I mean talent. Real talent. I don't mean being good, or really good. I mean being gifted. I guess every parent wants to think their kid is gifted, but actually, pretty much nobody's kid is gifted."

"I'm really not that kind of parent," Jane protested.

"Yeah, but Bryce probably is gifted."

Jane bit her lip.

"I can't totally tell," I said. I knew I should stop talking to Jane, but the Vicodin and champagne had me all revved up and I couldn't find my verbal brakes. "At her age, it's mostly about having facility for movement. Which is totally rare, by the way. You can take a million dance classes and never have it. And then there's the right body, which she obviously has. How tall is your husband?"

"Oh, um, about five eleven."

"She's not tall for her age, though." I found the conversation technically interesting, which was a distraction from the collision I was about to have with my own head. "That's good. If nothing drastically changes, she should be okay." I looked at Jane's cleavage, which, in her wrap dress, seemed fairly substantial. Of course that might be fake, or padded. But she didn't appear to have wide hips or anything bad like that.

"Well, however it turns out will be okay with me," Jane said, a little defensively. Poor thing, I'd made her hunch her shoulders forward and suck in her stomach. "I'm certainly not . . . invested in her becoming a ballet dancer."

"Sure."

"If she really loves it, I'll always be supportive," Jane said, hastily.

"Love chooses you too, though." I spotted Marius's head in the corner, surrounded by patrons and admirers. "You don't say, 'I am going to love this.' It just happens."

"But you must really love it, to do what you're doing," Jane insisted. "I mean it doesn't seem possible that you could work so hard and give up so much without really loving it."

"What am I giving up?" Stop, I told myself. Stop it.

"No, no." Jane again almost took my elbow. Was she afraid I would break at any normal human contact? Does she know something I don't know? "I don't mean . . . give up," Jane said. "It's a wonderful thing, what you're able to do. I just mean . . . well, you had to make sacrifices, right?"

"Yeah, but I didn't make them because I loved dancing. I made them because . . . because . . ." I looked around for someone to rescue me from the conversation. Gwen, behind me on the poster, hugged an ass.

"You were meant to do this," Jane interjected smoothly. "I get that. And obviously, it was all worth it, because you have this wonderful career. But there's no telling whether Bryce will have that opportunity. And if she gives everything up to pursue dance, and it doesn't happen for her . . ."

"Then what?" Somewhere, my sister was battling invisible demons. Somewhere, Wendy was acknowledging that visible demons had won. And there Jane was, anticipating heartache like it was a thing you could avoid. And there I was, not knowing the difference between visible and invisible, demonic, angelic, winning, losing.

"We just want her to have every opportunity available to her," Jane said.

"You're trying to cheat it." I was tired. I needed to go. Somewhere. Else. "You can't take it back now. It could happen that she succeeds as a dancer and she still wants to kill herself. My point is it's too late, Jane. You had her. You brought her into this world, which is mostly suffering. She's going to be in pain no matter what, and you can't do anything about it."

Jane looked at me like I had slapped her, which I guess I sort of had, but it seemed important she get some correct information. Wake up, lady.

"Maybe one day you'll understand what it's like . . ." Jane said, clearly trying to keep her voice level. "To love someone and want to protect them."

"Maybe one day you'll understand what it's like," I said, "to try to do that and fail."

I set my champagne glass down and started to walk away from Jane, but now it was Bryce coming toward me, followed by Mr. Five Eleven. Shit.

Bryce looked fragile, in her blue dress. It's not that I don't get it, Jane. I can barely look at your daughter's exposed arms, so unmarked, so pale, without wanting to cover them up. Bryce had a rose tucked into her ponytail.

"I just put your bouquet in the car," she explained. "So it wouldn't get hurt. But see, I put one in my hair."

"Beautiful," I said. I looked up and Bryce's dad was looking over my shoulder at Jane. Probably reading her face and trying to decode what he should be doing. Snatching his child up and running away from the mean, nasty ballerina?

"They have a TV monitor in our dressing room," Bryce said. "But I couldn't really watch you do Helena. But I know you were perfect. And when you dance Titania, I'll be onstage with you!"

"Well, don't get so busy watching that you forget your moves," warned the dad. Jane moved around me to join her family. I felt Bryce's embarrassment, Jane's embarrassment. My own.

"This. Is my husband. Steven." Jane introduced him to me without meeting my eyes. Steven, guy-like, oblivious, shook my hand.

Bryce moved next to me.

"Is it okay," she asked shyly, "if my dad takes our picture together? Dad, do you have my phone?"

Jane looked like she might throw up.

And just at this moment, Marius appeared, with Abby in tow.

"Ah, picture time," he said. "Perfect. They want one with me, and a member of the company, and a student. May I enlist you two?"

And so Jane and Steven watched as the company photographer took a picture of the three of us, Bryce in between me and Marius, like she was our daughter. Abby entered Bryce's name in her BlackBerry. "It would be for the school website," she told them. I could feel Bryce vibrating from the attention. Marius thanked her, in his best courtly manner, for being in his production.

I glanced over at Jane's husband. He probably just lost his daughter to Marius in like, that exact second. No "Your moves were spectacular" from him will mean as much as anything Marius says to her for at least the next seven years. The love we have is never as desirable as the love we want.

"Satisfied?" I asked Marius.

"With you?" He smiled. "Yes."

Bryce smiled at Marius, smiled at me, a mini victim of Stockholm syndrome. But I saw Bryce's face onstage tonight. She didn't even know how happy she was. You only know that kind of joy by its absence. And sometimes even when the curtain falls and the audience goes home and so do you, the perfume of that joy will linger. Like dead but still perfect roses.

25.

I took Wendell's class this morning. I just couldn't face Gareth and his approval and expectations and kindness and all. I needed something unforgiving and cold and critical.

Wendell gave me a nod of acknowledgment as I took a place at the barre. I couldn't have my usual spot in the corner by the window, because it was already occupied by Mariya Orekhova. She was a guest artist with our company a few years ago, and then went back to the Kirov. I think I exchanged about four sentences with her during her entire tenure with us, which is probably about three more than anyone else did except for the other Russians in our company. There are Russians, and then there are Russian ballerinas from the Kirov. Just looking at Orekhova, her ridiculously attenuated limbs and her icy, impassive face, made me feel fat and junky and clumsy. I watched her pull her leg to her ear (or rather, her leg just went there of its own accord, her hand merely along for the ride) and flex and point her remarkable feet. On another person this would look like stretching. On Orekhova it looked like she was issuing a threat. I massaged my neck. Wendell came up behind me.

"Pain?" he said.

"I'm doing something wrong," I said. "I keep hurting it."

"I'll watch," he said crisply, moving away.

About halfway through barre, he approached me again and stabbed at my collarbone with two fingers.

"Too far forward," Wendell said. I tried to bring my upper body back.

"Too far back!" Wendell shouted. "Don't exaggerate."

I stopped doing the combination in order to try to find the right position.

"Not forward, not back," Wendell said.

The combination ended, so now we had an audience.

"Just stand like a normal person. If you can."

Wendell smiled around at the class so everyone would know he was "being funny," and there were the usual sycophantic twitters.

I tried standing like a normal person.

"Fine, then just keep that, but dance," said Wendell, to another appreciative murmur of his wit. I glanced over at Mariya Orekhova, who raised one of her alabaster arms in a queenly gesture, turned her head, looked in the mirror to note blandly her own magnificence, and then turned back to the barre.

Why am I here? I thought. *I should leave.*

Except that Wendell was sort of right. I could feel the subtle adjustment work something different in my back. *Stop caring,* I told myself. *It doesn't make a difference.*

During center, Mariya passed by me, did a double take, smiled, and kissed me on both cheeks. I remembered Roger's joke that you could tell Mariya was a robot because if you got really close to her you noticed that she had no smell whatsoever.

Gwen, when I repeated this to her, laughed, but then asked, "Why do you think she's a robot?"

"Well, you know, because it's sort of alien, her dancing. She's so freakishly perfect, all the time."

I was curious, actually, as to what Gwen's opinion of Mariya was. Gwen was so used to being the local phenom. Gwen was freakishly perfect, but you could argue that Mariya was even more so, with her exaggerated extensions, her insuperable control.

"Is she?" Gwen asked.

"Have you ever watched her?"

Gwen thought.

"I guess she is," Gwen said. "But I haven't really thought about it. I mean, I can't tell. I don't know what it's like to be her, so I can't really tell about her dancing."

I put it down as another of Gwen's superpowers—her sometimes astounding lack of acuity that acted as a kind of protective shield. But there was something more to it. I couldn't think, because it was class, and I was still trying to hold my body like a normal person, but something tugged at my mind. It wasn't just that Gwen had difficulties assessing anything that wasn't herself, it was that it didn't even occur to her to do so. And while I was probably the one person Gwen could, in some sense, *see*, she couldn't actually *feel* me. I was feeling her all over the place, wearing her like a too-tight skin, sweating and tearing and twisting at her. And she couldn't feel that. She had no idea.

I watched, along with everyone else in the room, whether covertly or not, Mariya execute the grande allegro. Kirov dancers can jump. Mariya needs almost no preparation for elevation. With very little down, she can get very high up. I was easing my way to the door, head turned to watch, and bumped into Wendell, who was blocking my path.

"What can you say about that?" he asked me, pointing with his chin at Mariya.

I shrugged.

"That's right." Wendell nodded. "You should have something to say."

I didn't know if he meant me, or one in general, or if he was complimenting Mariya, or denigrating her talent as being too far beyond praise.

"Thank you for the correction," I said, mimicking the finger jab at my chest. "That was helpful."

"Give my best to your sister," Wendell said, walking away.

Dream again tonight. Helena. My moment of sharp clarity had passed and I was feeling somewhat unsteady, like I had been on a boat for hours and hours and was now on a dock, wondering at the earthquake happening in the still ground below my feet. I tried sitting down, but it didn't really help.

I was listing at my dressing table, pinning Helena's little

cap into my hair, when I heard the text message alert from my phone go off. Once again, I was sure it was Gwen, but this time I felt grateful that she had at last signaled me back. I waited until a swell had passed and then grabbed my phone.

Drink tonight?

It was from Gwen's boyfriend, Neil.
Drink tonight?
In a way, taken out of context, it was mysterious. Would I drink? Would there be a tonight? Even without the question mark it would have been compelling: *Drink tonight.* That had an urgency, a compulsion. Tonight. You must drink. Within context though, it was a scumbag move. Neil and his big dick. *I care about both of you.* I swallowed some nausea.

Onstage, I clung to Klaus in a way that was not entirely feigned, and actually worked very well. And his sturdiness was genuinely appealing. I hadn't given any thought to why Helena loved Demetrius, because it seems like part of the point of this piece is that love is a potion and it's quite arbitrary. When someone has anointed you with *jus d'amour*, you love whomever you see first. But tonight my careening, stubborn, determined little Helena physically needed Demetrius.

But then it was over again. Step, step, step forward. Right leg swings behind left, acknowledge the audience, curtsy. Step, step, step back, left leg swings behind right, acknowledge your partner, acknowledge the audience. A beat. The audience is still applauding warmly so step, step, step . . .

Back in my dressing room, I was truly lost at sea, with no horizons. Also a distinct sense that there was water coming in the boat, that there were too many holes to stop it.

Drink tonight?

Drink tonight.

You did hurt me sometimes, Gwen. You didn't mean to, but you did. Did I ever hurt you? Why would I want to do that?

No, I think sometimes you did mean to hurt me. Sometimes you meant it.

There was a knock on my door, Klaus stepped in, all leather jacket and freshly washed blondness.

"What are you doing tonight?" he asked.

"Oh, I don't know. Going home to bed," I said.

"Want some company?" he asked.

Klaus shut the door behind him. There was an awkward moment when I knew he was going to kiss me, and then he kissed me. It was soft though, so I couldn't feel it.

"*Whoosh,*" said Klaus, after I pulled back. "That's just how I imagined it would be."

Something. Adrenaline? Klaus kissed me again, this time pulling me to him harder, holding my head with both his hands.

Lift it off, take it off me.

"Stefan and James and I are going to grab a quick drink at Luxembourg," Klaus said. "Do you want to join, or can I come to you after? Or will that be too late?"

"No, no," I said, thinking about Gwen's apartment and how there was a mountain of my stuff piled on her bed, and, oh god, all those masking-tape Xs. "You guys go ahead and I don't know . . . maybe text me when you're done and if . . ."

Klaus kissed me again, this time grabbing my ass with both hands, although I was wearing a dressing gown and the silk didn't give him much purchase. Klaus reached inside it and grabbed my waist, but he's had his hands on my waist nearly every day for weeks now. It occurred to me that I had felt pretty much every part of Klaus's body except his dick. Was it going to be enough?

"I'll text you," he said. "Don't fall asleep on me."

Why not? I said to myself, over and over. Why not why not why not. It's something to share with my invisible movie audience. Why not? Give them a little thrill, poor dears. It's been such a dreary season.

I took a taxi, jolting carsickness made worse by the stupid TV monitor. I turned the volume off and lowered a window. "Thank you, miss," the cabdriver said. "It's so terrible, to listen to this all night long."

"God," I said. "God, yes, I would kill myself." I laughed.

Back at Gwen's I scooped everything off the bed and shoved it into the closet. It was like a comedy, things were falling, and I was tripping and I had one shoe off and was trying to find candles and then thinking that lighting candles was ridiculous and should I put on music, and if so, what, and wondering if I had time to wash my hair, no, hair wasn't crucial, but I should shower, but then what should I put on after, and should it include underwear, or just a robe, and throughout all of this Klaus was texting me updates:

At Café Lux.

Finishing up.

Getting check: what's yr address?

I combed my wet hair, brushed my teeth, found a pair of Gwen's yoga pants and a thin T-shirt that made my boobs look good, sort of. Well, this is life, I thought. No one can say I haven't tried. I thought about the last time I had sex, then the last time I had sex with someone that wasn't Andrew. I poured myself a glass of wine and hastily tried to imagine having sex with Klaus, who was apparently about two blocks away from having sex with me.

I was glad that I hadn't gone off the pill, but it did seem like a condom should be used. I hurried into Gwen's bedroom and checked the nightstand drawer. There were no contraceptives in there.

There was a rope.

A rope with one end knotted in a noose. Not expertly knotted. Would it have worked, even?

I greeted this object with resignation. I had been wondering where it was, actually.

I didn't touch it. It was lying by itself, not covered up or anything. There was nothing else in the drawer. Klaus was buzzing the intercom. I shut the drawer slowly and walked, quite sedately, over to the buzzer. Well, then, I said. Possibly out loud. I took a sip of wine. Things were beginning to feel a little fuzzy.

I showed Klaus into the living room, not really sure what to do with him or where to put him, or myself.

"Nice place," said Klaus.

"It's my sister's," I said. "My, um, I was living with my ex and we broke up so I'm sort of . . ."

"Couch surfing?"

"Well, no," I said. "There's like . . . a bed."

"That's good," Klaus said, taking off his jacket.

It became clear to me that there was a bad-idea component to the evening. On the other hand, if I sent Klaus away then it would just be me and the rope.

"So Klaus," I said.

"Kate."

"So," I said.

"Yes?"

This seemed like it could go on indefinitely.

"I'm not really sure if—" I began, but Klaus advanced, grabbed me by the back of the head, and pulled me to his mouth. I was reminded of something Andrew once said. "For a guy, sex is always something that's in front of you. I don't mean in the future. I mean physically in front of you."

There is no future. There is only what is physically in front of you.

Klaus picked me up and carried me to the bedroom. It was possible, I thought, that other drawers contained other weapons. Gwen could have the entire arsenal of the Clue game hidden. A candlestick. A lead pipe. A revolver.

Klaus took off my shirt, then his. Well, bare skin always feels good against bare skin, and Klaus was a very good kisser. No strange techniques or excessive saliva. As he worked his way down, his belt buckle dug in between my legs for a moment and this felt very good, so I held on to his shoulders, pinioning

him against me. Opening my eyes, I watched him struggling to
kick off his boots, but they were cowboy boots (of course they
were) and they really required two hands.

Probably not a gun. Gwen wouldn't have a gun. New York
isn't like Louisiana or something where you can just walk into
any old Walmart and pick up an assault rifle. We don't even
have a Walmart. You'd have to go to like, Hoboken or something. Staten Island? And it's not like guns come with instruc-
tion manuals.

Do they?

I slid out from under Klaus and scootched down to the end of
the bed to pull off his boots. Underneath them, he was wearing
white tube socks. Little-boy socks. I pulled them off. His feet
were very cold. Klaus undid his belt buckle and unzipped his
jeans. The top of his cock became visible. I brought myself into
the plank position over him. My wet hair fell past my shoulders
on either side of his face.

"You smell good," he said.

"Aveda," I explained. "Shampoo for blondes."

"But you're not a blonde," he murmured, sliding the yoga
pants off my hips. I buried my face in his neck. Even without
the leather jacket, Klaus smelled very good. We must use com-
patible products.

I couldn't picture Gwen purchasing the rope. I couldn't picture her forming it into a noose. Don't you need to make a
special kind of knot? I wondered if Gwen had a secret stash
of pills anywhere, and how much Vicodin you had to take for
it to knock you off. Would you just throw up all over yourself
and start to suffocate or would the ickiness of that make you
struggle and try to save yourself. A gun would be the best way.

There's probably only a moment of pain. What's one tiny little moment?

Klaus rolled me off him and stood up by the side of the bed in order to pull off his jeans. I kicked the covers down with my feet and propped myself up on one elbow to watch him. Klaus touched his erection proudly. It's a great-looking cock, I'll give him that. It was just, at that particular moment, I couldn't see that it had anything to do with me, other than being physically in front of me. Klaus climbed back into bed and attacked what was in front of him, which was, coincidentally, me. He pinned my hands above my head and sucked hard at my neck, my armpit, my breast. He flipped me on my side and shoved his cock against my ass, moaning. He brought one of my hands down in between my legs and, covering it with his own, rubbed both our hands against me.

An embroidered throw pillow in the oven, ribbons of blood unfurling in a bathtub. I never really believed Gwen was going to kill herself. Even when she was standing before me in the posture of one who was about to kill herself, I did not believe her. I didn't call Dad because I thought she was going to kill herself. I called Dad because I wanted to get rid of her.

"Are you on the pill?" Klaus whispered, rolling me onto my back and bringing my knees to my chest. I nodded, but Klaus's eyes were shut. His blond hair was streaked with sweat.

"I am," I said. "But shouldn't we—"

"It's okay," he said into my thighs, biting them. "Don't worry. I'll be safe."

I wanted to laugh. "Oh, really," I could have said. "While you lick my pussy I could reach out with one arm and pull a gun out of the bedside table. I could aim for one of the masking-tape Xs on the wall opposite the bed. I could aim for my own head." Then I remembered that it was a rope in the bedside table, not a gun. What a stupid thing a rope is. Couldn't you have left me something a little better, Gwen?

Klaus was inside me then.

It's chemical. An imbalance. Mine is spiked with Vicodin, what do *you* have, Gwen? Mom wants you to get off drugs altogether. You could have more electrolytes or antioxidants or oxidants or antitoxins or octogenarians or toxic orangutans. That would be funny, wouldn't it? If you turned out to be just fine.

I wondered what I could do that would make Klaus spend the night. I really didn't want to be left alone with the rope and Gwen hovering just outside my peripheral vision, daring me to prove how much stronger I am. Or am not.

"You're going to make me come," I told Klaus, who shook his head, tried to stop himself from orgasm, failed, caught it midway and enjoyed it, fell down on one elbow, shuddered, but theatrically, for the sensation of it.

After a minute I gently tipped him off, putting his chest between me and the nightstand.

Fall asleep, I willed him. *Fall asleep and don't wake up till it's morning.*

"I'm falling asleep," Klaus said after a few minutes. "I should get up."

"Okay."

His feet were still cold. I thought of his tube socks on the floor at the foot of the bed. I didn't want to watch him look for his socks.

"I'm going to get some water," I said. "Do you want?"

The kitchen tiles were very cold under my feet and the edge

of the glass felt very hard under my teeth. Klaus's arms, when he hugged me good-bye, were still a little sweaty.

"Hey," he said. "Just between you and me, right? I don't want any drama at work."

"Of course," I said. "No drama."

I smiled and shut the door. I heard him walk down the hall, cowboy boots on thin carpet. I imagined I could hear the creak of his leather jacket as he pushed the elevator-door button. I heard the soft ding, the uneven rumble of the doors sliding open. The doors sliding shut. That little ca-chung sound that signals descent has begun.

"Well," I said, turning around in the darkness. "I guess it's just you and me."

26.

I stood against the door for a long time last night. Eventually I sat down. I think I must have slept a little, at one point. I woke up thinking, *It won't ever end.* I got up, went into the bathroom, looked at myself in the mirror. Looked at us. How could it end? Here we are, forever clasped, like two boxers staggering around the ring. Too tired to let go of each other, eyes shut. Clinging to each other's sweaty backs, mouths open against each other's shoulders. We will die this way, neither submitting.

But neither of us is dying.

It's Wendy who's dying. And it's Wendy I went to see, because that's what you are supposed to do. You are supposed to just go until there's nothing left to go to.

Karine let me in, as before.

"Does she know I'm here?" I asked.

"I didn't tell her," Karine said. "Sometimes people change their mind and do not come, so I think it is better not, for sick person, to be waiting. She will be happy to see you." Karine patted my shoulder.

"I give her morphine now," Karine said. "So she might fade a little, but she might want to talk. Her friend was here yesterday. They have nice talk. Sometimes, it's very bad, the going, but this will not be bad."

"I brought some flowers," I said, unnecessarily, clutching them. "Is that stupid? Should I?"

"Yes. You go on now. Bring them to her and I will find a vase."

I watched my feet walk down the hallway.

"Wendy?"

Wendy's bedroom was bright, the curtains drawn back, all the lights on. I was expecting something somber, but rooms have no sense of occasion. They just go on being rooms no matter what happens in them.

Her bedroom had also gotten more crowded. Paintings leaned against the walls. A bookcase had been moved in, and stacks of other books were in piles on the floor. There was also, it must be said, a smell. I walked into it, trying not to flinch. Wendy's bed was angled into a half-sitting position, but her eyes were closed. I put the flowers at the end of her bed, in between the little mounds of her feet under the blanket.

"Oh goodness, Kate dear." Wendy licked her lips. Her head was covered with a silk scarf, yellow, with white daisies. It was sheer enough that I could see the pink of her scalp below it. Her skin still had that strange pearl-like sheen. But she looked smaller. She had been such a tall woman. Was. Was almost, still. Would soon be not.

"What time is it?" she looked worried.

"Eleven."

"Eleven in the morning?" Wendy looked at the window. I took her hand. I'm not sure that I ever held her hand before. It was cold, but her fingers moved in mine, gripped them. "Another morning," she said.

"Yes."

"But you dance tonight," Wendy said, with surprising energy. She sat up a little. "You dance Titania tonight. You should be preparing."

"Oh, you know," I said, leaning against the bed. "There's plenty of . . . I'm ready. I'm not. Don't worry about that."

"We were going to have it broadcasted on the radio," she said, shutting her eyes again and smiling. "Remember?"

"Like a baseball game," I said. "That's right."

"What do you think of my new decor?" she said. "Karine and I have been redecorating."

I looked around at the haphazard piles. Some things I recognized. The big oil painting from the library had replaced the one that used to hang opposite her bed.

"I always loved that painting," I said.

"Theseus," Wendy said. "I always thought that could make an interesting ballet. Theseus celebrating his triumph over the Minotaur. You remember the story."

"Right. King Minos and the Athenian youth who were collected and sacrificed to the Minotaur every year. And there was a labyrinth," I said, looking at the painting, which was not strictly representational. It was hard to look at Wendy and I couldn't just hover over her, staring at her, too obviously trying to commit every detail of her face to memory. "What's-her-name, King Minos's daughter, told Theseus how to navigate the labyrinth so he could slay the Minotaur. And she gave him a ball of string so he could follow the thread back out."

"Ariadne," corrected Wendy. "The string was called a *clue*."

"Right. Ariadne. Theseus dumps her on an island, right? After she saves his life, he sails away with her and then just leaves her somewhere. Naxos?" I looked over my shoulder.

"According to Hesiod, yes," Wendy said. Her eyes were closed. She was smiling. "Homer says that Theseus slew her, possibly because he learned she was already married to Dionysus. But we needn't feel too sorry for Ariadne. By most other accounts, Dionysus found her on Naxos, and married her, and she bore him children. So, things could have gone much worse for her, and you know they generally did for women, so it's really almost a sweet tale. Until Perseus shows up and slays her, although accounts differ there too. Some say she hanged herself. Tilt me up, dear? There's a button, I think? Some sort of control thing on the side of the bed?"

I bent over the side of the bed. I saw the little control device, hanging from a curly wire. There was a stick-figure man stenciled on it, his differing posture indicating what button to hit to adjust the bed. I couldn't operate it. I could barely see.

"I'll call Karine," Wendy said.

"No, no, here it is. I've got it." I can't do this, I thought. I thought it over quickly several times and then tilted Wendy a few degrees upright.

"Glasses?" Wendy murmured, reaching a hand out to the tray next to her bed. "Kate, would you?"

She took them from me and perched them on the end of her nose, looking at the painting, not at me. Which meant I could look at her for a moment. There was a thin blue vein underneath her ear, tracing its way into the collar of the nubby sweater she had on.

"I bought it at the gallery I love," Wendy said. "In Prague. It's by a Greek artist, not well known. I don't suppose it's an important piece, but I just love it."

"Me too," I said. "It looks like Theseus is dancing, sort of."

"He is." Wendy took off her glasses and closed her eyes. She began to recite:

> Now Theseus, in his return from Crete, put in
> at Delos, and having sacrificed to the god of the
> island, dedicated to the temple the image of Venus
> which Ariadne had given him, and danced with the
> young Athenians a dance that, in memory of him,
> they say is still preserved among the inhabitants of
> Delos, consisting in certain measured turnings and
> returnings, imitative of the windings and twistings
> of the labyrinth. And this dance is called among the
> Delians, the Crane Dance.

"Wow," I said. "Why did they call it the Crane Dance, though? Why not the Labyrinth Dance? Or the Hey, I Slew the Minotaur Dance?"

Wendy smiled, which was what I was hoping for, but then she looked worried.

"I can't remember the Greek word for 'crane,'" she said.

"It's okay," I said. "You just recited Homer. You're the only person I know who can do that."

Everything you say to a person who is dying feels like slightly the wrong thing. It's amazing how loaded our vocabulary is with words that can go wrong. Soon I wouldn't know anyone who could recite Homer.

"Plutarch," Wendy corrected. "Not Homer. But the word for 'crane.' I can't remember. It's . . . oh, this is really . . . this is very . . ."

"You'll remember it," I told her. "You'll be thinking of something else and you'll remember it."

"When?" she asked. "When will I remember it? I need to know it now, Kate. Oh, what is it? Why can't I remember?"

Her eyes weren't quite focused, because of the morphine, maybe. Maybe because she needed more morphine. She reached out for my hand, and I could feel that she wanted to grip it, but she wasn't strong enough. The feebleness of her grip seemed to make both of us panic.

"It's okay," I said. She shook her head.

"It's in the library," she said. "A Greek dictionary. Not the modern Greek. The ancient Greek."

"Okay. Ancient Greek dictionary. I'm on it."

"You won't be able to find it," Wendy said. Her breathing changed. "Oh, *why* can't I get up?"

"You should rest," I said. "I'll get it."

"You won't find it." Wendy tried to swallow. The effort it took her made it seem as if she were swallowing a boulder.

"I'll find it," I said. "Or wait, my phone. I can look it up. Look, here's my phone."

"Kate." I didn't know if she was crying or her eyes were watering.

"I know, just one second. See: ancient Greek crane. Oh crap, that's just mechanical cranes. Okay, ancient Greek dictionary.

Do you want me to call Karine? Do you need something for the pain?"

Wendy nodded a child's nod, her eyes locked on mine. I didn't want to let go of her hand. I tried to think of something to say. Something that wouldn't hurt.

"Kate, did you find it? I need to know the word. I can't remember it."

I looked down at my phone. Ancient Greek dictionary. I typed the word "crane" with my free thumb, hit the search button.

"I'll go get Karine," I said.

Wendy nodded again, but her weak fingers threaded through mine.

"Okay, here it is," I said. "Oh. Oh, it's in . . . the Greek alphabet. Here, you can read it." I held the phone out, but Wendy shook her head.

"Oh, your glasses," I said. But my hands were full. Wendy half turned on her side, pulling her legs slightly toward her body, trying, I think, to curl into a ball. There was a portable intercom on Wendy's bedside table, but I didn't know how it worked. Did I need to push a button?

"Karine?" I said. And then, louder, "Karine!"

"Just describe the letters," Wendy said.

"Okay," I said. "Okay." I held up the phone. The letters were so small.

"What does the first one look like?"

Karine came in, not running, but moving swiftly.

"All right now," she said.

"She's in pain," I said.

"She's not in pain," Karine said, placing a large hand on Wendy's shoulder. "Are you in pain, Mrs. Hedges?"

Wendy shook her head.

"No, I think she is."

Karine reached for a dropper on the plastic tray beside the bed. Gently, she placed it inside Wendy's mouth, holding her cheek.

"Ativan," Karine said to me. "For the anxiety. There now."

"It's fine," whispered Wendy. "But. Kate?"

"Yes?"

"The letters? For 'crane'?"

I leaned over the bed. Our faces were almost touching.

"The first one is like . . . is like a small-case *y*, and the second one is like a capital *E* with an accent aigu and then a small—"

"*Geranos*," Wendy said. But she didn't sound relieved. "That's it. *Geranos*. Why couldn't I remember it?"

"We all forget things," I said, hating words, hating them. "It's not important. You knew it right away."

"I think I might sleep for a little now."

"It's all right now, Mrs. Hedges?" said Karine. "You sleep for a little and when you wake up you will see the nice flowers your friend bring you."

"Thank you very much," said Wendy, very formally, shutting her eyes. "That's very kind."

27.

It was still too early to go to the theater. It was too early, and too late. I walked back to Gwen's across the park again, but this time quickly, not looking up or around or seeing anything at all. Life is just what is physically in front of you. I walked fast, as if I might catch up to what was in front of me, run smack against it, stun myself.

My phone was ringing as I let myself into the apartment. "Mom and Dad," said the screen. I wanted to let it go to voicemail, but I guess some part of me thought, "Mommy." It was the part that was still with Wendy, still holding her hand.

"Kate, it's me."

Gwen's voice. I pressed the phone hard against my ear.

"Kate?"

"Yeah. I'm here."

"It's me."

"I know."

"I didn't think you'd answer," she said. Nervously? There

was something. "I was going to leave a message. To wish you *merde* for tonight. Titania. You'll do great."

"Oh." For a second it occurred to me that it wasn't actually my sister who was talking. It was someone else, doing an impression of her, playing a trick.

"Kate, is that *you*?"

"It's me. You don't sound like you either."

"Yeah, well." The sound of a big breath. "I'm sorry it's taken me so long to call."

Still not really her.

"You want me to call back? You could not answer and I could leave a message."

"No," I said. "No of course not. Don't be silly."

"I just didn't want to do the big *talk*," Gwen said. "You would not believe how much talking I've been doing. I kept thinking that you sort of knew, in some way, that it was okay or something. Also I thought I'd save talking to you until it wasn't like, this huge thing."

Okay, that did sound like Gwen logic, where time erased everything and there were a thousand clean slates to be found amidst all the spoiled ones.

"Can I ask how you are?" I really was asking this of myself. *Can* I ask Gwen how she is? Can I do that? But Gwen answered.

"I'm about to go into my therapist's office," she said. "I'm sitting in the car with Mom. I just wanted to call and wish you *merde*. I wish I could be there. I *miss* you!"

"Me too," I said.

"You want to talk to Mom?"

"Okay."

"Okay. Bye, Kate. I love you."

"I—" I started, but I could hear Gwen saying something to Mom, and Mom saying something back, and the sound of a car door slamming. I felt unsteady.

"Hi, Katie-bird," sang my mother.

I walked into the bedroom. The sheets were still kicked around, things on the floor, Gwen's sweatpants in a crumple. I sat on the edge of the bed.

"Hi Mom. How are you?"

"Well I'm just fine and dandy, how are *you*?"

Happening? Not happening? It was hard to tell. I rotated my ankle until it popped.

"So, wow. That was Gwen."

"She wanted to call," my mom said. "It was her idea. We were driving and she said, 'I want to talk to Kate,' and I said, 'Well then you should.'"

"Uh-huh."

"How did she sound to you?"

"Mom, you were right there."

"I know. But didn't she sound good?"

"It was so quick."

"Well, she had her therapies to go to, but it's been on her mind. Because I know there are some questions about how she's going to manage things once she goes back to New York, and she just needed to talk to you about that. We all want to talk to you about that."

"Well, that's not my decision, though."

"Okay, I guess that answers my question," Mom said, somewhat sharply.

"What question?"

"Your sister is doing much better," Mom said. "*Much* better.

But she needs to stay on this medication and keep up with all her therapies and be healthy in her choices. We just weren't sure if she could do that all on her own."

"We?"

"I think it was more of an episode that had been building up," Mom said. "I know that's controversial of me, and I know she needs to take some medication, but I think she had all the feelings and they all just built up and overflowed and maybe even, in some way, she was wanting there to be a big thing so she could just get it all out. I don't know all the psychologicals, obviously. But, honestly, after listening to these doctors, I'm feeling like *nobody* knows what they're talking about."

"Do they have a . . . a diagnosis, or whatever?"

"Oh, well, obsessive-compulsive is a thing, or what they call psychotic depression, or dissociative personality, but that's just a name, and anyway the first two medications were not right, and were *way* too much. I think the antianxiety medication has worked the best. But she has to take it. That's what everyone says. She has to take it. We have to think of it like . . . oh, like any medication if you have some sort of medical condition."

"She does have a medical condition, though. Right?"

"Nobody really understands these things very well, Kate."

"Does she not want to take her medication?"

"Well, she wants to take it *now*. It's apparently a problem, sometimes people just decide they are okay without their medication."

"So someone needs to make sure she's taking it."

"She is responsible for herself," Mom said firmly. "That's what a lot of the work she's doing now is about. But, yes, I know your father and I would feel a lot better knowing you were there, when Gwen goes back to New York. We just wanted to make sure that was okay with you. Because you and Gwen lived together before, but maybe you don't want to do that anymore."

"Does Gwen want to come back and live with me?"

"She doesn't want to ask it of you, honey. But yes, I think she does. I don't know. Maybe the timing is right, since you and Andrew are taking a break. You two could look after each other!"

"This would be . . . when? When does she want to come back?"

"We can talk the ins and outs when you come home. You're coming home, right? When the season is over? My goodness, that's next week!"

"Yeah. Yes. Next week."

"Are you excited about dancing Titania tonight? We read the *Times* review online. Sounds like you and your partner stole the show!"

"Did it?"

"You didn't read it? There was a whole paragraph on you and that Klaus person. Gwen said the reviewer is hard on women, so that him saying you did good is really good."

"Did she?"

"She was so happy for you. We're all happy for you! I don't want that to get lost in all this. I know it's been . . . whew!"

Rage overtook me.

"It sounds like it's going to be okay, though!" I said, standing up. "It sounds like Gwen is really going to be just fine and it's all going to be okay!"

"One day at a time, still," Mom said, her voice gratefully swinging up. "But I just want you to go out there onstage and just dance your little heart out and know that we're all so proud of you!"

"Oh, that's so sweet!" I said, opening up the bedside-table drawer and yanking out the rope.

"And I'm glad you and Gwen talked. I think that was a big hurdle!"

"She really sounded good!" I said. "And she's been taking class and everything?" I walked back into the living room, looking at the ceiling.

"Yep! Well, listen, honey, I know you've probably got to get going."

"I probably should!"

"Have a wonderful performance tonight! I know you'll be just . . . wonderful!"

"Thank you very much," I said, formally. "That's very kind."

I dragged the desk chair into the middle of the room, under the lighting fixture. It's a nonfunctioning lighting fixture. It's not wired. There's a hook. Over the years, things have been threaded through that hook. Gwen and I used to hang dried flowers there sometimes. It was a place to string lights across at holiday time. Once, for a joke, I hung my bra up there. That was funny, wasn't it, Gwen? Are you amused?

It wasn't so very long ago, really, that Gwen and I left the theater together and walked to the subway. We said good night at the corner, and Gwen walked down the steps to the train. I crossed the street to descend on the opposite side. I was going downtown, to the apartment of Andrew's that I lived in. Gwen was going uptown, to this apartment that we shared and where I had abandoned her. We stood on the platforms of our sides, waiting for the trains, tracks and rails and columns between us. Gwen stood way back from the edge of the platform, as did I. Neither one of us could bear the sight of the rats scurrying across the tracks.

Gwen looked very small, bundled up in her coat with the huge fake-fur collar. Things were not good between us. There had been too many demands, too many late-night calls, summonses to her dressing room, to the apartment, to the bathroom at work.

"What is it?" I kept asking her. "What is it?" I was sick of her not being able to articulate her fears, only what she wanted me to do about them. I was tired of it never being enough. I was tired of everything. It wasn't that I didn't want to dance anymore. Or that I didn't want to be with Andrew anymore. I just didn't want to want anything anymore. I just wanted to disappear. Gwen's train came first. I was looking at her, she was looking at her feet. Then the subway car blocked my view of her. I heard the doors clatter open, the bell ring. I watched the windows of the car, waiting to see her figure. She sat down by the window, turned her face to me, raised one hand, and waved, slightly.

The train pulled away. My train came. I didn't get on it.

Gwen always hunched her shoulders and covered her ears when a train came into the station. She couldn't stand the screeching noise. Even if it was a newer train, and didn't make that horrible grinding noise, she still did it, holding her breath.

But that night she hadn't done it. She had just stood there, dwarfed in her coat, staring at her feet. Anna Karenina might have stood like that, just before the end.

I ran up the stairs to the street and started walking not really sure of what I was doing. I called her cell phone. I called twice, three times, four times. It was freezing, and I had forgotten my gloves at the theater. The cold chopped up my hands like scissors. I pleaded into my phone. "Call me." "Let me know you're okay." "I'm sorry." "I'm here for you." "I'm coming over."

I let myself in with my key.

Gwen was standing on that blue chair. That blue chair right there. Under that ceiling fixture. That iron hook, right there. The rope was around her neck. Was around the iron hook.

"Oh COME ON," I yelled, slamming the door shut behind me. "Are you SERIOUS? Get down from there."

"Go away," she said. "Get out."

And she moved, just slightly forward, but it pulled the rope taut and I froze.

"Okay," I said. "Now just stop it. This is ridiculous."

"You think I'm playing a game? You think I'm pretending?"

No, not pretending. And yet. I knew she knew I would come after her. I knew she had listened to my messages. Knew I had a key. She was waiting for me.

"I don't think you're pretending," I said to her. "But please stop this. Just. Just. Take that off."

"You don't understand."

"Then explain it to me," I said.

"You always say that but I know you don't want to hear it."

"Of course I want to hear it, Gwen. You can tell me anything. I love you."

"You always say that too."

"Gwen, please take that off. Here, I'll help you."

She moved again, leaning forward slightly on her toes.

"GWEN."

"I'm not safe."

"I'm right here. I won't let anything—"

"Don't TOUCH me."

"Okay. Okay, I won't touch you."

"You think you're better than me? You think you know everything?"

"No, I don't think that." No, Gwen. Never that.

"You don't care about me. You won't miss me. You'll be glad when I'm gone."

"That's not true."

"Go away. Just let me do it. Don't steal this too."

"Steal this too?"

"You steal from me. You STEAL."

"What, Gwen? WHAT have I stolen from you?"

"You watch me."

"You make me watch you," I shouted, begging. "How can I NOT watch you?"

"You take everything away from me."

"What," I said, crying now. "What have I ever had, Gwen, that you didn't have? What have I ever had that you didn't TAKE?"

"JUST GO AWAY."

"I would go away," I shouted, "if you let me."

"You can't help me," she said, stroking the rope. "You don't know how. You don't know what I know. You can't ever feel things the way I do. You are just pretending to be alive."

She stood there, swaying dreamily, fondling her rope. And I hated her. And I wanted her gone.

"Oh, just DO IT," I shouted. "Just go ahead. Do it right now."

"I will."

"DO IT then. You want me to watch? I'll watch. Do it."

"You don't know what it's like." She choked on her tears. "It's not right. I know it's not right."

"And when you're finished," I said, "I will pull your head out of that thing and I will do it too."

"You can't." She grasped the rope, possessively.

"What, you're going to stop me? How are you going to do that? You'll be fucking dead."

I was screaming at this point, but Gwen suddenly got very calm. She reached up and pulled the noose from around her neck. She stepped down. *Is that it, then,* I thought. *Is it over again? Again and again and again?*

"Here," Gwen said, making the gesture for deference, indicating the vacant space on the chair.

"You're right," she said. "You better go first."

I didn't do it then. I could do it now.

I thought back then that the feeling was strong in me, the desire to disappear, but I had no idea. I had no idea it could get this big, this strong.

"Strong" is the wrong word.

Easy. The thought of disappearing feels so . . . easy.

She left it for me. She left me the rope, and the Xs, and she even left me Titania. All the things she could do and I couldn't.

But she couldn't do this.

I guess hurting yourself wasn't enough, Gwen. It didn't hurt bad enough. So you thought if I hurt myself maybe it would make it better?

If I did it, would you be able to feel me, Gwen? Would you be able to know what it's like to feel me? Because I sure don't anymore.

I left the rope coiled on the chair. For the first time since I've been here, I felt like I finally had something to come back to.

I went to the theater. I went to my dressing room and did my hair, grabbing handfuls and yanking them upward. I put on half my makeup. Nina was leading a warm-up class onstage. I went down and took a position at the barre. In between combinations I practiced standing like a normal person, neither too far back nor too far forward. I should get it right at the end, I thought. I realized why Wendy wanted so badly to find the Greek word for "crane." You want to get these things right before you go. I went back to my dressing room. Selected shoes, just right, just right. I needed eyes. I needed lips. I did the work of a mortician. Mara stopped by, to wish me *merde*.

"Are you okay?" she asked. "What happened?"

"What do you mean?"

"You look—"

"Oh, I talked to Gwen!" I stuck a pin so hard into my scalp that tears came into my eyes.

"Hey," Mara said, kneeling down next to me, trying to grab my hands. "Hey, tell me. What happened?"

"Oh, she's GREAT." I said, twisting away from her. "Turns out, it's NOTHING. She's fine. Maybe a little bipolar, but not *really* bipolar. She just needs to take a pill, and as long as I stick around and make sure she takes it there will be no problems at all. She's taking CLASS."

"Okay, slow down," Mara said. "Kate, what's really going on?"

"You know what my mom sounded like?" I said, twisting the ends of my hair into pretty swirls to pin down. "She sounded like ME. She sounded exactly like me for the last ten years, only now we've got a pill Gwen can take. Or not take. That maybe works. Or doesn't. Or will for ten more minutes until she can get back here."

"That can't be right," Mara said. "Kate, listen to me. You know that Gwen needs help. I know it. Roger knows it."

"Roger's been chatting away with her on the phone," I said. "Because apparently she's not really messed up. She has some sads and bads from time to time, some delusionals, some ickies, but that's all of us, right? I think something is going to stab me in the eye. That's not normal either."

"I was there, remember?" Mara grabbed my leg. "You don't think I felt guilty, leaving you alone with her? I pretended it was okay. We've *all* been pretending."

"What if we were wrong?" I struggled to stand up, knocked the chair back, hit my wrist on the edge of the table. "All this time. All this TIME. And it turns out it's just something you can take a pill for."

I reached into the drawer and pulled out the bottle of Vicodin.

"These make me sick. I can't eat. I can't sleep. My mouth feels like it's filled with ashes and it makes me too fucked up to even dance on them anymore. But Gwen's got a pill that makes her feel totally fine. She's not crazy anymore. Look at what I've DONE TO MYSELF and SHE'S NOT EVEN CRAZY."

"Ladies and gentlemen, this is your half-hour call. Half hour to curtain for this evening's performance of *Midsummer Night's Dream*. May I have Kate Crane and David Resnick to the stage, please. Half hour."

"I've got to go," I said, grabbing a sweater.

"You're not dressed," Mara said. "Wait. Let me help you." She held out the Titania costume. I stepped into it. Mara put a hand on my back, trying to stop my shaking.

"It's fine," I said. "I'm fine. Just let me go."

David wanted to run a few lifts, so we ran a few lifts. Marius, crossing the stage with Claudette in tow, watched for a moment. He didn't wish us *merde*, that's not his thing. He made sort of a benediction gesture. Last rites.

"Shit," said David. "I totally forgot to get you flowers."

"I forgot to get you flowers too," I said.

Will that bother him later, I wondered. He'll bring me flowers then. A floral tribute. Maybe a wreath.

"You don't have stage fright, do you?"

"I feel anticipatory," I said. "I'm really looking forward to tonight."

Things got muddy in the wings, later, because there was Bryce, all eyes and downy shoulder blades. It would have been nicer of me to be cruel to her, but I couldn't. It's okay. Her mom will

explain what a horribly sad person I was. Deeply troubled. Not
the person Bryce thought I was. Not at all.

I swept onto stage, summoned fairies imperiously. Since I had
taken Gwen's part I thought it fitting that I pay her a sort of
artistic tribute, so I danced my first solo not as Titania but as
Gwen dancing Titania. I think Gwen danced very nicely, but
really only she can know what it's like to be her.

I argued with Oberon over the changeling boy. Perhaps not
totally convincingly. Oh, just take him. He needs a good home.
I danced some more. Deedle, deedle, deedle! Very, very good.
When you dance well, what is there to say? There's nothing to
say. There are no words. Eventually, Titania went to sleep, in
a pretty little conch shell with flower-petal curtains. I lay there
and listened. How funny it would be, I thought, if I just never
got up. If I just pretended to be frozen, in a sort of coma. How
long could you keep that up? Not long, really, because someone would stick a pin in you, or surprise you, or throw a bucket
of ice water over your head, and you wouldn't want to move,
but you would.

Don't move. Don't move. Gwen and I on opposite walls,
daring each other. What a stupid game. I'm going to win this
round.

Manny fluttered the flower over my head, shaking invisible
love potion, tricking me into being in love with the first thing
I see upon waking. I got tricked into loving dancing. But no
one ever came and took the spell away, so I had to ruin it all
on my own.

Things got harder dancing with Bottom. I felt tired. I had been asleep too long. To sleep, perchance to dream, ah, there's the rub. We should do a ballet to Hamlet. Too hard to stage? My ribs hurt. I don't like this part anymore. I wanted it to be over. Bottom crawled into the conch shell with me, and the flower petals covered us. We were wheeled offstage.

Little problem in the wings because I unexpectedly found myself reluctant to get out of the conch shell, and, once out, I sat on the floor. I wasn't really sure how I got there. Roger, in his donkey head, loomed over me.

"Is she okay?"

I looked up into the vacant eyes, trying to find the real eyes. Impossible.

"Kate?" he whispered. "Are you okay?"

"I'm okay," I said. "I'm sorry. That wasn't very good."

Mara appeared over the donkey's right shoulder.

"Sweetie," she whispered, gently. "You have to get up now."

"Is it over?"

Roger laughed.

"She's fine," he said over his shoulder. He boosted me up. "It was good," he said. "I mean, I have no clue what you looked like because I can't see a fucking thing, but it felt okay. What? It didn't feel okay to you?"

No clue. No clue. There was something? What was it? Oh, yes. Wendy told me that the thread that Ariadne gave to Theseus, to help him find his way out of the labyrinth, was called a *clue*. That was his clue. Now it's my cue. Words! Even now, at the end? I don't know anything.

Mara held my hands. I hugged her, feeling the muscles of her perfect back.

"Don't you worry about me," I said.

A dresser came up and adjusted my little wings. We crab-walked together while she was doing this over to the tissue box duct-taped on a plinth. I blew my nose, patted down the sweat. After a bit, I got back in the conch shell with Roger and we were wheeled back onstage. Puck appeared and sprinkled the flower juice over my head that would lift the spell. I woke up. Horror! In bed with a donkey! Laughter from the audience. I could have played it a little better. Shit. Shit.

More dancing. Curtain. Intermission, and then we'll have Act II. The marriage celebration of the mortals and the reconciliation of Titania and Oberon. It shouldn't work, really, this staging, because all the dramatic tension has been lifted. First you have tension, and then you have release. But it does work. It's very beautiful, this ballet that Marius has made. It's truly enchanting. The immortals weave in between the mortals, who don't see them, but who inspire them. The immortals are amused at the mortals. They feel tender toward them, benevolent. They've seen human beings come and go, and they're not so special, this group, not so extraordinary, but it's okay. We just go on. Falling in love, messing up, carrying on. In ballet you can get away with that sort of thing. You can also have people kill themselves at the end. Either way, as long as you do it beautifully. Either way is fine, it doesn't matter.

Because I didn't want the final pas de deux with David to look as regretful as I felt, I didn't dance it as well as I wanted to. I just danced the steps, the proper emotion arriving a little too late, when we were almost done, and then we were done.

And that's it. That was the whole deal right there. Curtain down. Applause, applause. Curtain up. Applause, applause. Lights

lowered, stage cleared except for the corps de ballet, still ringed in
the back. Soloists and principals ran on, in ascending order
of importance. David and I came on last. David kissed my
hand. We took our bow. I stepped forward and acknowledged
Fumio, who had been conducting. I stepped back to David.
We led the whole cast forward. They took their cue from me.
We bowed. We stepped back. Curtain down. "Hold Company,"
shouted our stage manager, gauging the applause. Okay, CUR-
TAIN GOING UP. Everyone forward, everyone back. Lights
lowered, but no, they were still applauding. Lights up. Bow.
Okay, please stop. Okay, yes. It's over. I know what's coming. I
am going home now. I am going home.

28.

"I'm sorry," David said, when the final curtain came down and we were leaving the stage. At first I wasn't sure what he was talking about. I felt drugged with anticipation. At last something definite would happen. No more waiting. My arms felt tired, as if I had been holding them above my head for a very long time, hanging, hanging. I didn't want to feel pain, though. I was worried about the pain. Well, I had enough Vicodin left that I could probably get myself to pass out with the rope around my neck and then I would just . . . fall.

"I was a little off," David explained. "I don't think we totally, you know, connected like it's been in rehearsal. But it's the first time we've performed together. It'll be better on Saturday. You did great."

"Oh," I said. "No, that was me. That wasn't you."

"We're a team," he said, kissing the top of my head. "We'll work it out."

I didn't want to think about this, so I just smiled. I smiled and smiled, all the way up to my dressing room. Once there, with the door closed, I felt a heavy, almost sensuous wave of fatigue take over. I let it, languidly taking pins out of my hair, dropping them on the table. No more pins. There was a knock on the door. I stilled, leaning back in my chair, eyes closed.

Mara. Still in costume. I could see her through my half-closed eyes, see a swash of rose-pink fairy tulle.

"We wanted to make sure you're okay," she said. I opened my eyes a fraction more. Yes, Roger behind Mara. Bottom the yokel's brown pants, daubed with orange.

"I'm okay," I said. "I really am. Thank you for checking on me, though."

"Mara told me," said Roger. My eyes opened fractionally.

"About Wendy Hedges," Mara said quickly. "About her dying."

"So rough," Roger said. "You must be really sad, baby."

"It's sad," I said. "But you know, these things happen."

"And with Andrew, and everything," Roger continued. "And Gwen's not here to—"

"We just didn't think you should be alone," Mara interrupted.

Friends. It's not that I don't have friends. But if I stick around I will lose these friends. I will watch them grow more anxious, then frustrated, then mad, then they will wish for it just to end somehow. If I were a nice person I would stick around long enough for them to get to that place, but I'm not a nice person.

"It's been a long season," I said. "I just need a good rest. I just need to go home and sleep and sleep." I took a deep breath and exhaled a smile. "Sorry I was sort of wonky tonight."

"Come out with us," Roger said, moving from behind Mara's tulle. "We'll get a glass of wine. It will help you sleep."

"Or tea?" Mara said. "You could come back to my place and I'll make you some tea. Mike had to go to Boston on business. You could stay over."

"Slumber party!" said Roger. "Come on, sweetie. I'll rub your neck."

Tricky.

"You guys are so sweet," I said. Actually, annoyingly, I felt a headache coming on. God. A stupid headache. I wanted to feel good. I thought I should open my eyes all the way, but I was worried about looking at them. Then I tried and it wasn't so bad. They were separate enough, removed enough now. They were lovely, whole, distinct people. They would be very sad. Very sad. But they would go on perfectly fine. I could see them, being perfectly fine. And it might even be helpful for them. The world is so utterly, utterly sad that it's useful to have very concrete things to be sad about, from time to time. There, and there, and *that* thing there. Feel bad about that. Cry for me and it might keep you from crying about the misery that is everything. And people say killing yourself is a selfish act. I faked a yawn.

"A long hot shower," I said. "That is my greatest desire right now. I've been all tense and weird, I know, but I actually think I got some of that out." I turned to Mara. "Thank you for letting me go off earlier. I just needed to get that off my chest to someone." I tried to ignore the fact that as soon as I said "long hot shower" I really did desire a long, hot shower. I needed to keep my head in the game. Eyes on the prize.

"Will you call me tomorrow?" Mara asked.

"Call us," Roger added.

"I will," I said. "I promise I will."

"Promise" is a word like any other. Words can go in any direction. It's only the body that is incapable of lying.

"Now, shoo," I said, making a funny face. "Shoo, chickens. I need to get out of this flummery."

As last words go, they weren't great, but time was essential. Roger leaned over and gave me a loud smacking kiss on the cheek.

"I TiVoed the dance show," he said. "It was the final tonight. None of us are on tomorrow night, so you are both coming over and watching it with me. I'm making risotto."

"Awesome," I said.

Mara lingered in the doorway. "Call me if you need me?" She made the gesture of helplessness, knowing I wouldn't.

I acknowledged her gesture with a queenly nod. She left.

Reassuring other people that you are not going to kill yourself is not that hard. Who wouldn't want to stick around for risotto? Unless, of course, the thought of eating and swallowing and dishes in the sink and the fact that you have to keep on eating and swallowing and putting dishes in the sink seemed so Herculean a task, so laden with so many gestures and sounds and smells that you just couldn't face it anymore. All the things before and after the event that is life.

Keith. My brother, Keith. I couldn't think. If I kept thinking then there would always be something, some reason. I had one more performance left of the season. Just one more. It would be cleaner to do it then. I could have a little more time to make everyone feel it wasn't their fault. No. It didn't matter. I had to think about myself. That was the important thing.

I took off Titania and hung her up, threw my tights and g-string into the net bag labeled "K. Crane." Someone would have to remove all the labels from my costumes. Would the next girl figure out that the slanting rectangle of tape on the door was something she should touch for luck?

Another knock on my door. This time I felt fine about answering it, because it seemed almost like a pleasant game. I felt proud of my secret, the thing tucked up inside me that was all mine. Just mine.

This time it was Bryce, in street clothes, but with her face still full of makeup, an enormous dance bag on her shoulder. She held a photograph in her hand.

"I was wondering," she said, blushing, "if you could sign the picture of us? My dad got it printed for me. See?" She held out the photo. In photographs I either look very pretty or like I just had a stroke. I was pleased to see that this was a pretty one. Since Bryce and I were both wearing stage makeup in the picture, we looked somewhat similar. Almost like mother and daughter.

"We look almost like sisters," said Bryce. "Sort of?"

"Come in," I said, sitting back down at my dressing table. Bryce's eyes took in everything on my table: the little dish I keep my jewelry in, the makeup spread out across a towel, deodorant, spray bottles of water and holding fixture for my hair, brush, comb, geisha pins and bobby pins and rubber bands, dental floss for sewing ribbons, a tomato pin cushion, the antique silver hand mirror from James, balms and powders and lotions and adhesive tape and toenail clippers and perfume. I watched her move on to the photographs and postcards and notes taped against the mirror and tacked onto the walls beside it, my costume hanging on the rack, my lineup of pointe shoes against the wall. Her eyes returned to the dressing table. I could see her wanting to touch things, a little girl wanting to try on Mommy's pearls, spray her perfume, unscrew her lipstick. But Bryce has a mother.

"I have a marker," Bryce said, handing me a black Crayola pen. I admit, the pen almost got me for a moment, but I carried on.

"I start pointe this summer," Bryce said, leaning against my dressing table. "For real, I mean. But I got my shoes last week and I've already been practicing in my room. They don't hurt at *all*. I don't need the toe covers."

I wrote carefully across the bottom of the photo, "To the most beautiful fairy, Bryce, with love from Kate Crane."

I handed it to her, watched her read the words. Her left cheek dimples when she smiles. I was both glad and sorry to have noticed this.

"Put something in your shoes, though," I said. "Because when you start working in them, they might hurt a little, till you get used to it. It hurts a lot if you get a blister. Don't pop your blisters, even if people tell you to. They'll take twice as long to heal. Tape your toes but take the tape off after class. Oh, and Epsom salts. Epsom salts and alcohol work better than any of that crap they have in the drugstore aisle."

Bryce took this in very seriously, as well she might. It was probably my last chance to be of any use. I felt very proud of myself. Socrates dispensing wisdom before gargling some hemlock.

Bryce glanced up at the pictures surrounding my mirror.

"I have an extra copy? Of our picture? If you want one, I mean?"

"Sure," I said, high on my own deathbed benevolence. "You'll have to bring me one."

But Bryce dug into her bag and produced a manila envelope.

"You'll have to sign it for me," I said, handing her the marker. And then get out of here, I thought. Keep walking and don't look back. But Bryce was hesitating now, wondering what to say.

"You can just sign your name if you like," I suggested.

"You are my favorite dancer," Bryce wrote, and then added, "ever! Love, Bryce Elizabeth Ford."

"Bryce Elizabeth Ford," I said. "Great stage name."

Since she was still watching me, I stood up, untacked a post-card next to the mirror, and hung the picture up.

"Okay, I've got to get going," I said. "Thank you, Bryce!"

"Me too," she said. "Bye, Kate. See you Friday!"

She actually skipped out of the room.

I sat back down. I needed to get the makeup off before it cracked into my face. Or should I just powder down and take off the lashes? I didn't want to imagine what my face might look like later. Maybe I should start taking Vicodin now? No, later. I needed to get set up.

Another knock on my door. Probably Rani, to collect my laundry bag.

No. Marius.

"Oh, good," he said, leaning elegantly across the doorway. "You're still here. Come and have a drink? I want to talk to you."

No, no, no, you cannot talk to me, Marius. You cannot want to talk to me.

"My god," Marius said. "Don't look so—oh, it's not about tonight! Tonight was fine, didn't you think? I have some notes for you. Little things. You're coming too far downstage on the bourrées, you need to cheat that circle with the temps levés a little, and I think you and David should run the Act II pas at some point on Friday, in costume, because it looked to me like he was fighting with your wings? Something. And a little too precious at the beginning, but that's probably more my chore-ography than you. Don't be afraid to put the Kate Crane stamp on it, it's what I expect."

A million, a hundred million reasons to stay alive, the immense pain I would be inflicting on my family, on my friends, on a ballet student who just got pointe shoes, all the horrible and seductive possibilities of life, and the first crack in my resolve comes from the thought that I need to fix the bourrées?

"It's not what I want to talk to you about, though," Marius said. "Come and have a drink, if you please. You look like you could use one. I know I could."

Twenty minutes later I was seated next to Marius at a tiny Span-ish tapas place in Soho where evidently he is well known. In the cab ride downtown, Marius had mostly been on the phone with a board member. I had looked out the window. No, of course I wasn't going to kill myself. Not that I still didn't want to, especially when I considered the extreme melodrama of my recent behavior. At one point, Marius touched my knee, and when I looked at him he made the gesture of apology for the phone call. I had almost forgotten he was there.

This was harder to do at the restaurant, as we sat very close together, at a corner table. I've sat next to Marius plenty of times, though never in candlelight, and never after a fantasized near-death experience. I felt self-conscious about being alone with him in a place where he, possibly, took women, and where my obvious ballerina-ness must mark me as one of "his" dancers. I felt self-conscious about still being conscious.

"Your eyes are bright," Marius said.

"I have a little bit of a headache."

"Eat something. Have an olive."

I ate an olive.

"So." Marius selected a piece of cheese. "Did you have plans for the summer?"

"In a manner of speaking." My body felt equal parts lethargic and restless. But then, I wasn't on any drugs.

"Can they be changed? You're not booked anywhere?"

"No. Things have been sort of . . . I'm possibly in a transitional moment." I thought of desire. A desire to have a long, hot shower. A desire to go to Roger's tomorrow and laugh at a stupid show and eat risotto. A desire to do the last pas de deux with David properly in *Dream*. A desire, still, in flares, to put an end to all desire.

"You know," Marius said, leaning back, "you were very good in *Leaves*. Tudor would've loved you."

I ate another olive. I wondered if Marius was going to tell me, once again, that he sees something deep in me and he wants me to work harder and get more confident. In some ways, the moment that I planned on killing myself was as confident as I have ever been.

"Anyway," Marius continued. "I have a job for you, if you want it."

It was regret, really, that I was feeling. I didn't quite want to leave my death behind me. It felt so unfinished.

Wait.

"You have a job for me?"

"I'm setting *Dream* in Amsterdam," Marius said. "This summer. July. I want you to come with me."

I selected a piece of cheese. Marius watched me eat it.

"Why?" I asked, finally.

"To have an illicit affair with me," he said. I choked on the last swallow of cheese. Marius motioned to a waiter to refill my water glass.

"To help me set the ballet," he said, when I'd recovered. "I need an assistant. Claudette is going a few weeks ahead, to teach the corps sections and the children, but then the woman really needs a holiday, and I'd rather have you, anyway. You're more fun, when you're not being irritating. You are a good coach, and I trust you. And it would be practice for you. For us. To see if we work well together. In that sense."

I needed something to do with my hands, so I reached for the bottle of wine on the table. Marius took it from me and filled my glass.

"Well, I'm not going to pay you very much," Marius said. "So don't get excited. It's a sort of preliminary internship, really."

"An internship."

I put down my glass and looked at Marius. Actually, because

of the candlelight and the strangeness and the rush of alcohol and some weird sort of adrenaline, I squinted at him.

"No one dances forever," Marius said. "Not that I think your career is on the decline. If you stay healthy you should be able to keep dancing for a while, and I want you to do Hagar in *Pillar of Fire* next season, so please stay healthy. But, yes, eventually, I see a place for you on the artistic staff. I want you thinking toward that, not toward whether I'm going to promote you. I have no plans to promote you, by the way."

I remembered a book that Keith used to always want read to him when he was little. It was called *Fortunately, Unfortunately*. A little boy had a series of calamities that were then abated by strokes of good fortune. As I recall, he fell off a cliff (unfortunately), but there was an ocean below him to break his fall (fortunately). There were sharks in the water (unfortunately), but (fortunately) he could swim. I couldn't remember how it ended.

"I need someone to talk to," Marius said, abruptly.

We looked at each other.

"Well, I don't need someone, but it would be nice. It can be very lonely, this job." Marius brought his arms back and folded them across his chest. I watched him slide his watch up and down his wrist.

"It's just an idea I had," Marius said. "A little plan. You'll come to Amsterdam and we'll set the ballet. And I want to do a new *Cinderella*. I've always felt the score was more interesting than the ballet, I want to do something darker, more Grimm, very theatrical. A year from now, next spring season. There isn't really a role for you in it, so maybe you could assist in rehearsals. Well, before, actually. I'd like to talk it over with you. I'm not entirely sure how it would work. Perhaps it was premature to talk about that. I always get like this at the end of a season. It's satisfying, but there's always something that's not satisfying, or I want something more. I tend to chase diamonds when I'm in this mood. That's you, Kate."

"I'm a diamond?"

Marius leaned back in his chair again and studied me.

"It comes and goes with you. It came back these past two months. The intensity. The sharp edges. The desire."

"Marius," I said. "Marius. I've been a mess this season. I've been"—to my horror, I felt my throat closing in—"I'm a total mess."

Marius, because he is Marius, produced an actual handker-chief from his pocket and handed it to me.

"Can you pull yourself together by July?" Marius asked. He put his hand on my back then, very gently. The combination of incuriosity and tenderness was just what I needed.

"I'm incredibly hungry," I said. "I need more food."

"Is that a 'Yes, thank you, Marius, I accept your generous offer'?"

I nodded, and then started to cry a little more. I was, undeni-ably, a total mess. I was likely to be messy again in the future. It seemed unavoidable. I would have to do many difficult things, including, probably, unclasp my sister's hands from around my back. And find some way to pry my own from hers. I would have to grieve for Wendy. I would have to dismiss my invisible movie audience. I would have to participate in all parts of this world, not just the event, but the thing before and after. Life, or whatever.

29.

Marius put me in a cab. I had a lot of things to think about, and I thought about none of them. I thought about what Marius had told me of *Cinderella*. I hummed the music softly to myself. Well, actually it got pretty loud by the end. One of the good things about New York City is that you can bellow Prokofiev at two in the morning without causing your cabdriver any alarm whatsoever.

Outside Gwen's apartment, I faltered. I didn't want to go in there. It was too soon, too much. In the end, I managed it by going directly from the front door to the bathroom without turning on any lights. I brushed my teeth and washed my face in darkness, still humming the overture to *Cinderella*. I felt my way to the bedroom, shoved everything on the bed to the floor, and kicked the comforter after it. I lay there. Nothing.

So I got up. I turned on all the lights and got a plastic bag from under the kitchen sink and walked around the apartment, unpeeling all the masking-tape Xs and stuffing them into the bag. Without looking at it, I added the rope, and moved the chair back to the desk. I undid the locks on the fire escape window and crawled out on the landing. I served the bag, overhand, into the alley below. It landed very softly, which surprised me.

I took a long, hot shower and when I crawled back into bed I made a few snow angels. And then I fell asleep.

30.

I saw Wendy Griston Hedges one more time before she died. It was the day after the final performance of *Dream*. At that point, she was sliding in and out of consciousness, but I described the performance to her anyway. It wasn't perfect, but I think David and I got the Act II pas de deux right. A few times Wendy opened her eyes, and once she smiled. I knew she wasn't smiling at me, but I was glad I was there to see it. She died the next day.

That was one year ago today. In her honor, I've come to the Met to pay a visit to Ugolino and his sons. It's very peaceful in the sculpture garden, all this white marble and light. And Ugolino sits in a storm of violence and wasted fury, his sons coiled around him like serpents, pleading, dying.

I never got a chance to ask Wendy what it was, exactly, about this particular piece that satisfied her so much. But I think things like this pick up where words fail us. I'd like to think that dance can do that too.

A week after Wendy died, her niece called me to say that it was Wendy's wish that I should have the painting of Theseus at Delos. It took about a month to come to me. I'm pretty sure Wendy's family had it appraised, to make sure I wasn't running off with something of great value. Wendy left a large bequest to the company too.

It's hard to miss somebody. I don't mean that it's difficult to feel sad at the loss of somebody. I mean that it's hard to feel like you're missing them properly, or purely, or with the right significance. So many other emotions attach to it.

I did go home to Michigan. Just for two weeks because I was looking for a new apartment and there were things to work on for taking *Dream* to Amsterdam. But I wanted to go, and my being there with Gwen meant that Mom and Dad were able to go see Keith play the best tennis of his life at the French Open. He lost in the semis, but everybody agreed that he showed a lot of heart. Gwen and I watched it on television.

Gwen took class every day I was there. I didn't, because I wanted to give my neck a thorough rest. That's what I told her, but really I was scared to watch her dance. I was scared she wouldn't look the same.

So I drove Gwen to class, and to her therapy sessions, and we did a giant jigsaw puzzle together, and cooked food, and at night we stretched and watched movies or television. Mom had told me that "sticking to a routine" was best, and I think it was best for both of us. In a way, it seemed like we were both convalescing.

But in the end, I did see her dance. She asked me to come to the studios, at the Grand Rapids Ballet, and watch her run through the first-act solo from *Giselle*. I couldn't refuse.

I sat on the floor. Gwen, as Giselle, pantomimed opening up the windows of her little cottage, smelling the air, running out the front door, dancing for the sheer joy of being young and alive and in love. A peasant girl who refuses to believe her heart is weak, who doesn't know that her lover is promised to someone else. A girl who will, by the end of Act I, go mad and throw herself onto the point of a sword.

When she was done, I stopped the CD player, and saw half a dozen students from the school pressed up against the windows of the door. Transfixed. Awed. I knew how they felt. But they couldn't know my relief. Or my pride.

When I turned back, Gwen was sitting on the floor, legs stretched out in front of her, massaging her knee.

"It's a little stiff, still," she said.

I nodded. I had seen the scars on her bare leg, still red around the edges. I went and sat next to her.

"Beautiful," I said. "Absolutely beautiful."

"You mean it?"

"Yep."

"Want to see me do the mad scene?" The self-mockery caught me unawares, and I didn't know how to react.

"Relax." She nudged me with her leg. "I don't think you have to *be* crazy to act crazy. I mean, look at you."

We laughed then, a little.

"Gwen . . ." I hesitated.

"Don't give Mom a hard time," she said, abruptly. "She's the easiest person for me to be around right now. She's so convinced that there's nothing wrong with me that she doesn't watch what she says. Dad's been playing the most awful chirpy music on the violin, but Mom's like, 'Oh, look at what Mrs.

Hendrick's got in her yard! Garden gnomes! That woman is out of her mind!' "

"Oh, shit, really?"

Gwen smiled.

"VI-sor JU-deeee," we sang together.

Later that night, as we lay on the couch together watching highlights from the day's tennis, Gwen asked me, very shyly, if she seemed okay. Did she seem different?

"I think you seem good," I said, carefully. "How do you . . . how do you feel?"

Gwen sat up, straightened her legs in front of her, flexed and pointed her feet.

"You know, they don't actually know what's wrong with me," she said. "That's why it's taking time, to get the medication right. I'm not like, psychotic. Although I got a few of the questions wrong, on the test for that."

"There's a test?"

"Oh, Kate." She leaned over her legs. "You wouldn't believe some of the things they ask you. Like, say the first thing that comes into your mind. What do apples and bananas have in common?"

"Um, they both have skin?"

"That's what I said! And that's wrong! You're supposed to say that they're both fruit!"

"Oh. Well, duh."

"That's what I said!"

"So we're both a little psychotic. Or that test was made up by really boring people."

"I've met some psychotic people," Gwen said. "They're sort of boring. They always talk about the same thing. I don't think I'm like that."

"No. You're not like that."

Gwen folded her legs under her chin. I had brought her cat Clive with me to Michigan, and he liked to station himself on the back of the couch. Clive mewed and head-butted her shoulder.

"And you know," Gwen reached around and knuckled Clive's head, "even before, it went away. The bad feeling. On its own."

"Yeah. But it always came back." I said it gently.

"I don't know if it's gone right now because of the medication and the therapy," Gwen said. "Or because it's just . . . gone for a little while and it's going to come back."

I held myself back from telling her that she had to stay on the medication. I felt like the sentence was there anyway, hanging between us like a banner.

"So how *do* you feel," I asked. "In general?"

"Fine when I'm in class," she said. "The rest of the time, I don't know. Good, I guess. But, it's sort of like . . ."

Gwen held out a flat palm. With her other hand she mimed being on pointe, dancing on her palm.

"It's sort of like I can't quite feel the floor. And I know that's supposed to be better, because I don't get so upset and I don't feel so scared. I don't have that feeling like I can't stop everything from coming *in*, but. I don't know. It kind of feels like . . ."

Gwen dropped her palm and danced her other hand across the air, her fingers shaped like a pointed foot, searching for a floor that wasn't there.

And I think I was able to feel her, then. And then able, in my imperfect way, to grieve for her.

But I didn't know how to talk about the future. Neither of us did. It came out awkwardly, in a rush of half-truths, while we waited to pick Mom and Dad up from the airport.

"So you're going to Amsterdam with Marius," Gwen said. "That'll be fun."

I knew she was trying to sound normal, and it pained me. Gwen hates traveling.

"I was thinking," I said. "Maybe I should sublet your apartment while I'm away? There are always dancers coming for the summer program at the school."

Gwen looked down at the floor, frowning slightly.

"Not to a bunch of girls," I said hastily. "Maybe one girl and her mom, or something. I could put anything you wanted in storage, so it would be safe."

"There's stuff I need," Gwen said. "Like, I need summer clothes. Shoes."

"I'll send you whatever you need. Or. Do you think you'll . . . ?"

"I'm supposed to tell Grand Rapids Ballet like, soon, I guess . . . they've offered me a guest artist contract. They're doing *Giselle* in October. Just four performances. And then *Nutcracker,* of course. Some stuff in February and March. I haven't talked to Marius about it yet, so don't say anything."

"I won't."

"I know everyone thinks it's a good idea. For me to stay here a little longer. I guess I could tell Marius that . . . I don't . . . I don't want anyone to *know,* Kate. Nobody knows, do they?"

"Nobody knows," I said. "Except Mara, and she won't say anything. You could just say that it was general health issues? Or that you want some time off, that you need to . . . like, recharge or something."

"Yeah."

"Would you stay with Mom and Dad, do you think?"

"It might be better to get my own place? Someplace close to the studios? I don't want to have to drive. I don't think I even remember how."

"I might do that too." I held my breath. "Get my own place."

"Actually, I don't even know if I *can* drive," was all Gwen said.

The day I was leaving, Gwen handed me a list of things she wanted from her apartment, and said it was okay if I found a sublet for her. She looked anxious, and also like she was trying not to look anxious. I said, "Don't worry. I'll take care of everything. It'll be . . . everything will be safe."

And then we hugged each other, and pressed our cheeks together hard, and then we sort of let go. A little. Enough to know we had separated, and that this was how it was going to be now. Something lost. Something gained.

I found a girl from Texas, who came with her grandmother, and they stayed on for the school year, but Gwen is coming back to New York this summer. Mom's coming with her for a few weeks, to help her get "set up."

I imagine that I will try to lay down some boundaries, and that at least a few of them will get crossed. I'm trying not to anticipate, as Roger advises.

Amsterdam *was* fun. It was a lot of work, and I felt like I didn't get to see much of the city other than the route from our hotel to the theater, and the three or four places Marius and I always ate at, but I didn't mind. It was good to be occupied, and being in front of dancers all day in Amsterdam actually made me love dancers, and dance, in a sort of new way. Marius said it was like that for him too. That he loved dance more when he stopped doing it.

Mara says she doesn't know if she loves dance more now, all she can think about is how nauseated she is, but I'm thinking that after the baby she's not going to come back. Our joke is that by the time her kid is in school, I'll retire, become assistant artistic director, and hire Mara as ballet mistress. It's not really a joke. Although the part where I fire Nina and her deedles is. Sort of.

But I'm still doing it. Dancing. Gamzatti in *La Bayadère* this season. And Hagar, as promised, in *Pillar of Fire*.

Pillar of Fire is big drama. There are three sisters. The youngest one is all flirty and vivacious, and the oldest one is all stern and judgmental. Hagar is the middle one. She's the pillar, the fire trapped in stone. I could go on and on about Hagar, but anyway, she falls in love with the Friend— a nice young man—but her younger, more vivacious and flirty sister steals him away and Hagar ends up pregnant from the man from the House Opposite (it's a whorehouse) and the man abandons her, but in the end the Friend comes back for Hagar. So it ends well, but it's tense, and emotionally complicated, and claustrophobic, and painful. Tonight is the premiere. I'm going to tear that shit up.

·   ·   ·

I'm standing in my dressing room now. I am here. I am in the present tense. I'm not always here, and sometimes here is a very difficult place. Sometimes it is a labyrinth, or a Minotaur, or a rope I can neither let go of nor follow. It's hard to find the right words, but I guess I would say that it's something like feeling the floor.

And that it is my privilege to feel it.

Also from

MEG HOWREY

"A true gem."
—*Booklist*

Blind Sight

Set largely over one summer in L.A. where teenage
Luke meets his famous father for the first time, this
smart, funny debut novel is part coming-of-age story,
part family saga, in which the truth is not always
what it seems.

HC ISBN: 978-0-307-37916-0
EBK ISBN: 978-0-307-37961-0

Pantheon Books